Praise for
Night of Devoured Souls
and the Era of Shadows Series

[I]mmersed in a world … where magic and reality blend together. [T]hinking long after I'd read the book … I recommend it to anyone …

— WENDY

Easily pulled into the story and become engrossed into what occurs. Good characters that keep you wanting more …

— SHARON

I loved the characters I did not want to put the book down! I am looking forward to reading the next book in the series!

— VIRGINIA INGHAM

Enjoyed every word!

— VICTORIA TRAVISANO

[G]reat blend of mystery, suspense, horror and fantasy. The dual stories … is a … unique approach and cleverly shows differences and even unexpected similarities, in the cultures and our perceptions over the passage of time.

[T]he thing I liked the most … are the characters … caring about what they were struggling through.

I thoroughly enjoyed the antagonist character of Akhenaten, someone that you love to hate, much like I did with Joffrey and Ramsey in Game of Thrones …

— MATT

The reader … is left thirsting for the next installment of each story thread … the pharaohs are very well researched and give the reader a look into life that now only exists in books like this one. Eagerly awaiting the next book in the series!

— AMAZON CUSTOMER

[N]ever has a boring lull, so you are always engaged in the story. I know that books must end, but it left me excited for the next one.

— TIMARIE SIMMONS

[A]ction/adventure and historical fiction ... this novel was a perfect blend of both!

— ANTHONY RUDD

Needs a squeal—FAST

— PTF

Enduring gut-wrenching loss and the weight of defeat, the characters take us through their own journeys, embracing change and discovering the extraordinary power one can possess to change circumstances.

— LS VEALS

I loved the characters[.] I did not want to put the book down!

— AMAZON CUSTOMER

This book grabs your attention right from the start. It starts action-packed and suspenseful and does not stop.

— DANIELLE ROWEN

I found this book captivating from page one!

— VINCENT REYES

I was drawn in to the story and loved it!

— JACK V.

A fantastic read! The stories were captivating ...

— BRITTANY JOHNSON

I love the concept and ... story ... Unique ... bring[s] two worlds together. The writer is clearly knowledgeable ... [about] ancient Egypt ... [which] brings the book together adding to the depth and story.

— NATALLA ESCOBAR

Era of *Shadows* Series

BOOK TWO

Night *of* Devoured Souls

R.M. SCHULTZ

For information about this title or to order other books and/or electronic media, contact the publisher:
R.M. Schultz
email: rschultz.imaging@gmail.com
website: http://www.rmschultzauthor.com/

ISBN: 978-0-9988918-3-5 (print)
       978-0-9988918-4-2 (eBook)

Printed in the United States of America

Cover and Interior design: 1106 Design

To those who have lost their magic, may you find it.
To Matt, for crafting the story when I fell short.
To Creslin and Jocelyn for the magic in this
life—I hope you will always find yours.

Acknowledgements

T HANK YOU TO THE FOLLOWING people for their insight and help with the story:

Laura Veals, Barbara Kloss, Timarie Simmons, Neisha Lane, Jason Weersma, Serena Craft, Danielle Contreras, and Laura Robertson.

This story is based on numerous written records
referencing historical events and people of ancient Egypt.
The discovered monuments, temples, and architecture are factual.

Ancient thread character list:

Akhenaten: Pharaoh, son of Amenhotep III and Tiye

Aten: The sun and god

Ay: Nefertiti and Mutnedjmet's father, brother of Tiye the former queen

Beketaten: Akhenaten's sister, Nefertiti and Mutnedjmet's cousin, Pharaoh Amenhotep's daughter

Chisisi: The freeman leader working with the slave group

Croc: Heb's pet cat

Dark Ones or The Shadows: Mysterious monsters from children's tales

Devouring Monster: Creature that is a mixture of a crocodile, lion, and hippopotamus—from the underworld and devours the hearts and souls of men

Harkhuf: The muscular dancing dwarf brother from Nubia

Heb: Main character of ancient thread

Kiya: One of Akhenaten's significant foreign wives

Mahu: Akhenaten's chief of police

Maya: A scribe who oversees Heb in slavery

Mudads: Egyptian soldier

Mutnedjmet: Nefertiti's younger sister

Nefertiti: The queen of Egypt as well as Pharaoh Akhenaten's cousin, daughter of Ay, sister of Mutnedjmet

Paramessu: Egyptian military captain

Pentju: Akhenaten's chief physician

Seneb: The boyish dancing dwarf brother from Nubia

The son of Hapu: The royal magician

Suty: Akhenaten's bodyguard

Thutmose: Akhenaten's older brother who was to become pharaoh before his mysterious death, the son of Amenhotep

Tia: Slave woman

Tiye: Amenhotep III's wife, mother of Akhenaten and Beketaten, Ay's sister, aunt of Nefertiti and Mutnedjmet

Wahankh: Muscular Egyptian slave bully

Yuf: Elderly slave

Chapter 1

Present Day

"Come," the Egyptian detective said with a thick accent, waving us out of a room with a one-way mirror and adjusting his yellow tie. "You need to identify the body."

Aiden tugged his black socks up toward his shorts as he backed into a corner, his hands shaking. Kaylin and I followed the detective and marched down a flight of stairs, our slapping footsteps echoing along the walls.

Memories of Maddie filled my head. Was she really dead? My heart skipped several beats, the weight of tremendous guilt squeezing it like a constricting snake. I loved her—secretly loved her—the only other person I knew who shared my fascination with ancient Egypt. And she was the primary reason I was in this country.

We entered the basement of the building. The detective's quiet whistling carried down the hallway as we trailed behind him. One light flickered overhead. Double doors stood before us, opaque with Arabic letters running across the glass. My skin prickled with an eerie sensation and a chill. This had to be the morgue.

Images of a maimed body popped into mind. Had Maddie been murdered by her abductors as a warning for trying to locate the legendary Hall of Records? Those men had taken not only the girl I loved, but our group's strongest link. I didn't care about the Hall anymore, but I would find those men … and her, if this body wasn't really hers.

The detective flung open the double doors and strolled inside.

I fumbled with Maddie's fashionably sheer glasses—the only piece of her I still had, those she'd left behind at the site of her abduction. My wrist grew cold, the chill leeching from Dad's bronze bracelet and sinking into my flesh.

Kaylin shoved me through the doorway.

Bloodied surgical instruments littered a green-tiled room. The stench of formaldehyde funneled into my nose and turned my stomach. Bodies lay beneath sheets on metal tables … I imagined their lifeless faces turning to watch me as I entered. The room tilted and spun, and my abdomen contracted in a dry heave. I braced myself against the wall, but the sweat caking my palms made me slip against the cold tile.

The detective stopped beside a body, pivoted around to face us, and crossed his arms. He studied me—as if he thought we might be responsible for the murder and that my reaction would decide our guilt. He reached for the sheet.

My breathing stopped.

Fingers dug into my shoulder.

"Gavin?" Kaylin whispered, her blue eyes dilated with fear. A sick glow washed over her face, her skin blanching against silky blond hair as if she were about to vomit. "Why would anyone kill Maddie?" Clinging to me, she hid behind my arm. "I've been her friend since college. She's the sweetest person I know." She sniffed. "I'm s-sorry if I tried to use you and her to find the Hall. I was just …"

The detective flung the autopsy sheet aside.

My neck and jaw clenched with apprehension.

No—*Maddie, no …*

A woman lay beneath! Dark brown hair, petite …

I gasped, my vision flashing with light and darkness as my head bobbed and my knees buckled. Her skin was waxy under the incandescent light. Empty, bloodshot eyes. My breath caught in my throat.

My stomach cramped, as if in a vice, and vomit poured out of my lips, splattering onto the floor.

She was dead!

Wiping my mouth, I turned my face as I glanced back at the body out of the corner of my eye. I heaved for breath, but air would not enter my shaking body.

The green in the room still spun, but I forced myself to look.

Her ears were bigger, her face … different.

No—it wasn't Maddie! Similar build, but I didn't recognize this woman! My breath gushed from my chest in relief and—

"That's not her!" Kaylin said, hopping up and down and hugging me. "That's not Maddie!"

My limp body bowed under the force of her embrace, and I fell down, smacking the floor with my hands and knees. I forced a couple of deep breaths, and a twinge of guilt followed. "H-how'd she die?" I asked.

"Someone found her in desert," the detective said in his thick accent, stroking his short beard. "She not bring enough water or—"

Mr. Scalone—the treasure hunter who'd pretended to be our tour guide—threw the double doors open and strode in, speaking to someone on his phone. The doors banged into the walls as he flicked his hair back out of his face. Pacing around, he nodded at the phone, and his tattoo-encrusted arms flexed.

I sighed, long and deep. Should we even continue on this path to the Hall of Records in hopes of locating Maddie? Was this body a warning? Someone involved was very dangerous. And even our renowned treasure hunter hadn't been aware that they were tracking us. But the police hadn't helped locate Maddie either, and they didn't seem genuinely interested.

"No," Mr. Scalone said into his phone, stomping around the room of the dead.

Irritation made my face hot. "It's not Maddie, by the way," I said, loud enough to interrupt his conversation.

"Hang on a minute," Mr. Scalone said into his phone. His stubble-covered chin jutted back over his shoulder. "What?"

"The body," I said, analyzing him for some emotion. "It wasn't Maddie. She's still out there somewhere. Alive."

"I figured she wasn't dead," he said, his Italian accent thick as he marched out.

❄ ❄ ❄

Jolting up in bed, I wiped my sweaty brow on a pillow, the faint scratch of skin on cloth almost indistinguishable as my pulse hammered in my ears.

My head felt light as I swooned with panic. Another dark hotel room. Only faint artificial light streamed through the slits between the windows and curtains.

I kept having nightmares but couldn't recall what they were. Once awake, I only thought of Maddie and what'd happened to her. At least that wasn't her body in the morgue, but how much longer would it be until she met the same fate?

In the morning we'd be off looking for her again.

My hand ran over the peeling leather of an old journal lying on my chest, rough like scales of a reptile—the book I'd found inside the lost tomb of Amenhotep. The book that had a translated tale from ancient Egypt and that Dr. Shelsher's student had held in his death grip.

I opened the cover, but then slammed it closed. The tale was so fantastical. It might have been based on reality or someone's recollection of events in a time when most natural phenomena couldn't be explained—but it wasn't even close to a history textbook. It also wasn't complete. I'd skipped to the end before and found that the hieroglyphs ended abruptly, as if the student had been forced to stop his work at a moment's notice. And the story offered no clues to the path we were attempting to follow in order to locate Maddie.

Glancing around, I recalled Kaylin climbing on top of me a couple of nights ago, her blond hair draped over her upper chest. But even then I hadn't been able to stop thinking of Maddie—even if Maddie didn't feel the same way.

"If you get me to the Hall of Records and its treasure, I'll give you anything you want," Kaylin had said—probably all feigned attraction to manipulate me.

But I'd rolled out from under her, turning her down.

"Maybe once Maddie's safe, you'll be more eager to take me up on my offer," she'd said.

But even if Kaylin wanted the treasure, she did care about Maddie, given her demeanor at the morgue.

Grunting in frustration at everything, including my insomnia, I shook my head and snatched the journal. I staggered to the nearby chair and plopped down into coarse fabric that tugged at my boxer briefs. I clicked on the lamp and thumbed through the journal to my bookmark. My fingers ran over the hieroglyphs, and I translated words as if I believed I could absorb their meaning like some kind of magical Braille. The ink and rough paper rubbed against my skin with a scratching whisper. If only Heb and I could save Mutnedjmet and Maddie, escape our versions of slavery, avenge our fathers, and rise above our fate—what we were born into. If I could become an Egyptologist with the discovery of the Hall, and he a scribe ... Maybe somehow we could help each other. A tingle ran up my spine as my eyes closed. Ancient Egypt and the boy appeared in my mind ...

Chapter 2

Journal Translation

"GET OUT!" a toothless sailor yelled.

We'd traversed the Nile and docked at a rectangular lake, the western entrance of Karnak. I unloaded with the other slaves down a flimsy ramp. Our shackles rattled in the suffocating desert heat. The buzz of flying insects whirred overhead, and flies landed on my bare skin, the touch of their feet blending into the stinging sensation of the dirt in the wind.

"To the temple," the sailor said, making a quick exchange with a well-dressed man before leaving.

This new man, wearing a wig and carrying a writing palette, scrutinized us. "Take your places with the other slaves!" He pointed into the distance.

We stumbled away. Aches from my recent punishments, delivered by my former master, Akhenaten—now the Pharaoh of Egypt—and his bodyguard, Suty, wracked my body. The unyielding Aten sailed through the blue sky, its scorching rays crashing upon my head and back, raining down punishment and adding to the misery of the dry wind and biting insects. Still, my previous torment consumed every thought. Memories played in vivid detail, within the confines of my heart. Nefertiti, my love … was that really who you'd become? An eternal beauty who turned me down, turned down love, to be with a vile pharaoh for wealth and power? That was not who you were when we grew up together.

Rage ignited in my heart. But Nefertiti's younger sister, Mutnedjmet, took her place in my mind. Mutnedjmet's gentle face broke into a smile as she reached out for me. She had shattered her Bes amulet in protest of my treatment and against Akhenaten's reign. And I still wore Father's bronze bracelet—his last gift.

I needed to escape this new situation, make my former master suffer, and save Nefertiti from his consuming madness … but how? My gaze darted about. How could someone ascend beyond their God-given birth status? I'd tried with all of my being, and it had only brought me further down, from servitude to slavery.

✳ ✳ ✳

Days blended together as we slaves rolled enormous blocks of stone from a boat docked at the artificial lake to the monuments we were building for Pharaoh. The slabs were far larger than any man and must have weighed more than two adult hippopotami. I didn't possess the strength to offer much assistance in the pushing or pulling, so I placed logs along the ground to roll as makeshift wheels. I stumbled as exhaustion numbed my movements and delayed the response of my muscles.

Hobbling to the back of the block, I hefted a makeshift log wheel in order to recycle it to the front. Verbal assaults flew from the mouths of the surrounding freemen and slaves, telling me to run faster. My eyes clenched shut, attempting to block everything out. These men couldn't hate me already. But perhaps keeping the stone moving would make it much easier for those men who were pushing and pulling rather than having to initiate the block's movement from a dead stop.

Two Nubian—people from the wild lands far to the south of Egypt—brothers, and former dancing-dwarves, wielded greater strength than me and stood closer to the ground. They more easily picked up and placed their logs. As we rolled the slab up a steep ramp of packed dirt, the overseeing foreman—a short but stout man with stubbly hair—shouted for us to ease it into position. The foreman conversed with an architect who poured over parchments. Scribes tracked our progress, jotting notes on papyrus. They were all adhering to the instruction of the wise man, the son of Hapu.

My jaw clenched in anger. I hated that magician. His role in Akhenaten's scandal and the murders hadn't crystallized, but I couldn't trust him. The last time he'd spoken to me, he'd claimed he desired to help Egypt, but he kept appearing in positions of power. And if he controlled magic, why did Akhenaten spare him and no other magicians?

A shudder echoed through the stones of the monument as our team slid the gigantic block, already carved into near perfect shape, into the pylon—two towering walls that created a monumental gateway between them. It fit precisely amongst the other blocks, but a team of freemen moved in and chiseled, drilled, and sanded the top surface for contact with the next layer. Many of these men had sun-darkened backs—Egyptian farmers out of work during the inundation. But an Asiatic and Middle Eastern man mingled with them.

"Another one down," a man named Chisisi said, raising his hands in triumph, his thin arms and torso betraying his strength. His dark hair, cropped shoulder length, bounced along with his antics and framed his sharp features. He was not a slave. He, like most men here, received food rations for his work—more than one could eat in a day. But as slaves, we barely received enough to keep up our strength and continued for longer hours.

Longing tugged at my heart. To become a skilled laborer or scribe, I'd be well paid for my time. But given my history and birth status, I couldn't fathom a route to becoming educated and moving up this rigid hierarchy. Years of back-breaking servitude lay before me. And the harder I worked, the more they'd expect me to continue the pace. I needed something …

"Ants piling another grain of sand on their hill," Seneb, a boyish dancing-dwarf, said in a Nubian accent. He smirked as he wiped his hands on his dingy-white kilt, leaving a darker trail of dirt.

A thin woman in a white dress swayed closer as we descended, on our way to retrieve another block. The woman smiled, her dark hair blowing aside and exposing her demure features. Pretty, but nothing compared to what I was used to adoring … Nefertiti.

"Thank you, Tia," Chisisi said with a wink and smile as she handed him a vessel of water and one of nutritious beer. After chugging long gulps, the freeman handed the beakers off to a hunched older man named Yuf. Yuf reminded me of Father, with his flat face and short gray hair.

"Give me the drinks," a younger man named Wahankh said, his stern gaze moving up and down the man's frail body. He motioned with brawny arms and ran a hand over his stubble of dark hair.

"I …" I whispered, wanting to protect the feeble old Yuf who reminded me of my father, but I bit my lip. I couldn't fend the burly man off.

Wahankh jumped at the old man and smacked him on the back, tearing the pitchers from his hands.

Surprise and then anger made my breaths come in heaving gasps, the same anger I'd felt when serving Akhenaten. "Don't hit him," I said, stepping up beside them both.

Towering over me, Wahankh glanced down as if I were an insect.

I swallowed with apprehension. Acting like this was exactly why I'd ended up here at—

Wahankh elbowed me in the chest and sent me tumbling onto the ground with a jolt. Dirt stuck to my sweaty forehead, caking my skin like the makeup the royal family wore. Grunting, I raked my fingers through the dirt. I rose to my elbows and wiped my face, which drove more stinging grit into my eyes. I blinked to clear my vision just as Wahankh backhanded Yuf across the face. Yuf's head twisted sideways.

Harkhuf—a bearded dancing-dwarf from Nubia—jumped in and placed one muscular leg behind Wahankh's feet and shoved his torso, tripping him. Wahankh landed on his backside with a thud and grimaced.

"Respect your elders, Egyptian," Harkhuf said in a thicker Nubian accent than his brother. His striated triceps bulged as he sneered at the burly man and stroked his black beard.

Jumping to his feet, Wahankh tensed his sinewy muscles. His face was beet red, and spit flew from his lips. "He's a slave, dwarf, same as you and me! Freemen treat us like beasts, and so that is how I will treat to those beneath me. Pray it's only him and not you!" Balling up his fists, he stood nearly twice as tall as Harkhuf.

Seneb—the boyish dwarf brother with the clean-shaven face—leapt beside his comrade and spat on Wahankh's feet. "I'll take you down like a rat on an elephant's testicles."

Wahankh reared back and punched at Seneb's face. Harkhuf blocked the wide hook with a forearm and jabbed the man's groin or belly—so quick that I couldn't see. Doubling over in pain, Wahankh bellowed. Seneb kicked and pushed the man back into the dirt. This time he lay there, clutching his midsection.

"Hey!" the foreman shouted and snapped his flail at us. Its leather strands dangled in the breeze like serpents waiting to bite and tear open flesh. My muscles tensed. "Get the next block or you'll be working into the night!"

Harkhuf kicked dirt on Wahankh. Something pinched my insides with worry. This bully was not as big as Suty—Akhenaten's bodyguard, with his scarred face and ear, who had tormented me as a servant—but Wahankh reminded me of that monster. I knew what close enemies could do.

"Thank you," Yuf whispered, glancing from the ground to the dwarves. He grabbed the toppled beakers and downed the remaining liquid, releasing an "Ahh ..."

If only the dwarves wouldn't have to pay for their heroism with pain ...

I hobbled back toward the lake for another block, and the cracks in my dry feet opened again, bleeding onto my stained sandals. What would Wahankh do to them for revenge? To me? The entire incident reminded me of my former master and all of my mistakes. Could I have altered my fate if I'd gone to Nefertiti sooner, before Akhenaten had changed her, and taken her away with me? Pharaoh Akhenaten must've cast a spell on her in the later years or poisoned her mind, and I'd waited too long. I should never have returned for Akhenaten's dead body—only for him to be revived. Then I should've run away when the magician later gave me the chance ...

The vast city of Thebes spread out around us, workers toiling under the Aten stacking, carving, and painting stone. So many temples and pylons towered around us, to commemorate the Aten and Pharaoh.

A face I never wanted to see again stared back at me. A sculpture of Akhenaten emerged from stone—thin build with a potbelly, elongated face, sunken cheeks and eyes, plump lips ... Workers rolled his statues into position beside the pylon walls in construction. My chest burned with pain and rage, as if the Aten rose inside my heart. The man responsible for every wrong in my life, and for my current situation. I wanted to knock the sculptures over, break off their heads, and smash them into dust. But I'd use the last head to crush Akhenaten's other minions: Pentju, the lying doctor; then the son of Hapu, the magician; Mudads, the guard; Suty, Pharaoh's bodyguard; and finally, I'd use it to crush Akhenaten himself.

Chapter 3

Journal Translation

JUTTING MY CHIN OUT, I studied the statues of Akhenaten, my former master, and swallowed my hatred for him—although it felt as if a lump the size of a rat was forced from my chest down into my stomach. I marched away for more blocks of stone. As I attempted to stand straight, my lower back spasmed, pulling me down into a hunched posture. And my legs and knees throbbed with a dull ache.

After sweating and working through the day, with a short break in the barracks during the scorching afternoon heat, workers broke up into factions. Freemen divided into laborers, scribes, or craftsmen.

A foreman cracked his flail. The snap sent a ringing through my ears, and my skin tingled as I imagined the biting pain of the dry leather. He then pointed at us slaves and motioned, driving us into a line.

Pain from the day's work radiated from my ankles through my neck with a burning sensation. How could I make it through another day, much less a lifetime of this?

The hearty aroma of beer and bread wafted by. My stomach grumbled so loud that the old man behind me, Yuf, laughed. Slaves waited, hunched over with knotted or missing fingers and gnarled joints. Many were foreigners. How did they push on? Something must still drive these men—perhaps just a survival instinct. But wouldn't death be more merciful than this existence?

Trying to peek around a larger man in front of me, I stood on my tiptoes and leaned forward. He muttered and elbowed me back.

A woman dropped a meager hunk of bread that thudded when it hit the table. Snatching the slice, I stumbled as others pushed me on. I grabbed a cup of watery beer and shuffled inside the cramped confines of the barracks.

Crunching and slurping filled the enclosure, which teemed with odiferous men whose rank stench stung the inside of my nose. I dropped onto the dirt floor in the corner, and a sense of loneliness and of being lost overcame me. Poor Croc, my orange and white cat and only brother, my best friend … He wouldn't show up here, jumping through the window to sleep with me like he used to. I hoped he could've survived Suty's strike, and a broken leg—

A loud burp rang out. The two dwarves huddled together and wolfed down their meals. Easing over beside the nicer one, I bit into bread that tasted like old sandals—and that had a similar texture.

"Get away from us," the muscular one snarled through a mouthful. I froze but didn't move away either. Seneb reached out to his brother, but the bigger dwarf slapped his arm away. "I'll only warn you once, boy, then you'll get a beating."

My lips gaped in disbelief. "What?" I didn't think he would hate me, not after we'd helped Yuf.

Harkhuf's face contorted like a jackal-headed Mummy Maker's snarl. I backed away to an empty corner, and someone shoved me into the wall. I hit with a thud, and pain shot up my chin into my face. Wahankh grabbed the cup from my hand and pried the bread from my fingers. Chuckling, he shoved it all into his mouth.

I braced against the wall, dumbfounded. Anger sparked and heat rose in my cheeks as I studied the much larger man. He'd destroy me if I tried to fight back. Was this what life was like outside the comfort of the palace? People still took from the less fortunate, but here they did it much more savagely. I needed food, or I'd never survive.

Guards stood beside the doorway, but they didn't turn around to help. They probably didn't care what happened in the barracks, as long as we didn't run away. Pity dripped from the faces of a few men around me, but others grinned, and some even laughed and pointed. Yuf averted his wrinkled face as he gummed the bread he'd dunked into his beer. Pressing myself against the wall for security, I turned my back to the room and slumped down. Tears burned my eyes. I couldn't live like this, but I'd defied my old life, and Akhenaten would never take me back.

I lay awake on the gritty floor, the jumble of rank-smelling men snoring in conflicting rhythms. Intense itching arose on the inside of my leg, and then the back of my neck and head. Biting insects or lice. Disgust sent a shudder through my spine as I rolled onto my side and scratched my skin raw—leaving spots of blood under my fingernails.

Exhaustion from the long day and preceding weeks wracked my body, but my mind was the more battered. Moonlight swept through the window as sleep was unable to take me.

Creeping over snoring bodies to the doorway, I peered out into the night. Watchmen stood on duty, hovering around the slave quarters. Picking my way back over to the window, I jumped and clung to the sill. More armed guards. I wouldn't be able to escape my current predicament as easily as I had in the past. Sighing, I studied my bracelet—Father's actually—but something blue caught my eye. Tucked into the waist of my kilt was the ostrich feather, the Feather of Truth. I twirled it between my fingers. Akhenaten had given it to me so I could recall my betrayal, but I remembered it much differently. I remembered his vicious taking of the throne; a false plague of snakes and scorpions; killing Father and then the crown prince; taking Nefertiti, his own cousin … Slumping down, I curled up and closed my eyes. Hours later, I drifted off.

The beating of wings filled the night—giant wings—flapping like a ship's sail. A shrill call rang out. I stood in a vast desert where figures wandered around a foggy periphery, hunched and toiling with internal hardships. Nefertiti and Mutnedjmet walked beside me, whispering. Sheer beauty … Smiling with delight, I reached out to hug them. But something thudded into the ground behind us.

I whirled around as a giant bird's taloned feet leapt at us. Its head was human, a ba—the bird-like portion of a human soul that could travel. And this ba was one of the few people I'd ever loved.

"What is that?" Nefertiti screamed, scrambling away in fear. Dirt flew from beneath her feet, but she couldn't run.

"Father!" I yelled, squeezing the bronze bracelet upon my forearm.

"Can his ba help us?" Mutnedjmet asked, her eyes wide as she stepped up to the creature.

"Listen, Heb—" Father's head said from atop the giant bird's neck.

"I'm lost!" I said, collapsing to my knees. "What've I done?"

"Hear me!" he replied as a shudder waved through the sand like footfalls from a giant and vibrated the air around me. Dark clouds blotted out the sunlight. The outline of a tamarisk tree grew beside him, twisted and gnarled. The few pink buds that had newly formed popped open to reveal black petals ...

A wandering soul stumbled between us. Its mummified head lifted and empty sockets gazed into my eyes. I shrieked in horror. The chubby face of Amenhotep, the deceased pharaoh preceding Akhenaten, stared. Other hunched figures advanced through the fog. The watermelon-headed doctor, Pentju, grinned behind rotting teeth. Suty's monstrous form lumbered from the mist, hatred smoldering behind squinted eyes and his pig-like ear. Stomping footsteps approached and my bones shook. A hollow scream echoed in the distance, followed by another. Father's ba wheeled around to face the unseen adversary. His mighty wings flapped in streaks of red.

"Father, help me!" I yelled.

A giant stepped from the darkness at the periphery and swung an open hand at us. Its palm stretched as wide as I stood tall, ensnaring and squeezing Father. He screamed, as if in terrible pain. Akhenaten's black-painted eyelids—as large as the giant hand—emerged from behind the shadows, appearing like a skull.

Another dark hand descended upon me.

Chapter 4

Journal Translation

S CREAMING, I BOLTED upright amongst the startled slaves sleeping inside the barracks. Another nightmare …

"Shut up!" voices grumbled around the room.

The dwarves glared. Rolling over in embarrassment, I closed my eyes. These dreams were growing more frequent. Or did Father's *ba* try to visit me, only to be intercepted by someone or something? Please, no more nightmares.

"Get up!" a lanky soldier yelled, clanging his spear on his shield. "It's time for you slaves to get to work."

Rubbing my eyes, I groaned and stumbled outside. I shoved down a meager meal of watery beer and old bread before anyone came to take them.

※ ※ ※

Days dragged on, long and hot, blending together into months.

My limbs grew even thinner, and my energy waned as my body burned and darkened under the sun, although a layer of grime and purple bruises always hugged my skin. Blood stains seeped over my sandals as blisters ruptured, and calluses ravaged my hands along with nonhealing cracks. How long would it be until I fell down and died? Death seemed a welcome option compared to this horrid routine of toiling all day, collapsing at night as my joints gave out, and trying to eat my meager rations before Wahankh snatched them.

"I thought they were changing to *talatat*," Harkhuf said, eyeing a stack of smaller stone slabs by the dock. "The new building blocks were supposed to be able to be carried in two hands." His upper lip wrinkled.

"We'll be using the *talatat* soon enough," the foreman said, motioning for us to each lift a new block, as if it should be easy. "They're carving them now, before shipping."

"The stones are getting smaller so we can build faster," Seneb, the boyish dwarf said, crossing his arms. "But these aren't small enough to carry very far."

Three of us grunted as we hefted a rock weighing as much as a full-grown man and placed it on Wahankh's back and shoulder. He shuffled across the desert, straining and heaving for breath.

Chisisi balanced a slab on my shoulder. I nearly collapsed under its crushing weight. Wobbling over a short distance, I dropped the block and leapt away so I wouldn't be smashed. Sweat streamed from my brow.

"You all need to carry your weight now," the meaty foreman said, pointing at me and walking closer as he raised his leather flail. "No more using your weakness as an excuse. You either, old man." He pointed at Yuf. The other slaves all glared at us.

Tia swayed by. The foreman's large eyes focused on her chest, just below his eye level, then moved on to her backside as she passed. Whispering something to her, the foreman smiled as he smacked her buttocks and grabbed hold, squeezing. Tia's head hung, her cheeks flushing as if she were ashamed. Memories of Akhenaten and Nefertiti, and his physical power over her, flooded my mind. My teeth clenched to suppress my rage.

I jumped and grabbed the pitcher from Tia, yanking her away in the process. The foreman straightened and cleared his throat. I took a long drink as the foreman's flail rose over his head. Dropping the pitcher, I spun away for another block.

"Wait!" the foreman shouted. "There," he pointed at Wahankh, who had dropped his block in the dirt and rested his muscular frame against its shaded surface. "Give him two lashings." He held his flail out to me, handle first.

My hands fell limp in disbelief. "I can't."

"Do it," the foreman said, shoving the worn leather grip into my hands. "Or you'll get more than two, and so will this slave woman." He nodded at Tia. "We know someone in this very group is stealing rations from the storehouse. I don't know who it is yet, but I'd bet it's Wahankh. He can get a taste now, but once we catch the thief in action, they'll be very sorry."

My eyes closed as my fingers hesitantly encircled the weapon—the braided skin of an animal meant to tear the flesh of man. Stealing food? How could a slave even do that … Wahankh made sense for the thief, though.

"Get away from me," Wahankh said, standing and clenching his fists as I inched up to him.

"You better turn around and lean against that block," the short foreman said with a grin, "or I'll give everyone here a turn."

Wahankh's eyes narrowed as he swallowed. A flame ignited behind his irises, threatening retaliation. Slowly, he pivoted and placed his hands against the block, leaning against it.

I rapped the strands of the flail against his bare back without much force. Leather landed without a snap.

"Every lash that is too light adds another whipping," the foreman said, folding his arms across his chest as he stood beside me. "Now he gets three."

My breath rushed out in disbelief. Wahankh's face peeked back over his shoulder with a vile sneer. "Get on with it," he growled. "You'll get yours later."

I lashed his back, breaking open his skin. Red ran in streaks as he grunted in pain. My insides tingled with fear and remorse, and my hand trembled. I reached back for another strike.

"I thought you'd be more interested in something else," Tia said, offering her other pitcher to the short foreman.

He smiled and whispered something in her ear. She slunk away, and he smacked her on the buttocks before following her, leaving.

I dropped the flail and ran away from Wahankh as fast as I could, back to the lake for more stone blocks.

✳ ✳ ✳

That afternoon, I cowered inside the barracks for our rest during the heat. Wahankh would come for me … But who could be stealing rations from a storehouse, and how? What would their punishment be, when they—

Hooting and hollering erupted as a soft hand settled onto my back. I shrugged it away and curled up to protect myself, but the touch returned. The demure features of Tia appeared. She was carrying an armful of cups. The slaves whistled when she bent over to pick up our discarded drinks, but she slipped me a half-full cup of brown liquid. I gulped the beer as suspicion rose inside me like the liquid. Why would she help me?

"Thank you for standing up to the foreman," she whispered as she took the empty cup. "That's been going on for a long time, and no one else has done anything. I led him away to his superior, who doesn't want him touching me, because ..." She swallowed. "But the foreman had thought I was taking him somewhere else." After clearing her throat, she said, "Anyway, he won't be touching me for a while. You, on the other hand, need real help. It's hard to fit in and make friends with those you don't have anything in common with. But you need to survive." Her petite eyebrow arched onto her forehead as her chin motioned at the dwarves. "What could you offer him? They seem like your best chance for an ally in our group."

The angry dwarf who hated me? "An outlet for his anger?" I asked, brushing my hand along the dirt floor. The faces of the slaves started to wrinkle with anger or jealousy as they watched us.

"You could be his chew toy if he wants to be a dog, but learn why he is the way he is. People have reasons, whether you think it's deserved or not." She patted my cheek. "The mightiest phoenix can be ripped from the sky by a storm, but the sparrow who learns to bend with the pressure can endure the harshest wind."

She smiled and stormed out of the barracks with the clay vessels, holding her head high as men glared and yelled, "Whore!"

My mind muddled with thoughts about her words, but the desire to protect her rose inside me. I wanted to kick the jeering men, but I couldn't fight them all. Curling up into the corner, I shut my eyes.

Perhaps Seneb's acceptance of me threatened his hateful brother. Did Harkhuf fear losing any part of Seneb to someone else, someone not like them? What could Harkhuf and I possibly have in common? Should I be mean, or try to befriend someone else? Chisisi? Yuf was even weaker than I.

That evening, after multiple short bursts of hauling my first large block, I settled an edge onto the emerging wall of some temple or monument meant to commemorate Akhenaten's divinity. Two men slid the stone into place. Aches ran across my lower back, and a twinge of pain shot up my spine. Sucking in a deep breath, I grimaced and ambled away.

Maya, a young scribe, jotted notes onto papyrus as Harkhuf marched up the ramp with his fourth block. My stomach cringed as a sense of worthlessness spread over me. Is that why he hated me, because I couldn't keep up with him?

Using the other end of his pen, Maya brushed dark hair from his oval face, revealing pale skin. He tucked his long locks behind jutting ears and furrowed his brow.

"Are we beating the other groups?" I asked, forcing a grin that tugged at the cracks on the edges of my lips.

Tapping a sandal beneath a full-length dress, he said, "No one wins. I just track progress."

Strange symbols and lines scrawled across the parchment in his hand. Fascination blossomed in my heart, like a lotus opening for the Aten. I'd seen such images and words many times. In my past life, Father had wanted me to become a scribe ... Regret arose and wrestled with my other emotions, swirling to anger.

"You must be really smart," I whispered.

He frowned. "I've spent my life studying. It's more dedication than brains."

"Could I learn, then?" I asked, leaning closer.

"No." Maya shook his head and stepped back. "The lower classes and slaves cannot learn such a skill. Return to your work." He pointed toward the lake.

My shoulders slumped as I followed Chisisi.

Night finally descended, and our exhausted group limped to the barracks.

"Boy!" a voice called from behind.

My heart leapt into my throat. Had Wahankh come for me? But as I spun around, the face of the trickster himself emerged.

Chapter 5

Journal Translation

THE MAGICIAN—THE TRICKSTER—stared back at me. Spider web markings encompassed his broad face, and the black wig sat on his head again. Those pale eyes contrasted against the trenches of black-painted wrinkles, which appeared as deep as the Nile. A white cat sat on his shoulder, rolls of fat hanging from her lower belly. Towering behind them, a statue of Akhenaten guarded the southern border of Karnak—the stone devil and his demon minion.

"Heb, come here, boy," the son of Hapu said, waving me closer.

A lanky soldier outside the barracks grabbed my arm, holding me fast. "Sir, what brings you to the slave's quarters?" the soldier asked the son of Hapu.

"This is of no consequence to you," the magician replied, running liver-spotted hands across his shaven body. "Send the boy over. I'll return him to your watch in a moment."

The soldier released me and swallowed as he adjusted his rawhide shield and padded cap.

"Heb," the son of Hapu whispered as I neared. "I know you've reason to question me, but I require your services. I'm trying to help Egypt … and you."

"I've heard this before," I said, hatred searing through my eyes. "Why would I trust you? You wanted to usurp the throne. But you failed."

"Boy," he sighed, "I was appointed as the co-regent at the sed-festival by Amenhotep himself. Pharaoh discovered something. Don't you see? He didn't want Akhenaten to succeed him. He would've given the kingdom to an old fool not of his bloodline rather than to his own son!"

"Why's Akhenaten pharaoh now, then?" I asked, folding my arms across my chest, skeptical.

"I couldn't stop him." He held his palms out as his forehead creased under the thick wig. "Akhenaten has grown too powerful. A genius who wields magic. His are not common tricks, either. I've seen him scratch the surface, but I sense a vastness inside. One I have never felt. Secrets lay buried and locked away, deeper and darker than you could fathom. People question his direction, but he holds complete and utter control of Egypt's military. He enforces any command by the might of the greatest army on Earth, if not from his own power—magic like a great flood of the Nile, ever growing, gathering in fury. He'll consume Egypt in his wake, leaving nothing behind. No future, no past."

"What are you doing about it?" I asked. This magician talked a lot but never acted.

The cat on his shoulder let out a soft meow as she glared at me with unblinking blue eyes.

"I'm trying to work with him to remedy Egypt. Akhenaten cannot be dethroned by might. Only a united front of its people could stand against his immortal wrath."

"And why didn't his plague of serpents strike you down?" I asked. "If all the powerful magicians of Egypt are falling victim to his outbreak, why not you?"

"I've offered him complete servitude," the son of Hapu whispered. "Because he permanently removes those who oppose him. I'm acting in diplomacy in order to stay alive and help my country."

"I wonder what my dead father would think of your diplomacy?" I raised an eyebrow.

"Listen, boy, we're cloaked here by me, but I've only a short time to perform magic undetected. Pharaoh's been preoccupied as of late. But if he finds out I've talked to you or utilized magic without his permission, I'll go missing or be found dead and diagnosed with plague. Then all magic will be lost to this world forever."

"Help me escape," I said, reaching out to him.

"I gave you a chance before!" He leaned in close. "Your decisions were your own. You may blame others, but being stuck here is a product of your own choosing. You accepted the risk of love, or Nefertiti's lack thereof!"

Stepping back, my chin fell to my chest. How did he know?

"Many a man has fallen for the wrong woman, especially one so beautiful as Nefertiti. But you decided your own tragedy and fate. However, I do say: Do not be the leaf carried in the wind, or your life will be decided by others. Instead, be the wind."

My fists clenched in rage. "The threads of fate can't be altered!" I shouted. "Especially by one so insignificant as me." The words of Father, Mahu, and all of Egypt agreed on the matter.

"Passively accepting circumstance creates the weak and lazy," the magician said, his shaven eyebrows narrowing as he shook a long finger. "Hence, is there anything you can do to change your life? You'd sit here as a slave the rest of your days if you believed such rubbish!" He slapped me across the cheek. I stumbled back. His eyes narrowed and his deeply wrinkled face contorted. "You are one of the only people who hasn't stood idly by. Don't give up now."

"What else can I do?" I asked, holding my stinging cheek. Visions of striking the feeble old man raced through my mind.

"I cannot see what lies ahead. A darkness has descended upon all of Egypt. The mist is too opaque." He tugged at the white sash across his chest, and the cat slipped and leapt down to the desert. She sauntered over to my ankles and rubbed against them; its soft hair and warmth caressed my skin as only one creature ever had. Croc. "Your resolve in the face of impending disaster gave me hope that we could resist even this madness. I saw your raw will, the sheer determination of a mere boy, and realized mighty people still dwell beside the river, even if one cannot spot them with the naked eye. To achieve what you had at one time desired, you'll need to expand your mind. That cannot be done by huddling alone in a corner each night!"

I gasped in surprise. How did he know all this? I yelled, "All my fighting failed, and I've no will left. It's been drained out of me."

"Quiet!" The son of Hapu glanced around. "The louder you talk, the more energy I must expend to keep us hidden! He'll taste us soon. You must escape, but not yet. There's one who watches you. One of his conjuring, after

Akhenaten cursed you for the insults that cut gashes in his soul. That will never be forgotten. It watches day and night, does not tire, and does not sleep."

I swallowed in horror. "When I asked Nefertiti to run away with me?" My head hung.

"And tried to rise above the position the Aten granted you."

"Who's watching me?" I asked.

"Although I cannot see," he replied, closing his cloudy eyes, "I presume time will ease his anger. A lull in his animosity will create relaxation in his oversight. In the coming years, you may have a chance, but you'll need knowledge and skill to make any difference. That in itself will take decades—time we don't have."

"What are you talking about? Who's still watching me?"

"Him!" The magician pointed a crooked finger into the night.

Chapter 6

Journal Translation

"THE HUNTER," THE MAGICIAN whispered as he pointed into the night. "The Devouring Monster of the underworld."

Darkness parted like low clouds, revealing a spot of dim light. Atop a stone block in the distance, a figure cloaked in black stood watching. Folds of shadowy cloth billowed in a dry wind, the stench of death carrying to my nostrils. I dropped to my knees, terror crushing my heart like the jaws of a crocodile.

Blackness settled back around the figure. "He's seen me!" The son of Hapu pulled his white sash tight about his shoulders. His hands trembled. "I will not be able to openly speak to you for some time, if ever. But know this: The greatest heroes did not have only one mentor, no matter what the tales say. You must learn from those around you. Learn from everyone, even if it's how not to do things. If you desire to escape, you must press forward with all that you possess, no matter how little that is."

Reaching out a wrinkled hand, he clutched tiny, rolled-up sheets of papyrus. "You must keep these hidden. I don't know of anyone who can be trusted. When you've deciphered their meaning, I'll find you."

I snatched the minute scrolls and unrolled them. Jumbles of images. "I can't read!"

"You'll find a way," he said, hurrying off. Twilight crawled over towering pylons and statues of my former master. A cloaked figure leapt down and vanished into darkness.

"Hey!" the guard at the barracks barked, lifting his spear. "Get over here!"

Stuffing the papyrus into my kilt, I jogged to the barracks and lay down inside.

The Hunter was watching me? I shuddered as horror worked its way through my skin and into my bones like burrowing worms. How could I ever hope to keep my soul from the nothingness this beast brought upon its victims? There was no greater punishment than to have your heart eaten by the Devouring Monster. One would cease to live in any world, as if you had never existed at all and had never meant anything. But how could I ever escape this place and that monster? I squeezed my eyes shut.

✳ ✳ ✳

The following day, I ported a small *talatat* block in two hands, drenched in sweat and dirt, following the line of hunched slaves. Yuf walked just ahead of me. I marched before an architect and the foreman, who watched the unending line. After passing my block to the craftsmen at the temple wall, Tia handed me a jug of beer.

"Do slaves ever just give up?" I asked in a whisper.

Tia's dark eyes widened and she swallowed, as if she couldn't speak.

"Not unless they physically can't move from pain or cramps," Yuf said in a raspy voice. "Too much fear of the consequences." He rubbed his lower back.

"What're those?" I asked.

"You have to repay your debts to society by working until you can't. If you don't, when you die, Anubis will feed your heart to the Devouring Monster, and you'll be lost to the chaos, the nothingness." He shook his head and shuddered. "You haven't reached the end of hope already, have you, young man?"

I held my breath as tension rose in my chest. All slaves would be consumed if they didn't work themselves to death? I didn't respond for a moment. "Why are you here?"

"They say men work harder when pretty women wait at the finish line." Yuf smiled and nodded at Tia. She cocked her head and batted long eyelashes.

I shook my head. "No, that's not what I meant. How did you—?"

"I've been here for over three decades," Yuf said, shrugging. "Took some extra rations. My family—"

"Some?" Tia asked, raising a thin eyebrow.

"Okay, did it a few times, actually, when my kids were hungry." He placed his hands out. Peeling calluses ran across his palms like dry hills, interspersed with ravines of cracks and creeks of blood.

My stomach dropped, and nausea rose. This man was cursed to be a slave for the rest of his life because he took rations for his family? So similar to how I became Akhenaten's servant, torn form a life destined to become a respected scribe—a memory I still could not face.

"Turns out the man I was stealing from happened to be related to the high priest of Thebes," Yuf said and chuckled in a hoarse tone, followed by a cough. "Should've found out whose grain—"

"The festival's almost here," Maya said, jotting on papyrus with his reed brush. "We need to work faster."

"What festival?" I asked. Tia stood straight and proper, gazing off into the distance.

Maya frowned. "The one everybody's been preparing for. Pharaoh's first sed-festival."

"Akhenaten?" I asked.

Chisisi laughed as he strode past, dropped a block into place, and brushed back his shoulder-length hair. "No, the other pharaoh," he said, smacking me on the back and knocking me forward a step.

"It is strange," Maya said. "The first sed-festival typically occurs after a glorious thirty-year reign. Then we celebrate his divinity."

"How long's this pharaoh been ruling?" Seneb asked, wiping his smooth brow as he accepted a jug from Tia.

Maya rubbed his eyes and yawned. "Three years."

My chest tightened in shocking pain. Already?

"It's easy to track," Maya said, his long hair shining behind ears like cups. "The date is now based on his reign. Year One of Egypt, for the eons to come, began with Akhenaten."

"How can he bury the past?" a deep voice grumbled. Harkhuf shoved a block into place as Wahankh snatched the jug from Seneb, gulping the remaining contents.

"Could he even alter the future?" Seneb asked, standing still, as if paralyzed with fear.

"Pharaoh is God on Earth," Maya said.

Something burned inside me, knotting my stomach again as if I carried a disease. I leaned over and vomited a string of bile.

Maya cringed and stepped back, but Tia placed a hand on my shoulder and offered water. Sipping, I swished away the burning acid lining my mouth and throat, and I spat.

"He despises Pharaoh and Egypt as much as you," Seneb said to Harkhuf while pointing at me.

The muscular brother snarled and stomped off. "He can't handle the work."

"If you want to make friends, you have to be one of them," Tia whispered in my ear. "But control your temper. If you lose it, hatred could fester. Either be polite and ease your way in, or go in swinging. I've seen both work for different people, but I don't picture you doing the latter."

My mind wandered. This woman was smart, like Mutnedjmet. Was she advising me, just because I tried to help her once? What did she really want from me?

I nodded.

"Entice him," she said.

I stood straight. "That's easy for a beautiful woman to say."

She lowered her head and shook her locks side to side, and an edge grated in her voice. "It's easier for me with men, but they've also been taking advantage of me for years. They always desire something in return. You can use your own strategy."

"I don't think I can entice Harkhuf."

"You can influence people's feelings by expression and words." She cupped her chest and frowned, as if to say "save me from the foreman."

Pity rose in my heart. She was right. I should be careful with her, or I'd be used—like with Nefertiti.

"You can make them happy, excited, depressed, mad, or even angry," she said.

"I didn't make him angry," I replied, sighing.

"No," she said. "But if you're too happy, you could make his anger worse. Find another emotion, or another person."

"I've tried to talk to Maya, but he doesn't want me too close," I said, turning away.

"The upper class is different. Instead of finding something in common, win them over by serving them well while acknowledging their superiority."

An artist chiseled into the temple wall we were building, revealing a scene of fearful Egyptians bowing in the dust below a towering Akhenaten. Sunbeams offered *ankh* symbols to Akhenaten as a manifestation of life and dominion. The image of my nemesis twisted my soul. I'd tear this wall down with my own hands and bury it below the depths of the Nile. I would read the magician's scrolls tonight …

After sunset, I faced the wall of the barracks and unrolled the papyrus sheets the magician had given me. The fading sunlight and new sweat stains on the parchment didn't help, but images ran rampant over the paper like insects across a field. Recognizing birds and men didn't help me make sense of it, even after several hours. Cursing the son of Hapu, I rolled the papyrus sheets up and tucked them away.

The following day, people arrived by boat from all over Egypt and beyond. Feasting and drinking for the laborers, elite, and most of Egypt dragged on for days as people celebrated around Thebes. We slaves remained trapped in the barracks, as we were not supposed to be working and in the way of the party. But watched as we rested.

Pharaoh's gleaming figure appeared in the distance, at Karnak, surrounded by servants and guards. My stomach clenched, overwhelmed with a torrent of emotion. Akhenaten's body was gold—as if he were the embodiment of a god. Ascending a flight of stairs, Pharaoh slowly joined with an image of the Aten, reinforcing his supreme and unquestionable divinity for the world.

My insides crawled in anger and disbelief, the disease in my stomach—whatever it was—that I carried always responding first. The feather on my kilt felt hot, like fire. I couldn't think beyond Akhenaten and my last encounter with Nefertiti and her sister, Mutnedjmet. I'd grown to almost despise Nefertiti for who she'd become and for her choices, but all of that could've been Akhenaten's doing, even magical manipulation of her mind. And deep down, I still loved the real Nefertiti. It was Akhenaten who'd twisted her mind, making her the person he wanted her to be and corrupting her character, which was why she'd treated me the way she had. I'd just waited far too long, and by that time Akhenaten had pulled her too far into the darkness. But could she still love me, if I saved her?

Lying down, I pictured Croc's orange and white fur curled up against my neck. I'd stroke his stripes and under his chin, and his purring would settle me. That cat could always make me feel better—ever since I'd saved him from drowning when I was a child and he a kitten. My heart ached for him. He had to still be alive.

Days passed as the celebration continued. Examining the scrolls night after night inside the barracks didn't teach me how to interpret them. My face grew hot in anger, and I crumpled a scroll in my palm.

The visitors departed, and we were forced back to work, carrying and stacking blocks. I kicked through the dust, shuffled up the ramp, and huffed as I slammed a stone into place.

Maya raised an eyebrow and marked his parchment for the stone placement.

"What power do you hold?" I asked, pointing at his work. "To speak through images?"

The scribe smiled. "They say only a rare few possess magic, but the truth is something else."

"Do you command magic?" I asked, my eyes widening.

"Magic is in the eye of the beholder," he said, shaking out his writing hand. Turning the back of his hand to me, he extended and spread his fingers. His pen didn't fall. Rather, it floated against the backside of his fingers.

"You're a magician!"

Laughing, Maya turned his palm to me. The index finger of his other hand—which I thought had been gripping his wrist with the others—was extended and concealed, holding the pen and making it appear to float. "Not in the way you think, but words themselves are magic. Feeling and thoughts are expressed in the heart, but the ability to utter and communicate emotions and ideas to others, or write them down for the future, is no less than a miracle."

My forehead wrinkled as I took in his words and stumbled closer. I studied a strange image upon the papyrus atop his writing palette—a tube with symmetric rectangles. "What does that mean?"

"That is *sema*, the trachea and lungs," he said. "The unification of equal parts."

"Can I draw it? I don't wield magic, but this would brighten the life of a slave boy."

"You're nearly a man, and you have to get back to work," he said, tapping his chin. "Make it quick." Dipping the pen in black paint, he handed it to me along with his writing pallet.

My hands shook as my skin tingled with energy. The reed shaft of the pen was smooth, but the tip scratched at the parchment as I traced an outline, its magic flowing up my arm and into my soul. The resemblance was weak, but I shuddered with joy and hopped up and down.

Maya chuckled and took back his tools. "Good try."

"I'd love to draw something else, when there's time," I said.

He waved me off. "Get back to work, slave."

Striding off, a lightness grew in my steps. After working another hour, I found a moment to hurry away to the toilets—holes dug into the desert—to relieve myself. A few guards stood watch around the area, but I yanked a scroll from my kilt and hunched down over it. Unrolling the parchment, I saw the symbol.

Chapter 7

Journal Translation

THE SYMBOL UPON THE TINY papyrus scroll the magician had given me was the depiction of a trachea and lungs—the unification of equal parts. My limbs shook in anticipation. I'd solve the magician's riddles right now ... But *so* many more images were scrawled over the paper, and I couldn't make sense of any of the rest of them. My shoulders slumped. It would take far too long to be able to read these! Grunting in frustration, I closed my eyes. I crumpled up the papyrus and threw them all down.

After taking two steps back, I paused. A sphinx-shaped rock sat in front of me. Heaving with all my might, I lifted the torso-sized stone from the desert, and a stretching sensation pulled at my lower back. I dropped it on the scrolls with a thud. The sound, and the thought of them being flattened, made me grin—although the facial expression initiated a pain from tugging open the cracks running across my lips. *That's for you ... I only wish it were you under the rock, magician.*

When I returned, the other slaves hobbled over for their dinners. I took my place at the very end of the line and received the only remaining food— a sad piece of dark bread and a half-filled jug of beer. A guard pointed for me to go inside our hovel. Passing through the doorway, I was shoved into the dirt while my meal was torn from my hands. I attempted to stand, but Wahankh balled up a large fist and cocked it. Rage burned in his eyes as he punched my shoulder multiple times, sending waves of force crashing through my frail body.

Shoving the bread into his mouth, he washed it down with my beer before strutting across the large inner chamber. Everyone watched. This wasn't anything new now. I brushed myself off, the heat of embarrassment and anger burning in my cheeks. Could I entice that man, or become his friend? I wanted to punish him if I could, but perhaps he'd be a better friend than enemy.

The boyish dwarf, Seneb, shook his head. "I'd like to help, but you need to stand up for yourself, or it'll be the death of you. You're not a helpless old man." He paused. "How's that leg of yours?" He pointed to the wicked scar crawling around my ankle—the one from the hippopotamus bite.

"It doesn't bother me anymore," I said, pulling my knees up to my chest and scooting into the corner.

"Stop talking to the Egyptian," Harkhuf growled, then he drained his cup.

"Relax," Seneb said. "He's not responsible for your capture, or for the Egyptian slave trade."

Harkhuf's dark face paled, his eyes widening as they wandered and viewed some memory. Sweat dripped from his forehead, and his teeth ground together so tightly, a grating erupted from his head. Seneb rested a hand on his brother's shoulder, and the gruff dwarf swallowed, snapping out of his trance. "He's still an Egyptian and has it easy." His dark eyes focused on me. "Why don't you sit with your own kind?"

The bridge of my nose wrinkled with confusion. Who was my own kind? I glanced around. There were others from outside the kingdom, men with thin moustaches and beards and angular eyes or darker skin. "Do you mean Wahankh?" I asked. "I'm an Egyptian slave, rather than a Nubian, but I'm nothing like him."

"You can't tell the inside of this boy from his outside," Seneb said to his brother.

"If he wants to sit with us, he can't be a weakling." Harkhuf spat onto the ground. "They go easy on him."

My face flushed as anger mounted. Shouting, I climbed to my feet. "I may not be able to lift blocks of stone like you, but nothing is easy for me. I've lost my family, my friends, my love, and my cat! I've suffered more than you!" Harkhuf's face blurred as I fought off burning tears for my own self-pity.

Harkhuf punched the ground. Standing, his eyes turned wild as he approached. "Have you seen them come to your home? Dark Ones?"

I gasped in disbelief. Dark Ones? Childhood tales of mysterious spirits … But over the recent years, in my dreams, I'd repeatedly seen figures in all black, with white, linen-wrapped heads and glowing green eyes.

"You haven't endured anything!" Harkhuf advanced, his shoulders arching as he heaved for breath.

"Stop, Harkhuf!" Seneb said, grabbing at him. But the muscular dwarf shook off his brother. All eyes watched.

"I'll pummel you into the dirt," Harkhuf said.

"I don't want to fight you," I said, backing away.

"Run, you coward," he growled, advancing. "Run from your every fear."

Lunging for his brother, Seneb wrapped Harkhuf in a bear hug. But Harkhuf heaved and kicked, his foot burying into my stomach. The wind rushed out of me as I sailed out of the building into the sand. Coarse dirt tore off streaks of skin as I slid to a halt.

After I gasped for breath for several minutes, a guard dragged me back inside and flopped me down at the doorway. I huddled against the frame, clutching my throbbing midsection. Loneliness tugged at my heart. Perhaps some people would hate me, no matter what I did. Too much violence and anger.

Hours faded away …

Chapter 8

Journal Translation

UNDER THE EARLY LIGHT of the next morning, I leaned over with my hands on my knees. Warm sweat already dribbled down my face and chest, mingling with a gray dust smeared across my skin—from stone I'd carried. I gasped for breath.

"What'll you do when you get out of here?" I asked Tia as she handed a jug to the freeman, Chisisi. I'd heard the others talk about their futures, with hope, even though they must realize we'd never survive to see such fantasies.

"I'll probably sail the world," Chisisi said, arching his back in a stretch, "discover new lands. I've already run a successful farm, a jeweler, and a bakery. I was getting bored. Things other people struggle with are easy for me." He looked down over the rest of us.

"He was asking Tia," Harkhuf said, grunting and focusing on Tia. "We've all heard your stories."

Tia turned away and thought for a moment. The wind lifted her hair, and her locks danced about her face, shimmering in the sunlight. "I'll save myself. No man can do it for me. I despise the men I've encountered. The only man I ever loved, my father, was taken by a crocodile when I was a child. I cannot love another. Then, when I am safe, I'll open a pottery shop in the north." Her eyes grew distant. "I can taste the silence of shutting out the world and creating time as if it were my own to control. Thick clay wraps around my hands and fingers, molding and sinking deep as I fashion meaning, order from chaos. My mind drifts for hours that could be lifetimes. The sound of birds whistling and an earthy aroma sticks in the air beside the warm fire." She took a deep breath. "Only once my mind has cleared or accepted my darkness could I raise a family. But I am not even sure I want this. I think it is only what I'm supposed to desire." Blinking rapidly, the glimmer in her dark eyes returned. She forced a smile.

A crocodile had killed her father? My heart melted with sympathy. Poor girl. Then she'd become a slave, and a target for all kinds of bad men. No wonder she believed she couldn't love another man. A yearning arose from deep within me to protect her and make her feel something from a man other than lust.

"What about you, Harkhuf?" Tia asked.

The stout dwarf stood dazed, entranced with the simple tale of her dreams. His face was more relaxed than I'd ever seen it.

"We'll return home to our kin, under the drums of the valley, like the great herds coming home to winter," Seneb said, nudging his brother in the ribs. "We'll appreciate our way of life much more than before the fall, the Dark Ones, and the Shadows—"

Harkhuf silenced Seneb with a backhand to the stomach. The gruff brother's scowling countenance returned.

"What fall?" Chisisi asked, wiping his brow with a thin hand.

Harkhuf cast a warning glance to his brother. Seneb's lips twitched, struggling to remain silent. What evil lurked in the dwarves' past—other than murdering their former Egyptian master who'd tortured them? A greater atrocity—one that Harkhuf would want to hide?

"Well, I, for one," Chisisi said, glancing around, "will be looking for a wife after we're done here." He winked at Tia, but she rolled her eyes. He hadn't heard a word she'd just said.

"I'll find me another wife," Yuf said, shuffling over in his hunched posture. "Then I'll die a happy man."

We marched back to the lake. The thick wig of the magician stood out at the base of a temple. Pointing, he barked orders at a foreman.

As he continued to verbally lash the man who tried to explain some situation, I approached.

"The blocks need to be laid out on the ground in another layer first, before going higher," the magician shouted, and the foreman hurried away.

"The son of Hapu," I said.

A wrinkled face spun to scrutinize me, his naked eyebrows narrowing.

"I need assistance with the scrolls," I whispered. "I can't decipher them, and I've tried everything."

The magician yelled, "Paramessu, this slave boy is talking to me. Get him back to work!"

I tripped in surprise. A strong hand squeezed my arm and spun me around, forcing me back to my group. A snap filled the air as a flail buried itself into my shoulder with searing pain. Screaming, I fell to the ground, holding out my hands in defense.

The assailant's strong jaw framed a long, hooked nose and pale eyes. The short hair on his head burned red like fire. "Discipline is what society is founded upon," my attacker said as he raised the whip. "You will obey." The flail cracked again, and I scrambled away on all fours. Warm liquid ran down my back like streams across a burning field as I hurried to the retrieve another block.

Barely tolerating the pain from the lashing and the weight of the block in my arms, I stepped onto the ramp with spasming legs. Nowhere was safe, not here. And that damned magician had betrayed me yet again, even having me whipped for trying to read his scrolls—like he'd asked me to! I would enjoy seeing him suffer one day. My stomach twisted in pain, and my leg gave out. The block dropped with a crash as I rolled down the decline.

I lay still with acceptance. I couldn't go on. Akhenaten had won, and I'd lost Nefertiti to him. The Aten's scorching heat baked the life from me, and I no longer cared.

A soft hand touched mine. A whisper, a familiar voice. The image of Father appeared over me, silhouetted by white clouds. I gasped and blinked. The hand reached lower and grabbed my arm. Was I dead?

Pulling me, Father faded into the clouds. Maya had helped me to my feet, away from the line of block-toting slaves and laborers. I supported myself with my hands on my knees. The muscles in my lower back spasmed and burned.

"Take a look at this," Maya said, sifting through several sheets of papyrus before handing one to me. Only a few images and hash marks filled the empty space of the parchment. "I need someone to make a few copies to be disseminated to the appropriate people." He paused. "I could use your help, but you'd have to do it at night."

My eyes narrowed with suspicion. Did he need help, or did he actually feel sorry for me? "I can try," I said.

"Good, and I'll make sure you get more to eat." Maya glanced back through the dust to the toiling slave line. "So, if it is you who is stealing bread from the stores, please stop before they starve you in retaliation. I'll inform the guards you're working for me at night as punishment and to not let other slaves harass you during your assignments. A guard will supply you with the papyrus, pen, ink, and the original documents after dinner."

I nodded in disbelief and staggered to the block I'd dropped.

✳ ✳ ✳

Weeks became months, the days the same, although the meaning of time slipped away. I never saw a chance for an escape, remaining in a constant struggle to consume food before I lost it. My only joy came in copying Maya's documents under twilight.

"Your proportions of the *meseh* are off," Maya told me one morning before work. "The crocodile's tail is too long, his jaws and body too short."

I nodded. He'd always corrected my mistakes and showed me why.

Someone scoffed as they passed by behind us. Maya quickly folded up my parchment and tucked it away. "Back to work, slave," Maya said and cleared his throat.

My eyes grew wide with fear as I turned …

But the magician continued walking away, his white cat perched on his shoulder. He didn't even glance back. Images of the papyrus scrolls he'd given me, which I'd crumpled up months ago, sprang into my mind.

I jogged off to relieve myself before the others started hauling blocks for the day. The sphinx-shaped rock was still there, beside the outhouses in the desert. Heaving, I lifted an edge of the stone. There they were—flattened parchments. I snatched them with one hand just before the large rock smashed back into the dirt. Tucking the papyrus into my kilt, I ran back to work.

Settling into my corner that night, with my back to the other slaves— some argued while others sang songs under torchlight—I glanced at the guard. He stood at the doorway, facing outside. Pulling out one of the magician's scrolls, I teased the flattened surface apart. Images spread out before me. Thoughts and sounds formed in my mind: *I know what it is you desire!*

My body tingled with the discovery. Something I'd stared at for hours and that made no sense whatsoever had shifted, images forming like emotions inside me. I shouted with elation, not caring if the others stared. I opened another scroll.

Control your temper, boy. I could see the magician's spider-vein-encompassed face in my mind as I read his words. *The first rule of diplomacy: No matter what anyone throws at you, you never lose your temper. You are the master of your emotions, not the other way around. Anger leads to misguided words and actions that will not benefit your objectives. You were not taught as a child, like the soldiers and scribes who were born into their positions. They've trained for their tasks since they could walk or talk. You need to work harder just to equal the most mediocre of them. And if mediocrity is all you desire, I'll leave you alone as the slave you've chosen to become.*

I was reading—a previous servant, and now a slave, reading! I pored over the messages ten times. My beaming smile faded. Was I missing something, some hidden meaning that was supposed to help me escape? I read it all again. *The slave you've chosen to become?*

I stood, dumbfounded, my arms dangling at my side. There were no pearls of wisdom. The son of Hapu had put me through months of torture to learn basic reading and writing, just to tell me something this ridiculous? He'd had me whipped when I tried to approach him and ask for help. And after all these months and extra hours of work, he'd tricked me yet again! Ripping the scrolls to shreds, I threw them into the air and cursed his name.

I gritted my teeth, and my face ached as I lay down and imagined my revenge.

The following day, I hauled and stacked blocks in a frenzy, trying to impress Harkhuf. But he didn't acknowledge my efforts, and I grew weary. The son of Hapu appeared, talking amongst the artists of the temple. My rage burned anew. I wanted to hurl a block at the man's head. Attempting to capture his attention, I leapt down the ramp. He glared at me as if I were an insect and shook his head. I wanted him to know I'd solved his stupid puzzles. But he waved me off and left.

What did this old bat want from me? He wasn't helping at all. Perhaps he too wanted to make me suffer.

The noon sky faded into shadow as the sun blotted out, but it didn't match the darkness creeping into my soul.

Chapter 9

Journal Translation

I SHOVED A BLOCK INTO place upon the growing wall of Akhenaten's monument, and a puff of dust billowed out, stinging my eyes and making my throat burn. I coughed, like Yuf usually did.

The stifling heat of the midday Aten faded into shadow, and a tingling cold arose. Perhaps a large cloud was drifting by. I looked up. The light of the Aten itself slid into darkness, as if another disc covered it. The stars emerged, and the horizon all around us turned to twilight. What?

My knees quaked in fear as I shivered. What could possibly harness enough power to shade the Aten? Apep, the giant snake the Aten battled in the underworld each night so that the Aten could return the following day?

People screamed and pointed. Many fell to the dirt or ran for cover. I wrung my bracelet. How could one escape if the entire world were destroyed—if Apep consumed the Aten?

After another minute, the darkness slid away and the Aten shined again, swallowing the stars with its light. Silence draped over us like a blanket. No shouting, no wind.

"Amenhotep and the pharaohs of old m-may be d-displeased," Maya whispered, his voice cracking. "I must speak to the priests." He jogged away.

"I thought the world was ending," Chisisi said, letting out a long breath.

If the world ended, perhaps I'd be saved from my torment. I glanced around, hiding a grin. But would Nefertiti and Mutnedjmet be free of Akhenaten? Or was Pharaoh bringing about the end of the world as the magician had suggested?

"Like a cobra spreading its wings in warning before it bites a moron with a musical instrument," Seneb whispered, his face to the sky.

"Never, in all my days," Yuf whispered, shivering.

The guards, foremen, and architects rushed away. We hurried back to the barracks.

That night, I fell into a deep slumber where vile creatures lurked in the mist. Linen-wrapped faces with green eyes! But a familiar voice spoke through them. "Your life is about to change ..."

Soldiers woke us early, yelling and snapping flails as they drove us out of the barracks. We followed an architect and Maya to the west lake and passed the soaring but incomplete temples and pylons we'd labored on for so long. These structures stood proudly in the red light of the glorious Aten as if bathing in the blood spilt for their construction. I wanted to destroy them all.

Our group and another boarded a rickety boat manned by toothless merchants or smugglers who reeked of salt and sweat as heavy as any of us. Shackles clanked as they locked our wrists and all of us together with long chains. Sailing out from the canal into the Nile, we turned north with the current, toward Memphis. We docked at night and at a few smaller towns along the way to pick up more unfortunate men but never left the boat.

* * *

A toothless sailor carried a sack around the boat and poured its contents into the waiting hands of the slaves. Grain flowed out of the sack into my cupped hands, but the sailor moved on before my hands were full. I swallowed a mouthful—a meal smaller than even what I was used to. My stomach growled in hunger and tugged at my other organs, as if threatening to digest them. Perhaps they wanted to keep us weaker than usual so we couldn't create any resistance.

Wind whipped the grass and brush covered banks, which blurred by. The calling of birds carried over the gusts, their bright colors bouncing amongst the foliage. The blue ostrich feather at my waist reflected the sunlight. I tried to focus on my surroundings, but my broken heart returned; thoughts of Nefertiti and Akhenaten ruling together in happiness consumed every moment. Only by taking all of their evil laughter and smiles and crushing them would I find relief.

The Aten descended into the western horizon. Something moved along the bank. Another glimpse. A white form darted from a short tree into the brush. Standing, I strained to see into the dusk. Another flash of a small creature, perhaps orange.

"What is it?" Tia whispered, her long chains clinking as she stood.

"I'm not sure …" I said.

Chisisi and Maya, two of the few unbound men, shaded their eyes and scrutinized the bank. Wahankh and the two dwarves leaned closer to the edge.

"Is something out there?" Chisisi asked. "Something dangerous?"

"A crocodile?" Harkhuf said, grinding his teeth. His eyes showed more white than ever.

Maya squeezed Harkhuf's shoulders, and his knuckles blanched. Yuf peeked over them.

"Like the boy hiding from the father inside a girl's room," Seneb whispered.

My skin prickled in anticipation. Orange and white? Memories of Croc came flooding back—my cat, my best friend, my brother, and even my savior—in more ways than one. He'd knocked a jackal-headed monster off of me once … somehow. And Mutnedjmet had then been afraid of him, thinking she'd seen something else, but she couldn't quite explain it. I should've kept him closer after that, not letting him wander away all the time. Croc never visited me in Karnak, but he'd been left on the wrong side of the river.

I released a breath. No, it couldn't actually be Croc. Even if he'd survived Suty's attack and a broken leg, he wouldn't be here, running along the water. Cats take the easiest route to food and shelter. Maybe this was a feral or some other wild animal.

The wind rustled the reeds, but the creature remained hidden.

"A crocodile or hippopotamus won't come after us on a boat this size," Seneb whispered to Harkhuf.

"I hate crocodiles," Harkhuf said, shuddering.

"If a beast attacks, I'll sacrifice our scrawny boy," Wahankh said, gripping my arm. "Then we can get away. I've seen them attack before, outside of Thebes when—"

"If you slaves don't shut up, we'll start tossing you over," a sailor with a ratty beard yelled through a couple of remaining teeth.

After the boat sailed farther from the area, the deck hands docked us on the eastern shore. Others fell asleep as the wind howled and sharp smell of stagnant water floated around us. My fingers absently traced script and hieroglyphs on the hull, the action still bringing me comfort in spite of the magician's trickery. My backside grew numb, sitting on the unforgiving wood of the boat for too long. Something rustled the bushes along the shore.

After standing and scanning the banks of the Nile, I didn't see anything in the brush. My legs wobbled with fatigue. Lying down against the cold, hard wood, my eyelids grew heavy and I drifted off.

I stood before the chewing bull and the priest with the sword—the same old recurring dream I'd had since I was a young. Children huddled around me. I knew what was about to happen. I'd seen it many times. I tried to close my eyes before the blade fell, but the nightmare changed. The cold bronze sword weighed heavy in my own hand. I gasped in surprise. The weapon was in my palm. Laughing, the other children pointed at me. But the bull was no longer just a bull. Several beasts stood before me, without animal heads. They wore heads of men. The son of Hapu, Pentju, Mudads, Suty, and even Akhenaten. My hand rose and fell on its own accord, hacking and slashing. Blood spilled, and I smiled. The children screamed and scattered in all directions. I pursued them, laughing.

Something bumped me, and I jerked back into reality. The feeling of power and dominion faded. I grimaced in disgust at the dream and my emotions. My stomach clenched, and I almost vomited.

"You were twitching like you were with a beautiful woman." Seneb smirked. "I didn't want to interrupt, but then you starting whimpering like a scolded puppy."

I rubbed my eyes. What kind of darkness had crept into my soul and made its home there? How long could I keep it at bay?

We sailed, but for how many days I couldn't recall. We ran aground on the eastern bank. Desert and farmland stretched far north and south, ringed by mountains in the distance. Only a couple of mud-brick huts sat scattered about the area.

"Get out!" the ratty-bearded sailor yelled as he grabbed my wrists and unlocked the shackles. "This is your new home."

As we filed from the ship, another vessel docked, carrying militia and policemen. These guards made a quick exchange with the sailors who'd delivered us and ushered us away from the bank. Soon a multitude of artisans, scribes, laborers, and other slaves arrived and unloaded. A short man, withered by the sun, demonstrated how to create bricks from the mud of the riverbank. He scooped clay into a frame mold and baked it under the Aten until it hardened like rock.

"You'll be building a city," the man said, raising his hands to the sky. "The new capital of Egypt. The greatest city the world has ever seen!"

※ ※ ※

Armies of slaves and free laborers fashioned mud bricks by the tens of thousands. We erected houses and buildings in the driving sun, dust, and wind under the guidance of foremen and architects. The days were no easier, but the atmosphere felt different—a new frontier swirling with fear of the unknown.

"Can't you mark that we completed another house?" Chisisi asked Maya, running a thin hand across his sweaty forehead.

"No, I can't lie," Maya said, brushing his long hair behind jutting ears. "My scribe status would be revoked."

"We'd get more food," Wahankh said, veins bulging on his forearms as he clenched his fists.

"And everyone here deserves more," Maya said, "but if I start lying, we'll be caught, then we'll be punished. We need to keep accurate—"

"You don't give a goat's horn about slaves," Wahankh said, towering over the scribe.

"I do," Maya said, "but we have to work with diplomacy. I've spoken with our superiors and explained that we could work harder if we received more food, but the stores have run low. There're short rations for everyone until the next shipment. Plus, they've cut back on our group, as someone is still sneaking into the storehouses and stealing grain."

Still stealing food? How, and who? I glanced around. Tia stared into the distance as if trying to ignore the situation. Seneb and Harkhuf stacked bricks, appearing uninterested … perhaps on purpose? Yuf leaned against the wall of a building, his mouth open and revealing many missing teeth. My gaze lingered on Wahankh, and then Chisisi.

"It wasn't like this in Amenhotep's time," Chisisi said, kicking a stone.

"Quiet!" Maya said, placing a finger to his lips. "You, too, could be enslaved, or a slave could be killed, if such talk is heard by others."

"A freeman wouldn't care if a slave is killed," Wahankh said, spitting at Maya's feet. "If I catch who is stealing food, the man responsible for paring down my meals, I'll …"

"Wahankh." Maya stood tall, his large ears casting shadows across his cheeks. "You receive the same rations and take more, from those who can least defend themselves." He glanced at me. "I'll report you to the guard if you start trouble."

My throat constricted with suspense as the two men locked eyes. Wahankh's jaw muscles bulged. Maya swallowed.

Slowly turning, the slave strode away for another mud brick. I sighed in relief.

We returned to our endless work.

Gathering inside barracks not yet roofed, at least thirty slaves fought for space to sleep. Soldiers stood on night watch. My head sagged with depression. How could anyone escape from this location and hope to survive? We couldn't run and blend in with the people of any surrounding city—there weren't any. Nor could we flee into the desert. The entire region to the north, east, and south was encased with mountains, creating a natural fortress. The only way out would be to chance a swim down the Nile. And to venture into those waters without a boat risked death by a number of methods.

A faint green light streamed through the window, the glow carrying over and drifting out the doorway. My skin tingled with apprehension. I'd seen this before, with magic.

Standing, I crept over snoozing slaves to peek outside.

"Where'd he come from?" Harkhuf asked in a grumble.

I jumped.

"Where's he going," Seneb mumbled. "Tia? Where'd Tia go? Gone, like girls after passing wind."

Harkhuf's eyelids were open, but a glaze clouded his irises. Seneb's eyes remained closed. Waving a hand over the bearded dwarf's face didn't cause him to blink. The two continued to banter, sleeping. I snuck to the doorway.

Green light radiated from the outskirts of the ghost town outside. The wind died out, the air growing heavy. Everything lay quiet, but a chill crept into my bones. The watchman outside slept standing up against his spear. My tongue cramped as I inched past him, wandering east toward the mountains.

Could there be a sphinx out here just over the knoll, like I'd seen in Thebes before I'd been forced into slavery? Death seemed more inviting than my current life, so what did I have to fear?

Cresting the hill, I found someone waiting for me.

Chapter 10

Present Day

DAWN'S SUNLIGHT ANGLED through the outer glass doors of the hotel as I stepped from the elevator, buttoning up my shirt. Kaylin sat on a green armchair in the lobby. Aiden, Kaylin's brother, and Jenkins, their bodyguard, must've still been in their rooms.

"We'll be back on the trail today," Mr. Scalone said into his phone as he paced the quiet lobby, his boots clunking on the tiled floor. "We all want to find Maddie."

My fists clenched. This treasure hunter had lied and pretended to be a tour guide, then attempted to impede locating the Hall of Records so that he could remain in control of our group. But the worst part was that we still needed him out here in Egypt, as the rest of us didn't know much about exhuming artifacts, locating treasure, or dealing with locals.

Tossing back dark hair, he nodded and scratched thick stubble. "Either way, we'll keep on it." He hit a button and lowered his phone.

Kaylin jogged to Mr. Scalone, her long legs showing toned muscle below her blue shorts. "We need to get going," she said.

Mr. Scalone pivoted around, and his tight jeans bulged at the seams. "There's something we need to do first." Most of his white shirt was unbuttoned, which exposed his rippling chest and abdominal muscles.

"More important than helping Maddie?" Kaylin asked and tugged at his rolled-up sleeve.

"Someone might be able to help us," he said, "and if not, we'll get right back to searching for her ourselves."

He exited the lobby through the front doors and waved for Kaylin to follow, eyeing her up and down.

The bridge of my nose wrinkled in frustration as I finished tucking my stained shirt into my pants. Who did he know who could possibly help us find Maddie? She'd been taken from me far too early, just like my dad—whose letter and discovery had brought us all here—and just like Nefertiti from Heb. My teeth ground together, creating a grating in my head. But we didn't even know what Maddie's captors wanted. She was my main priority, but tracking clues in order to locate the Hall of Records was the only time these abductors showed themselves—probably trying to prevent us from locating the ancient secret. But why?

If we could get the abductors to show up again, we could set a trap and capture them or follow them back to Maddie. Continuing along the trail to the Hall would give us the best chance of saving her.

I ran outside after Mr. Scalone and Kaylin. Heat blasted my exposed face, as if I sat too close to a fire—a sharp contrast to the air-conditioned interior.

"Who were you talking to?" I asked Mr. Scalone as I slid into our silver SUV with the boxy frame.

"The Minister of Antiquities," he snarled over his shoulder as he cranked up the air conditioning and fan so that I could barely hear him from the back seat. The sudden chill tingled my skin.

"Why are you still talking to the Minister of Antiquities?" I asked, my jaw agape. "He may've been responsible for sending those two men to abduct Maddie. Remember, the ones we hired in Luxor to help excavate the tomb?"

Mr. Scalone scoffed and shook his head. His dark locks waved above his shoulders. How much resentment did he still harbor against me? He turned around. Black circles hung thick under his eyes—a gross reminder of my kick to his nose for attempting to stop me from climbing one of the Colossi of Amenhotep. He pointed at my chest. "Let me tell you this: He wants us to find Maddie and the Hall of Records. He's assisting me in ways you couldn't understand. You'll actually be inhibiting Maddie's rescue if you restrict our conversations."

"Why does he want to help us now?" I asked, my fingers digging into the soft leather seat. "When we originally met with him, he told us that exhuming artifacts carried stiff sentences and he could not allow it."

"The Minister of Antiquities cannot let random people, especially an ignorant boy like you, just come in and excavate historical sites," Mr. Scalone replied, turning back around. His knuckles blanched white as he squeezed the steering wheel. "But if we unearth the loot in the Hall, the wonder of people from around the world will come flooding back to Egypt. Egypt needs this as much as we do."

Mr. Scalone hit the gas, and I flew back into the leather, the acceleration tugging at my insides. We sped down dusty roads between low-rise buildings before turning left and veering toward the river.

"The minister has flown down to meet us," Mr. Scalone said over the hum of tires on asphalt, leaning back and driving with only one wrist on top of the steering wheel. "He's concerned about Maddie's disappearance and wants to help any way he can."

"Why would an antiquities minister get involved with an abduction?" I asked.

"Gavin," Kaylin said, turning around. Her long hair waved across her cheeks. "This Minister of Antiquities feels horrible that Maddie was taken, especially at a historical attraction. He might be able to offer assistance. You want all the help we can get, right?"

I glanced out the side window at the blur of buildings. Something twinged in my gut. Had Kaylin also spoken with the minister, or was she just assuming his feelings?

Mr. Scalone slammed on the brakes, and we lurched forward as he parked outside a Hilton hotel on the banks of the Nile. After jumping out, he led us into the air-conditioned building, strode directly for the lounge, ordered a shot, and downed it in one gulp.

"Paul, my friend," a man with only a slight accent said from a shadowy corner of the lounge. Standing, the man straightened his white suit and approached Mr. Scalone, who gave him a giant hug and smacked him on the back.

The Minister of Antiquities—in his white suit—smiled, beaming as he scrutinized Mr. Scalone. "Too long since I last saw you." After patting his wavy gray hair, he then pointed to chairs in the dark corner. "Come, my friends, we must discuss your circumstances."

Lowering myself into an armchair, I sank into the cushion as I studied this man and the two bodyguards who stood against the wall behind him. Something wasn't right. Women didn't receive much respect in this country, and I still wasn't convinced that these men truly wanted to help Maddie.

The minister clinked a spoon against the side of a ceramic cup and raised the steaming drink to his lips. "Tea?" He sucked in a bit of liquid, and an herbal aroma wafted around me.

Kaylin and Mr. Scalone reached for their cups.

"I am very sorry for this situation," the minister said as he brushed off the sleeve of his crisp suit jacket. "For the past few years, I've been assuring the world that Egypt is safe and that tourists should return. Now this happens." He sighed, his eyes closing above a hooked nose. "We don't want to hide anything, but we don't want this unfortunate incident scaring more people away. Egyptian families are suffering from the decline in tourism." He smiled at me.

The skin on my upper back crawled with distrust. His whole demeanor was calm and collected, as if he were in control …

"I remember you from our last encounter," he said. "Gavin, is it?"

I slowly nodded.

"I've been in contact with the ENP, and several close friends are assisting you," he said.

"The ENP?" I asked.

"The Egyptian National Police," he replied. "I am taking your friend's abduction very seriously. To me, it is an act of terrorism, and I will not tolerate anything of the sort."

"When we met with you a while back," I said, "you told us not to pursue any excavations. You told us we'd suffer severe consequences."

The minister forced a tight-lipped grin. "I have to say that kind of thing."

"So you didn't have anything to do with the two hired hands that Mr. Scalone found in Luxor?" My fingers dug into the bronze bracelet on my wrist. "The ones who took Maddie?"

"Gavin!" Kaylin kicked my foot. "He's here to help." She smiled at the minister and released an awkward chuckle.

"No." The minister spread his hands. "That is fine. No, Gavin. But we cannot let people without proper training, applications, and licensing exhume and destroy artifacts—our history. I cannot grant anyone who comes to me outside the appropriate channels these things."

My chest tightened. Maybe I'd jumped to conclusions. Anxiety about Maddie might be clouding my judgment. News of an abducted American would set back Egypt's reputation. "You had nothing to do with those men, or Maddie?"

"Absolutely not, young man," he said, not blinking.

"Mr. Scalone, your good friend"—I motioned at the treasure hunter—"hired those two men and said you'd recommended them."

"I never said any such thing," Mr. Scalone said, his Italian accent thick as he glanced at the minister.

But Mr. Scalone had, when we were back in the hotel after we'd escaped the tomb.

The minister sipped his tea and smiled. "I often make recommendations for friends, even if I don't know the people or business. I ask around as a favor." His eyes wandered, as if pondering something, before he put a fist under his chin. "But that fact may give us a clue. I will double-check where I had heard of these people. You are absolutely sure it was the same men?"

I nodded.

"I'm not sure," Kaylin said, her plump lips pursing. "They looked similar, but I have to admit, as someone who hasn't traveled to your country before, a lot of people in Egypt do."

The minister made a note on a tablet. "I understand. Egyptians who have traveled to the States have made similar comments. I don't see it, but I studied at your universities for many years."

"Reminds me of the '04 excavation," Mr. Scalone said, folding his large arms over his chest.

The minister chuckled before falling into a long conversation with Mr. Scalone, sharing stories, laughing, and clapping. The minister's eyes glowed as if his and Mr. Scalone's tales were toys and they were children. I twirled Maddie's black glasses, and a pain arose in my stomach, pain with the bite of acid—my Crohn's disease was probably acting up with all the stress. And unfortunately, my last infusion—to control the disease—was now due, which meant that soon there'd be increasing chances of a flare-up.

What were we actually doing right now? We needed to go out and find Maddie. The ancient bracelet on my left wrist grew heavier, dragging me down into the seat.

"We need to look for her, now," I said and stood.

"Gavin," the minister said, and I paused, "we will find this Maddie for you, and she will be fine. Egypt is now a safe country for tourists. And these criminals will pay dearly. Please, take this." He produced a document.

I took the paper, unfolding it as it crinkled between my fingers. A metal medallion of an eagle with a striped red, white, and black shield slid into my hand. Heavy and cold.

"This is a permit for excavating anything in Egypt that you believe will help you find her," the minister said, nodding at me. "I know you have great knowledge of ancient Egypt, but please don't destroy anything. If you show this to the local police, they will allow you entry to any site. I am offering you this only because I want to help in every way I can ... to remedy this situation."

My face dropped. We were free to pursue the path through ancient sites, without any hindrance? The minister was helping us. That was enough for me to start looking for Maddie.

I grabbed the SUV keys from Mr. Scalone and ran out of the lounge.

Chapter 11

Present Day

I MARCHED UP A DUSTY HILL in the desert in front of Mr. Scalone and Kaylin. The wind whipped around my fedora while tugging at my sleeves and pant legs, making them ripple like waves. Several other groups of tourists hiked the trails in the distance, headed to historical sites. Aiden—Kaylin's younger brother—carried the tiny fennec fox he'd purchased on this trip like a football, and Jenkins—the bodyguard Kaylin's dad had hired for them—struggled along in his slate-gray suit and sunglasses. The bodyguard's dark head glistened with sweat, and he remained as silent as usual.

Heat beat down on us from above, soaking through my pants, shirt, and hat, the temperature probably a hundred and ten degrees in the Valley of the Kings.

Mr. Scalone brushed past me and Aiden, slowing to study the fox in Aiden's arms. The fox was panting, her tongue lolling out of her mouth. But Mr. Scalone didn't grimace at the sight of the creature; instead, he reached out and patted the top of her head.

What? He'd hated that fox before, along with everyone but Kaylin and possibly Maddie. I stopped as the others continued on. Did he feel guilty now, and so he was trying to be a better person?

A single lonely cloud whisked by overhead. The wind transformed its appearance, light gliding through as it split in the center. A shifting white and gray abstract. Eyes and a face took shape, but maybe only in my mind. My breathing stopped.

Maddie.

Her features were as stern as I'd ever seen them. My heart fluttered with a swirl of emotion. She was still alive … driving me on.

I imagined her hiking the desert beside me. She was the primary reason I'd followed Dad's letter to Egypt—because she'd been pursuing the fieldwork portion of her PhD in Egyptology. The image of her in my head turned to me, and suddenly we were back in college walking through the falling maple leaves on campus. Her backpack bounced at her back as she carried her books. I tried not to look at her yoga pants, but rather tried to take all of her in as leaves floated around us in the gentle breeze.

"So, Gavin, what got you interested in ancient Egypt—from such a young age?" she asked me as I quickly directed my attention straight ahead.

I twirled a pen around my thumb as I walked. Yellow leaves crunched under our feet.

"You've been reading magazines with tombs and gold masks since your dad conveniently ordered you a subscription," she went on, "but kids don't always take up what their parents force-feed them."

I was silent. Was that really why I'd run across those images that had entranced me, before I'd even started kindergarten? My dad had said that because I'd spent hours looking at those pictures and asking questions, he'd get me my own magazines and books about the pharaohs. Was the original a trick, meant to entice me? My cheeks flushed. Maddie's insight made me feel naive.

"Gavin," she said again, adjusting her sheer glasses. "There had to be something more." Sitting down on a cedar bench, she opened some kind of vegetarian wrap and placed her water bottle beside her. "Sit down and open up." She patted the seat beside her.

I eased myself down, my nerves rising as I took a deep breath, attempting to be calm and confident. Pulling out my two cartons of milk, I took a big gulp of the cool liquid—I'd consumed the stuff like candy before it incited my intestinal disease.

"So?" Maddie asked, crunching on her wrap as her big, brown eyes bored into me. "You're a hard one to get to talk, especially about yourself."

I swallowed. She'd probably think I was a sensitive wimp, or weird … My mind raced for some macho story of bravery, like Indiana Jones, but I'd already made her wait too long. I couldn't come up with anything other than the truth. "I—I had a dog. Well, I've always had dogs," I said, taking a breath and then swallowing a forkful of rice. "But this was the best dog, a border collie who used to go everywhere with me. We'd play baseball, fetch, swim, Frisbee, or anything, all day, everyday."

She stopped chewing and studied my face, brushing her brown hair behind her ears.

"Tater was my best friend growing up. I didn't have any brothers or sisters, and we were inseparable." My eyes closed. "But he died suddenly when I was about eight. I just woke up and he was having some kind of seizure on my bed. We took him to the vet, and they scanned his head. He had a brain tumor. They offered surgery but told me he wouldn't be the same dog after that procedure. I wanted him, not a wandering ghost. And I didn't want him to suffer like that, just for me. So, after a day of seizing and never waking up, we put him down. My parents told me that I'd see him again when I went to Heaven." I looked away, blinking to clear the rising tears that stung my eyes. "But the next day at recess, my teacher asked me why I was crying. I told her about Tater and that I'd see him again in Heaven. She said it's a well-known fact that animals don't have souls, and so Tater would never have an afterlife." I swallowed. "I fell apart."

Maddie smiled but wiped at her eyes.

"That's when I thought of it: mummified animals in ancient Egypt. I'd seen pictures of them. The only way to ensure that I'd get to see Tater again was to learn everything I could about that time, including how to mummify his body. I'd make him immortal." I chuckled, biting back rising sorrow. "The problem was that I didn't find out until later that my parents had already had him cremated."

Maddie laughed, but tears burst out. Rubbing my shoulder with tender fingers, she said, "You'll see Tater again. People aren't as special as they like to think."

Her words warmed my heart. I loved her. "How about you?" I asked, coughing to hide the lump of sadness in my throat.

"I just really liked ancient Egypt," she said, smiling.

"What? No, you can't do that," I said, nearly dropping my plate. "You said I had to have some reason."

"Well, then I guess it's because of our lost connection to history and to our ancestors." She removed her glasses and cleared off the mist from her tears. "Understanding the greatest mysteries of our past will help with mankind's future. At least, I want to believe that more than anything."

I stared into those gentle eyes, wanting to kiss her …

But my memories of Maddie leapt forward. That weekend she was going to meet me at a party. I planned to get a few drinks with her and tell her how I felt.

I walked through the front door of a house with a guy friend. The beating music shook the walls as people stood under flashing lights, packed together like artifacts inside an undisturbed tomb. Grabbing a plastic cup, I filled it at the keg and downed the contents with one gulp. I wanted to be having fun when Maddie saw me. I filled—

"Gavin!" Maddie yelled over the thumping music, grabbing my arm and spinning me around. She hugged me and stepped back. "This is my boyfriend, Erik."

A guy four inches taller than me, with fifty more pounds of muscle, nodded as if he couldn't care less.

I felt smaller than normal, as if I'd shrunk before them.

"Gavin's the only other person I know who wants to be an Egyptologist!" Maddie smiled as she clung to her boyfriend's bulging bicep.

"Let's dance," Erik said, pulling her out into the midst of grinding couples. I couldn't help but watch. He grabbed her glutes as he pressed her up against a wall and locked his mouth on hers.

My stomach knotted with jealousy, feeling as if someone had kicked me in the groin.

One of Erik's eyes popped open. He stared at me, watching them.

Chapter 12

Present Day

STINGING SWEAT DRIPPED INTO my eyes, returning me to the present and to the rank heat of the desert. We still hiked through the Valley of the Kings. Wiping my brow, I trudged on and attempted to keep up with Mr. Scalone and the others. The tomb of Ramose lay ahead. I needed to save Maddie, but her abductors only came after us when we were walking the ancient, hidden path to the Hall of Records. So, my best option was to locate clues to the Hall's whereabouts and hope those men showed up again.

We entered the excavated side of a mountain and descended a long, sloping corridor. My skin tingled as goose bumps rose against the plummeting temperature. The tang of damp earth permeated the air.

Jenkins's clean-shaven head turned left and right, the dark skin at the base of his skull wrinkling.

Mr. Scalone clicked on a flashlight, waving the beam around. "Reminds me of the time right before I was trapped inside a tomb ..." His words trailed off as if he'd forgotten I was there for that situation.

"The descent of the sun and the glorious dead into the underworld," I whispered. "We follow their path downward." The hairs on the back of my neck stood up as if something watched me from the shadows. The souls of the past. Their breaths cooled the stagnant air and swirled the musty scent.

"This is creeping me out," Aiden said, pausing from chomping on a mouthful of gum. His fox's panting ceased. Silence.

Jenkins turned, slapped a large hand onto my shoulder, and squeezed for reassurance.

We crept downward, only the crunch of boots on dirt breaking the quiet of the inner sanctum. The confines squeezed in around us.

I grabbed the hot metal of my flashlight and clicked it on as I entered the inner chamber. Scanning the images upon the walls, I searched for secrets—secrets that had somehow been buried for millennia in these eternal shadows. There would never be enough sunlight to create shadow illusions down here, not like in the other temples we'd visited. My heart dropped. This was probably not the right—

An engraved image of the deceased stood out before me like a mural. Studying the details of the side view profile, I muttered, "Ramose was a close relative of the son of Hapu, the magician."

"The same dude with the pool of knowledge that helped us find that last hieroglyph on the statues of Amenhotep?" Aiden asked, clutching his couple-of-pounds fox to his baggy t-shirt. The fox yipped as her huge ears deformed against Aiden's chest, but she licked his hand. "The upside-down image of the sunrise that brought us here?"

I nodded. The magician's relative, Ramose, was an old man in the journal's story. And Akhenaten had killed Ramose for resisting him in the council. "The images on this wall were made in typical style," I said, passing my light over processions of Egyptians and a cluster of women who were wailing for the dead. "Then, as if Egypt transformed overnight, the Amarna era began." My light scanned the opposite wall, highlighting figures with elongated frames, necks, and skulls—like modern alien replicas. "There, Akhenaten, still named Amenhotep the fourth at the time, sits beside Ma'at, the goddess of justice and her Feather of Truth." Standing behind Pharaoh, a proud woman in a red dress held a papyrus staff and the ankh. The blue ostrich feather rested in her headband—the same feather that Heb carried with him as a reminder of his days with Akhenaten. Questions about the journal and the past floated in my mind. Whose history survived the ancient world?

My beam of light crawled across the paintings.

"Was she the beautiful one?" Aiden whispered, pointing. His smacking lips resumed as he chewed at his mouthful of gum.

In another image, a woman with exquisite features sat beside Akhenaten on a balcony. "Nefertiti beside her pharaoh," I said and scribbled some notes with a pen. My stomach cramped. "Ramose stands before them, being rewarded with gold—a repeating image in all of the noble tombs of el-Amarna."

"So that's, like, why you led us here first?" Kaylin asked, hugging herself and shivering. "You thought the hieroglyph we discovered at the colossi suggested el-Amarna, but the first signs of the era were found here?"

Mr. Scalone dangled an arm around her shoulder and chest, as if to warm her up.

I nodded as I popped chalky antacids into my mouth to calm my stomach—and hopefully ward off my rising disease. A fruity taste coated my palate. Maybe we should push on, but I needed to give myself ample time so that we wouldn't have to come all the way—

Aiden screamed. I jumped in surprise. He'd already been exploring a sloping passage in the corner. Jenkins sprinted off into the darkness, and I followed. Red dreadlocks appeared, bouncing above the buzzed sides of Aiden's head as he staggered backward. His flashlight lay on the ground, and he pointed into the shadows. The fox in his arms yipped. Jenkins held a handgun but aimed it downward.

I flashed my light over a mummified skull that rested at a grotesque angle within a niche in the wall, its deep sockets unyielding to the light.

"R-Ramose?" Aiden asked, his voice cracking. Green gum fell from his lips onto the ground.

"This is the burial chamber," I said, stepping forward and examining the human bones. No inscriptions on them.

"Do we need a clear pyramid to catch the light?" Mr. Scalone asked, approaching. "Like with those giant statues?"

I shrugged, my gut telling me otherwise. "Each clue that we've discovered has revealed itself in a new way. I doubt it. Not down here."

Mr. Scalone grumbled something, then louder, said, "I want to help Maddie as much as you do." He wandered off.

I scrutinized the chambers for hours, taking notes and using my flashlight to cast shadows across objects at various angles. Mr. Scalone photographed everything—an illegal act—but Maddie might need it, and, in some respects, we were now above that law. Turning on the camera on my phone, I videoed the scenes while altering the origin of my light. Nothing.

I sighed and scratched the sparse stubble on my jaw. Maddie would be able to figure this out.

Mr. Scalone grabbed his pack and marched out. "You have to know when to move on."

Kaylin followed him, flanked by Jenkins.

"C'mon, Gavin, it's probably gettin' dark out," Aiden said, sliding a couple of new pieces of gum between his lips and chomping on them with his mouth open. "We've been here for more than half a day, and I don't think those sun and shadow tricks will work down here." He motioned with a nod of his flat-billed cap, stood, and trailed after the others.

The prickling on my neck returned, as if something watched me. Glancing about the dark chambers, I imagined the processions carrying in the dead and laying him to rest. At what time had someone returned and left a clue to the Hall—the ancient Egyptian's greatest cache of wealth and knowledge? Or maybe this place only confirmed that el-Amarna was the next step on the path to the Hall.

Maddie's face arose in the darkness. I jerked upright in shock. No—it was only in my mind, another daydream. Taking a deep breath, I exhaled, my breath thick like fog. She sat still and silent, unblinking as her shiny brown hair dangled over her shoulders. Her eyes begged me to save her, pain visible in their depths. Where could they have taken her? I imagined the captors at her side, laughing, even groping her. Racing at them with blind rage, I'd strike one man down with a blow from my flashlight to the base of his skull. Bone would crack. The other would stumble back in fear as I approached him like a warrior, veins that I didn't know I had popping from my arms. The man would turn and run, and I'd scoop Maddie up in my arms and hold her close. I'd never let her go again.

But she was strong herself, not a princess who always needed saving. She'd hug me but push me away and snatch my flashlight only to chase after—

A gunshot exploded and echoed inside the narrow corridor, disrupting my daydream. My ears rang, and my head swooned. Dropping my messenger bag, I spun around.

Chapter 13

Present Day

I RACED UP THE SLOPING corridor of the tomb, toward the sound of the gunshot. Kaylin, Aiden, and Mr. Scalone stood motionless against the walls of the tomb.

Jenkins sat with his back to me, clutching his chest. His handgun was still in his grip. Aiming at something outside of the tomb, his hand shook, but he squeezed the trigger and returned fire. The bang rang my ears with a high-pitched buzz. A man screamed.

I couldn't move.

Jenkins groaned and grimaced as he fell to his back. Blood seeped over his hand and dripped down the walkway.

Rushing up to him, I grabbed his burly shoulders and sat him up against the wall. Mr. Scalone peeled the gun from his hand and ran back up the corridor to the entrance.

"What happened?" I asked, trying to move his hand and assess the wound, my palms slick with sweat.

"Someone shot me," Jenkins whispered, his voice airy. "I can't breathe." He gasped.

I tore his hand away from his chest, which revealed a small hole leaking blood. Wadding up the front of his jacket, I pressed it against the wound to stem the hemorrhage. Then I leaned him forward. The bullet had exited his upper back, and a large circle of blood encompassed the area, pooling across his clothes and painting the wall he'd been leaning against red.

My heart thundered against my ribs, and my breathing grew shallow. "Hold on," I said, trying to yank his jacket off.

Jenkins groaned, his face drawn and pale. "It's too late; my vision is fading." His tongue and lips were blue, hypoxic.

"No! Hold on!" I jerked his jacket and shirt back as Kaylin and Aiden helped maneuver him.

His sleeves slid down and off, forcing his arms back. He howled in pain. A gaping hole of torn flesh—like raw hamburger—showed through the ripped back of his shirt.

He gasped for air, as if he couldn't catch his breath.

My stomach squirmed as I also gasped for air. I was a medical student but hadn't seen enough trauma to be able to function without the shock of the situation.

Pouring blood. A fragment of a rib. The bullet had either punctured a major vessel and was filling his chest with blood—a hemothorax—or had punctured a lung and was filling the space outside of his lungs with air—a pneumothorax. Either way, he'd be unable to oxygenate very soon.

Leaping back down into the tomb, I rifled through my bag, searching for something to drain his chest.

"Hurry, Gavin!" Kaylin shouted.

I lunged back up, holding an exposed pocketknife and the hollow casing of a pen.

Jenkins's eyes were glossy and distant. His breathing turned shallow and quick.

"I don't know how to do this," I shouted. "A chest tube could be inserted between his ribs and drain his chest of fluid or air, but I've never performed one in real life." I angled the knife at his ribs and placed the pen against his skin. "This might make it worse. And even if I help him breathe now, he may bleed out soon after."

"Do something!" Kaylin screamed. "He's going to die!"

Jenkins's big head swung against his shoulder, his blank eyes staring into mine.

"I'm sorry!" I yelled. "I'm not a doctor."

His voice was barely a whisper. "Go." His chest heaved, his tongue purple. "You can't save me. Save the girl. They've taken her to a house in the desert. Question the man who shot …" He shoved me away.

"No!" I yelled and buried the knife as far as it would go into thick layers of fat and muscle that felt like warm steak. No blood or pressurized air spewed out from his chest. And he didn't even cry out in pain.

The light in Jenkins's eyes faded, and his body went limp.

Shoving the hollow pen casing into the hole I'd made, I felt around with my fingertip. Squishy, but no opening. The knife blade hadn't been long enough to pierce his chest cavity. I shoved the pen in harder, but his intercostal muscles and bone stopped it. Plunging the knife in deeper, I tried again. Nothing. No pulse. I started CPR, pushing rhythmically on his chest with my open palms.

Hyperventilating with fear, Kaylin tried to open Jenkins's mouth.

CPR would be useless without addressing the primary chest problem … so I attempted both for another five minutes. No response. I glanced around in disbelief, the lead weight of failure tugging my shoulders downward.

The handle of another gun reflected light—the gun Jenkins had confiscated from Mr. Scalone. It was tucked into the back of his pants.

Kaylin sobbed. Aiden stood dumbfounded, as if unable to move or even blink.

My hands fell limp in shock. I'd lost him. I was training as a doctor, but I still couldn't help him. What if Maddie had met the same fate?

I closed the soft skin of Jenkins's eyelids, covering his vacant eyes.

Shouting carried down the corridor. A man's voice chanted in Arabic, as if in pain.

Grabbing the smooth handle of the gun in Jenkins's pants, I pulled it out and gasped for breath as I ran up the sunlit corridor and exited the mountain. Mr. Scalone leaned over a man who lay in the dirt. This man was dressed in a *thawb*, his face pale, his breathing shallow. He wore a beard to his chest. I recognized him immediately—one of the two hired hands from our original excavation at Amenhotep's tomb.

They did show up when we walked the ancient path …

Another gun had been kicked out of the wounded man's reach. The man muttered something, but Mr. Scalone shouted in his face, spit flying from his lips.

I shoved the gun I'd taken from Jenkins into my pants and pulled out my phone. I recorded the wounded man's Arabic ranting.

Mr. Scalone pressed a large boot to the man's stomach. An area of his *thawb* was soaked in blood. Cocking Jenkins's other gun in the man's face, Mr. Scalone shouted, "Who are you? And who do you work for?" Then he shouted something in Arabic.

The wounded man's eyes were wild as he babbled.

Pushing Mr. Scalone off of the man so that my microphone could pick up his words, I asked, "Where is Maddie, the American girl you abducted? Where did you take her?"

The wounded man clutched his belly, the red circle on his left side growing. Maybe his spleen had been ruptured by Jenkins's bullet—a slower death than the bodyguard's. I applied pressure to his wound with part of his garment. His belly was tense. If I could save him, we might get more answers. But if I opened his abdomen here, without proper instruments, I'd never locate or stop the source of hemorrhage.

"Help me lift him," I shouted. "Let's get him to a hospital."

"I'm not saving that," Mr. Scalone said, spitting on the man. "I'll help carry Jenkins."

I gritted my teeth, suppressing remorse for Jenkins. "It's too late for Jenkins. And I don't really want to help this man either, but we need him if we want to find Maddie!"

Mr. Scalone picked up the wounded man's gun. Then, grabbing an arm each, we dragged the man across the dirt and down the trail; I stumbled under his weight.

The wounded man babbled for another few minutes before his head drooped onto his chest and he stopped talking.

We lay him in the desert, and I closed his eyes. We hadn't even made it down to the valley. Hopefully he'd given us some information in his last words … but what'd Jenkins said about a house in the desert, and how had he known that?

Mr. Scalone inspected the two handguns he now carried.

My eyes closed, and my gut twisted with apprehension.

Chapter 14

Journal Translation

THE SON OF HAPU sat on the ground amidst the desert night, his back to me. Bathed in his green light, he chanted as a candle burned in the sand beside him. I approached with caution. Something brushed against my leg. Leaping back in fear, I stumbled and tripped into the sand, a jolt of pain coursing through my elbow. A fat, white cat sauntered over and rubbed against my ankle.

"My boy, or young man, rather," the magician said without turning. "I trust your voyage with the mercenary pirates was tolerable." Wiping the dirt in front of him to clear the area of markings, he stood and gazed upon me.

"They tried to starve us, but I'm alive," I said. "No thanks to you." My teeth clenched and my fists burned as anger mounted within me. I wanted to pummel him, but he was an old man.

"You do look even more frail. But I hope the days on the water didn't kill your ambition." He smiled, his naked eyebrows arching. "Welcome to the city of the horizon of the Aten, el-Amarna."

"I don't see a city," I said, grinding my foot into the dirt as I stood.

"You're helping build it. Akhenaten witnessed the sun obscured in the sky that day at this very site. He was returning from Memphis and saw it as a sign. A prime location at the center of the kingdom between Memphis and Thebes. How else to better control both the north and the south? And only his most devoted worshippers will be at hand to help rule all of Egypt. I find myself once again the head architect."

"What did happen to the Aten that day?" I asked.

His chin wrinkled, deepening the crevices traversing his face. "A few of us have scientific suspicions, but Pharaoh won't hear of it." He shook his clean-shaven head. "After returning from Memphis, he acted out of sorts. More so than usual. The temples at Karnak were nearly complete, but he grew impatient and angry. Some Thebans weren't exuding adoration for the monuments, or for the Aten, as he had expected. He said the passing shadow marked the beginning and end of times, and he believes it's the most obvious of warnings to those who stand against him and his monotheism."

"Mono ... what?" I asked.

"His worship of only the Aten. It's been his objective for years, but now it's revealing its ugly head everywhere. He'll not hear of other deities in his kingdom and is erasing the priests, their demand, and their food supply. He's started a war with the pagans of Egypt."

My forehead tightened in disbelief. "What else do people worship if not the Aten?"

"You need a great deal of lessons, but we don't have time."

"Why've I only heard of one God if there are others?"

"I don't know," he said, placing his fist on his chin. "But I have my suspicions. You were Akhenaten's for as long as you can remember. I fear he may have formulated his plans long ago, and they included you, or perhaps even the servant before you."

A vision of the filthy old man in solitary appeared in my mind. He'd run in circles, alternating voices and personalities, as if he'd practiced the performance for years. He was Akhenaten's first servant. "How would obscuring religion for me help Akhenaten become pharaoh or assist him in murdering his older brother, Thutmose?"

"It is unclear. For many reasons, religion is of utmost importance, but it'll not help you in the ways we need at the present moment. You must be patient on this subject."

A sense of mystery flooded over me, like the night Father was murdered. He had wanted to tell me something important, and it'd had to do with the afterlife.

"Now it is finally time," the magician said.

My head lurched up to attention. "For what?"

"For you to prepare for what you wish to accomplish."

"I'll never be able to accomplish what *I* wish!" I yelled, anger rising as heat in my face. "It took months of tedious work to read your stupid scrolls, only for a few words of advice. This, after you had me whipped! I grow feverish, and my insides are poison."

"If that is what you believe, you will never succeed." He shook a finger at me, the entangled dark lines on his face twisting. "Vengeance seeps from your heart through your bones and tissues, rotting your insides like you would have it do to your enemies. Turn this poison against them instead."

"How can I escape this? Much less achieve—"

"And I didn't know the captain, Paramessu, would whip you. I told you the Hunter was watching us, and we couldn't do anything suspicious or we'd both be consumed." He paused. "You didn't listen."

The bridge of my nose tightened in confusion. "Why'd you bring me out here, then?" I asked. My stomach clenched, acid rising in my throat.

"I'm here to help. Why else do you think the guard was asleep?"

"Still pretending, are you?" I said, crossing my arms. "Why help me?"

"Because you saved my life, remember?" he replied, his clean-shaven body glistening in the green light. "Remember the sphinx on the great road? He who commands the sphinx rules Egypt, remember? Only the greatest pharaohs of old could do so. Tricksters sphinxes can be, but not liars. Not unless they're asking riddles."

My lips went slack as I recalled the encounter that night, when I wore the time bender's jaguar cloak of stars. "They told me I could save people, but everyone died!"

"I already told you this in Amenhotep's mortuary complex, remember? When you were unseen by others? The Hunter killed the magicians in Karnak, but you saved me by leading the monster away from Luxor Temple, so it didn't find me working with others."

Could I believe this strange man?

"Moreover, you know Akhenaten's mind better than any living person. You played beside him for years when he was young and vulnerable, in private situations."

I folded my arms. Did that make me special? A weapon of sorts? "Is the Devouring Monster still watching us?"

"Yes," the magician said and took a deep breath. The candle on the sand blacked out. Darkness. I swallowed, glancing around, although I couldn't see anything. The flame sprang back to life, creating a dome of green light that held out the night. "But not at the moment. Time has passed, and his watch has eased. He's still awaiting your death, to consume your heart per his master's orders, but the creature has other duties and expects a young man like yourself to live for many years."

Remorse pulled my eyelids down. After suffering for a lifetime, my fate would be similar to Father's but even worse—the worst punishment known to man. I couldn't stay here until I died and have my heart consumed, losing my soul to oblivion.

Jumping at me, the son of Hapu jabbed his walking stick into my stomach.

I doubled over, more in surprise than pain, but it knocked the wind out of me. I gasped. His cat nibbled and licked my toes. I tripped over backward, sprawling out across the rough sand.

"I've been searching long and hard." The magician's lips and forehead pulled back in a grimace. "You may not hold any chance, but I've found no better takers. The others are upset and filled with internal conflict, but they lack initiative, will, and action. You've surprised me because you hold the ability to change your fate."

Rising to my elbows, I regained my breath. "What?"

"I'll help guide you to do what it is you desire."

"I can't get out of this place," I said, motioning to the mountains and empty desert. "And you have no idea what it is I truly desire."

"In your current situation, you'll become a mindless slave until your body breaks with fatigue. Then you'll be consumed by the Devouring Monster. But you can still obtain the most powerful weapon a man can wield."

My eyes widened as my stomach lurched with excitement. "I want it!" I jumped up.

"Don't be impatient; such power only comes with years of toil, diligence, and sheer willpower."

"Magic?" My mind raced. Something had happened to Suty just before he'd forced me to board the sailor's boat to Thebes. I'd made the crocodile ward, and he had been shoved away by some unseen power.

"No." The magician shook his head, shadows dancing upon the crevasses of his face. "I could teach you about magic, but you'll never accomplish what you wish by that route. I'm talking about knowledge."

My body sagged with disappointment.

"You'll never strike Akhenaten down with a magic trick. He is too powerful." Pacing in a circle, his lips pursed, he said, "You'll never be able to sweep the military out from under him with a mighty weapon, and you'll never grow close to him without diplomacy."

"Close to him? I don't want to be close to him; I despise him more than anything!"

"I know what it is you desire!" He spun on me, flames of deep green flashing beneath his eyes. "If you wish to avenge your father, utterly destroy Akhenaten, and perhaps even seduce Nefertiti, you must listen …"

The magician could smell my hunger but couldn't know how twisted my soul had become. The Devouring Monster would either choke on my poisoned insides or enjoy them like the sweetest of fruits. "All right!" I yelled. "What do I need to learn?"

"Everything," the magician replied.

I kicked the dirt. "I've tried for so long already, and besides basic writing, I've learned nothing!"

"You've learned empathy and understanding from your peers, but your diplomacy needs work. Harness the ability of science, literature, art, hand-to-hand combat, and war."

"How am I going to learn all that?" I asked.

"Over a vast amount of time … many years."

"I don't have years!" I shouted.

"Even old wise men who say 'patience is a virtue' hate waiting." He rubbed his chin. "Your young body could hold out in your current state for long enough. But mentally, you may not be able to keep the blackness at bay—since you're building his monuments and cities. I'll show you how to cope."

"I can't!" Clenching my fists, I stared down the sky.

"We all run at our own rate of speed through time, and I've considered utilizing the time bender to slow yours, but I cannot locate him. Also, I fear you'd never want to return to your given speed, so with his magic you'd age to death in a matter of days. Therefore, you'll have to work diligently every night for years, as hard as you worked with the scrolls."

"I'm exhausted in the morning and find it hard to even carry on now," I said, throwing my head back in frustration.

"If you're going to achieve what you want, you'll have to put in a lot more effort!" He poked me in the chest. "The balances are set heavily against you, and I didn't make it so. You must work much harder for your achievements or just give up now."

"I'm too tired."

"I'll teach you how to rest the mind at times and the body at others. Your brain may recover during parts of the day while your body wanders in mindless labor."

"Magic?"

"Some would say so." His eyes stole a glance at the candle, still burning bright. "But others have solved the mystery. Don't you wonder how Akhenaten did it all these years? There are creatures who learned the process eons ago. They evolved and perfected the trait. Creatures in the great oceans rest half of their brain while the other functions, and then it alternates. They do not sleep! You have to completely let one side go, while performing duties controlled exclusively by the other. Humans need sleep, but you can get away with much less for a time. It'll take its toll on your body, but if your desire burns bright enough …" The candle flickered, and the son of Hapu jumped. "I must go; the beast draws near."

My mind raced with muddled thoughts. Could I believe a word this crazy old man had said? If it meant I could live out my desires for revenge and redemption, would I be able to push on? Perhaps those feelings were all that kept me going.

"Take the candle. A magical light will arise every night just after dusk. When the flame is steady, the guards will sleep and you may come out to study. When the light flutters, the Hunter is approaching. If it goes out completely, the beast is right behind you! I've left materials buried under a boulder overhang outside the outhouses." He pointed at the barracks. "I fear I won't be able to visit you for some time, but you must remain vigilant for when we receive a chance to act!" He disappeared into the night, his cat following after him like a ghost.

Snatching the candle, I rushed to the toilets. A donkey-sized rock sheltered a mound of dirt. Digging with all my fury, I uncovered a box with papyrus sheets, books, and a sack of food. I ate ravenously as I studied writings under the flickering green flame. What if I could achieve something in this life after all? My heart lifted with hope, opening up the world. "Hope can shape radiant dreams out of the nightmares of the present," Father had once told me.

✳ ✳ ✳

The next morning, I carried a spring in my step as I scarfed down my bread and threw back drink. Wahankh made his rounds among the meekest. He snatched my jug, but I stood in defiance. He shoved my chest with one hand, and I toppled into a cloud of dust and coughed. He downed the remainder of my beer and threw the mug at me. "Stay down, dog."

I squeezed the dirt beneath my fingers in anger. Hope didn't seem to help in this world, and neither would knowledge. But it wouldn't be long until I was gone from this place. Poison spread through my internal organs, burning. I heaved, as if I'd vomit blood.

Tia crouched beside me and offered her beer. "You have to eat faster if you cannot fight him," she whispered. "And if you don't fall down, there'll be a confrontation. He's intimidated you for a long time and needs you to be an easy target. If the others he bullies see you fight him off, he'd worry they'll try the same. Your stand will have to be the most vicious."

Yuf placed a cracked hand on my shoulder. "Take mine," he said, offering me a bite of the beer-soaked bread he'd been gumming. My stomach turned, and I dry heaved.

Chisisi laughed, raising his thin arms. Three servant women surrounded him as he spoke. "If anyone took my food, they'd be eating dirt for their next meal."

One of the women giggled as another rubbed his back.

My face flushed in embarrassment. Women seemed to think Chisisi could accomplish what he spoke, but what did they have to go on? He was a freeman, I guess, but he worked with slaves. Somehow his life must not be as amazing as he made it sound. Had he been placed here, or did he prefer the company of those lesser than himself—to feel powerful? Standing, I shuffled off to work.

After dinner, I wrote and made copies, which over time became easier and quicker. I'd wait for the candle to light and read for a few hours every night. Days and nights flowed together, exhaustion racking my body most of the time. Learning became the only source of enjoyment, although many times it was also the most miserable. I read papers on mathematics, physics, geography, history, military tactics, astrology, farming, architecture, poetry, and art. But the more I learned, the more questions I had.

Weariness tugged my eyelids and head downward like lead weights, my body desiring only sleep. For one night, I hoped the old bastard would not light the candle, but the glowing green shone around me. Kicking the candle over, I buried my head. A ringing rattled around inside my skull until I stumbled out beyond the sleeping guards. Now I understood why the Egyptian words for teaching and punishment were the same.

Our group toiled for months, and an empty city sprang from the desert. But the fateful day had arrived. Over the past two days, the candle's flame had flickered after being lit. The guard remained awake, but fear of him was nothing compared to the other evil lurking out there. I stayed inside. Frustration and a sense of urgency ate at my heart, which gave me trouble sleeping—even though I now had extra hours for rest.

As I staggered along under the sun, limestone grated through dirt. Freemen heaved and rolled large blocks in from the surrounding cliffs. These slabs would frame a temple or a royal palace. Other men carved the great road, running north to south, just inland from the fertile fields along the shore. This thoroughfare stretched wide enough for many chariots and ran for miles inside our protected realm.

Blinding light shimmered from the west. The golden hull of a barge settled onto the river's bank, flanked by a countless entourage of boats. They ran aground. Hordes of militia as well as councilmen disembarked.

Akhenaten, with gold shining over most of his body, held his scepter high as he stepped onto dry land and gazed upon his emerging city. My throat tightened in rage. It could've been months or even years since I'd last seen him, but it felt like ten lifetimes.

"It's arrived!" Maya said in a high-pitched voice, cracking his knuckles.

"What has?" Chisisi asked. "Pharaoh?"

"The *benben* stone," he whispered.

Chisisi and Yuf nodded, but the dwarves looked confused with their arching eyebrows.

"What is the *benben*?" I asked.

Maya's lips parted and fell slack. He blinked a couple times before responding. "The *benben* stone was the first piece of land, an island, to arise from the waters of chaos that surround the world. The great phoenix itself, the Aten incarnate, landed on the stone and called out. For a moment everything was cast in shadow—the beginning of time and existence. The cry of the phoenix could make the dumbest of men the wisest, and he could comprehend all the secrets of the universe. This person would understand what all the animals of the world and the fish of the sea are saying.

"The rest of the earth arose around the stone," Maya continued. "Now the Aten sails its barge across the watery skies in the eternal cycle of birth, death, and rebirth. This circle is the way of everything. But the day the shadow returns will mark the end of time. The *benben* stone made all of life and creation possible and holds the world's greatest powers, powers beyond all of mankind. Only the Aten itself harnesses more energy. Akhenaten discovered the stone's location and quarried it from its eternal resting place within the mountain. He constructed a room for the stone in Luxor Temple, but it never resided there. He brought it here, to el-Amarna ..."

"So the chicken did come before the egg," Seneb whispered, his eyes transfixed.

More militia descended from a boat, hauling a massive rock on a wood sled. The stone shone beautiful yellow but was translucent. It ensnared the sun's rays with its pyramid shape. Power radiated from the artifact, tingling my skin even at our distance.

"It's the pyramidion," Maya whispered, "the capstone of every pyramid and obelisk, where the Aten-phoenix landed to begin creation. We honor and celebrate its representation on every monument in hopes he'll land again and save us." Maya fell to his knees.

Stepping from a mass of royal soldiers, Akhenaten approached the stone with arms raised. His hands were not held out in adoration of the divine but to take. The living manifestation of the Aten touched the *benben* stone. A crack as loud as thunder erupted. People cried and fell to their knees. A shadow passed over the Aten, and all lay still. Sunlight flickered and returned. People cheered.

Akhenaten roared in triumph as he held his hands skyward. "The stone is mine, and it has finally found its home, our home!" The living god motioned for the men to haul the artifact north along the royal road, where a great palace and temple of the Aten were under construction.

Marching in the midst of his council and the royal guard, someone glided beside him. A woman. The scent of rose mingled with citrus. A sliver of her face revealed itself. Untold beauty. My stomach twisted and burned, bringing a painful spasm. Anger, jealousy, love, and desire swirled. It now felt like no time had passed at all, or at least time had not dulled my emotions. My heart sank into my stomach. Slumping over, I gasped for breath.

The royal ensemble approached. My comrades tripled their pace, stacking mud bricks to form the walls of a large building. I couldn't bear to have Nefertiti look upon me as a slave. After all I'd been through, I still yearned to impress her. Damn it! I didn't desire her sympathy or to scorn her; I longed to become the rich and powerful man she would admire.

Leading the entourage past our work site, the son of Hapu headed north upon the great road. Akhenaten's gaze swept over our group, then myself. No sign of recognition. I exhaled. Nefertiti's face turned, smiling. My heart pounded so hard my bones rattled in their cage. Her magnificent eyes fell upon me. In a brief instant, they, too, passed along to the city's buildings and workers.

A storm of rage, boiling blood, and spasming muscles compelled me. My body was no longer under my control. Squeezing my bracelet, I hefted a mud brick and marched directly at Pharaoh. I would see if this god-king could be killed or would die trying. I'd crush him into the earth.

Stepping between the outer perimeter of the royal guard, I hoisted the mud brick onto my shoulder. I pushed past another guard, unassuming in his wonder of this new city.

Chapter 15

Journal Translation

A HAND CLAMPED DOWN ON my shoulder and halted my progress—from attempting to crush my former master into the earth with a mud brick. The grip carried the strength of a giant. My body jolted in surprise. I pictured Akhenaten's bodyguard, Suty, but the ogre with the scarred pig's ear paced in front of me. So did Mahu, his chief of police. The Devouring Monster? I shuddered in fear. Spinning around, I intended to smash the brick into the offender's face.

I stumbled. In place of an expected demon, the magician grinned from ear to ear. How?

Somehow he'd moved around his procession and caught me from behind. And his halting force was more than physical; he had frozen my limbs. Surprise faded as I gritted my teeth in rage. Attempting to ram the brick into his frail old chest, my arms wouldn't yield to my commands. He shoved me. I fell into the dirt, smacking my face against the brick, which shot a blinding light across my vision and sent a thud through my skull. The royal entourage continued on without notice.

Ay—Nefertiti and Mutnedjmet's father and now Akhenaten's vizier, the second most powerful man in the kingdom—brushed the thick wig from his face as he passed.

The small hand of a young woman reached out from beside the handsome vizier. The gentle face of Mutnedjmet smiled, her bright eyes catching mine. Tears clouded their radiance. She spun on me, but the magician moved between us and whispered something to her father. Ay held her fast.

Time slowed as if the time bender worked against me. Mutnedjmet cried out and struggled against her father's grasp. Somehow, I witnessed my paralyzed body immobile in the sand, as if watching from someone else's eyes. Mutnedjmet's mouth moved as if she yelled to me with all her might, but no sound came forth. Something dangled from around her neck—the smashed amulet of Bes—the one she wore for me! I stared. My heart lurched and released warmth through my blood, something I hadn't felt in a long time. Was it comradery, or perhaps even—

But Akhenaten strode past, his most prized treasure at his side, my love. Nefertiti gazed in awe upon her new city while she floated by, vanishing behind buildings.

My heart melted into the sand, and hope faded like a dying man's *ka*. I loathed the magician yet again. Why did he teach me and keep telling me he was trying to help, but then assisted my nemesis, Akhenaten, every time he reared his ugly head? Rage itself would've ignited me, but there was nothing left to burn. My stomach squeezed in upon itself, as if a hippopotamus stepped on my abdomen. I vomited bloody bile. Collapsing onto the road, I lay still until Seneb rushed over. He yanked me to my knees and hauled me back.

"What were you doing?" Harkhuf yelled so loud the people of Thebes might hear him.

I remained silent.

"You looked like a hypnotized bee following its queen," Seneb said. "I don't think Pharaoh would appreciate that."

Maya hovered over me, as did Chisisi.

"Slaves!" A thin watchman with a potbelly—Mudads, the soldier who had watched over me in my past—yelled as he removed a flail from his belt. He must've arrived with the new boats. This man had tormented me, doing so out of fear of not being able to feed his large family if he didn't comply. "This is no time for resting; Pharaoh's here. Get to work!"

The others hefted bricks as I forced my feet under me and tried to walk.

I fumbled through the day, laying less than half the bricks of any other man. The acids of hate ate away at my stomach. When no one was looking, I engraved two symbols upon a mud brick I sat in the sun to harden. I put them on the top face, which would be covered, but the act brought a smirk to my lips—the only spite I'd have that day.

We returned to our open barracks, and Tia served bread. I chewed but couldn't swallow any food.

"What happened today?" Seneb asked me. "You moved like a three-toed sloth through a field of fresh dung."

The others stared.

"You go another day like this and I'll throw you into the river," Wahankh said, snarling. "We had to make up for your laziness just to eat dinner!"

"I saw Pharaoh and felt faint!" I shouted, standing and throwing my mug at the large man. Wahankh cowered from the sailing object. "My past ..."

Tense silence.

"You had something to do with Pharaoh?" Chisisi asked, crumbs tumbling out from his open mouth.

"I disappointed him as a servant, before he became the god-king," I said. I lay down in my corner as the others whispered amongst themselves. Someone sat beside me.

"Go away!" I said, not caring even if it was Tia. But Seneb was there, his boyish features wrinkled with concern. I swallowed, uneasy this close to him. His brother would tear me apart for not carrying my weight. But I didn't care.

"What happened to you?" Seneb whispered, his gaze moving across my face as if curious.

"I lost my family," I said, clenching my teeth. "My father was murdered and my best friend was punished. Perhaps he is also dead. My girl left me for another man, my evil master." Images of Father, Croc, and Nefertiti ran through my mind.

The dwarf's meaty fist reached for me. I flinched as it settled onto my shoulder with a crippling squeeze. "Maybe we're not so different after all," the kind dwarf said. "Perhaps you just need to stand up for yourself, and you don't know how. Harkhuf can help."

"What can a little man teach me about fighting? You or he cannot know suffering like I do."

Huffing, Harkhuf approached and lifted me from the floor. My feet scrambled, but as I placed them down, the dwarf kicked the side of my knee. My joint crumpled, and I toppled into the dirt. Leaping up, I punched at him. The dwarf knocked my sailing fist down, sending my arm swinging harmlessly away, and struck me in the throat. I coughed violently as my knees buckled.

"Have you seen them come?" Harkhuf growled. "Did they smoke you out and trap you in nets? Have you been dragged away from your family as your women and children scream for help? Have you lain helpless as they torch your homes with your family still inside, their screams of agony drowning out the roar of the flames? Have you smelled the burning flesh of loved ones on the wind as they take you away?"

My eyes bulged in disbelief as I rubbed at my throbbing throat. Perhaps I wasn't more tortured. I couldn't even fathom recovering from such an event as he described. "I—"

"You've haven't endured anything! Not until you've endured shame such as mine!" Harkhuf advanced, his shoulders rising as he heaved for breath. "You feel sorry for yourself, but you are a spoiled Egyptian boy."

Everyone watched. Heat rose in my face.

Harkhuf advanced. I leapt at him to take him down. He danced aside and deflected my sailing body. I flew headfirst into the ground, and a wave of pain shot through my skull and down my neck. Standing, I spit grains of dirt and said, "You're going to get hurt!"

I circled him, and the slaves erupted in cheering, making room. Feinting a punch to the right, I struck with my left. Harkhuf ducked and landed a jab on my midsection. More pain. I doubled over.

"It's not only size and aggressiveness but a combination of experience, knowledge, and skill that determines the victor," Harkhuf said, striding closer.

"All right, all right, I understand," I said, holding out my hand in truce. After a brief pause, I kicked his thigh. Knocking my leg aside, he landed a heavy fist on the back of my neck. I crumpled as my vision blurred and my head spasmed. The slaves hooted and hollered. I wobbled for several minutes before crawling up to all fours. "You made your point. I'm a weakling, but I'm still not sure you can teach me how to best real men."

Harkhuf kicked sand in my face, the sailing grit digging into my eyes as he growled. Seneb grabbed his brother and pulled him away to a far corner.

Tia touched my back, but I pushed her away. "Stay away from me!" I shouted. Her pale eyes gaped, and she ran out. Turning my back to the room, I lay down. A sinking feeling of disgust consumed me. A dwarf had even bested me, and I'd yelled at Tia. How could I ever face a god-king? Not in this life …

In an hour, the candle lit with a green flame and didn't sputter. Snatching it, I marched out past the sleeping guards into the desert. Tonight, I would break that manipulative magician.

Chapter 16

Journal Translation

THE SON OF HAPU SAT near my rock marker. I slowed my approach to hide my animosity. Wind and grit raged through the black around us. A cloud blotted out the moon.

"I'm sorry you had to see the royal couple today," the magician said, not looking up.

I continued toward him. "I'm sorry I've been your puppet for so long."

His deep crevasses narrowed in confusion.

"Today, when I had the chance to enact my revenge, it was you who stopped me. Akhenaten was mine!"

Grabbing the old man by the shoulders, I flung him down. I pinned him into the dirt and held his arms so he couldn't cast his magic. The magician's cat hissed and lumbered off, her rolls wobbling side to side.

"Heb, please—" he began as my hand ensnared his throat.

"I'm finished with your lies and treachery," I snapped, rage strengthening my limbs. "I'll ask you one more time: what are you really trying to do?"

"L-let me speak—" His words came out garbled.

"You won't trick me!"

"The mind … can only comprehend … what it understands …"

"What?" I asked, my grip loosening in surprise.

"What you need to know is that you don't know much at all!" the magician yelled as he jabbed a hand at my throat. Blocking his fingers, I pressed down on his neck. Fear jostled in his eyes—the first time I'd brought such emotion to another. He was helpless. A wave of power crashed over me, escalating my emotions and strength. Temptation. I'd gained power from all my suffering. Finally. The ability to not care about other's feelings.

His liver-spotted hands feebly pulled at mine. As I tightened my grip, the magician choked.

"I'll permanently relieve you of your duty to Pharaoh," I whispered.

His legs thrashed as his face flushed a deeper red than a rose. I grinned. Terror and helplessness stormed in his eyes like demons, a look I'd seen before—although not from my hand. The high priest of Thebes—before his heart and soul were devoured by Akhenaten! After the man had saved my life. How many others had felt the same emotion under Akhenaten's grip in the past years?

Moonlight flashed on the magician's pale face. Horror filled my soul. I felt vile, like in my dream with the bull and the children, as if I were Suty, Wahankh, or Akhenaten. I gasped at what I'd almost done, at what I'd become. I'd take my chances with magic rather than murder an old man, or I'd transform into someone I despised above all others …

Releasing his throat, I grabbed the magician's walking stick and stepped back. My body shook like a sapling in a gale. "Why did you deter me today? Again?" I asked.

Rubbing at his throat, he propped himself onto his elbows and coughed for a minute or two. The purple faded from his face. "I shouldn't be the object of your anger!" He fell into a fit of sputtering. "If you believe you could have made it past all the guards, Akhenaten's chief of police, and his bodyguard, and then smashed a brick into his head, you're beyond reason. I've wasted my time on you. Even if you did accomplish all of that out of utter determination, you'd be tortured and killed, and Akhenaten wouldn't die. He's God now. If his mortal body can even be destroyed before his time comes, you will need something much more powerful to slay him. And you have gained no control over your emotions! Without that, you can only lead others through fear and intimidation—like him!"

Nausea rolled over me like waves of the sea. Dropping to my knees, I let the stick fall. I should bury myself in the sand and die.

"I didn't want to lose one of my prime students and best hopes for Egypt to such a rash act, just because you're a victim of your ignorance and your overwhelming need for revenge!" He choked.

A different kind of horror tormented my insides—the feeling of causing terror, pain, and anguish to another, without justification. I couldn't rejoice in the emotion like others I'd encountered or let vengeance alter my morality. I would need to find another way to accomplish my goals, a way I had never seen. Swallowing, I tried to control my quaking body. "I-I'm sincerely sorry I caused you harm, but I don't fully trust you. You're telling me to follow my desires, and yet every time Akhenaten is around, you're his loyal subject."

The magician climbed to his wobbly feet and brushed himself off. "Unfortunately, my powers remain under surveillance. Tact is my only weapon. Diplomacy can be mistaken as allegiance, just as now I'd melt you to a pile of bones, but the Hunter would sense the magic I'd have to expend and immediately be sent after me!"

I cowered. "What is your objective then?"

"I want Akhenaten overthrown and Egypt placed into the hands of a leader who'll guide the kingdom into peace and prosperity. And I'll utilize the best method available."

"You should've let an idiot of a slave have a crack at him, then. Perhaps someone else would take his place."

"I don't need another mindless soldier at my disposal," he said, shoving his face against mine as spit showered my cheeks. "And a substandard one at that! The chance your attempt would've succeeded would be less likely than being struck by lightning, stung by a pack of scorpions, and bitten by cobras in the same moment." He stepped back. "I wish Akhenaten wouldn't leave his scar upon Egypt, but it will take many years for someone else to obtain enough power and influence over the people, the military, and the priests to attempt to rule them. Here in reality, it's the only way to reclaim the kingdom. He's plotted for a decade while we stood blindly at his side. Now we must give comparable time and effort to take it back."

My head drooped, and my shoulders slumped. I felt like a fool. "I'm not sure how much longer I can wait ... but what should we do?"

"We've been working at everything we can right now. You need to continue learning."

I nodded with regret and frustration. "How long do I sit and read before acting?"

"Always plan on enjoying and celebrating what you have in life as if you'll die tomorrow, but you must learn and train as if you'll live forever."

"I can't celebrate my miserable life," I shouted. "I must act soon, or die trying!"

The son of Hapu poked my chest with a gnarled finger. "Akhenaten appears so close now that he's in el-Amarna, but your plans remain distant. He's officially changed his name from Amenhotep the fourth to the Aten and the *ankh*—Akhenaten—a sign of his maniacal leadership. He's forbidden worship of Amun and talk of other gods. He desires control over every living thing."

"You didn't give me any books on religion, so I don't know these other gods."

"That's because you'd only be too confused to understand any of it," he snapped. "If you have no one to ask questions of or to feed you lies, where will you turn? Theology doesn't make the kind of sense science and laws of nature do." He folded his arms. "Tell me, young Heb, what is it you live for? What are your deepest, darkest secrets and desires?"

I tensed. If I answered, I'd be laughed at or heckled by the world's wisest man.

"What made you chance your very existence when I offered you an escape those years ago?" He paused. "That yearning must be your strength now!"

I swallowed. My desire to crush Akhenaten and win Nefertiti must be beyond what this magician was thinking.

"I know of Nefertiti," the son of Hapu said, pacing around. "Perhaps you desire her more than anything in this world. But what of Akhenaten? If everything worked out as you secretly hope, what would be your plans for him? What would be your plan for yourself?"

Embarrassment rose inside, igniting my cheeks.

"Oh," the magician said, a grin lifting his lips. "You do have what I'm looking for. But your need for revenge will not benefit you. It may drive you, but do not let a single emotion be what you live for. You'll never succeed, and vengeance may poison your goals. You must harness it."

"What're you talking about? I'm powerless and will never escape!"

"You already have." He patted my shoulder.

"I've escaped servitude for slavery. Not exactly headed in the right direction."

"Not all paths are a straight road. First you have to hike the trail." He pretended to walk on a tightrope across the dirt, toying with me.

"Stop!" I shouted.

He chuckled. "I need to know one thing before we continue."

The bridge of my nose furrowed with suspicion.

He peered deep into my eyes. "Why didn't you kill me?" The son of Hapu's face pressed against mine, and he dug a bent finger into my neck. "Yes, why didn't you kill me? Anger consumed you, and you believed I alone crushed your plans, plans you won't openly discuss."

I stepped back and stiffened. What was he getting at? Why did he want to know why I hadn't strangled him? "I felt horrible for inflicting fear and suffering upon someone I wasn't convinced deserved it."

"Will you be able to inflict it when needed?"

I bit my lip. Could he be leading me into some kind of trap? Could it be possible all he needed me to do was say what I wanted? What would happen then—arrest, execution, or perhaps his loyalty?

I said, "I could inflict punishment on the deserving."

"Suddenly very diplomatic." His chin jutted forward and he nodded. "I do believe of all the others whom I am training, you may be one of the better ones." He paused. "And you should always respect people affected by reversal of fortune." He wagged his finger at me.

Who were these others he was training, and how where they doing? I'd bet they were probably in easier situations than mine.

"Just because you're weak in this life doesn't mean it'll be the same in the next, or vice versa. If you torment the weak here and now, you'll pay for it later. Think of Suty. I know his personality and motives. If your roles were reversed, would you torment him?"

"I'd feel sorry for him, if he were decent. And I'd not be so harsh." I shook my head as images of the vile beast and his scarred pig's ear formed in my mind.

He handed me a sack. "You must eat and grow physically strong in this life if you're to command power over the judging masses. Many do not wield the mental capacity to understand the powers of the mind alone. They need to see to believe."

Tearing into grains and root vegetables with renewed vigor, I studied long into the night. My life did have meaning and purpose. But why'd this old man put himself out to educate me and the others he spoke of? Even if I knew the real Akhenaten more than anyone, there had to be better alternatives than me. And people didn't help the likes of me. They invested their efforts for rewards from those with power to grant such things. Or did he actually expect me to overthrow Akhenaten? My mind drifted in thought as my body tensed. I desired that too, but the magnitude of such a feat seemed far beyond the likes of anyone, especially me. And how many more years of slavery could I endure trying to become powerful enough to even attempt this? Desperation must've brought the son of Hapu to me, or he wasn't as wise as I'd been led to believe—rather, mad.

"Slave labor only exhausts the same muscles and joints over and over again," the magician said. "Soon you'll be a crippled old man. You need to strengthen your entire body and be prepared for anything. Utilize exercises when your short attention span falters with your studies." The old magician showed me how to execute a single repetition of a squat. "Now perform a set of thirty."

I performed the exercise, and more, lifting myself with my arms and legs at many different angles, in many different postions, until I collapsed.

"Repeat all the exercises for a second set," he said, departing. "And if you need guidance beyond this crazy old man and your friends, seek answers from the dead ..."

I fell onto my backside during a squat and glanced up at him in shock. "How can someone talk to the dead?" I asked, my tongue going dry.

"You can write to those who've passed," he said. "You have the skills. Ask for advice, or whatever it is you long for."

My chin wrinkled in disbelief. This old man was crazy. How could I write a letter to the dead? Could Father's *ba* really read it? Would he offer wisdom, or at least console me?

A disc sailed across the distance between us far too easily for his toss. I caught the object. A bowl held a reed pen and a container of ink.

"The bowl is your papyrus," the son of Hapu said and winked. "Write to anyone who's passed into the other realm. Then leave it at the rock, and I'll make sure it arrives at the appropriate tomb."

"But my father doesn't have a tomb, nor would Croc."

"I'll fill the bowl with his favorite food and wine, enough to sustain his *ba* for a brief visit." He strode north, fading into the night. "He's being watched, and his body was burned, so he won't be able to appear for long. But I don't need an official tomb. Where he's buried will suffice, which is near Amenhotep in the Valley of the Kings. I'll make haste."

My chin jutted back in surprise. Father's scorched bones were buried? "I don't know what to write!"

"Yes, you do; you just won't tell me. Listen to your heart when all's quiet and you lie awake. This is when your heart speaks loudest and you can best hear its desires, dreams, and aspirations. Silence your brain from worry and stress and let your heart guide you ..."

After walking two steps toward the barracks, I spun around. "Who's watching Father?"

Empty silence.

I buried the bowl and pen in the sand beside the rock and returned to the barracks. I listened for my heart's voice amidst the snoring of the other slaves, and images of Father ran through my mind—his broad, flat face and short gray hair. His kind smile lit up as he embraced me. Cold bronze from his bracelet dug into my skin, the one I now wore. The metal upon his arm glistened in my mind, like eyes I remembered. Those vibrating bright eyes ... of Mutnedjmet. So inquisitive and full of wonder.

I recalled a time I'd never thought of before. As children, Nefertiti and I had waited for Pharaoh outside the audience hall. Mutnedjmet was there, as always, even though I wanted to be alone with Nefertiti. A cool breeze blew behind us, rustling my kilt, and the scent of citrus and rose hung on the air.

"It's hot out here," Nefertiti had said, fanning at those beautiful cheek-bones sculpting her heart-shaped face.

"At least we're not with Akhenaten right now," Mutnedjmet said, skipping around a tamarisk tree so full of pink petals it appeared like a puffy cloud at dusk. "Did I ever tell you about the time I saw crocodiles stand up like men and walk out of the river?"

Nefertiti shook her head and closed her eyes in irritation.

I couldn't help but grin, which blossomed into a beaming smile as I touched the shaded bark of the tree. Rough, but cool and—

Someone lumbered in through the darkened doorway of the barracks, returning me to the present. The rasping of a parched throat filled the barracks as the outline of the intruder's hunched frame heaved for breath. The figure slowly settled onto the floor and made snoring noises too quickly to actually have fallen asleep. What the … Yuf?

Stomping feet preceded torches that appeared at the doorway, as well as two armed guards.

"We've got you now, thief!" Mudads shouted as he stepped inside, raising his spear.

Chapter 17

Journal Translation

SLAVES GRUMBLED INSIDE the barracks and sat up under dancing torchlight, startled from the soldier's entrance and threat of punishment for the thief.

Mudads and the soldier beside him scouted about.

"We saw the thief come from the grain room," Mudads said, his torchlight moving across the disturbed slaves as he stepped over them. "A hunched figure, like this old man!" He pointed at Yuf, whose eyes bulged like moons.

Yuf stuttered a few times, his toothless mouth trembling. "N-no, no, I'm too old and tired. I can't move around like that without someone catching me." He held up a gnarled hand in defense as Mudads advanced with his spear.

"An old man just has to urinate several times during the night, huh?" the other guard asked Yuf—this must have been how Yuf had gotten past the guard and out of the barracks.

My throat clamped shut with horror. Would they stab a helpless old man? I leapt to my feet. "It was me," I shouted.

Turning, the guards eyed me. Mudads shook his head. "The thief didn't move like you."

"I hunch when I run, to try to hide," I muttered, lowering my head.

"Boy," Mudads said, rubbing at his belly. "If you confess and allow another thief to get off, everyone in this room will have two days without bread. If you admit you didn't do it and that this old man did, we'll only punish him … although he may starve to death."

"Don't do it," Wahankh bellowed, pointing at me as his thick jaw muscles tensed. "You starve me, and I'll take everything from you. More than just your beer."

Others jeered in agreement.

My insides tensed with fear. Burning rolled through my stomach like fire. I dry heaved and leaned over. Was stealing from the stores really worse than stealing from the weak, like Wahankh did? I guess those in power didn't care as much that way. Should I let another old man, like Father, lose his soul—they would surely take it—or have everyone besides Tia despise me even more?

I forced a breath in through shaking ribs. "I-I did it," I muttered.

The slaves yelled obscenities.

Mudads's chin furrowed. "You did it to yourself, boy, although I don't believe you, and someone in this group needs to suffer the consequences. So we'll just have to punish everyone, and they will punish you all the more. No bread for this group for two days. You'll be sorry by the end." The guards marched out.

I turned my back and curled into my corner. The others screamed threats as I covered my ears. Rocks pelted my back with sharp stings. What had I done? I needed friends.

✳ ✳ ✳

The next morning, my stomach growled and spasmed with hunger as my energy drained. Tearing pain from sore muscles—from my exercises—made walking torture. My arms and legs burned, and my back ached much more than normal. I kept my distance from the others and studied the surrounding mountain range and then the river—shimmering purple light reflected off of the water, blurring my vision. Could I escape this place?

The royal barge blotted out a portion of the reflected light as it disembarked the shores of el-Amarna, sailing south with a fleet of vessels.

Where was Akhenaten headed to now?

That night, the candle flame burned steady. I dug up the bowl. But the magician would see whatever I wrote ... I didn't care anymore.

After scribbling a dark letter to Father about my situation and suffering, I exercised and read about other creatures we shared the world with. The horse was fascinating, a creature who could run like the wind and be trained to pull a warrior's chariot. One soldier would drive the animal and protect the chariot occupants with a shield while an archer disposed of adversaries. The chariot team of three comprised the most powerful weapon in the world.

What would the trembling wood of a chariot feel like beneath my feet as wind raced through my hair and pounding hooves struck the desert, pulling me into battle? And the cool curve of the bow, and the magic of the arrow in my fingers, or the supple reins controlling the mighty steed? How many other amazing things did this world hold, things Akhenaten had hidden from me, and that I'd never see as a slave?

The starvation days, with only liquids for sustenance, passed—although Wahankh took my beer. Many days and nights blended together, time disappearing more and more quickly. Seasons arrived and departed, and after months or perhaps years of teaching, the magician vanished. But I continued my studies and training.

※ ※ ※

A mountain of gold floated down the Nile, settling onto the bank just after dawn, likely years into my slavery at el-Amarna. Several minutes passed before I realized the great royal barge, with an exuberant overhaul, had returned. Hundreds of smaller boats followed in its wake.

"Like a diamond sitting upon a pile of donkey dung," Seneb said, watching the royal barge land at el-Amarna.

"Egypt's most faithful will inhabit the city," Maya announced, slinging his writing palette over his shoulder as the arrivals unloaded their belongings.

"Where will we be shipped off to next?" Chisisi asked. He stacked bricks with us in the southern outskirts. "Or do I have to return ... home?"

"I've no orders to slow our work," Maya said. "El-Amarna will surpass Thebes as the largest city in the world. We'll build outwards, and then upwards."

"The entire military's arrived!" Harkhuf said, pointing.

Towering ships of war docked south of the others, and vast contingents of armed men flooded the banks. Tens of thousands with spears, shields, swords, and bows marched the great royal road, headed north.

The day of grand entrances continued, but none compared to the next. A ray of sunlight sparkled on the great road, traveling with enormous speed. The mightiest army the world had ever seen fell to their knees, trembling. People exited their new homes to witness the first parade of the Aten. All of el-Amarna bowed and groveled in the sand.

A golden chariot, drawn by two white horses, raced along the royal road, reflecting sunlight. Gripping the reins, Akhenaten drove the creatures southward as all the world prayed from their knees. Pharaoh portrayed the living Aten, driving his chariot across the land instead of the watery skies. The blue feather of Ma'at at my waist felt hot and heavy, burning and pulling me downward.

Spinning wheels from the golden chariot neared. Hooves thundered across the desert beneath huge plumes of bright feathers atop the horses' heads. Slaves and laborers collapsed. The horses snorted as they galloped, their bodies dripping thick sweat. They reached the southern end of that nine-mile stretch of the great road. Whirling the cart back around, Akhenaten drove them back to his grand palace. Beside him, previously obscured, stood a shorter figure wearing a flat-topped crown. Nefertiti, the queen of Egypt. Smiling, she gazed over her people while holding on to her king in all his glory.

Her happiness struck me like a bolt of lightning. My stomach sank and a wave of nausea overcame me, causing me to lean over and heave. Returning to a standing position, I contrasted against the bowing masses. Her gaze fell upon me. My skin tingled. Whether she recognized me or not, I couldn't tell, but I didn't recall the hunger burning in her eyes.

"Get down!" Chisisi said. "Or you'll be struck dead!"

Chisisi and Wahankh cowered in the dirt. A rush of pride and defiance filled my soul. Only one other still stood, but he wasn't conspicuous among the bowing. Harkhuf spat on the ground, his short stature blending in with the masses.

Perhaps Nefertiti remembered me and didn't want me punished, so she said nothing. Or what if she felt pity for me? But the chance she'd recognize me after all these years, and from this distance amongst tens of thousands of slaves and laborers, would be miniscule.

The golden chariot of the Aten raced north in its divine cycle, parading birth, death, and rebirth by disappearing into the horizon.

Chapter 18

Journal Translation

W E WORKED THROUGH THE DAY, but I lay down to rest before the candle lit itself, signaling it was time to start training. My eyes closed, and I drifted off …

A fierce wind blew cold, carrying the scent of damp earth. The land was stark and bare. Haze floated in the air, clouding my vision. I sat alone. The gale intensified. Unseen objects whirled in gusts around me.

As I wandered an unchanging scene, dark shapes appeared in the distance. I struggled against the forces of nature, wind and fog, to look closer. Buildings emerged along the skyline, at first tiny dots, but I crept closer until they created a vast city, high rooftops all interconnecting and completely blotting out light. Darkness reigned. El-Amarna?

A faint shimmer of green light surrounded me as I walked into this city. Rubble and discarded items lay strewn inside buildings and alleyways. The city appeared abandoned, but I continued deeper. Someone lay on the ground. Inching toward them, I called out. No response. Grabbing for my bracelet, I instead touched my skin. Father's bronze was gone.

I leaned over to inspect this person. Bones from their face showed through mummified skin, their sunken eye sockets hollow.

I gasped in fear and tiptoed around the desiccated corpse. More shriveled bodies littered the narrow road ahead, curled into fetal positions with perfect north to south orientation, but facing west. How did I know direction inside this city of darkness?

The dead clung to each other in spooning positions. Movement flashed to my right. But nothing was there. Snickering filled the air along with humming, as if to a hymn. Shapes shifted just beyond the edge of my vision, but I couldn't see them in their entirety. I froze. Dark Ones, draped in black with linen-wrapped faces? I'd seen them enough in visions but never knew who or what they were. The voices surrounded me and closed in. I couldn't move. My heart raced, and the hair on the back of my neck stood on end. I attempted to scream, but nothing came out. A bright light blinded me, and the beating of wings sounded. I shielded my eyes.

"Heb!" Father's voice said! "I'm being detained and can speak for only a moment."

"Father!" I cried, reaching out. The light dimmed, and Father's face appeared atop a great red falcon's body. The dead city no longer surrounded me, only a misty desert.

"I heard you and will guide you with all my power. I would've explained more in life if I knew—"

"Father! I've become a slave and am hopelessly lost!"

"Follow your hopes and desires, Heb," he said. "Netjer imy.k."

"What?" I screamed.

"It means 'the god who is within you'. The kingdom burning inside you should be your guide, not external forces! Don't revel and wallow in this kingdom, but use it as strength. Do not plan for the moment, only live in the moment. Make your future! It's not only yours, but my last hope to shape a dream from this nightmare. Bring your friends home. Travel and understand not only Egypt but the world. Journey east, north, south, and finally fade into the west. You must find the clues themselves. There're no clear answers to these riddles. Then you will return!"

"I don't have any friends. And I can't travel anywhere!" I wailed. "The wicked prosper while the good suffer. I'm alone in a cruel, dark world and just want it all to end!"

"The answers are hidden inside you, inside everyone. Netjer imy.k. You're not alone. Find a guide, another who grows in the belly of your woman, one who'll be your greatest ally, and find yourself. If you cannot stay, then take your comrades and leave!"

A deafening boom rumbled, vibrating the ground. Father's ba glanced back in panic.

In the west, a tsunami of water so tall it could cover all the monuments of Egypt barreled down on us—

Springing to my feet with greater ease than I'd ever experienced, I glanced around. Everyone in the barracks snored. My candle lay dark. The guard paced outside, muttering to himself. Blood drained from my face in apprehension. The *benben* stone, Akhenaten, the guard, the late hour, and the unlit candle meant something was terribly awry.

Could the magician have delivered the bowl to Father's remains in western Thebes? Is that why Father had visited me?

Green from the candle's flame finally flickered to life.

The flame wavered as if a gust of wind blew inside the barracks. I peeked outside. It was dark, and the guard had dozed off. Sneaking out to the rock, I found a large sack with a spear resting against it. Inside the canvas was a jumble of books, papyrus sheets, brushes, a jug of beer, paint, a sword, bread, flint, oil, and a lamp.

A bow and arrows also rested in the dirt under the overhang.

Picking up the treated wood, I strummed the bowstring. Vibrations as beautiful as any musical instrument rang in my ear. Tingling seeped through my limbs, carrying up my veins to my heart as warmth radiated through my body. The weapon I had always wished to wield, to unleash its magic! Grabbing an arrow, I nocked it. With all my strength, I tugged the string and held it taut. Veins I'd never seen before popped along my arm—thicker than I remembered. The cord bit into my fingertips, but I tasted something, something just out of memory. How many enemies had this very weapon disposed of? I let the arrow fly. Feather and wood whistled through the night faster than a diving eagle.

Yanking the sack from beneath the rock revealed a letter. I grabbed it and read:

Heb,

I've been gone too long, overseeing the construction of the Great Temple of the Aten. I've been ordered to care of the *benben* stone, as only one with immense wisdom can be trusted with its power. Akhenaten doesn't have the patience. But I fear it. No one should control the beginning and end of the world. Time is drawing nigh. I fear Akhenaten's ascendency all the more since its arrival. He knows all, everything I now attempt—this is the reason why you have not heard from me in some time. I cannot put you in danger. We must overcome the power that has manifested as Akhenaten, the greatest Egypt has ever known. It will not be without turmoil and much patience. The dictator has grown supreme. I wish I could have taught you much more, but I have placed a spell on the back of this papyrus. You hold magic! Use it wisely. I know what it is you desire! Harness it and make it reality, for Egypt.

My hands shook in anticipation. Flipping the letter over, I read the spell, memorizing arcane hieroglyphs. It didn't make sense, nor hint at what it was supposed to do.

Another sealed note drifted to the ground. The outside read: *Do not open unless I am dead!*

Tearing through the papyrus and wax revealed a map. Directions and markings showed a location upon a hillside in the Valley of the Gates of the Kings. The writing on the back said: *My final secret. I would have told you when it was time, but if you are reading this, I have not succeeded. I've shared this with no one, but it could be the reason they came for me. The map will guide you to the resting place of Amenhotep, his unfathomable gold and treasure, and the weapon you must acquire. Utilize the rain. Locate the eye of Horus!*

At the bottom corner, something read simply: *The Mask: The touch of the underworld.* And several arcane symbols were scrawled beneath it.

My body tingled with excitement as I spun my bracelet. Gold? Could I locate this secret stash and become rich and powerful? The first step toward facing Akhenaten and Nefertiti. I shuddered.

Striding back to the barracks, I held my head high, like when matching Nefertiti's gaze. The son of Hapu was wise—far beyond me—but I couldn't toil in this pit while the vilest of beasts lived the life of grandeur and all-encompassing power.

I wouldn't be studying or training tonight.

Tonight, I would escape!

Chapter 19

Journal Translation

MY HEART RACED AS I STUDIED the supplies the magician had left for me. Sheathing the sword in my kilt, I hefted the spear and slung the sack over my shoulder. I kissed my bracelet, grabbed the flickering candle, and forced a deep breath. Time to escape.

The guard at the barracks remained asleep. My friends—as Father had mentioned? I pictured Mutnedjmet telling me to see my true friends. My heart ached. I missed her. But I couldn't go find the magician in the city. If I had anyone here, they were inside these barracks.

I snuck inside. Holding a hand over Seneb's mouth, I shook him. He tried to yell as the green light of the candle washed over his face, but I squeezed tighter. When he relaxed, I released my grip. He woke Harkhuf. The bearded dwarf's wrinkled forehead of confusion lasted only a moment.

"About time," Harkhuf said, grinning. "I've seen that look before, but not on you."

I searched the room. Should I wake Chisisi? He was a freeman, only avoiding his past life. He could leave by his own will when the city's construction was complete. Yuf? No, he was too old.

Creeping out, I slipped past multiple slaves I'd spent years alongside without ever really knowing. My head drooped as regret fell over me. Perhaps I should've tried to get to know them. Wahankh snored nearby, pacifying my remorse. They were mostly murderers and thieves anyway. But then again, so was I. All of our acts were judged only by those in power, those who possessed much more of everything, but who were no more, and probably often less, moral than us.

Stepping outside, I pointed to the sleeping guard and strode east into the desert. The brothers followed. Once we distanced ourselves, I'd explain my plan and let them decide if they'd risk following me.

"Stop!" someone yelled from the darkness. I wheeled around as Mudads appeared under green light and hefted a spear, racing at us. "Stop, or I'll be forced to skewer you!"

I dropped the sack, the candle, and my sword and readied my spear. The light of the green flame flickered but didn't go out. The guard's eyes popped open in surprise as he skidded to a stop and focused on my weapon. My hands squeezed the shaft in anticipation. I didn't want to harm him; he only performed his duties to feed his family.

Cocking his throwing arm, Mudads bellowed into the night. His weapon whistled through the air. I gasped. Metal flashed and a clang rang out. The shaft skittered harmlessly aside. Having deflected the weapon, Harkhuf lowered my sword.

Mudads leapt at me while reaching for his sword. I froze in fear.

The unyielding wood of the spear in my hands turned cold and slippery. I tightened my grip. The bronze of Mudads's blade glinted in the torchlight as he sneered and started to withdraw it from his waistline.

He would not hesitate to kill me now.

Lunging, I cut Mudads down with a strike through his throat—where the jugular veins and carotid arteries ran, just like in the diagrams in the books. The spear tip slid through his flesh with ease, too easy. His sword came out of his belt and fell. Blood poured forth, and the light faded from his eyes. He gurgled and collapsed. My hands quaked with terror. I dropped the candle. The magical flame sputtered as I sucked in shallow breaths. I'd read thousands of pages of papyrus—about war and killing—had been taught a great many things by the magician, and had seen monsters and magic, but I felt as if the doctor had just pulled me out of my dying mother and I'd laid eyes on the world for the first time. Shock and regret engulfed me. What had I thought would happen if I tried to escape?

"We better run!" Seneb said, turning to the desert.

"Wait!" Harkhuf growled as he grabbed my sack, yanked it away, and peeked inside. "We need to get Tia!"

Seneb lunged for Mudads's spear, and Harkhuf traded the sword for my bow and arrows. Both dwarves sprinted back to the city.

Shouting from soldiers pierced the light wind, not so far away. The flame of the candle still lying in the dirt sputtered faster. My heart raced with dread as I stumbled after the brothers.

"What're you doing?" a raspy voice asked from the barracks. Wahankh peeked his wide face out into the torchlight.

My stomach cramped. "Go back to bed, Wahankh," I commanded, surprising myself.

Sneering, he approached. I held out my hand for him to stop. Ducking my arm, he snagged my wrists in crushing grips and knocked the spear from my hands. Waving torches came closer.

"I have him!" Wahankh said. "I have the runner!"

He shoved and kicked my legs out from under me, and I tripped into the dirt. But this time I was ready. Dragging him down with me, I used my legs and his own momentum to kick him over the top of me. He crashed into the sand. Before he could stand, I wrenched his thick arm by the wrist and locked out his elbow in an arm bar, as I'd studied for months. The joint hyperextended, his arm digging into my legs and lower belly. His muscles strained and popped. Wahankh screamed in agony.

"Quiet, or I'll break your arm!" I said, surprise tightening my chest. The magician's knowledge had actually worked!

Wahankh gasped for breath between clenched teeth, his head sinking. I relaxed his arm and stood.

"You'll stay here, but we'll be leaving," I said.

"Take me with you!" he said, holding out his hand. "Please, I've nothing here!"

Mudads's body lay before me. A flap of tissue gaped open at his neck, revealing his trachea and the vessels beneath. A wave of nausea made me choke, but I clenched my mouth shut, trying to hide my weakness and rising guilt.

The dwarves dashed into the light with Tia, heaving for breath.

Shouting carried from the city's edge, growing louder.

"Like a kitten clawing a crocodile, only to find a sheep inside," Seneb said, pointing at me and Wahankh—still lying in the dirt.

Chisisi stepped from his hut and rubbed his eyes. "What're you guys doing?" he asked. Slaves peeked out of the barracks, their wide eyes reflecting the green of the candle. Yuf hobbled out, putting his wrinkled arm around Tia.

"We're leaving!" I said, checking the diminishing distance of the approaching military. "Chisisi, you're free but could still incite death if you run."

"You slaves are going to need a leader," Chisisi said, puffing out his chest. "To the hills!"

A single guard appeared under his own torch. Hurling his spear, he screamed as the weapon arced into the air. Harkhuf released an arrow, his weapon flying with much more velocity. The arrow pierced the soldier's chest—his shout turning to a wail as he toppled over. The spear buried into the dirt beside me with a loud thud, vibrating the shaft back and forth. I swallowed with fear.

I gathered my equipment and the candle, and I ran east into the darkness.

"How're we going to escape?" Tia asked, her voice airy between sprinting breaths.

"We'll climb the mountains," Chisisi said.

"At night?" Tia asked.

"Unless you can make the Aten rise in the next few minutes," I replied.

As I led the dash through pale moonlight with my flickering green candle, the forbidden mountains appeared—the shadowed guardians of the holy sunrise and the cradle of the Aten.

"We should've brought Maya," Tia said, sprinting faster than the others. Yuf had fallen behind, lost in the darkness. My heart dropped. He wouldn't be able to keep up. I slowed, knowing I could die if I went back for him.

"Sorry, my lady," Harkhuf said, his footfalls pounding twice as fast as mine as he appeared in the pale light, assisting Yuf. "But Maya's a scribe. He has a good life and wouldn't have wanted to join a group of outcasts."

"I would've asked him," Tia said. "If we'd had time."

"This was a beast of a surprise," Seneb said between struggling breaths, appearing on Yuf's other side. "Like waking up to a large, hairy woman after too much drink. We should've planned better."

The yelling of guards echoed as we reached the foot of the mountains and began to ascend. The green flame fluttered. I searched for the Devouring Monster, sweat dribbling down my forehead. The magician had said the monster was here when the flame fully extinguished … we were still ahead of it.

The candle grew brighter and steadier. Perhaps it was only the wind blowing the flame as I ran …

Chapter 20

Journal Translation

TORCHES MOVED RANDOMLY, wavering in the darkness across a great expanse behind us. Shouts followed and echoed off of the cliffs to the east. The guards from el-Amarna had probably found the dead bodies of their comrades, but it appeared they didn't know what happened or which way we'd run—if they even knew we'd escaped. Perhaps they wouldn't climb after us until dawn.

Some relief. My heart rate slowed, and the green flame of the candle in my hand turned steady. I contained its faint light with my hand and body.

We traversed rock and dirt slopes, feeling our way along through dense shadows. The cries in the distance grew faint.

Yuf's breath rasped like brown leaves.

"We need to take a rest," Chisisi said, sitting on a rock.

"We should put as much distance between ourselves and them as we can," I said, struggling over sliding shale.

"If you twist an ankle rushing up there in the dark, you won't make it very far," Chisisi said, grabbing my sack and tugging me down beside him.

Perhaps he was right. I gasped for breath. Yuf collapsed, his ribs heaving. My heart twinged with sympathy. We needed rest, especially Yuf.

Deep breaths brought cool air into my burning lungs, easing the strain. What had just happened? A whirlwind of death I hadn't planned for, and I'd killed someone … I'd been fantasizing about my escape for years, but had I acted too rashly, again not following the teachings of the magician? Had I brought the others down with me?

Glancing around in the magical light, my eyes locked on Tia's. She forced a close-lipped smirk, as if she were convincing herself she was happy to have run with us. But lines of fear lingered in her face like hot embers. Would she still be happy with the decision tomorrow?

Beside her, the dwarf brothers clutched their new weapons, which appeared as extensions of their hands—much more so than the mud bricks.

Yuf groaned as he sat up, his upper spine still permanently hunched. After all these years, he risked his soul? Why now?

Chisisi held a beaming smile, as if he was finally happy. Did he desire to lead men more than anything else? To have their respect? God knows I couldn't—

Soft footsteps approached, sending rock tumbling down the hillside. I clenched my spear, my hands shaking. The candle still burned bright. The dwarves stood and readied their weapons.

A muscular form appeared, outlined by moonlight. My heart lurched as my feet slipped.

"Why are you following us?" Harkhuf growled, his bowstring straining as he aimed for the man's chest.

Wahankh's chiseled face emerged, flickering in the shadows and green light from my candle. He looked like a ghoul. My heart raced, and my hands squeezed the shaft of my weapon tighter.

"Go back," Harkhuf said, "or die."

"Wait!" Wahankh shouted, raising his hands. Words spewed from his mouth, "I know you all hate me, and I deserve it. But I grew up in the slums of Thebes and had to fight for every meal … fight for everything just to survive. It's so much easier to take from the weak. I've tried to take from stronger men, and the small who fight. The truth is I'm lazy … and afraid! I won't make it on my own out here, or back there. I promise you I will be a better friend."

My insides churned in protest. If I would've just fought him once, he'd have left me alone? Perhaps, but he'd have preyed on someone else, like Yuf. Could I condone his horrid bullying, intimidation, and violence, which had almost killed me? I pictured Akhenaten's face as my hand settled onto the ostrich feather at my waist. Hot, but soft. Pentju's watermelon head and Suty's scarred faced appeared, sneering at me. I had enough enemies, and much more serious ones. I took a deep breath, and my hands relaxed. Perhaps all of Egypt needed forgiveness, all but one.

"If you make anything more difficult," I said, hefting my spear, "you'll be left behind for the guards. Or I'll skewer you quicker than I did with Mudads."

Wahankh's face paled under the green glow, but he nodded.

Harkhuf grumbled and relaxed his bow.

"If Wahankh could follow us, so will the guards," Tia said, standing, the whites of her eyes beaming.

"We climb," Chisisi said, pointing up.

After several hours of slipping, stumbling, and falling through dirt and rock, I pushed Seneb up to the notch of the mountain. The fierce wind atop the world whipped at his hair like the breath of freedom.

What wonders lay ahead—what could stretch beyond the edge of the world? More water? The underworld?

The green flame of the candle wisped out in a trail of smoke, as if a gust of wind had struck it. But the air near my chest felt still. The candle fell from my trembling hand.

The monster was here!

No, perhaps the howling wind at the top carried down to me. My heart thundered in my chest as I glanced about, crushing my bracelet. Cold sweat dripped down my neck, making the hairs stand on end. I grabbed my spear in both hands.

"What's wrong?" Seneb asked, reaching out to haul me up.

"N-nothing," I said, glancing—

A screech raced up the slope, piercing my ears. Under moonlight, a hooded figure jammed a blade of bone deep into Yuf's chest. Ripping his beating heart out from the gash, the monster paused. The old man's body crumpled. After bringing the pulsing organ inside a long hood, the sickening mush of teeth tearing through moist tissue carried out.

Screaming in terror, I froze. I welcomed death over my past life, but not the obliteration of my soul. Anguish for all I hadn't accomplished tugged at my heart as my life flashed before my eyes. Poor Father, Croc, Mutnedjmet, Nefertiti …

The hood lifted in my direction. A rotting smell of death and decay wafted upward, slapping me in the face. Springing up the ridge, the figure moved with inhuman agility and strength. The dwarf brothers thrust a spear and released an arrow, but the creature dodged the weapons and kicked the men aside like dogs. Tia shrieked. Wahankh and Chisisi scrambled away. Raising my spear, I stabbed, but the creature leapt upon me. I toppled onto sharp rock as he pinned me down. The serrated blade of the Devouring Monster rose above my chest.

Hot, rancid breath washed over my face as pointed teeth glistened beneath the shadowy hood. Yellow eyes with slitted pupils emerged. Death descended.

Chapter 21

Journal Translation

S CREAMS FROM MY COMPANIONS protested the inevitable. But the cloaked Devouring Monster stood upon me. A golden hilt flashed and its blade descended, its crocodile teeth tearing the air itself with a grating sound—as if it cut the fabric of space and time.

Pushing against the cloaked arms with the shaft of my spear, I couldn't match the creature's strength. Bone pierced my skin and fire burned through my veins. Something sucked at my heart and blood, drawing them out like poison. I attempted to scream, but the air in my lungs vanished.

The crushing weight on my stomach disappeared in a flash, along with the pain. Was I dead? Light erupted from the heavens, partially blinding me. Something else stood with its back to me, roaring over the mountain like a lion. But this beast was not the Devouring Monster. I struggled to sit up as shrieks of terror erupted around me.

This new creature whipped a long tail through the wind. Orange and white fur covered its body. Bounding away in a flash, it chased the other monster down into the darkness of the west.

My forehead lifted in shock.

I wobbled to my feet, and blood drained from the shallow stab wound in my chest.

"What was that thing?" Tia asked, setting down a rock with a violently shaking hand.

Everyone stared at me as if I knew. Tension climbed up my throat. "Th-the hooded creature I've seen before. He is a demon summoned from the underworld to perform Akhenaten's bidding ..." I didn't want to mention the Devouring Monster and terrorize them all even more. "The other thing—"

"Saved your life!" Seneb said, rubbing his smooth chin. "It looked like a lion, but stood on two legs."

"You're not telling us something," Chisisi said with narrowed eyes as he brushed off his thin torso.

Should I be honest with them? "I had a pet cat as a child," I said. "The coloring reminds me of him."

"A cat!" Chisisi shouted. His shoulder-length hair bounced with his animated movements. "I've had several cats back home before I ... everyone has cats!"

"I've been in trouble at times, and nearly died from a hippopotamus," I said. "Croc, my cat, never did anything. But then, once, when I was being chased by Mummy Makers, I think he scared them off."

Everyone's eyes were as wide as the waxing moon, but they must've been too terrified to speak.

"We should try to forget Yuf and what happened and get moving," Harkhuf said, his striated triceps bulging with tension. "Once the sunlight comes and reaches the western slope, the soldiers will climb. And those other things ... I don't want to see either of them ever again." Stroking his short beard, he followed the ridgeline. "In which direction are we headed?"

Everyone stared at me, and then looked to Chisisi. Anxiety escalated within me like the rising sun. I needed to find answers to many questions, to chase buried secrets and the magician's hidden treasure, but I couldn't tell them. What did they expect of me? "I can't save you, and you might end up like Yuf if you follow me. I just couldn't go on any longer with Akhenaten in the city, with her ..."

Tia's soft hand took mine, sincerity burning in her eyes. "I couldn't either. You don't know the terrors I endured. I'll follow you and Chisisi to any death, and I'd prefer it to the life that I lived back there. Lead the way."

Dark mountains extended over the far side of this summit, carrying toward the night as jagged peaks. If we headed east, we'd probably run out of water and die from the elements. "We go south ..." I needed a reason that wouldn't raise suspicion for my first objective—Amenhotep's treasure. "We can send the brothers off to their homeland and each find our own lives."

I marched.

"No!" Harkhuf growled. "You will not force the easiest task on me. We will first return Tia to her family, or wherever she would like to go. When she is safe, then we may return home."

Tia smiled and glanced downward. "I thank you, Mister Harkhuf, but I may have no family left. I was … taken many years ago."

"I do not mean to pry," Harkhuf said, averting his gaze.

"I will follow the group wherever we go," Tia said. "Chisisi? Are you ready to go home?"

"I … one day, but not this day," he said, studying the vast world below us. "The promise of a lush oasis teeming with life and joy was not the el-Amarna I saw. But I'm not crazy enough to return home … not yet."

"Wahankh?" I asked.

"The slums of Thebes?" he replied, shaking his big head. "Only if I have no other options."

"Right now we only have two choices," Chisisi said. "North or south along the mountains. Once we're safe, we can find the river and take a couple of skiffs."

"We do not head south in the direction of my home," Harkhuf said, grimacing as if in pain. "I will die before I leave the lady and let any more terror befall her. We will see her happy first."

I nodded. I would rather not argue with the dwarf. It might force me to divulge too many secrets. "Perhaps everyone can make a new home in Memphis," I said. "I've lived there. It's a massive city. No one will know you or your pasts. Or you may decide to make your home in a small farmland along the way."

The Aten rose in the east, across a great desert of mountains, and flooded the expanse with pink light. The edge of the world was an endless mountain range? Howling wind whipped my kilt as sunlight showered my face and hope lifted my heart. Warmth radiated through my body.

My companions still searched for the monsters. But the image of the world below and the one we had left behind, painted with flawless magic, stole my words.

"Like an eaglet opening its eyes for the first time and witnessing the entire majesty of the world beneath its soaring wings," Seneb said with a tear in his eye.

I choked back my own.

Chapter 22

Present Day

AFTER JENKINS'S AND HIS murderer's deaths, the Egyptian National Police arrived and brought us down to a station in Cairo—wasting a couple of precious days. We also met with the detective from Luxor, who'd been investigating Maddie's abduction, as well as with several other men. I didn't even know who they all were. Maybe we were even suspects—with an abduction and dead bodies piling up. And I'd submitted my phone to a translator for interpretation of our previous hired hand's ranting that I'd recorded just before he'd died. If only it could help us find Maddie.

The officers we met with said they'd taken Jenkins's body from the tomb of Ramose and were preparing it to be flown back to the U.S. Jenkins's funeral was going to be at his sister's, as he had no wife or children.

My heart ached with remorse. Jenkins. He'd been someone I could trust, a good man even if I'd only known him for a short time ... until he'd made that comment about where they'd taken Maddie. How had he known anything? If I were more skilled with medicine, could I have saved him and found out?

Kaylin, Mr. Scalone, and I sat before a desk inside a cramped office with a window. Aiden huddled in the corner, holding his fox, but his head hung to his chest. AC blew at full throttle, whipping the red flagging hanging from the vent overhead. My teeth chattered as cold seeped into my bones, too much cold for just AC.

Was that hired hand's body in a morgue here? Was Jenkins's?

I nearly crushed Maddie's glasses in my fist, my fingers numb with tension.

"I've analyzed everything many times," a man said, stepping through the doorway and sitting on the far side of a desk overflowing with folders and stacks of paper. He was a thin Egyptian man with a moustache, and his gaze focused away from us, as if he couldn't look us in the eye. He spoke with only a slight accent. "Much of what the man says is gibberish. But I can pick up a few things, such as: 'steps away. Holding her. Never find ... destroyed the second indicator.'" His fingernails drummed the desk with impatience.

My throat constricted with anxiety. Maddie was close! Maybe she was being held at one of the historic locations along the path, to stop us from proceeding? But did the translation mean that someone had recently destroyed a clue? No, the arms of the statues at Abu Simbel had been destroyed and missing for decades, long before we—

"They haven't been able to stop us so far," Mr. Scalone said, dropping his fists onto the desk with a bang. "I'm not worried if we're only a couple sites away from the Hall and that girl. I already know the next stop, and the clue should still be at that location." He smacked me on the back. "We'll find her. And I know a little Arabic. That man said something in his dying breaths, something about a small temple—before you arrived."

"Can you send police to the ancient sites in Egypt, to look for her?" Kaylin asked the interpreter, batting her eyelashes and leaning forward.

The interpreter shook his head, grimacing as he studied us. "There are hundreds, if not thousands, of sites in Egypt. We don't have that kind of manpower, but we are doing everything we can in this investigation. And the Minister of Antiquities has given us an order to allow you to continue searching." His upper lip curled, making his moustache protrude. "As a policeman, this irritates the hell out of me, but we will keep the minister happy and cooperate. If we gather information on where your friend may be, we'll send officers. Keep in mind, the locations that tourists visit everyday would not be likely, or someone would have seen something. Inform me when you decide what this second location may be or if you learn where your friend is being held ..."

My mind drifted, picturing someone destroying the clues along the path to the Hall of Records. How could we follow anything that'd been erased? I only had experience with erasing records once ... Dr. Banks, the surgeon, covering up our mistake of amputating the wrong foot on that old diabetic woman.

✳ ✳ ✳

It seemed as if we'd gone back in time and sailed the Nile like the men and women of old. The rocking waves slipped by like seconds on a clock. But we sat aboard a hired boat from Cairo, a small yacht with an engine that hummed just over the sloshing of the river. And el-Amarna couldn't appear fast enough. My bracelet weighed me down with impatience and guilt. *Dad, you were already taken from me far too young, and, Maddie, with each passing day, the chance that you remain unharmed drops precipitously.*

Mr. Scalone motored us south against the flow of the river, dark sunglasses hiding the fading bruises of his black eyes.

I found my hands pulling out the crinkling letter that my dad had sent to me on my birthday—the letter that'd started this entire ordeal. Dr. Shelsher, its author, and his colleagues had supposedly died in Egypt in the early nineteen twenties, trying to uncover a lost tomb. But their bodies had never been found—the mystery of their disappearance never answered. Had a distant relative of mine received Dr. Shelsher's original letter, or had my dad found it on one of his worldly trips—a lost secret that hadn't made it out of Egypt until recently?

The yacht bucked, jabbing my teeth into the soft flesh of my tongue. Salty blood ran inside my cheeks.

We'd finally docked at the shore of the ancient site of el-Amarna. Mr. Scalone anchored the boat and led us away, through the fertile banks and gusting wind, up across the hot desert to the ruins. Whether he was in a hurry to find Maddie or only the Hall, it didn't matter; he was devoted to a cause, and both were interrelated.

Aiden sauntered along, his head and dreadlocks hanging from under his cap. His fox trotted beside him, her huge ears shading her face like the *nemes* headdress. "I don't know if we should keep going," Aiden said, speaking for the first time in days as he shielded his eyes from the sun. "Someone else might die."

"Maddie's still alive," I said, convincing myself it was true, although my heart twinged with fear. Someone, or all of us, could be killed at one of the next sites. But we'd have to take the risk. "She needs us. And the police are taking too long, if they're doing anything at all."

"So, this is the place?" Kaylin asked, hugging her withdrawn brother as if that would make Jenkins's murder okay and continue to drive us on. She glanced around the empty desert, and her forehead wrinkled. Only the bases of small structures jutted above the surface. She wouldn't know that the ancient city was below the current ground level and had had to be excavated. "Where that pharaoh lived? The one who had something to do with King Tut?"

"Yes," I said, scanning the surrounding mountains. I couldn't stop picturing Heb and the others on this very same plot of land. My spine tingled with wonder, and my connection to Heb returned, the bronze on my wrist growing hotter even though it was covered by my sleeve. This was the place we needed to be. But Heb's life and mine had diverged after Maddie had been taken. How would locating a clue and Maddie compare to attempting to escape from slavery and find Nefertiti or Mutnedjmet? And Heb needed to discover a way to change the future, while I needed a way to find the past. I needed his magician now more than ever …

"Akhenaten's forbidden city of the rising Aten," I continued. "His capital. The peaks to the east and the sunrise brought Pharaoh, possibly from witnessing a solar eclipse at this very site. Amarna artists only captured images of a land of splendor, flourishing with life and abundance. Future peoples, tricked by the images of the original artists, and people at the time must've thought this place would be Heaven on Earth. But the dead found in mass graves ended up telling a different story."

"What story was that?" Kaylin asked.

"A life of tormented work and toil under the Egyptian sun," I said, marching on. "Most people weren't slaves, but the workers were still stunted from lack of nutrition, and many had evidence of broken bones and backs— worked to their deaths."

"Like, how did this pharaoh get all his people to up and move out here?" Kaylin asked, jogging to catch up with me.

"He convinced them this was where God wanted the faithful to live and prosper. He also used tricks that modern-day terrorist organizations use to attract young people."

"Anger and a new family who understands them?" Kaylin asked, scrutinizing the area. She must've thought that there was nothing out here, as it appeared we now stood in the middle of nowhere.

"That embracing your hate for others is righteous," Mr. Scalone answered this time, marching beside us. "I spent time traveling in Iraq and Afghanistan during the wars. I wasn't always hunting treasure. Terrorists tell troubled people there isn't anything wrong with them and that they don't need to control their emotions, but rather it is other people's fault those troubled people are so filled with rage. Young men everywhere fight for social ranking and power, but when it gets too hard, some give up and seek revenge against society. They are tricked into believing that these other angry men will love them if they become part of the same tribe. They trick women by offering a more profound sense of family."

Aiden's feet scuffed through the dirt, his gaze on the ground.

"I worry that your brother might be one of those young men, Kaylin," Mr. Scalone said, reaching out and smacking the flat bill of Aiden's cap.

"Paul," Kaylin said in a high-pitched voice, grabbing the treasure hunter's arm. "Leave him alone. He might be lazy, but he's not a terrorist. I think the ordeal with Jenkins is just still affecting him more than you."

Mr. Scalone grumbled something.

"Where do we start looking?" Kaylin asked, glancing at Mr. Scalone and then to me. "This place is huge, like Karnak but without many buildings left."

Mr. Scalone put a hand to his forehead above his sunglasses and surveyed the blinding desert.

"The highlights are multiple boundary stelae," I said, pulling my fedora lower over my sweaty forehead. "Some are on the west bank, but most are on this side. There's also a Great Aten Temple and tombs up in the mountains."

"We go to the tombs," Mr. Scalone said, taking a swig of water and pacing off.

"I don't think so," I said, stopping. "The tombs have been studied in detail. Akhenaten's tomb was unfinished and never put into service. I don't think we'll find anything up there."

Mr. Scalone slowly pivoted around as his tattooed arms folded over his chest. His recently swollen nose—which was no longer crooked—looked fine. Had he reset it? Did he still have the black eyes under his shades, or had they transformed into the urine-yellow of a fading bruise? "You've been wrong most of the time so far. You got lucky once. I'll take your word one last time, but if you're wrong again, you only offer your knowledge of the past. No more decisions on where we go." He glared down at me through his dark aviators. "Maddie's life is depending on us."

My fists clenched with rage. That was crap. I'd figured out more than he had. Only Maddie had discovered more than me, and she was no longer here to help. "The boundary stelae," I said, "are mysterious. Maybe we should start down here in the south and work our way north."

We trudged under the relentless sun, across rock and dirt that reflected scalding heat and light back up at us.

Worn hieroglyphs emerged, carved with precision into a rock cliff face ahead. The structure towered over us but was nothing more than a giant rectanglar region of chiseled stone within the desert-brown mountain.

"Is this the stela?" Kaylin asked, twirling her hair beneath a long-brimmed hat.

"One of them," I said, wiping my brow with my sleeve. I examined the proclamation of Akhenaten, telling of his city, the Aten, and Egypt's new affiliations. At the top, Akhenaten and his family stood bathing under the rays of the sun, which were offering ankhs—the sign of life and dominion—to the royals.

"What are we looking for?" Kaylin asked and leaned her chest against my arm.

I shook my head. "I have no idea." Frustration rose inside me, and my upper lip wrinkled. Maddie couldn't wait for me to figure this out. And the crux of the situation was that I needed her to solve it. But now I had to do it in order to find her. I kicked a rock, and it clattered as it rolled across the ground—my big toe throbbing in response.

After an hour of photographing and videoing the inscriptions in the rock wall, we pushed on to the next and then the next stela, spending shorter and shorter amounts of time at each.

Stela-S lay along the cliffs that ran back toward the eastern horizon and was one of the best preserved. Two large cracks ran across and up its length, and there was a missing chunk in the lower right region. Smaller holes dotted the hieroglyphic message like cheese that rodents had gotten into. But this stela included Nefertiti and two of Akhenaten's daughters on the right with only Nefertiti and one daughter on the left side. According to experts, these were supposed to be mirror images, but that wasn't the case here. Other stelae had shown between one and three of his daughters beside him, but each side had appeared identical. What did the bizarre asymmetry mean?

The bridge of my nose tightened as pages of history flashed through my mind. The stelae had been created in different years and showed his daughters at a specific point in time. But why a different number on each side? I bit my lip, thinking. I didn't see, nor remember reading about, any stelae showing a son. And Tut had no tomb or other specific monument here either.

"Send us food, water, tents, and sleeping gear," Mr. Scalone told someone over his phone. "This kid keeps leading us astray, and our friend's life is hanging in the balance."

Chapter 23

Present Day

I SHOOK MY HEAD IN DISGUST at Mr. Scalone for blaming me for not finding any clues so far. What had he done to locate Maddie or help us out?

We moved across el-Amarna to other stelae in the cliffs until the sun sank below the horizon. The heat slowly released its compressing grip on our skin and lungs.

I crunched on a handful of mixed nuts as my stomach growled, and the salt caked my tongue. At least my stomach's protest was from hunger, not pain that would lead to vomiting. I'd better not get sick out here, or it would be more than a day until I'd get to a hospital and find relief. And Maddie didn't have time for that. Unfortunately, my infusion for my Crohn's disease was overdue and the chances for a flare-up had spiked.

Mr. Scalone lit a fire in a metal cylinder with pink goo inside. "At least some of us are prepared," he said as flames danced and crackled under his thick stubble and long hair. "Reminds me of the time I tracked deserters in the mountains of Afghanistan."

Kaylin stared glassy-eyed into the growing darkness. "That'll last all night, right?"

Mr. Scalone shrugged.

Darkness settled in around us. Besides when I'd been trapped in Amenhotep's tomb, this would be my first night camping away from civilization since I was a child.

"How long could this take?" Kaylin asked, opening a candy bar by the firelight. The wrapper crinkled as she sat, and melted chocolate seeped across her fingers like blood. Licking off the brown sludge, she said, "To look at all the stelae and tombs here?"

This site could take days to study. "It's big," I said, picturing the boundary stelae, the tombs, the city, and the Great and Small Aten Temples. "And we don't know what we're looking for. Whoever left this trail wasn't going to make anything easy, either. Anyone looking for the Hall of Records was going to have to dedicate a large amount of time and effort to their search."

Her chewing stopped. She lay back onto a fleece blanket—our only protection from the elements.

The night's chill began to sink through my sweat-encrusted skin. I scooted closer to the small flame and its meager warmth. The pink goo inside the burning canister released smoke with a chemical odor.

"What kinds of animals live out here?" Kaylin asked, her voice high-pitched.

Grinning in the firelight, Mr. Scalone said, "Snakes, scorpions, rodents, jackals, that sort of thing." He pulled out one of his guns and set it on his fleece blanket.

I reached inside my messenger bag and found the gun I'd taken from Jenkins. But I shook my head. A gun wouldn't save us from a cobra. If only Jenkins were still here, but he'd been terrified of the possibility of crocodiles in Lake Nasser, even more so than the rest of us. And he'd been the only one who hadn't dived in.

"Kaylin," Mr. Scalone said, winking. "You might want to sleep next to a real man out here."

"Who were these people that lived here?" Kaylin asked, not moving. "If we understood or empathized with them, could we better understand where or how they'd hide something?"

My thoughts swirled, my fingers brushing through the gritty dirt. "It's difficult to see how." I took a deep breath. "Artists, architects, workers, scribes, and military. The royal family, slaves ..."

"Was there anyone back then who could've been huge, like muscular big?" Aiden asked, jolting up as if he'd been kicked awake. His neck twisted about as he peered into the darkness. "Or were they all smaller dudes?"

Images of a hulking man popped into my mind. Scenes from the journal played like a vivid movie in my head. The scarred ear, pointed like a pig's—Akhenaten's bodyguard, Suty.

"And did they have doctors and policemen?" Aiden asked, sinking his teeth into a granola bar. His chewing stopped, his eyes darting around. "Did the pharaoh guy have another woman who started a big fight?" His face was more pale than usual, standing out against the night like snow.

My eyebrows pulled together in confusion. Why was he asking, and how did he know all that?

"The names of important people were recorded in this city," I said. "Suty was Akhenaten's bodyguard in el-Amarna. Pentju was his chief physician, and Mahu his chief of police—the ancient Egyptians had an actual police force. A lady Kiya came from a foreign land and created quite a stir with Nefertiti, until something happened between them." I swallowed. There's no way Aiden could have coincidentally asked about these things. "Why?"

"And another pharaoh?" His eyes narrowed and his shoulders quivered.

"King Tut was born here," I said. "How do you know this?"

"I thought I saw shapes moving out there," he said, hugging his fox against his chest. The animal's eyes were closed. "At first I thought I was just seeing fog in the dark, but now I think it's more than that. And I'm not high …"

My throat constricted with surprise and fear. What did he think he saw? I glanced about. Only thick blackness surrounded us … and silence.

"What?" Kaylin gasped, sitting up and smacking his thigh. "Aiden, why would you say something like that?"

"There are spirits still wandering the area," Aiden whispered, his expression dropping flat. "They've come out in the darkness. I've seen them since Jenkins's soul left his body." His eyes widened with terror.

Kaylin scooted over so that her side touched Mr. Scalone. The treasure hunter smiled and put a big arm around her shoulders. "The kid's probably never camped in his life," Mr. Scalone said. "I'd be shocked if he weren't scared out here. I'll take watch so no one sneaks up on us tonight."

Kaylin turned her back to the fire and watched our surroundings.

Something howled off in the distance.

Laughter erupted.

I jumped in surprise.

Aiden slapped his knee. "You guys were so freaked out just by the thought of it!" He fell back onto his blanket, giggling.

But his hands were still trembling ...

How could he pull a joke like that when Maddie's life was in danger? Or was it not a joke—was he trying to make us feel better after having seen something?

The fox's head popped up from beside Aiden. Lifting her little lips, the creature released a vicious snarl. She stared directly east, into the night.

Chapter 24

Present Day

W E HUDDLED AS CLOSE TO THE FIRE as we could, hoping the night in the desert of el-Amarna would pass swiftly. My eyes grew heavy …

I jerked awake. *Cold.* I hugged myself and rubbed my arms, shivering.

Sunlight lit up the east, painting the sky behind the mountains in oranges and yellows while reaching for the western stars. A gust of wind carried through my fleece blanket.

Kaylin hadn't budged from her position with her back to the now dead fire. Mr. Scalone had a hand on her hip, sleeping. Wasn't he supposed to be on watch? I released a low grunt of confusion. Kaylin had at least been pretending to be physically interested in me—to entice me into locating the Hall. But with a real scare, maybe she felt safer with the treasure hunter.

I kicked at Aiden, who'd buried his head under his blanket.

He groaned and rolled away.

Had Aiden really just pretended to see that stuff last night? But how had he known those things about the dead? "We need to get moving. Maddie's depending on us."

"I couldn't sleep," Aiden said, rubbing his eyes as his teeth chattered, his lips blue. The fox had curled into his armpit for warmth. "And I almost lost a testicle to frostbite." Brushing his dreadlocks back, he scratched the buzzed sides of his head and pulled his cap down.

After chomping down a quick breakfast of sugary granola, we hiked to several more boundary stelae and glimpsed parts of the ancient ghost town of el-Amarna. Chills slid up my spine despite the sweltering heat. But the day dragged on without a breakthrough. The only interruption was for two men packing in our requested camping supplies from their boat. No tourists way out here, not yet anyway.

"Wait a minute," Mr. Scalone said as I ran my fingers over the depressed hieroglyphs in a rock cliff. "We've been marching a repeatable distance between all of these markers."

"So?" Aiden said, feeding a jerky treat to his fox. "Fence posts around a property have the same distance between them."

"So, we're searching for an answer to a riddle, and it seems odd to me, you idiot," Mr. Scalone said, tossing his hair back with a flick of his thick neck. "Like, what lies at the perfect center of all of these things? Movies always use that as a clue." He waved at the stela in front of me as if it were an irritating insect. "Get me a map of the area."

My eyes wandered. Could he be right? Props to him if he actually helped save Maddie. Digging into my bag, I pulled out my laptop and cracked it open. I ran a quick search and found an aerial view of el-Amarna from a world satellite website. The connection was very slow but still active with my cellular hotspot activated. Waiting for the images to load took longer than what I imagined the first Internet connection in history would've taken. I groaned in frustration. But even in the middle of nowhere, we still had this technology. What'd Heb and the people who built this place had? Would it've made their lives easier, or would people like Akhenaten still have found a way to control it, and them?

"Put this location in," Mr. Scalone said, noting our current coordinates on his GPS. "Zoom out and mark all of the stelae."

I dropped pins on the boundary stelae locations. The markers didn't appear random, but they didn't create any kind of obvious sign.

Mr. Scalone paced back and forth, rubbing the thick stubble ravaging his face. "What's at the center?"

"Nothing," I said as I added the north, south, and royal tombs. Still nothing obvious. I sighed. Then I put in points for the Great and Small Aten temples. Then the royal palace.

"Now we're getting somewhere," Mr. Scalone said, leaning onto my shoulder and crushing me. "I can make out a lot of rectangles between these points." He brushed his locks back with a meaty hand. "Is there a reason that would be important?"

My fingers froze on the keyboard as my mind connected different dots. Taking out a pen and pad of paper, I drew the images. "The Aten temples were all created in that same rectangular configuration," I said, and my breathing stopped. Was the layout the son of Hapu's or Akhenaten's master-architectural plan? "El-Amarna itself was one giant temple to the Aten ..."

"Just like crosses for old Catholic church foundations!" Aiden said, pushing past his sister. "I told you before!"

"But what does that mean?" I asked. "That we search the remains of the Aten temples?"

"That's a better option than what we've been doing with these things," Mr. Scalone said, shaking his head at an engraved cliff face.

"Wait," Kaylin said, her finger thrusting against the screen. "What is that?" She pointed to the most eastern marker.

"The Royal Wadi," I said. "Akhenaten's would-be tomb. He attempted to create everything Thebes had right here, including a replacement for the Valley of the Kings. But like I said, his tomb was never used. No one has ever discovered his mummy or his final resting place, although archeologists have found nearly every other pharaoh and royalty mentioned in ancient writings. And there isn't much in his tomb here." I fell silent for a second. "But maybe it is time to move on to the temples, or the north or south tombs for other—"

"No," Kaylin said, shaking her head. "I might not know much about ancient Egypt, but I've been told that I'm pretty smart ... for a blonde." She grinned and batted her eyelashes. "That point is the tomb of this sun-worshipping pharaoh, right? Where the sun rises over the mountains?"

I nodded.

"What if you drew lines not only to make the rectangles, but also from every point to that tomb?" she asked, motioning on the screen.

"I don't get it," Mr. Scalone said, crossing his arms under his exposed pecs.

"Oh my God," I said, my mouth gaping. "Kaylin, you may not be Maddie, but right now you're a genius." I drew a line from each pin that I'd dropped back to the tomb, which created equally spaced angles originating from the Royal Wadi. "Rays from the sun," I whispered. "Sunbeams coming from the tomb of Akhenaten, to shine over the entire land. And everything's attention is focused on his tomb. There is no question what, or rather who, I should say, was worshipped in those temples and this city. Akhenaten believed he and the sun were one and the same. And his tomb was located at the eastern horizon, where the sun rose each day. The clue *is* using light … in a sense."

"And you thought we shouldn't look in his tomb," Mr. Scalone said, feeling along his abs and taking a deep breath. "I told you, that's the last time we listen to you." He thrust a big fist into my face. "The only time you open your mouth is to offer historical information. I make the decisions, for our safety and Maddie's."

My chin fell to my chest, the hollow sucking sensation of failure filling my core. I couldn't do this alone—find Maddie and be her hero. Kaylin and Mr. Scalone had figured out something I should've been able to. I'd let my dad down again, and I didn't even deserve Maddie. Mr. Scalone probably was her best bet, and it seemed like he really wanted to help her even more than find the treasure. I should just … No, Maddie had said something about me always running away from things.

Shaking my head, I climbed to my feet, slung my pack and supplies over my shoulder, and shuffled after the others—heading for the tomb in the mountain. Aiden hesitantly followed, glancing back as if he expected to see another armed man pursuing us.

Chapter 25

Present Day

SWEAT RAN DOWN FROM UNDER my fedora and onto my cheeks in warm streams. We'd traveled the metal road—meant to preserve the trail to the el-Amarna tombs—and stood before the entrance of the Royal Wadi. Modern channels had been dug long ago, on either side of the opening, to divert flash floods away from these royal burial chambers.

Still no other tourists, although this wasn't exactly a prime historical site even when Egypt was at the height of its tourism. There was nothing left inside that needed to be guarded, either.

At the end of a flight of steps leading downward, stone columns, shaped to look like giant papyrus stalks, supported the mountain overhead. An open doorway led into the earth.

I sucked in a deep breath. I'd never seen images of the inside, only read about nothing remaining.

"Does sunlight reach all the way inside the burial chamber?" Kaylin asked, not waiting for an answer as she jogged down the stairs. Mr. Scalone followed her. "This has to be the place."

"Yes," I said, following Mr. Scalone. "But like all of the tombs here, it was never completed. If it had been finished, the light would've been blocked."

Inside the mountain was a long corridor—the metaphorical descent of the Aten. This decline allowed sunlight to enter and shine upon Pharaoh's burial chamber, in true Akhenaten form. Why would he have wanted his tomb covered or sealed? This would've blocked out the sunlight …

Mr. Scalone placed his hand in the sunbeams streaming inside and studied the shadows.

"Why wasn't it finished?" Kaylin asked.

I shrugged. "Only one tomb in all of the nearby complexes was completed," I said. "And none of the five chambers down below in this royal tomb were finished." I descended. Aiden shuffled along beside me, looking back to make sure no one was following us.

"Whose was that?" Aiden asked. "Whose tomb was finished?"

"It was probably for Kiya, one of Akhenaten's closest wives," I said. "Or Beketaten, one of his sisters. No one's sure why Beketaten was more important than the others. Nefertiti's tomb was supposed to be down here too …" I pointed to a branch in the corridor. It ran off into the darkness. "There are a few unfinished rooms that way."

"What happened to 'em?" Aiden asked, pausing from chomping on gum and squinting into the black of Nefertiti's tomb. "I mean, if their mummies weren't here, where are they?"

"No one knows," I said, the hair on the back of my neck sticking up again. I could not convince myself that the feeling of someone watching was just my imagination.

More steps. We entered the pillared burial chamber intended for Akhenaten. Only thin rays of sun lit the center and cast shadows around the periphery. My eyes gaped in wonder.

Most of the images on the walls were desecrated or had been destroyed by historic floods. An indentation lay in the center of the floor. "That's where his sarcophagus was located," I said, pointing. "Images of Nefertiti and the Aten were engraved into its granite and protected the dead. But it was destroyed, smashed to bits in ancient times." I scrutinized the chamber.

Hours ticked by as I videoed the walls under the passing sunlight and shadows.

I clicked on my flashlight and jogged to the other dark rooms. Aiden followed. Images of the controversial pharaoh, his wife, and three daughters were everywhere. One mural showed a deceased baby lying in the arms of a nurse. "This female didn't survive childbirth," I said, focusing the beam of my flashlight on the dead baby in the image. "Neither did her mother. That happens more often when the mother is also the daughter of the father of the child."

"Wait, what?" Aiden asked, scratching his head by pulling the flat bill of his cap up and down. His fox rested in the crook of his other arm.

"He married his own daughter, and that is their child," I said. "Both women died."

"My God," Aiden said, covering the eyes of his fox as if she should not be subjected to this hideous truth. Then he coughed, and deep echoes rattled around the chamber before carrying up through the corridors.

We spent the entire day searching but found no answers. I pitched my tent near the base of the mountain, but away from the ditches designed for flash flooding. The floods at the tomb of Amenhotep were still too fresh in my mind. And my bronze bracelet seemed to grow heavier, tugging my arm down into the dirt as if Dad's disappointment in my abilities channeled through it.

Howls emerged off in the night over gusts of wind. I held my breath as we sat in a circle around a crackling fire. Aiden buried his head and ears inside his new sleeping bag. Did his fear and remorse over Jenkins affect his reasoning and cause him to see visions?

"Gavin," someone said. "Gavin!" Kaylin poked me. Her hair was back in a ponytail, her skin dirty.

I blinked, and my previous thoughts vanished.

"Did you hear me?" she asked, scooting over and rubbing up against my side.

I shook my head and lowered my fedora so that shadows would hide my face, and hopefully my emotions.

"Do you remember that time you, Maddie, and I went on that trip after finals?" she asked.

"Skiing?" I said, looking up at her. Why was she asking about that?

"Well, I snowboarded, but you might have skied," she grinned, twirling her blond hair.

"I remember," I said. "It was my biggest fantasy come to life. A chance to go away with Maddie and do something other than school."

"But she was, like, dating that big guy." Kaylin's eyes narrowed, searching my face, as if surprised by my words.

"She was always dating one of those guys; so were you."

"I don't get what she has that guys find so attractive," she said.

My forehead tightened with suspicion. Was she jealous? Kaylin, the gorgeous blonde? Maddie was sweet, smart, and cute, and I was drawn to her because of our similarities and something deeper, intangible. Kaylin just wanted to manipulate me.

"We did have fun, though," Kaylin said, her lips lifting into a smile. "Those were some of the best runs I've ever had. It'd snowed about four feet overnight and the powder was like boarding on clouds. I could carve down the double black diamonds, and when I fell, it felt like a cushion."

"Except on one run off in the trees, the tips of my skis got so buried that I fell face first," I said, staring up into the sparkling stars. "I couldn't pull my skis out because of the weight of the snow. And the snow was so deep that I couldn't even push myself up to the surface to get a breath. I panicked but somehow decided after a few seconds to somersault over, which pulled my skis back out of the tracks they'd been driven into."

Kaylin laughed and slapped her knee. "After you finally tumbled out—looking like a snowball—you hyperventilated for a bit, threw your poles, and screamed obscenities over and over. And Maddie fell over beside you, laughing hysterically."

"That wasn't funny … at the time," I said, but the pressure of an emerging grin tugged at my lips.

"Then remember when we went out that night and her boyfriend tried to embarrass her by putting her name in for karaoke? It was a song only she knew. We couldn't even back up her vocals."

"She hates singing in front of people," I said. "In the car is a different story. But if it wasn't that song she never would've done it."

Kaylin laughed again and snorted. "Somehow she was drunk enough that we got her up there by herself and she tried to be all emotional and melodramatic. She was terrible. What song was it? 'Collide' by Howie Day?"

"I wish; that's a much happier song," I said, shaking my head, remembering it much differently. "It was 'Alive Tomorrow.'" The title seemed fitting for her now. In my mind I could see her on stage, singing her heart out, looking as if she were yelling into the microphone. But her voice caressed my ears like velvet—although with a haunting beauty. Back then, I'd wished she'd been singing only to me. My heart twisted with pain. "I took a guitar lesson that next weekend—in hopes of getting good enough to play music for her and make her feel the same way she'd made me feel when she sang that night."

"You did?" Kaylin's mouth gaped open. She chuckled. "I had no idea you used to be that crazy about her. Did you get any good? At the guitar, I mean."

I was still that crazy about her. "No. I tried for a few months but couldn't sing and play well together. You must have to stick with it a lot longer or start a lot younger, like with everything in life. Or be born with talent. I eventually realized that I'd never be able to make her feel the emotion she brought out in me. I only wrote a song for my dad." I swallowed. "I tried writing a couple for Maddie, but I couldn't make them say or give off the feel that I wanted them to. Then I stopped and never picked it back up."

"But you wrote a song for your dad?" Kaylin asked, cupping my neck with tender fingers. "That's sweet. How's it go?"

The heat of embarrassment rose in my cheeks, and I glanced away. "I don't remember."

"Oh, c'mon, Gavin," Kaylin said, rubbing my arm as she leaned into me. "No one else will hear you over this wind, and I need a pick-me-up. These past few weeks have been way too hard, because I feel like Maddie's abduction is my fault. I wanted us to stay and keep looking for a clue inside Karnak. She wanted to leave because she was worried about those men. And I talked you into taking my side."

My eyelids fell shut and clamped tight. It was true. But it wasn't because I'd chosen Kaylin over Maddie; I'd just wanted to find the clue and the Hall. I'd chosen that over Maddie, just like how my dad had put his crazy dreams above his family, especially my mom.

"Just a couple lines," Kaylin said, her voice shaky with emotion.

I swallowed and cleared my throat. Singing in a whisper just over the howl of the wind, an old rhythm—I had no idea where it came from—poured out.

"My old man was indeed a king, whose memories we now sadly sing.
His love was deep, his mind too keen.
His humble life beyond my reach.
But on this day he's gone away.
Where he went no one can say.
But in the darkness there's a shining star, and here now is where we still are ..."

Chapter 26

Present Day

WE HIKED AWAY FROM THE TOMB under the morning sun and examined the remnants of the Aten temples in the ancient city of el-Amarna. The temples' stone walls were worn down by time, and all of the surviving artifacts had been removed. The Great Aten Temple was now only a crumbling foundation. A few tourists in long-brimmed hats, an Egyptian man in uniform with a beret and a large gun, and an English-speaking guide toured the area for a couple hours before departing.

I wandered and found myself in the southern part of the ancient city, alone. The sun beat down upon me, punishing me with its searing heat, like it had done to Heb, and forced my head and shoulders down.

I retrieved the peeling leather journal from my bag and cracked it open as I took a step backward to sit. But I tripped over the base of what would've been an ancient house and landed on my back. Hot sand caked the back of my sweaty neck, burning. Groaning in frustration, I sat up and wiped my neck clean, which sent some of the grit rolling down inside my shirt. Then I brushed a layer of dirt from the mud-brick base of the house—to clean off a spot to sit. There was something in the mud brick.

I blew away more dirt. The distinct image of a feather, the ostrich feather of Ma'at, was engraved into the top face of the block ... and another image. A dwarf figure with hair and a beard resembling a lion's mane—Bes. I gasped and, in a frenzy, brushed away the gritty dust and dirt from the surrounding mud bricks, even digging deeper and checking all of the surrounding surfaces. Nothing else. Nothing at all. But a memory sparked. These were the exact images Heb had mentioned carving into a block. My heart lifted, and my mind floated with wonder. He was right here, right where I stood, toiling with a hardship, just like me. This journal was as real as the stone, as real as the life around me now. The lives of the past. Were they all still here?

My mind drifted under the pounding rays of sun as I chugged water and pushed my fedora back from my forehead. The wind howled in my ears …

I remembered when I was about seven or eight years old. It was early in the morning on my birthday. My dad was traveling and had been gone for months, again. Sorting through a pile of brightly wrapped gifts, I gave each a shake—trying to guess their contents before my mom came downstairs. I reached for a package covered with clowns dancing on yellow paper. But the corner of a brown envelope stood out like an old book at an Apple store, hidden beneath the stack. I yanked it out. As I eased open the crinkling parchment, I gasped with excitement. The letter was addressed to "Gav" and said "Happy Birthday!" Only Dad called me Gav. A photo slid out. Black and white. Me as a young boy, standing proudly beside my dad—both of us in fedoras. I beamed for the camera in front of the backdrop of a fake sphinx—from a traveling King Tut exhibit.

Dad! The warmth of love radiated from my heart out through my limbs.

I pulled the card from the envelope. A brown dog was on the front, and music played when I opened it. The dog's eyes lit up. "Gavin, it's your birthday!" it sang to a melody.

Tater—my dog and favorite companion growing up—barked at the talking card and cocked his head to the side in confusion.

My dad had written, "Sorry I can't be there today, Gav, but I'm always thinking of you. Just trying my best to support you guys while living life the only way I know how."

I took a deep breath, knowing he loved his traveling gig, even though I wanted him with me. He and mom fought about it every time he was home—she trying to convince him to stay.

The rest of the birthday card said, "I got you something special. Look inside."

Digging into the stiff envelope, I felt around and shook it and the card out. There was nothing. But he wouldn't trick me like—

"Put that card away and enjoy the real things you have here," my mom said, stomping down the stairs and swiping Dad's card out of my hands before dropping it into the trash. Her red face and stern eyes sapped the warmth from my body.

I played the video game my mom had gotten me and ran around with Tater until late into the afternoon, but I still couldn't forget that damn music and Dad's promise. I waited until my mom went to bed. After sneaking downstairs, I dived into the trash and dug out the now stained envelope and card. Ten minutes of annoyance followed, and I threw the singing card across the kitchen, then peeled it apart—the tearing of paper bringing some satisfaction. Black electronic pieces sat inside; a microphone and a tiny rectangular thing. I tore these off, the glue peeling an inner layer from the cardboard. The singing stopped abruptly, but the dog's eyes still flashed.

Something else, something shiny that'd been hidden within the card, shimmered in the overhead light. My heart fluttered in fascination. What was this? I ripped and tore at the outer layer.

Gold!

A thin sheet of gold leaf slipped out—the first time I remembered laying eyes on the precious metal—although I knew exactly what it was. I turned the square the size of my palm over, and light reflected into my eyes, causing me to squint. Tiny slits were cut into the metal. My mouth gaped. Was this on purpose?

I held the sheet up to the cartoon dog's flashing eyes, and red light shone through the slits. But it didn't make any sense. Would Dad give me a thin sheet of gold as a present? How much was it worth?

Creeping upstairs and past Mom's room, I then went into Dad's old office. The floor squeaked, and I paused. Mom had turned his office into a storage room, but there was still a computer. I turned the computer on to look up the value of gold. The room was dark. As the screen flashed to life, light trickled through the slits in the gold leaf. I placed the sheet over the screen, but the light blurred as it exited the thin slices—possibly letters?

Dad! What were you trying to tell me? And how could I read your message?

I searched the room for anything that might help and ran across a stack of film the size of the computer screen. X-rays—or radiographs, as Dad said they were correctly called. I'd been fascinated with the images of bones made by some of the machines he sold. The first time I'd seen these, he'd taken a flashlight and put the beam up to his hand. He'd then turned off the lights in his office.

"Let's pretend that the light coming from this flashlight is x-rays," he'd said, his voice high-pitched with enthusiasm. The shadow of his hand had been huge and blurry against the bare wall behind him. "And pretend that my hand is all bone. Where the x-rays don't penetrate makes the picture on the wall."

"It's really blurry, Dad," I'd said. "X-rays don't look like that."

He'd smiled. "That's right. So you need the object you're imaging very close to the surface of the picture." Moving his hand close to the wall had shrunk its shadow and had made the edges crisp. The image on the wall had then been as clear as his hand and fingers. "That is basically how x-rays work, except they still go through bone—only to a lesser degree than soft tissue ..."

I snuck back down the stairs of our house and grabbed a metal flashlight out of the closet. Racing into the bathroom, I clicked the flashlight on. Then I held the slick sheet of gold against the light source. Blurry images of letters stood out on the shower wall. I positioned the gold leaf closer to the wall and the letters clarified:

'I rest beneath the kissing plant.'

What? My heart dropped. All this and now Dad still wasn't going to give me my present? I stomped off, having no idea what he was referring to—and being unable to sleep that night.

Over the next few weeks I tried to search for, and offhandedly ask Mom, about plants that kissed. She had no idea what I was talking about.

Dad finally came home to visit a couple of months later.

"Dad!" I had yelled, running out the front door and flinging myself at him. His wiry arms crushed me in a tight embrace. "I still haven't gotten my birthday present. It's too hard!"

He stroked his moustache, which overhung his upper lip, as he patted my back. "I can't do this for you anymore, Gav. If you still dream of finding lost tombs, like when you used to obsess over books of Egyptian discoveries, you'll have to learn how to follow obscure clues."

"Dad, I hate you!" I shouted in anger as I spun around and ran away. "And I don't want to spend time with *you*, either!"

That night, I hid and sobbed as I watched my parents from behind the opening of a cracked door.

"Look at what you've done to him," Mom said, folding tense arms across her chest. "Why can't you just get a job here in the city?" She paced the kitchen, and the floor groaned beneath her. "Then we'd be able to see you everyday."

"I'd die after a couple years of doing the same tedious work," he replied. His moustache brushed his lower lip as he swallowed a mouthful of beer. "It would suck the life out of me. I'm sorry that I didn't settle down, as you'd hoped, after we accidentally had a child. That's just not me." His eyes grew big and teary as he reached out for Mom's hand. She jerked away.

My heart felt hollow, like an empty present. Dad had never even wanted me?

"I love Gavin more than anything," he said and took another swig, which was followed by a loud gulp, "but I'm doing the best I can every day to sell medical supplies around the world. I'm helping the less fortunate in other countries. The salesmen in the States want to destroy the old equipment—scopes, surgical instruments, imaging machines—so that everyone has to buy new."

"Then go, and keep helping those people while ignoring your own family," Mom shouted, planting her hands on her hips. Her lips thinned. "Why shouldn't we get divorced? I never see you. And we don't need you."

Dad slowly pivoted around and shuffled out of the house with his head down. The front door didn't fully close, but the screen door banged shut.

I jumped at the sound, and something squeezed on my heart like the bite of the Devouring Monster. Dad was doing good for the world, but were his adventures and helping others really more important to him than seeing us? At the time, I hadn't realized that my parents would get divorced and that I'd barely see my dad again—and he would never look the same as he did that day.

Not until a couple of weeks before Christmas, when I was watching a movie, did I get a break on Dad's birthday riddle. "I'm standing under the mistletoe," a woman on TV said, and the man kissed her.

"Mom!" I jumped up. "What is mistletoe, and why do people kiss under it?"

"It's an old tradition," she said from her spot on the couch, knitting something long and teal. "Your dad says it goes back to ancient Greece and has to do with fertility. But actually, it's a poisonous plant and is invasive. We have some growing up in that old apple tree in the back yard."

I grabbed a flashlight and dashed outside into the wet darkness of a northwest winter. After locating a shovel in the shed, I ran to the overgrown apple tree. Thick plant material hung on the upper bows, absorbing my beam of light. I planted the shovel into the sopping ground and jumped on it. The tip sank in an inch and clanked against metal, jarring my hands … something was buried here. My heart jumped with excitement. This treasure was resting, like a mummy. Tearing at the muck with my shaking hands, I pulled out a silver box. I ripped it open, peeked inside, and found the …

I couldn't even recall what was inside—because I ended up treasuring the path more than the actual gift. Some toy maybe, one I'd long forgotten.

Dad had been training me since I was child. Everything he'd given me every birthday, Christmas, Easter—any holiday—was a string of clues finally leading me to some present or treat. He'd known all along that the path to the Hall of Records was real. My stomach twisted with guilt.

The cold bronze of his bracelet felt like a ball and chain, weighing my arm down to the earth and returning me to the present. I'd said that I hated him for preparing me for *this*. Just as Heb's father had prepared him for a better life—to be a scribe. And now that I was actually in Egypt, I was a disappointment.

Shaking my head, I blinked and stood, continuing to search the ruins of the temples and the palace of el-Amarna before returning to the royal Wadi—the tomb meant for Akhenaten.

"This is ridiculous," Mr. Scalone said in his Italian accent and cursed. He paced about the inner chamber of the tomb and stirred up a cloud of choking dust. "The entire path to the Hall is crap. There's nothing in this city or its tombs." Leaning backward, he yelled, and his voice carried out and echoed down the valley.

I cringed. Every living thing down there now knew where we were.

Sitting down on the steps leading into the mountain, I opened my laptop and examined the map with its markers. The rays of sunlight, the rectangles … these fit Akhenaten perfectly. But was it Akhenaten who would have laid a path to the Hall of Records?

I studied the points of the stelae, the temples, the tombs. Such a perfect image. I slapped my forehead in frustration, the sting carrying across my face.

Then there was another image. The markers on the far bank were blocked from my vision by my hand. The points to the east of the Nile had a broad base and tapered to the royal Wadi, it's summit … or pyramidion. My throat clamped in suspense.

"Gavin," Aiden said, approaching. "Whatcha got?" Then, louder, "He's doing that thing again, that thing he does when he's thought of something."

I leaned back. That thing? I glanced at the beanpole teenager and his fox, narrowing my eyes.

"You go to a different place," he said with a shrug. "Like, your body tenses, your breathing gets fast and loud, and you lean forward and tap your foot. You're in the moment, like a rapper feeling his beat."

My foot was tapping the floor … I shook my head. "Look," I said, pointing to the screen.

Kaylin hurried over.

"If we only look at the points on the eastern bank," I said, my fingers trembling, "I could be reaching here, but it looks like a—"

"Pyramid," Kaylin said, gasping. "Akhenaten's tomb is also at its apex."

I nodded. "Figurative sunbeams originating from Akhenaten's tomb are showering every point in el-Amarna, as well as the image of a pyramid."

"Does that mean we go to Giza?" she asked, her fingernails between her teeth.

"Because there isn't anything else here in the Wadi," I replied, "I think this is the clue. But the pyramids at Giza seem too obvious and popular a place to hide anything. Plus, this isn't a perfect pyramid like those three."

"How's this an imperfect pyramid, and what's that tellin' you?" Aiden asked, pressing against my shoulder. His fox panted in my ear, her hot breath rolling across my cheek.

"The sides of the pyramid in this line image, if you connect all of the markers," I said, pointing, "have irregularities or steps in them. I thought that may be the best the Egyptians could do in positioning the stelae against the cliffs, but every tomb the ancients made was perfect … except for some of their original works. And everything we've followed was perfect."

"Older pyramids?" Aiden asked, leaning closer to the screen. The fox's soup spoon of a tongue moistened my neck with warm liquid.

"Yes," I said, pulling up my collar. But should I tell them? There were at least two options. And if I chose, I'd probably be wrong again. "Two immediately come to mind. And Akhenaten wanted to return to the old ways, the ways of the Old Kingdom. There's a bent and a step pyramid."

"Bent?" Kaylin asked, staring at me.

"The original pyramids were made in layers of decreasing size as they went up," I said. "This made the edges look like steps to heaven instead of the straight sides you probably think of with the Giza pyramids. Then there was a transition when the ancient Egyptians attempted to create pyramids with perfectly smooth sides. During their first attempt, the pyramid started to show signs of instability and was going to be so tall and heavy that it would've collapsed on itself. So the architect altered the angle in the top third or so—to make the peak happen sooner—with less weight and less blocks. It looks weird."

"We're going to the step pyramid," Mr. Scalone said and pulled Kaylin away.

Chapter 27

Journal Translation

"COME," SENEB SAID, tugging at my kilt. We watched out for monsters as we climbed down the hillside for Yuf's corpse. Shale gave way and slid under my backside and palms, making the descent quick. Yuf's chest was ripped open, his ribs protruding outside his skin. Everything was covered in blood. My stomach rolled with nausea and heaved.

"We have to hurry," Tia said from above as she squinted and scrutinized the slopes.

Scooping up handfuls of loose dirt, I let the grains trickle out between my fingers. The wind caught the sand, sending a light coat drifting across Yuf's body. Seneb lowered his head.

"He was kind to me," I whispered, a tear burning at the corner of my eye. "When no one else was." Images of the old man filled my thoughts and how he'd kept working for so many years—similar to Father. Their resolve was beyond me. I respected them for it. I could never have done that. Yuf had worked so hard and long, toiling to avoid the fate of an unbalanced life and losing his heart and soul to the Devouring Monster. But somehow, he'd ended up receiving that exact, worst punishment. The Aten, our God, was brutal. Or was it all my fault, for letting him come with us? I should never have tried to lead anyone, just run away myself. "I failed him, just as I failed my father."

I swallowed the lump in my throat, feeling like a serpent swallowing a beautiful bird. One day soon, I needed to somehow make things right. But could I ever save their souls?

"We need to distance ourselves from el-Amarna," Chisisi said, waving us back up, "before the heat sets in. They're probably tracking us by now." Turning, he led our party of six north.

We traversed the eastern slope of the ridgeline so as not to be spotted on the horizon.

Seneb had retrieved his thrown spear and twirled it over his head. The weapon swooped through the air like the wings of a great bird. "Still trustworthy," he said, "like a beaten dog."

I handed the sword from the magician to Chisisi. Chisisi attempted to spin his weapon around his thin torso, but it flew out of his hands and smacked into Wahankh's shins with a ping.

Wahankh grimaced and grabbed his leg. "What about me?"

"I wouldn't give you a weapon, even if I had another," I said.

Wahankh stared at the blade, his wide frame leaning over.

My fist tightened on my spear.

"Don't touch it," Harkhuf growled, nocking an arrow.

Wahankh froze.

Seneb jumped and snatched the sword, handing it back to Chisisi. "You better hold on to this," he said. "We may have to actually fight."

"Perhaps someday when we trust you," I said to Wahankh, handing out a meager bread breakfast from the magician's sack. "Tia, we'll get you something too. We may all need to defend ourselves."

"I was a woman of Egypt," she said, holding out supple palms. "I know nothing of combat."

"Neither do I," I said, "but the dwarves will train us ... and Chisisi."

Chisisi sneered behind his long hair and puffed out his chest. "I've fought many men. This sword is unbalanced—a piece of junk."

A high-pitched hiss carried on for several seconds, echoing across the valleys and mountains to the east. I shuddered, glanced at my companions, and marched faster.

"Did that monster really eat Yuf's heart?" Tia asked, her eyes wide.

"I believe so," I said, my sweat drying the moment it reached my skin. Pain stung my heart as my eyes closed in remorse.

"Like the Devouring Monster?" Tia asked, her hands trembling as she clutched her dress.

"I've seen Akhenaten do the same and claim to wield such power," I replied.

"You saw Pharaoh eat a man's heart?" Chisisi asked, utilizing his sword like a walking stick.

"He wields great magic," I replied as I doled out water from a sheep's bladder.

The heat of the Aten grew fierce, pounding down on my head and back. Everyone slumped under the beating rays.

"We need to pass the valley of el-Amarna before heading for the river," Chisisi said, "or they will see us."

"And how will we eat?" Wahankh asked, touching his protruding abs. "Steal food?"

"We can hunt fowl and fish at the river," I said, recalling Akhenaten's hunting expedition years ago—how he had butchered so many birds and just left them there to rot. "Perhaps we can trade extra meat for grain."

"We can go without food for a time," Harkhuf said, climbing up to peek over the summit. "But we won't make it far without more water."

A creature hopped over the ridge in front of us.

Harkhuf screamed and jumped back, snatching and hurling Seneb's spear. But the weapon was thrown in haste and the creature was nimble. Bronze slammed into rock.

An orange and white cat pranced in a circle, purring. It was Croc!

Crying in excitement, I jumped up and down and spread my arms wide. He rubbed around my ankles, his coarse fur dragging on my skin as he hopped up on his hind legs. Collapsing in the dirt, I hugged him. Tears burned my eyes. I stroked his cheeks and kissed his head. He was alive! And no broken leg, although one had a lump and appeared shorter … But he squirmed from my grip and backed away from the attention. Definitely Croc.

I scooped him back up and turned him over, studying his anatomy. My little pet? Memories of the Mummy Maker sailing off of me in the dark, way back in Memphis, after which Croc had appeared, and the orange flashes I'd seen on the boat to el-Amarna replayed in my mind. But he was just a feral cat I'd rescued when his biting and scratching had caused me to drop him into the river. My forehead furrowed. Could he actually change into a beast the size of a lion? No—but magic had showed itself in mysterious places in this world. Perhaps it flowed within this little creature. Perhaps he was some kind of guardian.

"This little thing couldn't become a lion and walk on two legs," Harkhuf said, keeping his focus on the cat. "But it's weird that you mentioned him and he shows up now."

Chisisi chuckled. "Aren't Nubian dwarves in Egypt versed in animal husbandry?"

"We cared for all the animals at the estates," Seneb said, his boyish cheeks pulled back in a smile. "Both large and small."

"Never an animal like that," Harkhuf whispered, keeping his distance and his hand on an arrow as he marched away.

Croc flopped over, spread his legs, and licked under his tail.

"The sun will drain our internal fluids," I said, recalling survival tactics I'd read about as I handed out the water skin again. I took a gulp. Warm liquid trickled down my throat and wetted the parched sensation.

"Make sure Croc gets water too," Tia said, her demure nose wrinkling. "Even if that other lion-thing is somehow bound to him, he's earned it. Our souls …"

Harkhuf nodded but gave the water skin to Seneb, who poured a few drops into his hand for Croc to lap up as he purred. Seneb stroked Croc's back, warily.

"Thank the son of Hapu for our supplies," I said, "or we'd have had to turn for the river by now. I never wanted any of you to suffer." Tears might have clouded my eyes if I weren't so dehydrated.

"Suffer?" Harkhuf said, his beard jutting out. "We'd all still be doing plenty of that down there. This is the best rest I've had in years." Forcing a smile revealed his crooked teeth and cracked lips.

"We need to travel as far as possible before the Aten sinks into the underworld," Chisisi said, his order stern, "and hiking this slope becomes too dangerous."

We marched on. Following us in quick bursts of speed, Croc would stop, flick his tail, and glance in all directions.

In the late afternoon, Chisisi finally held up a hand and motioned for us to approach the ridgeline. I climbed and peeked over.

Desert opened up below. We had nearly traveled the length of the el-Amarna valley. A large regiment, appearing as dark spots, scoured the mountainside above our new city. Far below, the Nile's glistening waters traversed the land, making my tongue grow dry with thirst. But white billows skimmed along the blue, like clouds. Military ships!

Were they guarding our life source, knowing the heat would flush us from the mountains? Did Akhenaten know it was me, his defiant servant, who'd run away? Or perhaps Pharaoh worried the escape of slaves and the killing of his soldiers would make his new capital appear weak.

"Are all those ships looking for us?" I asked, pointing with the tip of my spear. Sunlight caught the copper and sparkled like a torch in the night, momentarily blinding me.

"No," Harkhuf shouted. "Cover your weapon!"

Trumpets bellowed from the west. My throat constricted in panic. Another mistake. The boats ran aground, and dots of men spilled out as if ants from their hill.

"Run!" Wahankh yelled.

"They'll cut us off if we try to outrun them to the north," Tia said, holding up her hands. "And others follow us from the south."

"We must head east," Seneb said, nodding at the mountains.

I shook my head. "We will die in the desert."

"Better to die free men than be murdered as slaves," Harkhuf said, heading down the far slope.

Sliding and tumbling, we descended the far side. The arduous ascent up the next mountain was much slower. Glancing back, I feared the entire Egyptian army would appear on the horizon. We needed to crest the opposite peak before the soldiers made it to the top of the one behind us and saw where we were headed—

"Stop looking back," Seneb said, shoving me onward. "Climb like a billy goat chasing its mate!"

Hours passed. Croc was gone again. But if he could keep track of me all these years and still save me, he was the least of my worries. Heaving for breath, I continued upward.

Cries and trumpets rang out. My stomach jolted in fear. Yelling across the void, fifty armed men atop the peak at our back shook fists and weapons or clanged spears against shields. They plunged down the slope in pursuit.

Night descended.

Continuing our flight to the northeast, we headed deeper into the mountainous terrain. Days passed. We rested during the scorching heat, being far too close to the Aten, and staggered on during the cooler parts of the day and at night. But every time we spotted the soldiers, they'd closed the distance between us. Our water lasted longer than any small vessel could actually hold, like magic. But the bread disappeared.

My stomach gurgled with hunger and my throat felt like the bed of a dry stream—cracked and peeling.

Tia tripped and fell. Reaching out, Harkhuf caught her by the arm.

"I can't keep going," she whispered, her breath hoarse. "I'm not used to the exertion like the rest of you." Desperation and fear clouded her face.

"They'll give up, or we'll find a way around," Harkhuf said, attempting to sound confident.

Gripping Tia around her waist, Harkhuf and I helped her climb. She didn't weight much, but the added effort cut my stride length in half.

Chisisi stumbled, rolling and tumbling down a long slope before lying on his back. After picking my way down, I knelt beside him. Would we have to leave him behind or drag him with us and slow our pace?

"You okay?" I asked, nudging him.

"I made it down pretty fast." His sand-covered face lifted into a grin, but his eyes were cloudy.

I offered him my water skin and he finally emptied it. But he continued to gulp, his cheeks sinking further and further into his mouth.

Wahankh paused at Chisisi's side, grabbed him under his arms, and hefted him over his broad shoulders.

"You shouldn't carry him," I said to Wahankh. "It'll be too exhausting, and neither of you will make it far. Just help him walk."

"He is our leader," Wahankh whispered and marched away as he patted Chisisi on the back. "Pretend you're of the royal family member and I am your servant. We'll be back in the palace in a couple of hours."

My mind grew fuzzy as I stumbled along after them. We would be overtaken by the Egyptian soldiers before nightfall.

Chapter 28

Journal Translation

I COULD NOT RECALL EVERYTHING that transpired the remainder of the day. A haze clouded my mind as we fled the soldiers of el-Amarna. Rummaging through my sack in desperation, I discovered the spell the magician had given me. The woven reeds of the dry papyrus crinkled against my fingers as I read the arcane and traced hieroglyphics in the air.

Everything went black. My mind shuddered in protest. Had the Aten set, or had I passed out in the sand? But then the desert floor moved beneath me as if I were sprinting through the light of the Aten. A panting sound rang in my head along with patting footfalls. I looked left and right, but I didn't control the movements. Chirping from a bird stung my ears, but the feathery form was far too high on a ledge for its calls to be so loud.

Cathedral-like cliffs emerged and jutted skyward for what seemed like miles. I approached a narrow passage, not visible from a distance. Squeezing between walls of stone, I followed a winding crevasse. Walls pressed in around me. Angled sunlight pierced through the cleft high above, creating long shadows. I turned a corner, and a shallow pool of water rested between the rocks. Droplets trickled down the ledges to accumulate at the base. I wanted to plunge my face into the brown liquid, but I couldn't. Instead, my long tongue lapped up water.

Screaming, I grabbed my face. My vision returned to the stark desert. The others stumbled along without notice, in a daze of their own.

Something loomed in the valley ahead. A towering wall of rock brushed the heavens.

"F-follow me," I said, my voice cracking like sunbaked dirt as I trudged away.

"Are we giving up?" Harkhuf asked. "We'll never be able to hide against those cliffs. But I'd like to kill a few Egyptian soldiers before I go."

"There's something down there," I replied. "A place to hide."

Within twenty feet of the cliffs, I still could not see the opening. Was the vision another trick of the magician's? I stepped around a small outcropping, and the break in the wall emerged.

My heart leapt with hope. No soldiers in sight. Waving everyone on, I wedged myself through the aperture. Shade engulfed my sunburned body like a cool blanket as the temperature plummeted.

Tia hugged the cold rock.

"There's water ahead," I whispered.

Narrow twists and turns kept us at a crawling pace, but the walls offered our weakened bodies support. The path opened up. A pool of brown water rippled against a shaded wall. I hurried to dunk my lips into the liquid, but a creature jumped in surprise near the water's edge. It stared with wide eyes behind a pointed nose, sniffed, and something slipped from between its teeth into the sand. I crouched, tensing.

This was not Croc but a tiny dog. It was so small it almost resembled a rodent, reddish-tan with substantial ears.

Harkhuf lumbered to the brown pool, unaware of the creature. Snarling, the tiny fox yipped.

Harkhuf's eyes bulged as he froze. "What does it want?"

"You're threatening it," I said.

"Is it venomous?" His deep voice turned high-pitched.

Tia laughed. "It's so cute! A desert fox. They don't attack but will bite if cornered."

Releasing a long sigh, Harkhuf inched over to the water. The fox darted off.

Dunking my face into the cool wet, I helped suck the pool away—as did my companions. During a short break, I filled the water skin with the dirt-liquid mixture.

The light above waned before my mind cleared of fog.

"We'll be trapped if the soldiers find the entrance," Chisisi said. "Let's keep moving."

"I'm drained," Wahankh said, flopping over onto his broad back. "I need to rest. They won't find this place. If they do, you all can run and I will hold them off for as long as I can."

"We could see where this chasm leads," Tia said.

"You tall, thin people may be able to slide between these rocks," Harkhuf said, "but I got stuck a couple times. Seneb had to shove me through. I don't want to go any farther, or I might not get out."

"How did you know to lead us into this place?" Seneb asked, staring at me.

I swallowed, my thoughts racing with the visions that had appeared in my head. The memories were murky. Magic? Or some premonition? I recalled seeing, as if through the eyes of a small animal—perhaps the fox we'd just encountered. But I shouldn't tell them all about the magician, my training, and the spell—they might think I was too different. Or it might scare them, or they might pry into my true desires for love and revenge against Egypt's most powerful. They'd all figure out soon enough that if they helped me, we'd die and lose our souls, just like Father and Yuf.

Seneb scooted closer to me, stood, and pulled me up with a strong grip under my arms. Whispering, he put his arm around my hips and guided me away from the others. "You don't have to talk right now, but I have a feeling you're going to have to explain a few things before too long."

I nodded, thinking of something to distract him from questioning me. "I never meant to lead any of you away. And trying to make decisions is harder than I'd thought. I'll leave that up to Chisisi. I just wanted to run away and be alone."

"It'd be pretty hard to survive on your own out here," Seneb said, patting my shoulder. "We can barely do it together."

True. How could I accomplish anything by myself, even if I managed to bring them all home and kept my secrets hidden? I pictured myself crossing the mountain range alone, the sun at my back as I entered el-Amarna. All of the Egyptian military would await my return for Nefertiti. Akhenaten would be smirking, grabbing her by the waist. Bleak ... "I want to help see everyone home, if I can," I said.

Seneb squeezed around my midsection. "Harkhuf and I really do want to return home, he's just afraid his wife and daughter might be dead. And I'm afraid he may not be able to go on if that is the case." His throat clicked as he swallowed. "He carries too much shame."

I nodded. "Me too."

"Ah." He waved his hand, as if he had no cares. "I've accepted the truth. The past can't be changed. It is the future that scares me. I mean, what happens when we get home? What will we do? What happens when I die? What will happen to Harkhuf?"

I angled away from him so I didn't have to divulge more of my past and stepped on something hard in the sand that cracked beneath my sandal. I stepped off of it. A shell … a scorpion! Leaping back, I yelled.

"What is it now?" Harkhuf asked, his face wrinkling with irritation.

I pointed at the arachnid, but it didn't move.

Seneb poked at it with his spear. It was dead. "The fox was eating it when we arrived. It's just the shell, nothing's left inside … like my grandfather's head."

"Why are you so scared of little bugs?" Harkhuf asked with a raised eyebrow.

I wouldn't discuss my past encounters and Akhenaten's plague now. And Harkhuf was not one to talk about not fearing animals. I shook my head.

A pair of eyes glinted from around the bend in front of us. The eyes did not blink, staring into my soul. My muscles tensed.

"The little guy is back," Tia said. "Weird, because desert foxes are skittish."

"Maybe he can't get out that way," Chisisi said, pointing ahead.

I inched closer to the bat-eared fox, and its nose twitched. Crouching, I held out the dead scorpion.

"Careful!" Harkhuf said, nocking an arrow. "He could tear your face off at that height."

"Put the weapon away!" Tia said.

The fox took a cautious step forward and paused. I tossed the scorpion into the dirt in front of him. After sniffing it, he lay down and crunched on the body like a greyhound with a bone.

"We should use the night and run for the river," Chisisi said, rubbing his cracked feet and brushing off his sandals. "The pool's dry and this is our best chance. The soldiers have probably passed us by."

Wahankh groaned, his deltoids popping as he sat up.

"He's right," Seneb said. "If they don't see us tomorrow, across the next valley, they will turn back, like flies to manure. Then they'll search until they find our hiding place."

My stomach churned with worry. I stood and inched back through the tight crevasse to take a peek, and the others followed. Firelight shone outside, glowing against the dusk. I glanced around the corner of the entrance. Fifty soldiers camped in the expanse, utilizing the rock walls as protection.

"Turn back," I whispered. "We'll never make it out alive."

Chisisi said, "I've had my share of experience sneaking past—"

Yellow teeth lunged for my hand, but I yanked it away. Snapping ensued with flinging saliva and curled lips. I fell back against the stone wall in surprise. Barking rang out across the camp, piercing my ears. Dogs.

Thrusting the shaft of my spear between the snapping jaws, I used the weapon to hold the jaws open.

Another muzzle poked into the gap, teeth yearning for my flesh. Soldiers shouted.

"Run!" I yelled, my heart leaping into my throat.

"They'll pin us in," Chisisi said.

"We're already trapped," Seneb shouted, shoving him back.

"I'll welcome them!" Harkhuf yelled, his chest heaving. "In this channel I could take them one at a time. I could take them all."

"You'd take down many," Seneb said, patting his brother's back. "But they'd eventually overcome us, like bees on a rat."

We dashed back into the shadows, and I kicked Harkhuf through a narrow turn. He grimaced in pain as he left blood on the rocks but popped out the other side. Echoes from the pursuing army rattled off the cliffs.

Barreling on, we navigated the winding path long into the night. Then I felt my way through the darkness, along the stone. My fingers fell into several carvings—chiseled hieroglyph warnings. We never should've pressed on, but I kept my mouth shut. Chisisi was right again; we'd be trapped.

Dogs barked from just around the last bend.

The passageway opened into an expanse ringed by the soaring cliffs. Moonlight arced onto roofs that shadowed a small city. I had seen this city somewhere before.

Chapter 29

Journal Translation

OONLIGHT ANGLED DOWN INTO A massive cavern where houses of stone spread out and continued into the mountain. Fear paralyzed my limbs. Yipping from the pursuing dogs barely registered.

"It's a village!" Tia said, racing forward.

"Or a ghost town," Wahankh said, slowing. "But if there are inhabitants, we don't know if they like strangers. And given our trek here, I'd guess they probably don't."

"Don't go in!" I said, my teeth chattering. Not a single torch burned inside. Where was Croc now? I glanced around for his orange and white fur. Nothing.

Baying from the army's dogs grew louder, as did the echoing footfalls of men.

"We don't have a choice," Chisisi said, leading us in.

"Every fortress is like a human," Seneb said, tugging me along by my arm. "They all have a back door."

Yellow eyes glowed from the edge of the stone city. Jumping in surprise, I raised my spear to throw. The fox appeared in the moonlight and sat on her haunches. I lowered my weapon. We approached and passed her, but she remained sitting as if she knew not to enter. But she yipped at Harkhuf's heels. Stumbling as he spun around, the dwarf fumbled with his bow and fell to his knees.

"Don't let it bite me!" Harkhuf shouted, crawling backward with eyes as wide as bowls.

The fox then trotted around us and disappeared into the darkness of the city.

Standing, Harkhuf brushed himself off and grumbled.

"I thought dwarves were the caretakers of all animals," Chisisi said, yanking on Harkhuf's shoulder to keep him moving.

"If you'd seen the animals of Nubia, you'd be more respectful!" Harkhuf said, shaking off his grip. "The smallest creatures can poison and kill a man in seconds."

Seneb nodded, but the moonlight reflecting off his teeth gave away his grin.

We passed between two small guard stations, which both appeared empty, and entered the massive cavern. Digging through my sack, I found the lamp I'd used for reading. I struck the flint and lit the oil.

"Tia, be our eyes," I said, handing her the light. "The rest of us need our hands free for …" An image of the dead city from my dream played through my mind. Were the Dark Ones here, cloaked in black, with white linen-wrapped faces and glowing green eyes?

Our light chewed at the darkness but could not penetrate very far. My fingers crushed the wooden shaft of my spear. I glanced inside buildings carved from stone as we headed for the base of the mountain and the heart of the city.

Remnants of broken furniture were strewn about the houses, but a layer of dust covered everything. Where had the people all gone, and why? And how long ago had they abandoned this place?

Something lay across our path. Black cloth. It didn't move. Harkhuf's bowstring creaked with tension as he led the way. Gooseflesh rose across my arms and legs, as if something watched me. I glanced up a pillar, following the stone to the underside of the roof.

Darkness.

Tia screamed, the sound echoing into caverns that stretched for miles. Harkhuf turned the black cloth over with his foot. Bones clattered on the stone walk. A skeleton, twisted upon itself in agony. It still had some mummified skin and hair adhered to its face. Its sunken eyes looked familiar … my dream! We shouldn't be here, but we couldn't go back.

"Now every rat in this city knows we're here," Wahankh said, huddling behind the dwarves with shaking, empty hands. "We better move—" He cocked his head, crouching.

I heard something too, a vibrating or fluttering sound. Black forms filled the air, screeching. I collapsed in fear, covering my head as creatures sailed by. Hundreds or thousands of them, with wings that sounded like a raging river and flicked at my skin as they passed. Then silence.

"Bats," Seneb said, brushing out his hair. "Keep moving."

We eased past the body, and another corpse appeared. Then another. Curled into fetal positions, they faced what I thought was west. An eerie déjà vu sent a tingling from my queasy stomach up my spine. Not all of us would make it out of here alive.

The bodies thickened, clinging to each other in the streets. The passageway ended in a rock wall with lanes veering left and right.

"Which way?" Harkhuf asked from the lead.

Silence.

The patter of soft feet sounded, and the fox appeared behind us. It sniffed the air.

Harkhuf traveled left through an open building. Dust billowed into the air with our footfalls, and the smell of death drifted by. A blur flashed in a corner of my eye. Stifling a gasp, I glanced over. Nothing but a smashed table propped against a wall. Could something be hiding behind it?

"Wait!" I said.

Everyone froze, their heads turning in all directions.

"In the far corner." I pointed to the edge of our light. "I thought I saw something duck behind the table."

"Perhaps we should let a stone sphinx lie," Wahankh said.

"I don't want someone sticking a knife in my back," Chisisi replied, the sword in his hand trembling.

Veering for the broken furniture, the brothers suddenly stopped.

The table shifted.

Dashing out from behind the cover, a pale blur disappeared through a doorway. I gasped with fear as my throat clamped shut. What was that? It moved fast, at the periphery of our light.

"In the name of the Aten." Tia's lamp clattered to the ground and spilled precious oil. Our light wavered and dimmed.

I held my breath in horror.

No one answered. She fumbled, trying to retrieve the flame before it went out. Bronze grated on stone as she picked it up.

"Let's get out of here," I whispered. "We should run for our lives."

A low growl came from behind us. The fox glared at the doorway and snarled, drool stringing from its lips. Images of Mummy Makers—with their jackal heads and human bodies—chasing me raced through my mind.

"Not that way," Tia pleaded, her face pale under her flickering flame.

Sprinting out the far exit, we entered an alleyway and jumped over the discarded dead. Our light wavered.

A faint hum sounded in the walls. As we ran on, the vibrations grew louder and more musical. We passed an alleyway on my left, and another pale creature flashed by. A large room opened up. In the center, steps led to a dark altar. Behind the platform was a doorway, and another exit opened to our left.

"That could be a way out," Wahankh shouted, pointing behind the stone altar as he huddled near Tia—wedging into the middle of the group.

The humming gathered outside, and the fox growled.

A pale figure darted along the walls with an apelike gait. Wahankh screamed as my blood turned cold. Remaining knuckled over, the figure peered at us. It was humanoid with pale blue skin and eyes as dark as the area beyond our lamp.

Harkhuf's bow creaked with tension as he took aim. Chisisi's sword trembled as we backed away to the far wall.

Slinking in, another ghoul stared at us. The humming outside grew to a crescendo, shaking the walls.

"There must be hundreds!" Wahankh said, cowering but then bolting for the far exit.

Another creature appeared from the darkness. Wahankh tripped and slid across the stone. Scrambling, his feet churned as he skidded to a stop before the monster. Hollow eyes focused on him, and its upper lip lifted to reveal rows of pointed teeth. The big man scurried back.

A vile snickering erupted, louder than the humming. Glowing eyes peered in through all three doorways. An army waited outside, their decaying stench suffocating. I couldn't breathe, and the bronze on my forearm bit my skin with cold.

"Come on, you demons!" Harkhuf bellowed. "Get this over with!"

The snickering ceased, and a larger ghoul entered, scrutinizing us. It spoke in a crackling tone, like embers in a dying fire. "You have come for the cursed?"

"I …" Seneb said, the spear in his hands clutched tight to his body. "We …"

"W-we were," Tia said, her teeth chattering, "only trying to obtain passage north through the desert."

"You have come far out of your way," it answered. "But you are here for a reason."

"We mean you no harm," Chisisi said, his face as white as his kilt.

"Of course you don't. But you are afraid we'll harm you." The creature stared into my eyes, smelling my fear as my heart drummed in my chest. Cold sweat dribbled down my forehead. "I know what dark desires this one seeks."

"Don't let him play tricks on us," I whispered, holding my spear out and forming a back-to-back circle with Tia in the middle. She held her light high. The fox snarled while making darting lunges at the leader.

"Not all that is evil hides in the dark," it said with a hiss. "Some bask in the light."

"I'll drop him," Harkhuf whispered, his teeth grinding. "And maybe the others will disperse."

"Our hearing has grown sharp in this darkness!" the leader snapped, glaring at Harkhuf.

"What is it that you creatures desire?" Tia asked, steadying her lamp by holding it with two hands. "Gold, beer, bread, solace?"

"'You creatures'?" the leader asked, putting a hand to his heart in feigned surprise. "What could you offer us that would change our minds about consuming your flesh?" The humming outside amplified and the tempo quickened—his army poised for their signal to attack.

"I'll kill you, at least," Harkhuf said.

The ghoul smiled, baring rows of long, pointed teeth. "You are already in the beginning stages of a feeble attempt at the Aten."

"Wh-what?" Tia asked.

"I know your leader's objective, but the rest of you"—he motioned to us—"do not, do you?"

The butt of my spear smacked into the floor in shock. Me, or Chisisi? I wasn't a leader. Did this thing know about the magician and Akhenaten?

The creature hissed and the humming died. He cocked his head to the side. "What have you brought here with you?" Its needle-like teeth gnashed together.

"An army is trailing us," Chisisi said. "That's why we're here."

"Why is the Egyptian army pursuing you?"

I swallowed, attempting to mask my terror. "I-I am an enemy of Pharaoh himself," I said, aiming my spear at the ghoul leader's chest. "My companions and I are fleeing Egypt!"

"Has it really been so long?" The creature held his chin with long-clawed fingers, as if lost in thought. "Time is like children's games in here."

Silence.

"It has no significance," he snapped. "Time drains by in your world, but we remain banished in here." His black pupils sucked in the surrounding light. "But you already know you will die!"

Chapter 30

Journal Translation

THE WOOD OF HARKHUF'S BOW groaned under added tension as he sighted this ghoul master at the edge of our flickering light. Catching the brother's shoulder with numb fingers that barely responded to my commands, I whispered, "Not yet." Then, louder, I answered the ghoul leader. "W-we don't need to die today."

"No, not today," the creature croaked. "Unless the army catches you. But you must destroy the necromancer, and not only for our sake. And to determine if that is even possible you"—he pointed at me with a gnarled joint—"will have to die. But before you pass, you will need the book."

"I don't understand," I said, my forehead wrinkling.

The humming commenced again, the tune familiar—ancient or sacred.

"We trained the necromancer ourselves," the creature said, limping about in a tight circle. "His education at Heliopolis cultivated his power and beliefs." It shook its head. "You may pass." The ghouls near the far exit stepped aside. "But beware the hunters; they are everywhere and sniff out magic." Tossing us an object from its waist, it smirked.

A rolled sheet of papyrus skittered across the stone, stopping several feet short. Pointing my spear at the ghoul, I inched forward and bent down without losing eye contact with the creature.

"Do not fall prey to the temptations of power," it said, pausing and staring.

I leapt back with the others and unrolled the crinkling parchment. It appeared similar to the magic spell the magician had given me. The heading read: *Revealing the Truth.*

"Do not waste your weak powers here," the ghoul said. "The answers to our secrets are of no consequence. Go, before I sense the impossibility of your desires and change my mind. I'd very much like to feast on the flesh of someone so disgraced and damned."

Maintaining our circle, we crept for the far doorway. The creatures surrounding the opening glared and snarled.

"Make a move and three of you will die before I fall," Harkhuf said, his bow still drawn and ready to fire.

The humming escalated.

Slipping through the doorway revealed a dark tunnel. We jogged away, but I kept glancing over my shoulder, expecting pale figures to emerge at the margin where darkness blended with the light of our lamp.

Terrifying screams erupted in the musty air. My mouth went dry. The bloodcurdling howls of horror and death came from the cavern behind us. Echoes of men and monster intermixed with spear and shield. We broke into a sprint.

Faint light glimmered ahead. Rays of red sun streamed around a large boulder and into the tunnel. Sliding against the massive rock hiding the opening, I emerged onto a mountain slope. By the location of the morning Aten, we'd angled northwest back toward the Nile.

We marched in silence for an hour, dazed with disbelief.

What had just happened? Would I wake soon?

Sitting on her haunches, the fox panted. The others' faces were pale, covered with cold sweat as they heaved for breath. Perhaps they'd never encountered monsters before. The Mummy Makers didn't seem so horrid now.

"What was that?" Wahankh asked, his hands on his knees, still trembling.

No on answered.

"Let's return to the river," Chisisi said after forcing a few deep breaths—his eyes red and bulging. "I think, in our dehydration, we're seeing hallucinations. And they shouldn't be expecting us this far north."

Walking for hours up and down the mountains in silence, we kept a steady pace. Croc sat waiting for us atop a mountain crest. Purring, he rubbed against my leg.

"Where were you?" I asked, picking him up and kissing him on the head. His coarse fur stuck into my mouth, making my tongue squirm. He meowed, but his orange stripes froze as he glared at the fox. Sniffing, his hackles rose and he wiggled out of my grip, falling and landing on all fours. He paused, studied the rat-dog, and flopped down on his side in the dirt, sprawling out.

The others pressed on down the slope—except Tia, who took my hand and looked into my eyes. "Heb," she whispered, "I'd like to thank you for what you did for us … with anything I can offer."

My hand tightened with awkward tension as my insides tingled. Did she refer to friendship, or something else? She was beautiful, but not Nefertiti. "Thank you," I said with a smile, sliding down the summit.

Her smile faded. "Where is it that you're taking us?"

My lip twitched with suspicion. Did she desire me, or did she attempt to coerce me, like she did with other men, into revealing what it was the ghoul leader had suggested? No, she didn't love me; that was impossible for her. I swallowed. Would love still be possible for Nefertiti?

Images of Nefertiti and then her sister Mutnedjmet's face and innocent smile filled my mind. My lip relaxed. I would not hold it against Tia and turn friends into enemies. "I am trying to take each of you home, and then return to my own … after they've forgotten about me."

"What's waiting for you at home?" she asked, her eyebrows climbing onto her forehead.

"I need to accomplish something I've yearned for all my life," I said, my fingers wringing the shaft of my spear. "You'd think I was a fool and laugh. Such dreams are not meant to be shared, even among friends."

One corner of Tia's lips lifted in a smirk, but then her face drooped. "I'm afraid to return to mine …" She stumbled as she descended the incline after the others.

Wait—why?

The fox stared at the ground beside the brothers, yipped, and rotated her head back and forth. Then her feet moved and the canine sank into the sand.

"No!" Harkhuf yelled, jumping and reaching for the small animal. His meaty palm grabbed only air. The fox had disappeared into the ground.

"Quicksand!" The dwarf lay flat, his eyes wide as he poked at the desert around him—testing its character.

I rushed to them.

Popping out of the ground, the fox shook, and a layer of sand splattered across Harkhuf's face and beard. The fox pranced away, lay down, and crunched on a black beetle the size of my hand. Harkhuf blew a cloud of dust from his mouth and wiped his face. "She's a little trickster," the dwarf grumbled, climbing to his feet.

I grinned as Tia laughed and Chisisi snorted.

Harkhuf shook his head and marched away.

The day and heat wore on as we hiked northwest.

Yelling and the clash of metal arose, carrying up the mountain. At the foot of the incline, a road extended east and west through an expanse of bland desert. Nothing in sight.

"I'm not ready for another shock," Wahankh said, hugging the shadows of the slope as he followed us west, in the direction of the ruckus.

"Then you shouldn't have run from el-Amarna," Harkhuf said, stroking his dark beard as his biceps contracted, bulging. "Perhaps I'll need to use this." He drew and nocked an arrow.

Chapter 31

Journal Translation

WE CREPT ALONG THE DESERT ROAD to the commotion and rounded a mountain bend before witnessing the carnage. Twenty impaled bodies of Egyptian soldiers lay strewn about. Another ten disheveled, dead bodies in stained kilts surrounded an overturned chariot, the body of a white horse toppled over beside it. Three spears protruded from its massive torso. So much death …

"People lying everywhere," Seneb said, "like the morning after my teenage girl had gotten together with her friends and stole my wine."

"I am still armed," a voice replied, coming from behind the chariot. "I am a captain and the son of a general, and if I do not return, an army will be sent to wipe out you pirate scum!"

An Egyptian soldier? If we helped him, would he just turn us in?

Harkhuf patted Seneb's back and grumbled, "We don't help Egyptians, even if—"

"Any man who owns a horse and chariot," Wahankh said, creeping up behind Chisisi, "and leads a platoon of Egyptian soldiers down the trade route to the east must carry something of value."

Tossing his bow aside, Harkhuf took a thicker bow from the dead Egyptian chariot archer and gathered arrows for his quiver. He also grabbed a spear. I snatched my bow back, but I also discarded my spear in favor of twin swords—as I'd read about this seldom-used and less-expected alternative. Cold bronze sat in both of my hands as well as upon my wrist. Chisisi searched through the remaining weapons, hefting a rawhide shield and sword as Tia and Wahankh took spears and shields. My palms sweat with nervousness. The bully with a long, sharp weapon …

Tia tucked a knife into her dress as the fox trotted up and sniffed the dead. Croc was gone again.

"These pirates or mauraders or whoever you say attacked you are already dead," Chisisi said in the direction of the overturned chariot. "We are travelers."

No response.

"Are you hurt?" Tia asked.

A head with closely cropped red hair peeked over the side of the cart. My forehead furrowed. I'd only seen red hair on Akhenaten's mother, Tiye, and one other. My stomach knotted with anxiety. The guard with the flail, who'd whipped me all those years ago, after the magician told him I'd been talking to him?

Two pale eyes appeared, then a long, hooked nose and an overbite with a strong jaw. It was him, the unique-appearing man who'd whipped me. "Who are you, then?" he asked, looking us up and down.

"Mercenaries traveling the great desert road," Chisisi said, smiling. "We're returning to Egypt after escorting a caravan to the east."

"I have no gold or food," the captain said. "I will not be able to pay you for your assistance."

"We didn't say anything about helping you," Harkhuf growled.

"What happened?" Chisisi asked.

Standing, the soldier examined each of us, then looked into the desert as if searching for something. "We were sent to the road to head off a few slaves who'd escaped from the new capital. I am Paramessu, and I led these soldiers east before we were ambushed." He held up a shield pocked with arrow shafts and feathers. "I am a captain and one of the best chariot drivers and horsemen of Egypt. But they took my steed." Clouds filled his eyes as he laid a hand upon the shoulder of the powerful equine. He gathered his shield and spear and inched from behind his cover.

My hands squeezed the hilts of my new swords. Would he try to bring us in? Wahankh rested his spear and shield, smiled, and assisted the soldier.

"Why do you travel with a woman ... and a fox?" Paramessu asked, one eyebrow rising suspiciously onto his forehead.

"All men need women," Chisisi said, his sword extended before him as he forced a grin.

"She can hold her own," Harkhuf said, lowering his bow. "So don't even think about touching her."

"I wouldn't dare," Paramessu said, his jaw clenching.

Harkhuf growled, "I know what you Egyptians—"

"The fox I raised from a pup," Seneb said, pulling his brother back. "He's like a basenji but doesn't require water. Makes for a good desert pet—only needs a few insects here and there."

Paramessu's eyes narrowed. "Please, if you wish to accompany me back to my ship, I will feed you. If not, safe travels." He nodded at the dead soldiers littering the road. "I will return and bury them." Pivoting around, he strode away.

I exchanged glances with Tia and the brothers, and the moisture returned to my palms. Did this soldier suspect we were the slaves, and was he trying to trick us by luring us back to his comrades? Could he possibly have remembered me, after all the years and hundreds or thousands of slaves he must've encountered?

"Why would you offer us beer and bread?" Chisisi asked as my hands fumbled to hold on to the slick metal of my new swords.

"I have sworn an oath to the Egyptian army, like my father, a revered troop commander," Paramessu replied, waving us on. "If you assist a captain, you will be rewarded, sir ..."

"Chisisi," he said.

"We encountered a small group of men several miles from here," Tia said, following and putting on her best smile. "They would not speak much but begged for water, with nothing to give in return. We offered them as much as we could as we were headed back to the river. This group, whom we believed were beggars, were unarmed and headed east. They were very polite but could have been the slaves you seek."

Paramessu stopped. His shoulders tightened. "I will have to go after them if I am to redeem myself with Father ... the general. But I won't be able to retrieve them by myself. Your group would be greatly rewarded if you accompany me back to my ship, gather supplies, and then ride east to capture these thieves and murderers."

"We're not sure those are the men you're looking for," Tia said, catching up to him. "What did these slaves look like?"

Paramessu inched back around to face us. "I was informed that six unskilled slaves and a free laborer killed a couple of Egyptian policemen and ran into the mountains east of el-Amarna. They are to be brought back to the capital for Pharaoh himself. They couldn't have crossed the mountains and reached this road for another three days, at best. That is, if by some miracle they survived without water."

"The people we saw must not have been the slaves you're after, then," Chisisi said, glancing at me out of the corner of his eyes.

Paramessu nodded. "Follow me. The day grows hot, and we have miles to cover. Your seasoned crew may have supplies, but I do not." Donning a hide cap, the young captain strode away.

Could we pass for Egyptian soldiers if we dressed like them? Removing a leather helmet from a body, I placed it on my head. The others followed suit. After gathering the dead's water skins, Chisisi motioned for us to follow the captain. Our only lasting escape would be via the river.

"We're not exactly camels, but we have enough water for another day or so," Seneb whispered. "We don't have to do this."

"I don't trust him," Harkhuf said, lifting his bow. "We hold the weapons of his dead comrades, wear no head protection from the Aten, and travel the trade road during the heat of the day. He may look naïve, but I don't think our lies fooled him."

"I trust his word," Chisisi said, nodding and bouncing his long hair. "We're helping him."

"Perhaps where you're from, someone's word is binding," Wahankh replied, repeatedly jabbing the butt of his spear into the ground. "But here, they'd turn you in for a loaf of bread, and this one has to please his father. Currently he's a failure."

"He can't overcome us alone," I said. "And the river is our only real hope. Who wants to follow him?" I lifted my hand. Something gnawed at my stomach with insecurity, but the burning deep inside didn't have the bite I'd felt as Akhenaten's slave. Would I lead more people astray? Chisisi's lip wrinkled. What was he thinking? How terrible a decision-maker I was, leading men not only to their deaths, but forfeiting their souls?

Chisisi and Tia raised their hands. Seneb and Harkhuf hesitantly followed. Wahankh shook his head.

"You can go your own way, Wahankh," Tia said. "If you believe that is best."

"I will die out here on my own," Wahankh replied, wiping his brow.

"They aren't looking for only one slave," Harkhuf said as he admired his new spear and bow. "You can tell anyone you're a farmer or trader."

"I'm coming," Wahankh said, his eyebrows narrowing.

Paramessu glanced back. "Follow me, my friends," he shouted and smiled, motioning us west.

Chapter 32

Journal Translation

WE FOLLOWED THE TALL SOLDIER with red hair down the great trade road, hiking for hours under the relentless sun. Green trees and brush finally sprang up in a distinct line. The Aten sank into the horizon.

"We're almost there," Paramessu said, draining his water skin. My companions drank theirs as well, but I saved the magician's inside the sack, in case we needed to run.

After the scrub brush, farmlands stretched to the Nile. A great warship lay anchored in the distant shadows. Paramessu waved his arms over his head as if to catch someone's attention.

A sinking feeling rose in my stomach. Perhaps several soldiers remained with the boat. As we approached, I caught glimpses of a single man moving around the hull. I let the others go ahead.

Kneeling beside the fox, I stared into her eyes, and the animal sat on her haunches. I whispered, "I don't know how you are bound to me, but I am going to ask something of you."

The fox cocked her head and ears to one side.

"Will you stay behind, and, if possible, let me see through your eyes?" I asked, half expecting someone to burst out laughing. "If that is even possible. I wish to keep watch on el-Amarna and Pharaoh."

She shook herself off. Red dust lifted into the air and caught a light wind, tickling my nose. A musky scent and something strange, something I did not recognize, wafted into my nostrils. I reached out. The tiny creature let me pet her on the head and along her back. Her wiry hair tugged at my calluses, but the touch warmed my insides.

She licked my hand and trotted off.

"What happened to your chariot?" the man aboard the warship shouted as the others sopped through the bank. I followed them.

"Much has happened," Paramessu replied as he ascended a ramp into the vessel.

"Those are not our soldiers!" the man shouted, disappearing into the hull.

As we climbed aboard, the other soldier approached with a spear cocked, ready to throw. "My captain, are you a prisoner?"

"Drop your weapon!" Paramessu said, pointing at the man. "I will explain, but we are parched. These men … and this woman are here to help. Bring beer and water."

"But they have our comrades' arms," the man replied.

"Our comrades no longer need them," Paramessu said, folding his arms across his chest.

The guard's eyes bulged as he turned away.

Wahankh inched onto the boat, shaking.

The soldier returned carrying armfuls of food and drink. We sat and wolfed down honey bread and thick beer as Paramessu explained his encounter with the bandits of the trade road.

"These travelers arrived out of thin air, just as I was praying to the Aten," Paramessu said to his comrade. "Anyone delivered by the Aten is deserving already, but they also scared the remaining pirates into the desert."

My mind muddled in confusion. Had we really scared off some remaining attackers and saved the captain? I hadn't seen any other pirates, but perhaps they'd had a scout who'd seen us coming. Or was he trying to confuse us so we'd reveal something? No, being raised in such a privileged life, this young soldier shouldn't be a talented liar or actor.

The young captain turned to us. "Why is it that on a daily basis we all compete with each other, but in a time of crisis we become something else and help?"

I shrugged, thinking of Yuf and Mutnedjmet. "I have experienced the same … infrequently."

Swallowing, Paramessu ran a hand over his short red hair. "I do not have the gold to reward you, but will you sail with me? I'll need another horse and chariot, as well as a troop of soldiers, so I must return to my father like a dog with its tail between its legs. The only way I'll reclaim any dignity in his eyes is if I catch the slaves before the corps from el-Amarna do … But for you, his gratitude for saving my life will prevail."

We needed to sail far away from here.

"Where is your father?" Chisisi asked as we shared a nervous glance.

"We can't sail now; it's growing dark." Paramessu nodded at the horizon. "Tomorrow we embark for el-Amarna. Most of the military is now stationed at the capital, protecting the *benben* stone and the temple of the Aten … per Pharaoh."

"We will accept the gift of your food and drink," Chisisi said, looking Paramessu in the eye. "But we must return to the road. A trader is waiting for us to escort him and his cargo."

Paramessu's red eyebrows rose. "You travel between Egypt and the Red Sea?"

Chisisi nodded.

"Stay the night here. And by my word, I will find a way to repay you all someday. Please visit el-Amarna when your lives allow."

"We must depart," Chisisi said, and my companions stood.

My eyes closed in frustration. The captain probably wondered why we came aboard and were now suddenly looking for this trader before dark.

Smiling wide, the captain clasped my arm and helped me to my feet. "One day they will follow you," he whispered and then turned and bowed to the others.

I stumbled back. I only led men to their deaths …

The others loaded up with as much food and water as we could carry. "We nearly ran out during the last crossing," Tia said.

My limbs shook with dread when I stepped to the ramp. Something wasn't right.

Chapter 33

Journal Translation

THE BOAT'S PLANK WOBBLED as we descended, leaving the red-haired captain behind and heading back for shore.

But my vision blurred and faded. I gasped and tensed. Then a light reappeared, and what I saw was not from my own eyes. I was sitting in a field, panting, as if seeing through the fox again. Disorientation made my head light. Long shadows had set in for twilight, obscuring a pair of eyes—poised and unblinking. Foliage crunched as footsteps drew near. The wind rolled through my hair. A figure cloaked in black strode through the farmlands, the reflection of gold protruding from a long sleeve. I glanced up. The warship we were exiting was not far away. There I was, my body, Heb, stooped over on the plank, standing like a—

My senses returned to my body in a snap. I stood straight, shaking my head to clear the fog. Cold sweat trickled down my back. Pointing, I shouted, "Get on the boat!"

Pulling the brothers back, I leapt into the hull. As I was about to kick the ramp over, an orange and white cat emerged from beneath a flowering tree. Croc stretched, yawned, and sauntered up the ramp.

"What is happening?" Paramessu asked as he approached, his hand on the sword at his belt.

A dark form appeared, sprinting through the fields below.

"I'm sorry, Captain," Chisisi said. "We don't mean any disrespect to you, but we are commandeering your vessel."

"What is that?" Paramessu whispered, his mouth gaping as he watched the Hunter.

"Nothing you would ever want to come face to face with," Harkhuf said, sighting down the shaft of a drawn arrow. The arrow tore through the air in a whistling arc. Ducking just before the arrow embedded into its head, the Devouring Monster didn't alter its momentum.

"Push off!" Seneb yelled. "We need to get into the water, like a dying fish!"

After shoving at the bank with an oar, Paramessu started rowing.

Harkhuf drew another arrow, a grimace contorting his face. "This thing evades even my skills."

The ship angled north with the current. "Row!" Chisisi screamed as I ran to the stern and grabbed the handle of the rudder. The boat jerked as my companions and I rowed out of the sink.

Diving into the water without slowing, the black-cloaked figure disappeared beneath the rippling surface. Fear closed its icy grip upon my heart as I struggled for breath. Who would die this time?

The boat crept out into the belly of the river as I waited for the creature to reappear. Waves sloshed under us, tilting the boat to and fro. Croc released a high-pitched hiss, which made Harkhuf jump.

"You will not steal our boat!" the other soldier onboard said. "Captain, this is a trick!" Pulling a spear from beside him, he pointed it at Seneb.

Seneb shook his head. The boat jolted beneath us and wood creaked. The soldier lost his balance, falling to a knee. Hissing again, Croc paced along the bow while glaring into the water.

"Row!" I yelled, maneuvering the boat into the current.

"Drop the oars!" the other soldier shouted.

"Drop your weapon and help us," Paramessu said. "That's an order!"

The hull bucked. Something inhuman and unrecognizable in the fading light clutched the starboard railing, tilting the entire warship. The soldier and Seneb toppled into the railing, the taller man somersaulting out into the water with a splash. Water pelted my face.

Wahankh shouted and pointed at the hair-covered hand as it continued to pull the edge of the boat into the water. Croc yowled, his tail puffing up to the size of my arm.

Harkhuf stabbed at the lion fur with his spear. A hooded head lifted over the rim, and another hand grabbed the spear, snapped the tip from the shaft, and flung the metal blade into the water.

Heaving, the beast pulled itself up. Croc's teeth buried into its finger, and his claws flashed in blurry strikes. An inhuman scream filled the night, and the creature retracted, sinking back into the river as Croc released its hand.

A swirling wave of red erupted from beneath the surface. Harkhuf grabbed another spear and lunged to the edge, searching. I drew my swords.

Paramessu's companion did not resurface. "My soldier is gone," the captain said. "Row!"

Croc yowled again. My skin crawled as if beetles scurried through the muscles. Would Croc turn into the beast we'd glimpsed atop the mountain outside el-Amarna? I prayed he would.

The current snagged the stern and ushered us northward against a howling gale.

Twilight eventually faded into moonlight, but we dared not dock. My eyes strained into the darkness, hunting for obstacles. Croc lay down and closed his eyes. Time slipped away.

My heart settled, and my mind drifted. Who were those cursed ghouls in the city of the dead? If I ever saw them again, it would be too soon. I'd seen too many monsters, including those in human skin. But magic did flow in *my* veins! I'd seen through the eyes of a desert fox, and I'd used the crocodile ward against Suty before I'd entered slavery. I hadn't been sure at the time, but something had shoved him away. Perhaps I *could* be more than just a servant boy … and could Croc keep the beast at bay so we could return Tia home and make her happy? She'd be free, escaping the horrors she'd endured—as only a woman in slavery would know. Would everyone return home, and then could I—without the aid of the son of Hapu? Perhaps helping others could absolve my soul for causing Yuf to lose his, and for Father's burning. My heart ached as if Yuf's gnarled hands ensnared it and squeezed. My breath came in shallow gulps, but my stomach didn't ache …

The Aten rose in the east, lifting my heavy eyelids.

"You don't know what you're doing, do you?" Chisisi asked as he ran a hand along the boat's railing.

I shook my head.

"You were a servant to Pharaoh when he was younger?" His eyes narrowed as he leaned closer.

"Yes," I said.

"You do anything else, such as make decisions for people?" He tapped his foot. "Not what they were going to eat, but decisions that affected their safety?"

I swallowed. "Only for myself, not for others."

"You should look to me for any big decisions," he said, crossing his arms. "I've led men in business, travel, and protecting others, and I've excelled. You"—he paused and motioned to the others—"and they will all be better off for it."

I nodded. What did I know?

Chisisi straightened like a pole, pointing behind us. "Look!"

A small fleet of warships trailed us from the south.

"My comrades," Paramessu said, waving with both hands over his head.

"Those ships must have been moving before dawn," Chisisi said. "Boats do not sail the Nile in the dark, unless …"

"We should stay well ahead of them," Wahankh said, shading his eyes as he stared against the morning sun.

"My good men," Paramessu said. "I am sorry, but we must stop this vessel. The military will offer us aid."

"You're no longer in command," Harkhuf grumbled, nudging him with the butt of his spear.

Paramessu's hooked nose wrinkled as his jaw muscles bulged.

"We may not be who you believe us to be," Seneb said, smirking. "And if you try to stop us, you will be bound like a rodent by a constricting python."

"Or thrown overboard," Harkhuf said, pausing, "like someone we want to get rid of."

Seneb studied his brother and shook his head at the comparison. "How about like bad bread, or a stone, or an empty crate."

"You've summoned a great evil against this ship," the captain said, shaking his head and short red hair. "Who are you?"

"A group of kindred spirits trying to find home," Tia replied, running a hand through her black hair and winking. She put a fist to her heart as if this were the only thing she'd ever wanted.

"Why is that," Paramessu said, walking away, "that *thing* after us?" Hunching down at the far end of the hull, he scrutinized the fleet.

No one answered.

Sunlight waned over the course of the day, and the pursuers gained considerable ground.

"They must be rowing as well," Wahankh said, rubbing his arms, nervous.

"Is this normal military action, if they are not pursuing us?" I asked the captain.

The tall redhead remained silent.

"We must sail through the night," Wahankh said, pacing the hull. "Or they'll catch us."

"Teach Tia to steer," Seneb said as he grabbed an oar. "We'll need all the men to row."

"With only five or six men rowing, you'll never outrun a fleet of soldiers trading shifts," Paramessu said, not moving. "It is futile."

"If we sail through the night, we should be able to lose them in the dark," I said.

"Or we could lose them within the delta," Chisisi said. "My home is there, and I know the maze of branching water."

"The fork in the river leading for my home will come sooner," Tia said. She swallowed and sat down, as if hiding something or still too afraid to consider returning.

Fields and intermittent houses blurred by as darkness descended. Croc slept atop the portside railing, his snores eventually mixing with the wind.

Tia tried her hand at the rudder, practicing turning left and right. Her first attempt cut deep into the water, nearly turning us sideways. I grabbed her arm. The snoring dwarves rolled across the hull and grunted. Scrambling, Croc clawed into the wood to hold on as he skidded to the edge.

But within half an hour, Tia guided us with ease. "You can take over in the morning," I said. "I'll need to sleep, but I want to go at full pace tonight."

Her hand brushed mine as she let go of the oar. Tender fingers ran up my arm and onto my chest, sending a tingle across my skin.

"Heb," she said. "We can find our home together. I can offer you things ..."

I glanced from Tia to the river, hair and water both twinkling with moon- and starlight. Was she offering herself to me if I'd find a new home with her? She was attractive, but my heart longed for another. "I'm sorry," I said, leaning away. "I ... can't."

"Are you in love?" Tia asked, taking my hands. "A wife back home, perhaps?"

"Something like that," I said, picturing Nefertiti and the time we'd stood on top of the watchtower overlooking the vast world and the blue ribbon of the Nile. She'd let me indulge in her unrivaled beauty, studying her face and curves for moments that lasted a lifetime—as if we were the only two people in the world. And she'd kissed me. My heart skipped as warmth flooded my chest and the tingling inside spread throughout my body. My eyes must've spoken of my feelings. "She held the power to make me, a mere servant boy, feel as if I were king of the world. She might again."

"Well," Tia said, her head reeling back, "I might not make you a king, but we could all try for a new life. Perhaps if I had someone at my side, returning home wouldn't seem so daunting."

"I won't be able to give you what you deserve," I said, shaking my head.

"I don't need anything from any man," she replied, jerking her hands away. "And I couldn't love you either; I just want someone there so I ..." Slinking off to the front of the boat, she lay down beside Paramessu and the dwarves.

My eyes closed with regret even though I'd tried my best not to make her feel as if she had been turned down. The decision might not have always been hers, and she was called a whore because of it—another side of this world that I once thought was only unfit for me ... She wouldn't trust any man and might even hate us all. But not jumping at her offer must've cracked her belief that she had only one power over us. I sighed.

Steering through the moonlight, I attempted not to brake with the rudder—so that the pursuing military ships wouldn't close the gap between us. But I risked a blind crash at full speed. When morning finally broke, my scratchy eyes scanned the horizon. The fleet had eaten up more of the distance between us, appearing larger against the ribbon of blue in the distance.

"Wake up!" I shouted.

"Damn, what is it?" Harkhuf grumbled. "Having the best dream in years. I was back home with my woman and little girl ..." He blinked and grimaced, as if in excruciating pain.

Seneb grabbed his brother's shoulder and squeezed. Harkhuf shrugged it off. "What happened?" Seneb asked.

"I don't know," I said, pointing to the military ships. "I kept us at full speed all night."

"How far away are they?" Wahankh asked, scouting into the distance.

"They will overtake us tonight, or tomorrow at the latest," Paramessu said, emotionless.

"We need to start rowing," Chisisi said, motioning with his thin limbs.

Tia snatched the rudder from me without a word.

Stretching the weariness from my muscles and joints, I took up an oar beside Seneb and Chisisi. Harkhuf and Wahankh manned the other side. Our vessel picked up momentum, propelling through the water.

"I owe you my life," Paramessu said, "but I cannot disobey the military. And I am not lying when I advise you: You will not outrun them. You will tire long before they do."

"What should we do, then?" Tia asked, glancing back over her shoulder as the wind waved through her hair.

Paramessu shrugged. "Give up."

"We could push on until nightfall and use darkness as our ally," I said.

"Like last night?" Chisisi asked, rolling his eyes.

"We could turn around, open our sail, and speed south," I said, "utilizing the strong wind and hugging the shores. We could sneak past them before the Aten reveals we've disappeared or—"

"Even at night they'd spot our white sail," Chisisi said, shaking his head. "And then we'd be headed back to el-Amarna."

"If we could make it all the way to Nubia, we might have a chance," Seneb said, his eyes growing distant. "But it's far, and we can't sail the entire way. You said 'or' like you had a second idea."

"Trying to hide our vessel as soon as night falls," I said, my forehead wrinkling with skepticism. "We could run far away into a city, which would be the best place to hide in Egypt."

"We won't reach any cities this day or night," Paramessu said.

"We'd be stuck running through the desert again," Chisisi replied, his lips thinning. "Leave the planning up to me."

Paramessu's eyes widened. I froze as I studied him. The captain now knew without a doubt that we'd been on the run from someone already. He must suspect we were the slaves he was looking for.

"At least we're armed this time," Harkhuf said, "and we have food and water."

Chisisi planted his hands on his hips and shook his head.

My oar dipped into the river. The liquid felt firm and unrelenting as I pulled the wood handle, attempting to propel us into the gusting wind. My muscles burned like acid as the hours crawled by. Only the occasional cacophony of quaking ducks protesting our passage interrupted the howling of the wind. The military ships came closer and closer before the sun set and darkness settled around us. We couldn't keep running.

"Dock here," Chisisi said, pointing.

Settling onto the western bank amid the brush, our warship protruded well beyond the foliage, but its sail was collapsed. The wind had died, leaving only raspy breaths to break the tense silence. Darkness.

Rippling waters gave way to dark shapes. Three military boats emerged from the black without a whisper, visible only by reflected moonlight.

My mouth went dry. Were they slowing down, or was apprehension playing tricks on me? Seconds dragged on like hours. The bow of the first boat crept past, then the hull, then the stern. The second and third ships were even with each other as they glided by.

Silence and darkness.

A tense breath escaped my lips, and my shoulders relaxed. I smiled and hugged Tia, but Wahankh's face paled more than the moonlight. He trembled as he pointed.

A great ship erupted from the mist. Two others trailed close behind, headed back for us.

Chapter 34

Journal Translation

WARSHIPS SKIMMED THE dark water, searching for us as if reapers coming for the dead. They collided with the shore, and timber groaned in agony, piercing my ears. Soldiers used the momentum of their impact to leap out of their boats onto the soft bank.

"Like babies flying through the air when their mothers trip," Seneb whispered from the darkness.

Thirty men charged onto our vessel with weapons drawn.

"It's empty," a soldier shouted.

"Where'd they go?" another asked.

"Sphinx north, Jaguars west, and Scorpions south," a deeper voice bellowed. "The first to site them or locate their tracks, sound your trumpets. Search every bush!"

Fanning out, the legions diverted as they hacked at the brush. They would find us soon.

Holding my index and little finger pointed at the water around me in the crocodile ward, I forced myself to believe I held the power to fend off beasts in the depths. The alternative was too horrendous. The hippo attack I'd survived on that trip with Akhenaten and Nefertiti ran through my mind in vivid detail—the boat tilting and throwing us over into the cold murk, the silence of the underwater world, the algae that clung to my arms and face like a net, the piercing tusk as it grated my bone …

I shook my head to dispel the images and peered through the rippling water—from beneath the surface. Light reflected amongst the brush at the river's edge. A single eye slunk into the water, coming toward me. The blood in my veins froze, and my throat constricted. The eye sank below the surface in a slow, deliberate motion, and the glow faded. Then everything was still. My heart raced with fear. Something was in the water with us!

But thrashing would not only create noise, it would draw the crocodile in—sensing wounded prey.

Spitting out the hollow reed I'd used for breathing, I surfaced. Cool liquid streamed down my short hair and face, stinging my eyes as I waded through the murk. Harkhuf released an arrow. A single guard remaining aboard our warship tipped over backward and plunged into the Nile. The splash, which I expected to resonate through the night, was muted.

Seneb had slowed the falling victim, catching and easing him below the surface. Harkhuf shot more soldiers—each remaining military vessel had kept one man on board. A soldier fell into my waiting arms, knocking me under with a small splash. As I resurfaced, the last soldier crashed into the hull of his boat with a thud. Heaving, I scrambled aboard one of their warships and hurried to the rudder. I back-paddled as Chisisi, Tia, and Wahankh shoved at the bow in hopes of dislodging it from the bank. Splashes sprang from the water around me—the brothers fulfilling their part of the plan.

A minute or two later, Paramessu coughed as the brothers shoved him aboard. He was gagged and bound, and he was soaking wet like the rest of us.

"Can't let him tell his comrades where we went," Seneb whispered, climbing aboard.

Trumpets blared in the distance. My shoulders tensed. They must've heard our commotion.

The boat budged and inched away from shore. A cat leapt from the reeds and into the hull without a sound.

We glided into the belly of the river, and the current grabbed us and spun us northward—even though the call of treasure still beckoned me south.

Soldiers stormed aboard their two remaining ships and Paramessu's smaller boat.

"Run them down!" the deep voice shouted.

"Where are the paddles?" another yelled.

I smiled as I let the current take us away. The brothers had thrown the oars from the other ships overboard before bringing Paramessu with them. As the soldiers gathered their paddles from the river, they might also find their store crates floating. Less supplies might hinder their desire and the length of time they'd be able to pursue us.

Harkhuf lifted his fists over his head before squeezing Seneb's neck in a rough embrace. Tia clapped, and Wahankh and Chisisi even patted each other on the back as they shouted with glee. The thrill of victory spread through my body like spilled lamp oil. We'd won, for now.

Tia gathered drink from the ship's stores and passed out cups as the warm wind whisked by. Seneb cut Paramessu's bonds, but the soldier didn't move, staring at the hull for hours.

✳ ✳ ✳

When I woke, the sky was still littered with stars. Grating snores interrupted the gusts of wind. I rubbed my eyes and took the rudder from Tia, who stumbled off and lay down.

What would we do now? And how could we ever face all the evil in this world?

Grabbing my bow, I nocked an arrow. I drew the sinew string to my chest as it bit deep into my fingertips, sighting a rock on the moonlit shore. The old wood of the bow's frame creaked in protest. I loosed the arrow. Whistling carried through the night, but the arrow landed far short and to the right of the target, skittering off of shale. But if an enemy had stood there, I would've impaled—

"You will only reap the power of the bow if you can *hit* your enemy," a voice said from behind, making me jump. "The worst archer in the Egyptian army could hit that rock from this distance."

I spun around. Harkhuf yawned and propped himself onto his elbows.

"But Egyptians aren't the world's best bowmen, are they?" I asked.

Harkhuf's eyes lit up as his bushy black eyebrows climbed his dark forehead. "The kingdom of Kush is home to the world's best archers."

"Is that where you're from?" I asked.

"I *am*." His voice reverberated, distant. "The wood and sinew run in my blood and extend from my limbs like arms. The timber of the ebony tree glistens in my hand amidst the rolling brush of the plains. Herds fill the fields like portraits, and my enemies quake in fear." His face relaxed as he swallowed, but the darkness in his eyes returned. "My size is a disadvantage with many weapons, but the bow equalizes me. I use thicker wood and heavier string to make up for my disadvantage in draw length."

I smiled. I'd read about the bow and the people of Kush and correctly guessed his heritage. "Could you teach me your craft?" I asked, attempting to sound as sincere as I was.

"One day we'll all fire arrows together, side by side, under peace or war, either in this life or the next. Slavery be damned." Harkhuf grinned as sunlight expanded across the horizon. He stood and approached me. "But first you must understand and respect such a weapon." He ran a finger along the frame of my bow as if a father wiping away his daugher's tears, and he described how the bow worked, the force angles and physics, what material was used to make the weapon, and how the greatest frames were crafted. In his excitement, I couldn't even tell that he hated me.

Taking up the bow, Harkhuf drew the string. Veins popped from his left forearm as he braced against the grip, the wooden limbs flexing under such force they might snap. His fingernails rested against his cheek, his elbow high. He eased his hand back to his ear, and the arrow sailed. The howl of the feathers ended in a ping as the bronze and wood arrow shattered and splintered against rock.

"Only the rare man who devotes his entire life to archery may master it," he said. "Few in history have done so, but you'll know you've mastered it when …" Pivoting and moving in a flash, he released three arrows before the first struck its target: the trunk of a scrubby tree far in the distance. The arrows almost simultaneously punctured three knots in the tree trunk, forming a triangle. "When you can release three arrows before the first has landed and can puncture both eyes and the open mouth of an enemy while pinning him against something."

An arrow dropped from my hand in sheer amazement. The Kush were the greatest archers in the world. "You are a master," I said, my mouth gaping.

"Speed and accuracy are of utmost importance with any weapon, but especially the bow," Harkhuf said, unable to hide his beaming smile. "But, no, to truly be a master, one would have to perform the same feat in combat … when your limbs tremble with fear, your mind is overflowing with doubt, and distraction is everywhere." He swallowed. "I have not accomplished this with a real enemy in the midst of war."

As I practiced, my fingertips rubbed raw against the bowstring, and dark, painful bruises arose on the inside of my left forearm from its punishing reverberations. I released another arrow and it arced into the sky as the first rays of light danced across the river.

"We need to get you, Chisisi, and Wahankh trained in basic combat," Seneb said, biting into a tuber and handing out breakfast. "Before we find real trouble. Otherwise we'll look like monkeys fighting gorillas."

When the Aten reared over the eastern hills, the military fleet were only dots on the horizon. Wahankh pointed. "I bet they're angry now."

"You're a good day ahead of them," Paramessu whispered. "But you'll all eventually suffer for what you've done."

"Will we make it to the delta?" I asked. "Or do we jump off at Memphis and hope to disappear?"

"We must be close," Tia said as she gripped the rudder so tight her knuckles blanched. Sweat condensed on her forehead. "Unless we already passed my river in the darkness."

"We'll be far enough ahead that they won't be able to see us dock at Memphis," Chisisi said, looking over everyone. "We can trade this boat for a small one and sail for my home in the delta. It will be much easier to disappear in a different ship while they search Memphis for us."

Wahankh frowned.

We sailed for days before nearing the city of Memphis. The branch of the river to Tia's home must have slipped by during the night. Water accumulated in the hull—from damage when the soldiers crashed their ship into the shore—and rose over my sandals, wetting my toes. And our pursuers had again closed much of the gap.

Gliding between the great white walls of awe-inspiring Memphis, a sense of nostalgia created a hollow, sucking feeling in my chest, threatening to swallow all of my memories. The feather at my waist felt hot. My heart yearned to visit, to relive a simpler time … before I had defied Akhenaten, and when Nefertiti still loved me … the nights exploring the city with Mutnedjmet as we trailed the cloaked man, Croc at our side … Father. I smiled.

"They're too close now," Chisisi said, stomping up and down the hull and splashing water across my shins. "We won't be able to switch boats without them seeing."

Only a few locals glanced up from their work and noticed our warship. We skimmed past the guardian sphinx and beyond Memphis. The Nile opened before us like a new world. Hours sped by amidst the waves before the river diverged into many paths. Which one led to freedom? I hoped Chisisi really knew.

The Aten descended into the underworld.

Chapter 35

Journal Translation

THE PURSUING WARSHIPS WERE close behind, somewhere in the darkness engulfing the river. But we approached the delta region.

As we gained speed from the current, I shoved the rudder against the waters below and steered us into the tributary Chisisi pointed to. Day finally broke as we passed a small city and another town. The three military ships still gave chase, now just out of arrow shot.

I groaned in frustration. Where would we go?

The river opened up. Nothing but blue water lay ahead.

"The sea!" Paramessu shouted and stood. "We must turn back! Even an undamaged warship may not survive her power."

Choppy waters stretched as far as I could see. My body tensed. A sense of hope, but also fear, gripped me.

"Will the military follow us beyond Egypt?" Seneb asked, poking Paramessu with the butt of his spear.

The captain shrugged. "Depends on who is giving their orders."

We emerged into the wild blue, and water rolled beneath us, making our boat climb and descend the waves. I threw open the sail. A gust of wind sucked us away, but the water in the hull slowly grew deeper.

The soldiers followed, their white sails billowing like clouds. We rode into the unknown, endless blue for many days.

On around the fifth night, darkness fell and the winds rose to a roar. Waves bucked beneath us and sloshed into the hull, spraying us with their salty mist. Even after collapsing the sail, our vessel thrashed about. Water rose up to my calves as lightning crackled overhead. Dread overcame me.

Clinging to each other and to the mast in desperation, we trembled in terror. What had I done?

Croc's claws dug into my shoulder, but I barely registered the pain. Tia's scream pierced the howling gale. Would I die here, die a freeman, never again to see Nefertiti or Akhenaten?

A towering wave smacked into our port side with a clap and splintering of wood, capsizing our vessel. We spilled out into the dark sea. Hanging on to Croc with all my might, I righted myself and broke out of the water just as a wave crashed into the back of my head. Spinning in the turmoil, I hugged the overturned hull of the boat.

I screamed for the others, but the wind and waves deafened me, like lions roaring in my ears. Another wave smacked my head into the unforgiving wood of the vessel. My memory faded …

I awoke to a blur of light. Sucking in a deep breath, I blinked to clear my vision. My limbs were numb, my mind cloudy. I still clutched the capsized hull, bobbing in now calm waters. Croc was curled beside me, his soaked fur dangling in clumps around his scrawny frame—not resembling any kind of powerful beast now. The dwarves lay facedown, hugging the mainmast, which had snapped off and floated free. The military ships were gone. A few hundred feet away, a mountain loomed up from the placid sea.

"Land!" I shouted, but it came out as a sputtering cough. The dwarves grumbled and looked up. I attempted to paddle the hull in by stroking with a free hand, but if we moved at all it was only in a slow circle. When I reached for Croc, he hissed in warning, but I grabbed his scruff, tucked him against my chest, kicked away from the wreckage, and backstroked for shore.

I kicked through a surf of crashing white water, and my back scraped along the rough sand and rock of a beach. Facing the clear sky, I lay prone with exhaustion and disorientation. What had happened? Would everyone be all right?

The dwarves crawled to shore, across a stretch of the open sand. Paramessu's red hair stood out beside Wahankh and Chisisi, who stumbled onto shore farther away. A strange but familiar smell hung on the air, a scent I'd not experienced since serving the royal family. Olives and oil. Struggling to my feet, I wobbled for my companions as Croc sat in the sun, licking his wet fur.

"I feel like a sewer rat after a monsoon," Seneb said, flopping onto the sand with a splat.

I scouted for Tia. Nothing else moved. Stark brown land with rock and scrubby foliage surrounded us, extending farther than I could see. Towering mountains protruded from the center.

Where was Tia?

Had the storm gotten her? My heart sank, growing raw with remorse. Dead but having her soul intact hardly made me feel better. Another lost life that was my fault.

Harkhuf marched beside me, his black beard turning left and right. "I don't see Tia," he said. "Not another woman … I wasn't with her. But I couldn't swim and save her and hang on myself!" He heaved for breath. "Like a daughter … I won't be able to … She has to be alive!" He raced away down the beach screaming, "Tia!" over and over.

Seneb stood and trailed after him, stumbling along.

I turned and marched in the other direction, in hopes of locating her. There was no one else.

I focused so my mind wouldn't wander with thoughts of what could've happened to her. Rocks protruded from the water just offshore, breaking waves into white foam and spraying mist. Something washed in, bobbing to and fro. A bundle I did not recognize. Curiosity crept into my heart. I grabbed and teased the sopping fabric apart. Clothing. But these clothes—a full body robe with gold adornments and sparkling jewelry amidst sopping wrinkles—were not Egyptian. This must've been the garb of a wealthy man or woman. Probably not from any soldier chasing us.

While I wadded up the garment, wreckage from our ship and supply boxes washed ashore. My sack of supplies rolled up onto the black pebble beach beside me. Opening the leather, I expected all of the books and parchment inside to be ruined, but everything was as dry as the Egyptian desert. This sack *was* magical.

Tearing through the damp wood of a crate, Wahankh and Chisisi ate what hadn't turned into a salty paste.

"She must be gone," Chisisi said through a mouthful.

Wahankh nodded.

Voices echoed behind us. I jumped in surprise, glancing back. A tanned man's long gray hair floated in the wind as he utilized a walking stick to assist him down the hillside. A boy followed behind.

The man shouted in a strange tongue. But when we did not answer, he stopped, and his eyes grew wide as he scrutinized us. He then yelled at the boy and waved his hands, as if scolding him. The boy ran back up the hill and disappeared before the man faced us again and said, "Egyptians and Africans?"

Picking his way down a goat trail, the old man spoke in a heavy accent with strange inflections, delaying my understanding. "You are a long way from home, my friends." He smiled, spread his arms, and said something in another language as he nodded at the dwarves. Harkhuf nodded back and Seneb bowed. "What brings you here?" His pinky finger trembled against his walking stick.

"Our boat capsized in the storm," Chisisi replied, pushing his soaked hair behind his ears. "I am sorry if we are trespassing. We will happily be on our way if you can provide or direct us to safe passage."

The old man examined us. "You do appear rather haggard, and without a ship." He motioned at the planks washing ashore. But his eyes longed over everything, as if he were searching for something specific. "Ah, it will be lost amongst all this," he whispered and flicked his wrist, then said, "I am Dedalos."

"Did you see a woman?" Harkhuf asked, squeezing the handle of his bow.

"Many, but probably not the one you are thinking of." His dark eyes softened. "I am sorry for your loss."

The pit of my stomach clenched. We were extremely fortunate to be alive, but Tia must not have been strong enough to hold on to the wreckage. Harkhuf sniffed back emotion, attempting to hide the sound by clearing his throat. Tears rolled down Seneb's boyish cheeks.

"Where are we?" Chisisi asked, wringing out his soaked kilt.

"Keftiu," Dedalos said.

"The island?" Paramessu asked.

"Yes," the old man replied.

"A damn big island," Harkhuf muttered.

Dedalos smirked. "One of the biggest."

"Can you get us back to Egypt?" Chisisi asked.

Wrinkling his chin, Dedalos scratched his head. "You must ask the mightiest of kings for assistance."

"Egypt is friendly with your people," Paramessu said.

"Yes, but the king has requested to meet any unannounced visitors," Dedalos replied, waving for us to follow as he hiked back up the hillside. "I am merely an old merchant, having traded oils around the world. Come. I will bring you to the magnificent palace within the city of Phaistos."

"Should we go with him?" I asked, whispering to the others.

"What choice do we have?" Chisisi said, pointing to the sea and our wreckage.

We followed Dedalos along the trail, up the brown slope, and continued across scrub-covered hills dotted with trees and through small valleys. The Aten shone between passing clouds of white, but its rays didn't bring searing heat down upon my skin. Harkhuf dragged behind, his head hanging. Croc had disappeared again. But that cat could probably take care of himself, even on a strange island.

At midday, we traveled a paved road. A city of stone sat upon a nearby hilltop, its shimmering palace towering over the land. The backdrop of a mountain soared into the heavens, reaching higher than any in Egypt. The tip was capped with something white. Stone, way up there?

Smiling again, Dedalos motioned for us to hurry. But his fingers still trembled—with apprehension?

Chapter 36

Journal Translation

AS WE PASSED THROUGH THE open road entrance to the island city, guards put their hands on their swords. A sharp sea breeze wafted by, and a salty mist landed on my lips. Dedalos muttered something to the soldiers, and they relaxed but still eyed us as if we had wronged them.

No walls around this city? Were these island people overconfident in their prowess at war? Or was this country not violent, unlike Egypt?

We continued through crowded streets filled with sun-darkened men who were either naked or wearing small white cloths. Women were more concealed, in faded purples and reds. The buildings, which appeared so magnificent at a distance, were collapsing. Toppled stones cluttered around leaning shops and ragged pedestrians. This once-glorious city must've reached its golden age long ago. The slums of Memphis popped into my mind, and the night with Nefertiti and Mutnedjmet, and the scorpion plague ...

All the inhabitants stared as we passed. Tension and distrust permeated the air, perhaps even hatred. I shivered.

We ascended toward the outer gates of a palace, although in its most lavish state, the palace would not surpass the temples of Egypt. Multiple stories of stone were laced with spiraling staircases, but cracks ran through the foundation like a giant spider's web. Chunks of stone were missing from slumping columns that stretched to the roof.

The heat of the midday Aten did not warm the chill growing in my heart.

"Welcome to Phaistos!" Dedalos said as he held up a liver-spotted hand. "We were allies with Egypt during the reign of the great Amenhotep."

The guards outside the palace appeared like sphinxes—unmoving as the old man whispered and passed. Lifelike frescos splattered the interior of the palace as we traversed a maze of open and roofed corridors. But all their color was faded by time. In their prime, the paintings would've rivaled the greatest Egyptian works of art, something I wouldn't have believed about the outside world of barbarians and chaos. Beauty had carried beyond the edges of the known world, in places beyond Egypt. But serving Akhenaten, I'd have never seen or heard of any of it.

A courtyard littered with withered trees and dead flowers opened before us. What must've once flourished was now sickened by the spirits of dead flora. What had happened to this place, these people?

Gray leaves crunched under my sandaled feet as I walked.

"I will inform King Radamanthis of your situation," Dedalos said, pointing to an open doorway. "Wait inside."

We stepped into a cramped room streaked with the rays of the Aten. Guards with spears and shields took positions outside as stifling humidity pulled sweat from every inch of my skin. A servant with a hairy chest and limbs delivered olives, soft cheese wafting a rank odor, and wine more robust than Egypt's. My stomach grumbled in hunger, but I hesitated. If these people did not even keep themselves free of body hair, how dirty would their food be?

Wahankh stuffed his mouth full of green olives and spewed pits. The others followed suit—except Harkhuf, who slouched in the corner.

"We may still find her," Seneb said, placing a hand on his brother's back. "No body washed ashore with the rest of the vessel."

Hope ignited an ember in my heart. Could Tia have washed up farther away or after us? Or had she been washed out to sea? "Perhaps Tia is a freewoman on this island, searching for us," I said.

"I think we'll see her and Egypt again soon," Paramessu said, raising an eyebrow as he touched a chunk of odiferous white cheese to his tongue. His nose wrinkled. "But it seems strange that this king wants to meet a few stranded sailors. Kings typically only make time for important guests."

Paramessu probably knew we were the escaped slaves he'd been hunting, but, at least for now, he didn't seem to care. Perhaps once we made it back to Egypt …

"From the looks of this place," Chisisi said, "I don't think they've had important guests for quite some time. I've seen dead people's houses look more welcoming."

"What will they do with us?" Wahankh asked, chomping through plates of food.

A long, drawn face appeared in the doorway. "I have convinced the mightiest of kings to grant you an audience." Dedalos said, "but you must dress decently and leave your weapons with the guards."

Servants stepped in and laid down white robes. The fabric slipped between my fingers—softer material than I was used to, and my kilt was torn and stained.

Harkhuf donned the local garment. It draped two feet onto the floor but would not close across his chest or waist. "I can stomach the robe but will not surrender my arms."

"We need assistance if we ever hope to return to Egypt," Paramessu said as I dropped my twin swords and bow. All of my arrows had been lost to the sea. "They aren't going to let armed strangers meet their king."

Harkhuf's fingers parted as if nearly frozen, his spear and bow clattering onto the stone floor.

Dedalos clapped, which echoed throughout the crumbling labyrinth of a palace. "We will dine with the mightiest king in the land." His gray hair wafted in the breeze as we followed him down long corridors and across the courtyard, finally entering an enormous hall of stone. Wooden tables the size of boats lined the walls, and a purple carpet led to an empty throne.

Servants hefted and shuffled the tables into the center of the room. Dedalos motioned for us to sit and took a seat beside me. Other men entered, most with gray hair and wrinkled faces. Platters of pale fruit, vegetables, and seafood—mostly finger-sized silver fish—were set before us. The aroma of the oils they doused the food in warmed my nose. My tongue tingled, and my mouth wetted with saliva.

The other attendees spoke to each other in a language I could not understand. Ten minutes passed, and no one ate. Seneb's stomach growled so loud that everyone in the room must've heard. Chisisi motioned for him to keep quiet. A burp escaped Seneb's lips, and he shrugged.

Silence descended.

Fixating their attention on the far side of the room, the attendees stood. A hunched man with a rim of long gray hair encircling his head emerged from another entrance. Assisting him by the arm was a fit middle-aged man and a young woman with long dark hair and pale skin. The slouching older man was adorned in a stark white toga covered in gold, silver, and a rainbow of precious stones. The king.

The king did not say a word. He slumped into the seat at the head of the table, his wrinkled face transfixed on his plate. The woman tied her hair back and revealed striking dark eyes and an ivory face.

Tense silence held a crushing grip on the room and my breathing.

A crack sounded. I jumped in my seat. King Radamanthis pounded the table again with a gnarled fist. He yelled with a raspy voice, his cry so loud I almost wet myself in surprise. Echoes radiated off the walls, spiraling down the corridors.

"Like a baby who hasn't slept," Seneb whispered, his eyes wide in shock.

Springing to attention, servants loaded his plate with fish and olives. King Radamanthis dug a hand into the food and shoved it into his mouth. Chisisi and Wahankh ate whatever they could find while the rest of us chewed for appearance's sake—except Harkhuf; he still didn't eat.

"Why have you come?" a voice rang out in Egyptian. I tensed, and a miniscule fish slipped from my hand. The king's dark eyes—young and vibrant, although dark and terrifying and similar to the woman's beside him—bored into mine, then Chisisi's. "Why are you in my kingdom?"

"I—I ..." I stuttered.

"We were in a shipwreck and washed ashore," Chisisi said, sitting straight. "We'd gratefully return to Egypt, if we could ride with a merchant headed in that direction."

Staring, Radamanthis gnashed his food, and chunks of oily fish dropped from his lips onto his hairy chest with a splatter. "Many come to my island to take things from me. But they have all fallen, and I remain strong! Our city and palace is the pinnacle of resolve and strength. The times of trade have passed. You will take nothing, and you will not report back to your armies. We have fended off the Greeks, but the other cities on the island of Keftiu have collapsed and turned into barbarian hordes. These savages attempt to undermine me and drain our resources. But no one can defeat us. We have been here for centuries." He paused. Then, he screamed, "You will not return to Egypt!" And food flew from his mouth in wet chunks, landing on nearby faces.

Chapter 37

Journal Translation

THE THUNDERING WORDS OF King Radamanthis threw me back in my seat. My head banged into the unforgiving wood. I could not move or utter a response, as if Akhenaten had ensnared my throat and chest with his crushing magic.

Standing on steady limbs, the king snatched his plate and marched out of the hall much faster than he had entered.

The other attendees grabbed their plates and exited. Only my companions, the young woman, the middle-aged man who'd escorted the king in, and Dedalos remained.

Dedalos cleared his throat.

The striking woman spoke to Chisisi in a foreign tongue.

"Princess Scylla apologizes for her father's demeanor," Dedalos said in his strange accent with low-pitched inflections and shrugged. "She says he's been feeling a great deal of stress and has changed recently. He's always been strong but has grown blind to the truth. We as a people are failing. The end is nigh."

"We understand," Chisisi said, nodding. "We too have been through a great deal of suffering and only wish to find passage home."

"We could try to make our homes here," Wahankh said, glancing around.

My stomach cramped. I needed to return to Egypt, Akhenaten, Nefertiti …

"In this festering hole?" Harkhuf said, shaking his head.

Dedalos winced.

"We lost our friend," I said, nudging Harkhuf to curtail his insults. "A woman. We'd like to find her, if she survived, and return home."

Dedalos relayed my message to Princess Scylla. She discussed something with the other man beside her. This man, who had a rat-like face, narrowed his eyes.

Dedalos turned back to us. "Princess Scylla and the youngest of her brothers, Prince Catreus, cannot discuss our situation. You may have to remain on our island indefinitely." He whispered something to the royal pair.

Prince Catreus rose from his seat and stormed out. Dedalos and the princess shouted after him, but he did not respond. Motioning for us to follow them, Dedalos and Princess Scylla crept out of the throne room and down long corridors.

Light faded, and my sandals scuffed along the stone path into the wasting courtyard. The stench of decay sprang up as we picked our way through brush to gather behind a withered tree with bark the color of a storm cloud.

Shadows crawled across Dedalos's face as he whispered, "Prince Catreus would not like outsiders to know of our faltering situation."

Chisisi nodded, and his thin jaw muscles contracted.

Running a hand through his thin hair, Dedalos said, "You seek aid to return to Egypt, and you seek your friend. I saw your garb before you changed into ours." He nodded at Paramessu. "You are a military officer of Egypt, here with your soldiers. The princess and I could use the skills and services of ones such as yourselves. In exchange, we will help you."

Paramessu's head drooped.

"You are correct," Chisisi said, stepping forward and brushing past Paramessu. "But I am his commanding officer. Tell us, and I will decide if we should help your cause."

Dedalos shifted his attention to Chisisi, his eyes narrowing and his lips pursing. "The other cities of the island of Keftiu have toppled. There are many to blame: the Greeks, other outsiders, and the great eruption, now many generations ago, but that sent us spiraling downward. We could still regain our former power, but something inside our own land is working against us. The Keftians from the other regions have become savages and attempt to destroy the last civilized area on the island, our city. We are the last hope for the civilization of the Minoans." He took a deep breath. "Radamanthis's eldest son and his soldiers are missing. We believe they were taken by the hordes they were fighting to the west and to the north, across the great mountain. It is hard to imagine barbarians defeating well-trained military men, so we believe the prince and some of the others are still alive."

"And you wish for us to find him?" Paramessu asked.

Apprehension ran through my body, tightening my muscles.

Rubbing his hands together, Dedalos cast Paramessu a wary glance. "We have no army left, only a few guards who protect the city. Someone must find the last of our soldiers and the king's son and bring them home."

"Then you will grant us passage to Egypt?" Chisisi asked.

"Ships to and from the island have grown infrequent," Dedalos replied, "but by the time you return, I will have found you safe passage."

"I will go!" Harkhuf shouted, tugging at his beard. "If we search the island, we could find Tia. As long as I get my weapons back. How much time could it take to travel across an island?"

"She's gone," Chisisi said, patting Harkhuf's back.

Harkhuf shrugged off Chisisi's thin hand and elbowed him away, then whispered, "She's still out there, the same as my wife and daughter ..."

Sympathy tugged at and slowed my beating heart. Poor Harkhuf—so hard on the exterior, and yet there was a deep tenderness buried within. Excitement and life had returned to him for a fleeting moment, in hopes of finding Tia, but when he finally gave up and accepted that she was dead, would he collapse into eternal depression? Would the darkness in his past—his capture, while others in his tribe were murdered—and now this be something he'd never recover from, as Seneb feared? My eyes closed, and I groaned. Yuf had died and lost his soul following me, and now Harkhuf's soul—although not in immediate danger from the Hunter—appeared just as dark. I should've never tried to lead anyone.

"This is going to be more dangerous than he is leading us to believe," Chisisi whispered, stepping away and back into the courtyard—out of earshot of Dedalos and the princess.

"Can't we just wait for passage at the docks?" Wahankh asked, approaching. "An island like this has to have docks where some merchant ships still come and go."

"My suspicion is we won't be able to find passage anywhere, not unless we help them," I said. Plus, this would give Harkhuf hope for a little while longer. Perhaps over time, his wounds for Tia would heal.

"We can still make our lives here without taking on such a treacherous task," Wahankh said, waving his hands at our surroundings.

Chisisi nodded. "As Egyptians, we have more experience and knowledge than they do. We are superior and could prosper in a poorer country such as this, one filled with savages."

"We are helping them!" Harkhuf yelled and then gritted his teeth with a grating sound that radiated through his skull and made me shudder. "We will find Tia."

"You may not consider my opinion," Paramessu said, folding his arms over his chest as the sunlight waned, "but I need to return home to my father as soon as possible. I've already failed to return the slaves, and if the military finds my massacred troops without me ... they will believe I ran like a coward and am too afraid to face my father. They already know that I was only made an officer because I was *his* son." His pale eyes pierced mine, dripping with regret and longing. "I believe helping these people will be our quickest route home."

Biting nostalgia sank into my gut. Home. Where was that? Nefertiti ... My heart thundered in my chest. I also needed to quench the fire of revenge burning within me as quickly as possible—before it consumed me.

"We will return your arms and fit you with everything you need," Dedalos said, crunching through the brush and smiling as if he'd heard every word or knew this was our only option. "You will need blankets, as the mountain is cold. A burro will carry your supplies. Rest tomorrow and recover. The next morning before daybreak, you will disappear before Radamanthis can stop you. The princess and I will defend you, but we may not be able to prevent your imprisonment if the king decides that's what unwanted visitors deserve. So you must remain hidden. When his son returns, you will be safe."

Goose bumps rose on my arms, and I squeezed my bronze bracelet. Was this place what Father's *ba* had been referring to when he'd said to head north before returning home?

The princess shouted. Speaking sternly to Dedalos, she pointed at us. Her hands and arms flailed.

Dedalos's gaze fell to the ground. "There is something else you must know."

I swallowed.

Dedalos's expression wrinkled so tightly that it appeared painful. "Tales say a creature was brought forth onto this island, summoned from our king's own brother at the city of Knossos. A beast resided in the labyrinth but has since been slain. You should not encounter another such as he, half-man, half-bull, devourer of children. But the princess wants you to know that dark magic flows like a river across our lands. There are many things we no longer understand. If you fail, perhaps only travelers in the distant future will discover the mysteries of how the Minoans crumbled."

I gasped with disbelief and rotated the bracelet around my forearm, searching for guidance. The pessimism this man held for his own people, and the beast—

"We will travel the island and find your prince and his army," Harkhuf said.

Dedalos and the princess led us back to our room and departed.

I drifted into a restless sleep. Images of ghouls, the dying island, Nefertiti, Mutnedjmet, and Akhenaten's black-painted eyelids filled my dreams. A half-man, half-monster terrorized children. I saw Tia, alive and waiting for us with tears and outstretched arms. The sopping wet clothes I'd picked up on the beach streamed blood down between my fingers. Something wasn't right …

My companions spoke over cold vegetables and olive oil, waking me. Blinking, I sat up, relieved for the interruption of my nightmares. I crawled over and retrieved my stained kilt, now dry. Beside it lay the clothes from the beach. I studied the jewelry. It was similar to what Radamanthis had worn—deep red and light blue stones ran along the arms and neckline. Unfolding the garment revealed the gash in the back, encircled with a red stain.

This was a noble's robe. A queen, or the missing prince's? And why were Dedalos and the princess willing to help us, while the king and other prince were not? What truth were they hiding, and were we being used for something larger than what they'd told us? Princess Scylla had seemed to insist on Dedalos giving us more information, but she wouldn't know how much he'd actually revealed if she didn't speak our language. If I could converse with her, would she tell me more? Or were all of my assumptions off base?

✳ ✳ ✳

"It is time," Dedalos said, waking us before dawn the following morning. The guards outside slept against the walls, reminding me of the guards put to sleep by the son of Hapu's magic during the months or years of my tutelage. Was Dedalos also a magician?

We followed the old man under the waning light of the moon, through the labyrinth of corridors, and beyond the city. A laden burro waited, tied to a post. Wet wind whipped across my legs and face. Seneb stroked the donkey's neck, untied the creature, and led it by a rope.

"Godspeed," Dedalos said. "Bring the prince home so that we may rebuild."

"Where is the queen?" I asked.

Dedalos's white eyebrows climbed his forehead, his voice raspy against the gale. "Why do you ask such things?"

"I didn't see her at dinner," I said.

"The queen," he swallowed, "has been gone for some time. Now be off, before the king imprisons you."

"Which way?" Chisisi asked as he stretched his legs, his eyes betraying his skepticism.

Pointing, Dedalos said, "That is west. I would venture around the margins of the mountains, which run east to west across the center of the island. Passage over them to the north will be arduous and dangerous. Only climb the peaks if you do not find the answers in the hills and valleys around the sea."

I glanced around. Hopefully Croc was out there somewhere and would find us before we departed. Brushing my short, dark hair back into a salty gust, I followed my companions west into the unknown.

Chapter 38

Journal Translation

W E PLODDED ALONG A STONE ROAD leading us west across the island, the bricks at our feet uprooted and worn by decades. The crumbling city had faded into darkness before the mighty Aten rose. And even though the heat hung heavy, the light seemed distant, as if choked by fog. Perhaps the Aten was less intense here because God favored Egypt and its peoples over this place.

Traveling for days, we crossed the rolling brown countryside. Buildings and houses crumbled beside the road, but there was no sign of human life. We marched until we reached the western edge of the island and the sea and stared over a rocky bluff into the vastness. Was there an end to these waters? Other islands or worlds in this wine-dark sea—had I heard that before somewhere?

The sun sank below the horizon, its fading pink and purple rays arcing across time and space. My old feeling of being a juvenile crocodile thrust into the endless river of the world returned. I still searched for meaning, forced to fight for survival in this world that was unfit for me. *Father, where are you?* Forcing a deep breath, I gazed upon haunting beauty, beauty like Nefertiti's—that which you would have to lay eyes on yourself to truly appreciate in all its grandeur.

An island shimmered in the distant twilight, probably too small to support civilization, but the sight forced my salt-caked lips into smile. Longing and curiosity stirred inside me. There was more out there. I'd probably never comprehend the immensity of nature and our world, never accomplish what I'd set out to do. There was too much power stacked against me. But would hope, as Father had said, and my burning emotions be enough? I needed to return to Egypt, but the thought sent shivers up my spine.

"The wind in the trees, the sunlight on the leaves, the babble of the sea, and time slipping by," Paramessu whispered as he stepped beside me, his eyes cloudy as he gazed into the distance. "That is art to me."

"We should move on," Harkhuf grumbled, slapping me on the back so hard I stumbled forward toward the cliff. Waves sloshed below as if sending a false message of gentle nature. "If we sleep here, we'll be damp and freezing by morning."

I studied the muscular dwarf with his stern face and short beard. Did the same questions I had bubble up within his soul?

Paramessu, the soldier stolen from his homeland who was forced to flee with a group of slaves—what did he hope to accomplish? Did he only desire to follow discipline and please his father?

Seneb's kind face met mine. His boyish smile bore off-white teeth that stood out against his dark skin as he tugged on the burro's lead rope. The burro stomped its foot to shoo away flies as it nibbled on brown grass.

Then there was Chisisi, an arrogant man with a hidden past and desire to lead.

Wahankh, the scared bully with the frame to overpower any of us except perhaps Harkhuf.

Where had Croc disappeared to, and what kind of creature was he?

And Tia, lost to the empty or perhaps bustling world beneath the sea. My heart ached. My greatest love, Nefertiti, was also lost to the depths of Akhenaten. What about her curious sister, Mutnedjmet, whom I did not understand? What path would she follow?

I wished Father's *ba* could see me now, the man I'd tried to become in spite of everything in my path. Even when I failed, I hoped he would be there to carry me with loving arms into the next life. The fingers of my right hand brushed the bracelet on my left forearm.

"Let's go!" Harkhuf said, making me jump and nearly plummet into the sea. I blinked to clear overwhelming emotion. "We've gone as far west as we can, unless you want to swim. We should get off this windy bluff." He strode away.

I turned to follow. A pinkish, twilight hue reflected off of the towering peaks ahead, blurring my vision. The mountains appeared inviting, like other things of beauty I'd beheld. Would they also make me suffer?

I sat to take first watch.

Seneb lay down beside me, tugging at a pile of blankets.

I nudged him with the toe of my sandal. "How does Harkhuf hope to find his wife and child still alive?" I whispered. "Didn't he say they were trapped inside a hut and burned?"

Seneb groaned, but his eyes opened. "I'm not supposed to talk about his past. He'll kill me." He sighed. "But I can tell you that Harkhuf's hut had a secret escape route. That's why he's convinced they escaped. He was also the only one who might've known that the Egyptian slavers were coming …"

"How could he have known they were coming?" I asked.

Biting his lip, Seneb's head flopped down. He didn't speak for a minute. "I've accepted that my family didn't survive, but some of the tribe were out gathering, so they weren't all killed. A small village probably still remains, living off of the plains of waving grass like we used to. Harkhuf is my only family now. I'd like to see him happy again, but I can't help him. His shame runs too deep, for what he once was …"

"A Nubian warrior?" I asked.

More silence. "If his family didn't survive, I don't think he'll be able to go on. We need to find Tia." Rolling over, Seneb turned his back to me.

Hours passed.

After trading watch, I fell asleep to the lull of the sea—the peaceful sound betraying its wrath, the ability to take lives without mercy.

Mutnedjmet, Nefertiti, and their cousin, Beketaten, giggled as they ran across the sand in my dream and disappeared over a hill. I followed after them and crested the rise. Darkness filled the other side, but a fire sprang forth and emitted a green flame. A face lined like a spider's web appeared at the margins of shadow and light. I gasped. The magician! And Croc was curled up beside him.

"I've lost sight of you, boy," the son of Hapu said in a tense whisper. "I don't know where we are, and I fear you have either died or fled to the edges of the earth."

"I was shipwrecked at sea, fleeing the Hunter," I said. "You disappeared."

Cocking his head, his eyes stared past me, as if he didn't hear or see me. "Wherever you are, I hope you are continuing your training in preparation for your return. No one can force it upon you."

"I've been preoccupied," I said, my eyes closing.

"Do you still not understand the difference between a wish and your will?" he asked.

I shrugged in confusion.

"Will is utter devotion to your wish." His pale eyes flickered as if he were vanishing. "Wishes fade with time and hardship. But a strong, devoted will never yields. And I do not speak of your opinions—they are meant to be bent. But you must persist in spite of everything."

My forehead knotted.

The fading reflection of the magician stood. Holding a bow, he nocked an arrow, displaying grace that betrayed his old bones. "In this world you will need experience and skills as well as knowledge and strength. Do not waste—"

The magician disappeared, and I awoke under my blankets. My companions snored as the orange light of the Aten burned the eastern sky. I pulled several books from my sack and read about mathematics and medicine before performing exercises until the Minoan sunlight hit the western sea.

The others woke, and we ate before hiking a narrow animal trail headed for the lowest valley between the mountains. Dedalos had said to check the northern areas before submitting ourselves to the peaks. The grade grew steeper.

After leading the donkey to a patch of green, Seneb shouted, "There's a cave!" He pointed to the base of a towering cliff.

Sunlight angled inside. Shadowy. Stepping under a rocky overhang of the mountain, I drew my swords. The air turned humid and rank.

Chapter 39

Journal Translation

ARKHUF AND SENEB STEPPED in front of me to investigate the cave. I breathed out in relief. I wouldn't have to go first.

A screech rang out. Leaping from the darkness, a figure bolted away while screaming louder than the shrillest pig, ringing my ears.

A frail woman with sun-wrinkled skin and wispy hair spewed curses from a toothless mouth. She shrieked, pointing to the mountain, the cave, to herself, and to us. Then she fled over a ridge and disappeared.

The burro snorted as it blew air through flared nostrils, its eyes wide.

"What was she screaming about?" Chisisi asked as he rubbed his ears.

Paramessu shrugged.

"Like a single Egyptian woman with too many cats," Seneb whispered. "Crazy."

That night, although we desired the warmth of a fire, we dared not give away our location. Huddling together in the provided blankets, the others slept in a hollow while I studied and practiced.

The next morning brought light, but not much warmth—a bitter chill crawled through my skin and into my bones, making me shiver and pull a blanket over my shoulders. As we climbed higher, we navigated around a gorge by staying to the animal tracks that had worn a dirt path through the brown grass. The white-capped peaks remained thousands of feet above. We crested a ridge, and the sparkle of the sea greeted us across a vast distance of mountain slopes and rolling hills. Northeasterly, an extensive city sprawled outward, and a single humanoid statue towered over everything.

We trudged downward.

"That colossus of a structure guarding the sea," Paramessu said, waving to the water, "it instilled fear in me even from the mountain. If there are still people here, I imagine they'd live near it."

"The king said the city was abandoned," Chisisi replied, his hair swinging back and forth as he walked. "We can stop there, but when we find nothing, we must scour the rest of the countryside. They must be hiding in caves or roaming around like nomads."

Harkhuf grumbled. The spark that had returned to the dwarf's eyes when we set off on this expedition faded again. Was he losing hope for Tia?

✳ ✳ ✳

After a couple days of traveling down mountains and across brown countryside, the humanoid behemoth of a statue towered against the horizon. My breathing paused in wonder. This god, the height of a large hill, stood with his feet spread and anchored upon stone pillars rising from the surface of the sea. His enormous legs were spread far enough apart that a warship could pass between them, a stone hand stretched toward the sea with a palm open to persuade any approaching vessel to stop. A spear as tall as he stood beside him. A shudder of intimidation ran up my spine. Who would dare come to this island with that guardian?

As we approached, piles of boulders appeared, littering the area—having fallen from the mighty statue. Sea spray and white corrosion covered its chest and face.

Silhouettes from normal-sized men blotted out the dancing reflections of the waves. I froze in surprise.

"We found someone," Harkhuf said, drawing his bow. "Or they found us."

Three silhouettes approached.

"Lower your weapon," Seneb whispered. "Our only hope to find the prince may be to befriend the locals, like a meerkat joining a new pack."

Sunlight settled on their haggard, weather-beaten faces and exposed skin, as they only wore only dirty loincloths. They paused twenty feet away, their long locks blowing in the wind.

"We are travelers," Chisisi said, stepping forward. "And we seek the Prince of Phaistos."

"I doubt they speak Egyptian," Paramessu whispered.

The barbarians stared. One approached, muttered something, and pointed to the city.

"I'm not following savages into a deserted city," Wahankh said, his knuckles white against the shaft of his spear.

"We came to find a prince," Harkhuf said, marching for the ruins.

"He's been looking for one of those all his life," Seneb whispered and smirked.

We followed Harkhuf, and a tightness arose in my chest. What would these barbarians do to us?

Shadows hovered around this fallen city of Knossos and crawled between all of the buildings like ethereal bridges, making the city of Phaistos appear inviting. A horde of disheveled men emerged from behind toppled columns and houses—a hundred or more of them. The island's chill crept back into my bones, instinct screaming for me to run.

A hulking man stepped from the group, wielding a spear with an enormous head of shiny bronze. He spoke incomprehensible words. Smiling, he revealed cracked teeth as he tossed long, dark hair over his shoulders. "Egyptian, perhaps?" His accent was made the words garbled.

"Yes," Chisisi replied, puffing out his chest.

"What are you doing in this cursed land?" the barbarian asked as his draping shoulders tensed.

"We won't be able to take the prince from an army this size," Paramessu whispered in my ear.

"We're mercenaries washed ashore by a storm," Chisisi said. "We desire passage back to Egypt, but we agreed to find the Prince of Phaistos in return."

The Minoan barbarian laughed, a deep, hearty roar. "The six of you and a donkey will accomplish this? Did the King of Phaistos make this promise?"

"Dedalos and the princess did," Chisisi said, stepping in front of me.

"Radamanthis is no king," the barbarian replied. "The island would fall to the Greeks if it were left up to him and whoever is giving him orders."

"What do you mean?" Chisisi asked.

"Come," the barbarian said. "If you truly seek the prince, you may be of value, but there is much you need to know."

Pivoting around, the hulking man strode into the city.

"I thought these men and the prince were at odds," Paramessu said, leaning over to my ear. "I assume they have him ... or killed him."

"If they wanted to kill us, they could have already," I said, following.

Trailing the barbarian leader, we walked around and stepped over the fallen stone of collapsed guard stations, continuing down broken streets before stopping at a large piazza. The peripheral and central statues were toppled over. The rest of the savages paused at the vicinity, surrounding the expanse and blocking any escape. Leaping up a few steps near crumbling columns, the leader spun about and faced us.

"If you are not Mycenaeans or Greek," the leader said, his voice resonating off of the surrounding stone buildings, although the words were difficult to distinguish, "then you have nothing to fear from us. Step forward! The King of Phaistos and I may not be on the best of terms, but we are not enemies, as you may believe. We both fight for our island country ... at least we used to."

"Radamanthis said your people are destroying his civilized culture," Chisisi said, holding his spear in front of him. "He believes you want everyone to become barbarians."

"Barbarians?" Throwing his head back, the leader bellowed with laughter. "Is that what I look like to you? A hairy, animal-skin-wearing brigand from the north?" He thrust the butt of his spear into the stone at his feet, which issued an echoing crack.

Chisisi shrugged.

The Minoan said, "You can call me Sea Shepherd. That is what my men call me, although in our language." He pointed at Paramessu. "You are an odd-looking Egyptian. And Nubian dwarves. Aren't you their entertainment?"

"The last man who believed that was killed by my hand," Harkhuf growled and slammed the butt of his spear onto stone. The echoing matched the leader's attempt at intimidation—the sound bouncing around the perimeter of the piazza.

"Well, my Egyptian mercenaries," Sea Shepherd said, winking, "we have seen hard times, but we are still fighting and educated. We do not use the palace in Knossos any longer ... after the bull-monster and the children ..." He fell silent. "But although we have rid ourselves of the evil, curses remain. Torment advances from all sides. There is magic here you cannot comprehend."

"I've seen magic," Chisisi said, planting his fists on his hips.

Sea Shepherd's eyebrows rose like peaks onto his leathery forehead. "You will not find the prince here. His legion obeyed the king's orders and attempted to wipe us out. I desire revenge, but not against the prince. That is what the king or someone inside his council longs for. Someone or something yearns for us to be at war ... so we will all fall."

Silence settled over the piazza like the calm before the tempest—the one that had struck our boat on the open sea.

"Why would King Radamanthis want to sacrifice his own island?" I asked, stepping alongside Chisisi, my voice weak in comparison to the others.

"I do not know," Sea Shepherd said, pacing along the edge of the step. "His brother passed away, but that was some time ago. Radamanthis and I were once good friends, but his actions divide us. I believe it is not his mind at work."

"So you would not be opposed to us bringing the prince home?" Chisisi asked, elbowing me back.

"Only the prince may wrestle control from his father and whomever it is in his ranks who poisons us," Sea Shepherd replied. "I encourage you to find him."

"Where he is hiding?" Chisisi asked.

"We drove his legion from our city, back into the snowy mountains, weeks ago." He pursed his lips and scratched at dense stubble. "They have yet to return. We both lost many lives ... and friends. But if they were bent on destroying us, they would've returned. And if they were too devastated by our forces, they should've fled to Phaistos. I fear that the heart of any dark magic lies within the highest peak but hope you do not have to venture into the depths of the snow up there."

"We must've covered half the island in the past weeks," Chisisi said. "Are there other cities? Other tribes?"

"You covered the unpopulated areas to the west, perhaps, on purpose? There are ... or were other cities, many ports and trade routes to the east," he replied. "But none could stand against Phaistos's army. And yet the prince never came down from the mountain."

My mind raced with images of retreating troops, fleeing these intimidating men. And why had Dedalos sent us west, away from the cities?

"Was the prince wounded?" Chisisi asked.

Sea Shepherd shrugged. "Whatever darkness the Minotaur left behind after devouring our children is engulfing this land. Go find your prince so he may flush the traitor out of Phaistos."

"Princess Scylla, Prince Catreus, and Dedalos appeared to be closest to the king," I said from behind Chisisi.

"Prince Catreus is shifty but has been beside the king longer than the king's mind has been soured," Sea Shepherd replied, his eyes narrowing. "And just because old Dedalos can speak to you doesn't mean he's telling you everything. Do not trust anyone. Prince Gortys, the one you seek, had a brother, Erythrus, who was said to be born disfigured—a mistake of his mother's own doing. It was something she ate when she carried him in the womb. Someone convinced her this something would make her son strong. The boy was hidden from society and fled the city years ago, after a feud with his father and brother. Erythrus has never been seen again, but within a year of his absence, the gray began to descend on the island. Some say he cursed us, but others have heard rumors of strange magic and strange creatures. Erythrus desired to rule the island and detested his family, running away in search of aid. They say he found what he was looking for and is gathering strength to rise against us. Others say the king and Prince Gortys murdered Prince Erythrus themselves to be rid of his abomination. People whisper that the royal family's murder brought a curse upon us all." He paused and looked at the dwindling Aten. "You may stay the night here but must be on your way at first light."

"We will set out for the snowy mountains tomorrow," Harkhuf said.

"I can spare none of my men," Sea Shepherd replied, motioning at the crumbling city around us. He marched up the steps and disappeared between the columns of stone. The other Minoans had already vanished.

Chapter 40

Journal Translation

"WE AREN'T REALLY GOING UP the mountain, are we?" Wahankh asked, his lips hanging open as he stared into the dusk at the white-capped peaks that Sea Shepherd had referred to as 'snowy'. "We should head for one of the ports to the east and wait for a ship there. Egypt is a paradise compared to this savage wasteland."

"If we're going to get lucky and get what we want," Seneb said, winking, "we need to cook dinner for the lady first."

Paramessu cleared his throat, blushing. "Seneb means to say that we will need an ally in order to obtain passage from this island. A merchant ship will not take on unknown mercenaries. The king will have to grant us passage or lend us one of his vessels."

"We go up the mountain," Harkhuf said, his returning sadness not apparent now. "We will find them all."

My chin wrinkled with skepticism. He was probably still thinking only of Tia.

"Agreed," Chisisi said, folding his arms across his proud chest. "In the morning, we go to the mountain."

Wahankh kicked dirt from a worn cobblestone and lay down in a corner of the piazza. The rest of us sat and ate before huddling in our blankets.

I pulled out the jeweled garment I'd found on the beach and studied it by torchlight. Who'd worn this when the bloody strike had landed? And what tale about Phaistos was true? Had this deformed Erythrus been murdered, possibly by his own father or brother? Then, perhaps, to cover their own atrocities, the palace had told its people the deformed brother had run away. Our mission could be in vain, and I didn't know whom to trust. The princess seemed sincere, but Dedalos could've been telling us something completely different than what she'd actually said.

I leaned my head back and fell into a restless sleep.

"Heb ..." someone whispered, although I couldn't see anyone.

A green light shone before me. I stepped into the light, and the Lake of Eternal Fog unfolded across a misty landscape—although I didn't know how I knew the lake's name or what it was. I paused in wonder. Everything disappeared into the fog just beyond the water's edge. The stubble on the back of my neck stood up with fear and prickled my skin, as if someone watched me. How many millennia had this lake been shrouded, and why?

I paced along the shore, and sucking muck clung to my sandals and feet like cold honey, attempting to hold me fast. I lifted my knee, and my foot slipped free with a pop. A wooden bridge emerged from the mist, leading over the water. Its path was obscured. I inched onto the bridge, but my sandals pounded on the wood, issuing hollow thuds. I continued across for what felt like an hour. The planks stretched forever onward.

A board wobbled. Icy liquid seeped over my toes. Leaping back, I gasped. The fog floated away on a ghostly wind, revealing that the bridge was only a trail of rotting timber.

But something was in the lake.

Veiled by mist, black figures stood in rows within the placid lake. The mist lifted like dew at dawn, and the figures' drooping heads became distinct—faces bound in white linen.

I froze, gooseflesh rising on my arms. Hundreds of dark figures with arms crossed over their chests stood still, holding crooks and flails. I'd seen these creatures before, but why did they keep reappearing? Perhaps they didn't know I was here ...

A single head lifted. Green eyes glowed through the tight cloth wrapping its head and face. And the eyes focused on me. Its otherwise-featureless face elongated and emitted a screech so shrill that my bones jolted.

The Dark Ones. They advanced.

I spun around and sprinted back along the bridge as murky
water sloshed over my sandals. Figures constricted in around me
like serpents, wading through water without a single splash or
ripple. Complete silence. The bridge and lake stretched as far as
I could see. But the figures closed in. My breaths came in gulps,
and my heart raced as my legs spun. The figures clawed at the
planks, reaching over the walk for me. I leapt into the air, but
one of them caught my ankle with cold fingers that froze my skin.
It yanked me down into their midst—

The Aten rose beyond the edges of the endless sea, disrupting my
nightmare. I wiped cold sweat from my forehead and rubbed my dreary
eyes. The crumbling piazza remained empty.

After the others woke, we gathered our belongings and exited the ruins.
We faced the mountain range dividing the island into north and south.
Peaks towered over us like the great pyramids.

Hiking up the mountains made me sweat, even though the temperature plummeted and the chill that'd crept into my bones burrowed deeper.
We traveled up and down slopes, across plateaus, and through valleys for a
couple of days before heading for the highest peak.

"I need to catch my breath," Chisisi said from behind, his voice raspy.
His chest heaved for air, similar to the others. Cold air burned my throat
on its way down, but my lungs hadn't given out—my self-inflicted torture
of physical conditioning was paying off.

"We're only about halfway up now," Wahankh said between gasps.

"I've been on a Nubian mountain at night," Seneb said, handing out all
of the blankets that Dedalos had supplied us with. "And draping yourself
in blankets is barely enough to keep you from freezing to death."

A biting wind thrashed my robe against my legs, pierced the layers, and
froze my perspiration. My hearing faded into the gale, and my eyes stung
and watered. The burro held its head low, folding its ears back.

"I've never felt such cold," Paramessu yelled, yanking his blankets tight
around his shoulders and shivering.

We trudged on as the cold clawed its way into my feet and hands. The
sensation was much worse than the night I'd spent alone in the desert cursing

the Aten for allowing Akhenaten to take advantage of Nefertiti. How many more new adversities could this world still throw at me? And could men survive these elements in a place devoid of the Aten's heat?

As I approached the white layer coating the upper slopes and summit, cold radiated from it like heat from a fire. I stepped into this snow and my feet sank, the icy wet slipping over my sandals. My feet burned as a painful cold turned my toes blue and climbed up my legs. I jerked my feet out, and my sandals slipped. I landed on my backside, the white stinging my skin.

"We shouldn't hike in this," Chisisi said. "And anyone up there will stand out like black on white. Let's circle the margin and keep an eye out for the prince and his army. God knows why they'd be up there."

No one argued. But still we braved wind, rain, and falling flakes of water mixed with the white stuff on the ground before starting a fire with lamp oil and huddling beside it.

Night passed in a blur of chattering teeth and intermittent dreams.

Similar days and nights followed.

"Do you remember me?" I asked Paramessu one morning as I chewed on a handful of brown olives, my hands shaking with cold. He glanced up from the crackling embers of our dying fire, and his pale eyes narrowed.

Silence.

"Discipline is what society is founded upon," I said. "That is what you said to me."

"I've said that many times in my life," he replied, his hair as red as the embers, his strong jaw clenched. "But I don't recognize you from before our encounter in the desert, nor do I remember uttering those words amongst this group."

"What if you were whipping someone?" I asked before biting my lip and marching away. The captain must not remember punishing me for speaking to the magician when I was a slave.

The rising sunlight remained veiled behind a canvas of gray clouds before me, but hours passed and the light faded. The sky turned white.

What was this magic? Was the precipitation's only purpose to make men suffer with the opposite feeling of the midday Aten? Flakes clouded my vision of the mountain, but something caught my eye. There were tracks in the new layer of snow—an unmistakable trail of footprints twice the size of mine. They led toward the highest peak.

"What would drive anyone up there?" Harkhuf asked, flinging snow from his beard as he outlined the tracks with a swollen finger.

New fluffy flakes fell into the prints, making them harder to distinguish. "We should follow them," I said, pointing. "Or we'll lose the trail. And I have a feeling these people don't come and go often."

Wahankh groaned.

"Night is coming," Chisisi said. "We could die up there from the cold, if we get lost, or if we can't see a cliff in front of us."

"It's the first sign of people we've seen in over a week," Paramessu said.

"We better not lose it," Harkhuf grumbled and stepped into the white with a crunch. He sank up to his ankles but made no display of discomfort or pain.

I gritted my teeth and followed, the cold of my skin now nearly matching the snow's. But we'd have to be swift if we hoped to make it to the peak before dark.

My chest heaved as the air thinned, each step like climbing five sets of stairs. The footprints were fading. We'd backtracked many times in recent days to avoid impassable areas, but the person we were now tracking had picked out a narrow path amongst rocks and gorges—without veering off or second-guessing any step along their route.

Hours passed before we neared the last slopes—the burro scrambling up behind Seneb like a mountain goat. The footprints we followed were now covered, and only inconspicuous depressions guided us in the waning light.

"If we don't find shelter, we will die up here," Chisisi hollered over the howling wind. "And a fire won't start in this wind and wet."

"Someone lives up here," I said, my teeth chattering. "They must have a roof and flame."

"I don't think they'll invite us in," Wahankh replied, his ears blue and his lips caked with frozen blood.

"If you wanted to turn around, you should've done so an hour ago," Harkhuf growled. "You'll plummet to your death trying to descend in the dark. And our own tracks are getting buried."

I clung to icy rocks for the final ascent, and the biting cold climbed into my hands and forearms. My fingers were numb and twisted.

Flakes blew sideways in the deafening storm surrounding us so that I couldn't see more than ten feet. My blood turned thick with fear. This was a mistake. I should've listened to Chisisi. Feeling would fade into numbness, and we'd slip into death without ever knowing it. I'd lead everyone to their deaths, like with Father—because he'd wanted to tell me something and Akhenaten had been forced to silence him with a fake plague—and Yuf … and Tia. No wonder Nefertiti hadn't chosen to follow me; she must've seen something inside me, something I didn't know about myself—not until recently, anyway.

The last stretch to the summit was too steep. We'd need to scale rock buried beneath ice and white. My eyes closed in frustration, my fingers barely responding to my commands.

"There!" Paramessu shouted, pointing.

A faint light—not in the direction of the setting sun. Someone had a fire!

We nestled ourselves into a gulley. The wind and blinding flakes diminished.

"A cave," Harkhuf said, grabbing for an arrow, but the arrow fell and disappeared into the knee-high snow. "We might need our weapons. Warm up your hands." He attempted to bend fingers as thick and purple as raw tubers, but they barely moved. Instead, he blew on his hands and rubbed them together like sticks he attempted to start a fire with.

I did the same, and my fingers felt like someone plunged them in boiling water. I grunted in pain. Laughing, Seneb smacked me on the shoulder.

Taking up my twin swords in weak grips, my hands stuck to the cold metal. I followed the dwarves, who crept to the cave's entrance. Terrors flashed through my mind: Mummy Makers, the Devouring Monster, ghouls, a half-man and half-bull Minotaur, the Dark Ones …

Holding my breath, I peeked inside. Only the reflective flicker of distant fire. Wisps of smoke floated overhead. The stench of rot burned my nostrils. I gagged as I reached to steady myself against the inner wall, but I tripped. A large bone—like a human femur—skittered away. Deep cuts from a blade ran along its length. Teeth imprints surrounded the shaft, like a vegetable someone had gnawed on. The stench turned my stomach, and yellow fluid spewed from my lips, burning my throat and tongue as it passed. Wiping my mouth with the back of my hand, I closed my eyes and grimaced.

"Get a hold of yourself!" Harkhuf said, stepping past me with his bow and a nocked arrow. The limbs of his weapon creaked with tension as he drew the string. "Did you expect rainbows and butterflies?"

Seneb chuckled. "I haven't seen any of those since Nubia." He led the burro into the entrance and dropped the lead rope.

"Did the army turn into cannibals?" Chisisi asked, kicking at a pile of bones. The sword and shield in his hands shook, rattling against each other.

"Let's sneak in and take a peek," Paramessu said, holding his shield before him. "If we can find the prince, or his brother, we should take them and run."

Where was Croc now? No, he wouldn't climb way up here, not into this cold.

I inched around a bend, and the air grew warm. Rumbling voices echoed off the walls. I peeked around the corner with only my left eye … something flashed, disorienting me.

Chapter 41

Journal Translation

I WAS NO LONGER INSIDE *the cave upon the snowy mountain. A vision of Egypt opened before me, appearing through another's eyes. The scent of the rose and citrus …*

My most hated enemy from what seemed like a lifetime ago stood before me.

Akhenaten!

He stood inside a high window above a crowd at my level and smiled under the fading light of the Aten. His elongated eyes and sunken cheeks were cast in shadow, the crowns of Upper and Lower Egypt resting atop his head. As his eyes narrowed, his black-painted upper lids grew like the empty sockets of a skull. The most beautiful woman in the world clung to his arm, smiling with more vibrance than I'd ever seen from her. Flames burned in her eyes. My stomach twisted with anger and jealousy. She still enjoyed fame, power, and wealth above all … the only means to stealing her heart.

Thousands of Egyptians cheered from below, worshipping and praising Pharaoh with all their love and energy as they groveled in the dirt and raised their palms in the sign of adoration. Something squeezed my heart.

The scratching of a pen was so loud, it sounded like my ear lay against papyrus. The vision shifted to the side, and as I saw through another's eyes, I was unable to control what I looked at. Short bushes partially obscured my sight as if I were once again the fox, and Maya, the oval-faced scribe with big ears and long hair, hovered nearby, jotting something down with a reed pen.

The vision refocused on the window. Beside Nefertiti stood her handsome father, Ay. Gray streaked the hair beneath his wig. Mutnedjmet stood at his side, frowning.

The tingle of nostalgia rose in my core ... If only we were children again, running around Memphis. I'd thought I had it bad then ...

A hulking man stepped past, a scar covering his shaven head and deformed ear, which resembled the pointy ear of a pig—Suty. Beside him, the entrenched face of the magician broke into a smile as he waved to the people. His pale eyes gleamed with sincerity. Confusion clouded my thoughts. Still helping Akhenaten rule Egypt? Although I owed him much, he still didn't appear to be pursuing our objective—at least not my objective. What was his—when all the mystery and secrets were stripped away, his insides and innermost thoughts exposed like raw emotion?

Beketaten's horse face leaned onto Akhenaten's shoulder. My stomach turned with nausea. Within the darkness during my last night before slavery, she'd deceived me into believing that she was Nefertiti. A boy climbed into her arms, and she held him high in presentation to the people, like a golden ankh. Thunderous applause erupted. My ears rang with pain. Only female children surrounded Nefertiti.

The only boy-child of Akhenaten's ... the new crown prince of Egypt!

I strained for a gasp of air. Was this vision of the past or the present? My previous visions through the fox's eyes had only been of the present, but I couldn't claim to know how magic always worked, especially now in a far-off land. And did it matter? Akhenaten had a lineage. Would this poor boy be cursed to live surrounded by evil, like I was? Or would this child embrace it and become as monstrous as his father? And why had they waited so long to present him, he was a boy and not a babe? Did he carry *deformities like his father and they wanted to hide them, or make sure that he would survive his early years first?*

Wait ... I'd spent the night with Beketaten. My throat constricted in panic. Could her son be mine? No, it must've been too long, unless this vision was from the past. Love, hate, desire, revenge, jealousy, anger, distrust, and ambition coursed through my veins. I tried to scream, but nothing came out. I attempted to run but couldn't move. The vision blurred and faded ...

Someone whispered and dragged me by my feet and legs. I slid across rough stone. Squeezing my eyes shut, I wished for the vision of Egypt, even with all of its torment, to return. But the face of my only love was gone. In her place was dark skin and a rough beard—an ugly dwarf. I gasped, dazed.

"What did you see?" the gentler face of another dwarf asked. The whites of his eyes shone like beacons inside the dark cave. "What was so terrifying that it made you faint?"

Shaking my head, I realized my companions had pulled me away from the inner chamber of the cave within the snowy mountain. My left temple throbbed, and warm liquid gushed from my nose and pooled around my mouth, as if I'd fallen and smacked my face.

"What's living in there?" Paramessu asked, pointing his spear at the reflection of flickering firelight ahead.

"I ... I don't know," I whispered, crawling back to the inner chamber. I didn't want to reveal my visions and let anyone know I possessed some sort of magic, even if it was weak.

Around the next corner, flames danced against rock walls while smoke billowed to a ceiling supported by stalagmites. The cavernous chamber stretched as large as any throne room. A large spit sat over the fire with the charred body of something as large as a man. It was half-eaten. Skulls sat upside down on tables—bowls of brain soup. Wooden cages lay about the periphery, and figures slumped within. The stench of rot lay thick. Nothing moved.

Harkhuf stepped around me and entered. Forcing a deep breath, I followed and avoided a pile of discarded bones as tall as I was as I crept to the first cage.

Within the cage, two haggard men lay still.

"Hello," I whispered as warm sweat dribbled from my brow, the heat in this room like the Egyptian desert. Neither captive moved. Something scuffed on the other side of the crackling fire.

A fearful voice spoke in a tongue I did not understand.

My body tensed as I whirled around.

Paramessu already led the way around the fire. More cages were filled with bodies. An emaciated man peered through the bars, light flickering across his sunken features. He rambled, his eyes wide with terror.

"We are Egyptian and do not speak your language," Paramessu said. Others moaned inside their cells.

"Egyptians?" the emaciated man asked in a thick accent that had strange low inflections—like Dedalos. "What do Egyptians desire here, other than to profit off of trades and take our oils?"

"We are mercenaries sent to find the Prince of Phaistos," Chisisi said, stepping forward. He jammed the butt of his spear against the stone ground.

Another captive rose to his knees and whispered to his comrade. The first emaciated man stuck his face through the bars and said, "Then you are too late. The prince is gone. But if you help us escape before they return, I will help you find him. We were part of the Phaistos military, trapped by the monsters."

My skin crawled. Monsters?

"What monsters?" Chisisi asked, glancing back at the rest of us. Wahankh slipped into the shadows.

"The Hidden Ones," the emaciated Phaistos soldier replied. "I do not have time to explain. Please get us out of here! They have been feeding on us, and there are few of us left. We are weak and weary."

While quietly slicing into the sinews holding the cage closed, I kept glancing back to the entrance. The dried tendons were tough. Churning rose in my stomach. Where had these sinews come from?

We freed nearly fifty sickly men from inside the vast chamber, but another thirty remained motionless.

"We need to get out of here," the emaciated soldier said, pushing strands of oily hair behind his ears. "In spite of the blizzard."

"The storm is too vicious," Chisisi said. "We can't leave until morning."

"The going will be treacherous," the prisoner replied, assisting another comrade. "But is nothing compared to what awaits you if they return. We just have to free the others first." He pointed with a blackened nail to the back of the cavern. A shadowy tunnel led deeper into the mountain.

Digging out my lamp, I said, "Tia, can you hold this … ?" Pain twisted in my chest. For a moment, I'd forgotten she was gone. I glanced at Harkhuf out of the corner of my eye. Had he heard my slip up?

"What others?" Chisisi asked.

Limping for the passageway, the emaciated man's gaze fell to the ground, as if hiding something. He picked a stick from the fire to use as a torch. "The women are here for …"

"What women?" Harkhuf asked, glancing about as he spun wildly.

"They are using our women to breed an army of their own kind," the soldier replied. "An army of magic wielders, to conquer the island."

"It would take generations to build an army by that method," Paramessu said, following the man. "Unless there're hundreds of women back there."

"These monsters are different," the emaciated soldier replied with low inflections, leading the way. "They've been working on this for years, and with their powers, they'd only need an army of a hundred to destroy all of humanity here."

"What powers do they possess?" I asked, my fists squeezing my lamp and sword.

"It came from combining the herb and the meat," he said. "The woman who bore the prince's disfigured brother was tricked into eating the foul weed left by the Minotaur. Tricked by a jealous queen. If the ingestion is timed correctly, the fetus is too strong to be killed by the toxins, but becomes … distorted. In return, the vile offspring is granted size, strength, and untold magic."

"What kind of meat?" I asked, my lips quivering.

"They come and gather us like sheep and fire us on a spit," the emaciated soldier said. "Then every so often a screaming child is brought into the world from the depths of Hades."

Was Hades their underworld?

"Pitting the men of the island against each other," he continued, "these creatures remain hidden and watch as war rages."

My knees trembled in horrid shock. I stumbled over a stone.

"How many of them are there?" Harkhuf asked.

"Ten or twenty," the emaciated soldier replied, "but don't let the numbers lead you to believe that they can be easily overthrown."

"Where are they?" Chisisi asked, glancing about. Wahankh was nowhere in sight.

"They go out into the storms," the soldier said. "That's how I knew it must be snowing. The weather gives them power. They will bring back more men ... and women."

Swallowing, I turned a corner. A large cage lined the far wall of a blind chamber. At least twenty women huddled together, trembling. Straw beds with posts and ropes surrounded a central fire, now smoldering. Its green smoke wafted up in billows, burning my nose and throat—the stench like rotten eggs. My stomach heaved with disgust.

"Anyone who still has the desire to live, stand up," the emaciated Phaistos soldier said, hobbling to the cell. Shrieks carried out as some captives scrambled away to the far side. Others sobbed and clung to the bars.

Racing over, I cut through the cage. Young women ran out, still in good physical condition. The bulging bellies of several pregnant women made my stomach flip.

"Follow me!" Chisisi said, ushering and then leading the women down the cavern.

The Phaistos soldier stopped, along with several comrades, and scooped up piles of shriveled plant material.

"We must go!" Chisisi said.

Carrying the herbs to the smoldering fire, they dropped them in and returned for more. Plumes of choking black smoke filled the air, stinking of skunk. These men were not going to stop.

Sprinting over, I loaded my arms up with the vegetation—dried leaves that resembled gargantuan cabbage. Still yellowish green, but the leaves crinkled under my grip, their rough surface tugging at my skin like Croc's tongue. The dwarves assisted, dropping more into the flames—so did Paramessu, nodding to me in recognition. "Crimes against women are the most heinous form of disobedience," the Egyptian soldier said, his hooked nose wrinkling as his jaws bulged.

We set all of the herb on fire and darted back through the passageway.

"What about your comrades who're too weak to move?" Seneb asked the emaciated soldier.

"As much as it pains me, we'll have to leave them," he replied. "We cannot risk hauling them down the mountain, or none of us will make it." He limped away.

Harkhuf cut open the other cages in the larger chamber and placed a knife in one man's palm. The victim's eyes remained closed, his body limp. "If you cannot make it out but still have any will left," Harkhuf whispered, "cut them ... or cut yourself."

"Don't let them take you like a tadpole from a puddle," Seneb added.

Wrinkled eyelids opened enough to reveal faint white. The corner of the man's cracked lips twitched. Harkhuf patted the victim's chest, but Seneb yanked his brother away.

The exit to the outside world opened on the other side of a long tunnel. Cold sweat dripped from my forehead.

Chapter 42

Journal Translation

WE FLED THE CAVE THROUGH clouds of smoke that seared my lungs. Several women pushed past me, racing out of the sweltering heat into the biting cold. Snow fell in sheets. Wind whipped my face like an icy flail. In the ebbing light of our torches, dark forms lumbered through the white. Harkhuf shouted as he raised his bow.

"For all that is sacred, run for your lives!" the emaciated man yelled, putting his arm around a woman and forcing her in the opposite direction of the monsters. Those two disappeared into the storm.

Three of Harkhuf's arrows whistled at the approaching figures, but there were no shouts of pain. The plodding monsters persisted, nearly upon us.

Lunging away with the others through knee-deep snow, I ascended a gulley. Bolts of light arced from the sky. With a flash and deafening crack, snow and rock exploded from the earth. Men and women screamed.

"Their magic!" someone yelled over howling wind. "Scatter!"

Taking another step, I fell into emptiness. My stomach rose into my throat as I plummeted. Blackness surrounded me.

I landed with a puff—a cushion of white saving my life. But it gave way. Sliding, I twisted and tumbled down a slope. Screams from unseen men and women surrounded me like the night as I flailed to gain control, smacking into objects. Pain erupted inside my head.

✳ ✳ ✳

I awoke to a faint light. My ears rang and my head pounded. Numbing cold had clawed its way up my limbs and reached for my core with fingers of ice. Blinking, I tried to focus. The pink light of the Aten glimmered through dwindling precipitation. I lay on my back near the snow line, having plummeted a long distance. My bad ankle, from the hippo attack years ago, was twisted and ached. Hobbling up and onto my hands and knees with limbs that barely responded to my commands, I searched for the others.

A man with a protruding spine under wasted muscle lay face down. Did I dare yell? I shook him, and the cold of his skin sank into my heart. Broken ribs stuck out of his side.

"Harkhuf! Seneb!" I yelled, glancing up and down the mountain. A mixed group of gaunt and full figures ran across a plateau far below. My breath escaped its prison in relief. Amongst them ran a few armed men, likely my comrades. But there were no dwarves. Limping along below the snow line, I hunted for my friends while watching the upper ridges for monsters.

Harkhuf ran in the distance, shouting. Halting, he jumped into the snow and fell to his knees.

I ran as fast as I could, pain tearing through my lower leg with a squishing sensation. The burro lay still, in a heap in the snow, two of its legs protruding at impossible angles. The beast's upward-facing eye was wide, its nostrils flaring for breath as its legs thrashed in an attempt to rise. Grimacing, Harkhuf plunged his spear into its head. The animal took a deep breath, sighed, and relaxed. Harkhuf dived into the snow beneath its body and dug like his only escape route lay beneath.

"Seneb!" he bellowed. Tears rushed down his hardened face like crystal raindrops down a desert cliff.

After several minutes, he stopped digging, his face drawn. He fell back to a sitting position, teetered, braced himself with his hands, and whispered, "The old, wise people of our tribe say that the time you are your truest self is not when you are alone—because you have no one to interact with—but when you are alone with an animal. You are then free of the masks we all wear in public, as animals do not judge and cannot tell anyone else about what you've done; whether that is love them or abuse them." He swallowed, his lower lip trembling. "Seneb was the kindest soul I've—"

Something moaned to my left. Out of the snow popped a humanoid form covered in a layer of white. As I reached for an arrow, my breathing ceased. A puff of steam spewed from its mouth, clearing a hole as a hand wiped at and revealed a face—a boyish face. Seneb!

Harkhuf yelled, jumping on and squishing his brother in an embrace. Hoisting Seneb from the powder and ice, Harkhuf carried him below the snow line and eased him down.

"I'm fine," Seneb said, brushing himself off as he wobbled. "Soft landing, but my head's foggy like …" In his dazed state, he failed to make a comparison.

I scraped together scattered arrows, packs, and weapons before turning to descend the mountain. Utilizing my bow as a crutch helped with my injured ankle. Seneb placed a hand on the burro and whispered in a strange tongue, closing its eye. He stroked and patted its shoulder. My heart twisted with sorrow for the loss of innocent life. I had felt less witnessing dead men …

We hiked downward as fast as we could manage with rock and frozen ground slipping underneath our feet.

Hours later, I spotted the group just ahead as they fled down to the foothills. Chisisi and Wahankh led them. Paramessu held a soldier's arm around his neck and tugged the soldier along. I released a deep breath, relief starting to sink in as we hurried along and joined them. No one spoke. Only Tia was still absent from our group, and I'd had no delusions that she was in that cave—although Harkhuf had probably hoped she was. But the Phaistos army was smaller than when we'd led them out. Many either hadn't survived the monsters or the descent.

"We need to continue day and night," the emaciated soldier said to me and Chisisi. "The monsters travel at night and will pursue the women and their unborn offspring. They will no longer wait in hiding. Those who've seen the monsters," he pointed at his people, "have now escaped and could band all the people of the island together against them. These monsters will realize that and will now come to take our lives while we are still separated and weak."

We marched east for days, toward the sea.

Journeying amidst nearly dead men, my companions and I helped keep them moving and fed them from our diminishing food supply. The women were filthy, but in much better health than the men. I focused on my surroundings, not wanting to imagine what they'd had to eat to stay that way.

The crumbling city of Phaistos, which held Radamanthis's palace, emerged, as well as the pungent smell of the sea.

"Home," the emaciated soldier said, pointing at the city on the horizon. "I never thought that on an island I'd be able to miss her so much. But we must be quick. The monsters will arrive this night, when we are at our weakest."

A trumpet blared from the tired city as we approached and its guards spotted us. Then the faces of other people appeared, and howls and cheers erupted, echoing in my head like sweet music. The people of Phaistos ran out to greet us, hugged the returning soldiers and women, and carried them away.

The emaciated soldier pushed away from two men who were trying to carry him and said, "We will amass every able body—even women and boys—and defend Phaistos from inside the palace walls. The city is unprotected, and the battle will eventually be decided at its capital."

As we limped through the gates of the palace, guards beat their spears against their shields in our honor. The clanging of bronze and wood synchronized like precise drumbeats and resonated throughout the city. Warmth filled my chest and soothed my stomach.

The emaciated soldier froze in his tracks.

Princess Scylla's pale face appeared, her dark hair floating in the wind. Gray air surrounded her, backset by a withered tree. Remaining motionless, she didn't even blink. Beauty that rivaled Nefertiti's caused me to stare in awe. I felt neither love nor lust but couldn't look away.

She said something to the emaciated soldier in their native tongue.

The emaciated soldier embraced her in a warm hug, his ribs rippling under his skin. His head fell onto her shoulder as he sobbed and replied. Then he stood straight and, in deeply accented Egyptian, said, "But I've seen things I did not imagine could dwell on this earth. He is coming."

The princess studied us and said in perfect Egyptian, "My brave heroes"—a rush of warmth returned to my face but disbelief rose with it—"please assist us in our final hours. Both of my brothers are coming home."

Chapter 43

Journal Translation

I WRAPPED MY TWISTED ANKLE in a cloth bandage—the added support—easing my pain—before we were ushered inside the palace at Phaistos to take council in the hall of the king. The emaciated soldier we'd rescued, Princess Scylla, Dedalos, and the other council members took their seats as servants laid out platters of food. The king had not yet arrived.

"We have scouts at the edge of the city," the emaciated soldier said as he piled up a plate of olives, bread, and vegetables while pushing aside the miniscule fish.

"Prince Gortys," Dedalos said, "do you not long for the taste of fish?"

Prince Gortys? The emaciated soldier was one of the two royal brothers!

"I'll never be able to eat meat again," Prince Gortys answered.

"Why did you not tell us you were the prince?" Chisisi asked, standing and folding his arms across his chest.

"I'm a sliver of my former self and was not the prince inside that cave," he replied as he sat down beside the princess. "And I needed to know why you foreigners were looking for me."

I nodded in understanding as oily olives slid across my tongue and produced an earthy taste but with a sharp bite. Everyone on this island pretended to be someone else. The princess had acted as if she could not speak Egyptian before we departed but spoke it with ease on our return. Dedalos probably knew something about the monsters all along and probably wasn't a merchant—given his influence with the king. Did the barbarians and Sea Shepherd also know more than they'd told us?

The chomping and lip smacking of the feasting attendees paused. The weary king entered, glared at his guant son, and spoke in a roaring voice that betrayed his physical body. My head jerked back in fearful surprise.

Then the king spoke in Egyptian. "They are coming. You invited an army of monsters to our doorstep, Gortys. Scouts report that hulking shadows wait for nightfall at the base of the mountains. You have brought too few men back with you. There is no hope. We must run like dogs."

Prince Gortys's eyes darkened, but a fiery rage sparked as he gazed upon the rat-faced man beside the king—Prince Catreus.

"Mighty king," Dedalos said, standing and interlacing his fingers. "Do we forfeit the city we've held since the beginning? Do we hand over the ashes of our fathers, allow our history to pass into the hands of the vile, without a fight?" He then spoke again in his own tongue.

"There is no need to fight and die when there's no chance of winning!" the king roared, forcing Dedalos back into his seat. Raising a tankard, the king downed the red wine in a mighty swig that dribbled over his cheeks. He stumbled up to Prince Gortys and wiped his mouth with the back of his hand, his eyes bloodshot under heavy lids.

Prince Gortys's head slumped to his chest.

"You're already dead," the king said, collapsing into his seat at the head of the table. He pointed at each of us. "I dine with the dead. Gortys departed with a mission to clear the island of barbarian filth. They drove him away. Then our prince allowed the Hidden Ones to capture our army—*my* army!" Smashing his fist onto the table sent a boom through the hall. "Now there are so few of us, we'd fall to the barbarians if they attacked our city."

"My brother, your other son, is coming for us," Princess Scylla said softly to her king. But her volume amplified as she stood and paced. "He is strong, yes, and has amassed a force to be reckoned with. He holds the evil magic bestowed upon him when he was cut from the womb of his dying mother! But I will not let my island fall! I will not betray you!" She pointed over the heads of everyone. "Father would have us drink ourselves stupid, to ease our passing in the way he has these last months!" Her voice rivaled even the king's in his own hall. Utensils clattered to the ground as everyone leaned back with wide eyes. "What tempest of depression has settled over you,

Radamanthis? One where you cannot see that your own son and daughter will stand and fight, whether under your orders or not?" She glared at the hunched king with folded arms, unblinking.

Tension stiffened the air around me.

The emaciated prince rose beside his sister.

"Sit down, Gortys!" Radamanthis screamed, his face darkening to the purple of storm clouds. "If you wish to usurp the throne, you will not succeed. Not before I am dead. But I will be there soon enough. We all will. Dead." Leaping to his feet with the agility of a young man, he retreated into his chambers. Catreus, the rat-faced prince, followed.

Silence.

"You will prepare for battle," Princess Scylla said to us. "This will not be the last night of the Minoans!" She then spoke in her own tongue to the rest of the room.

Feeble clapping followed. But Harkhuf and Seneb added their meaty palms to the ensemble. This spurred the hope within me, and I joined, standing. Paramessu, Chisisi, and Wahankh stood. The old men of the council glanced at each other. I had been warned that someone here was a traitor to their city. Who was it?

Celebrating with Prince Gortys, Princess Scylla, and Dedalos, we ate but drank only water. I studied everyone, trying to find a clue as to who stood against their own.

"Perhaps my mother ate the wrong weed," Seneb said with a boyish grin as he patted his protruding belly. "Instead of bigger and stronger, I grew shorter and wider." He bellowed with laughter. Some of the councilmen's faces went pale.

A thin man rushed into the room, out of breath. Shouting something in his own tongue, he placed his hands on his knees. From our time here, and my studies, I picked up some of the words, "West! In the hour!"

Princess Scylla said something in her language, in an even tone, that might've been, "Remain calm, my soldier," and followed it with much more. I picked up scattered words, and then she switched to Egyptian to tell us, "Remember their weakness. Size and strength twice that of a man, but their deformity also gives them vulnerability."

My skin squirmed as visions of hideous monsters hurling lightning bolts filled my mind—lightning like we'd seen atop the mountain.

"The bow will be advantageous against magic and monsters," Harkhuf said.

"We are honored by your service," Princess Scylla said to the dwarf. "Now it is time to prepare. May the gods be with us." She curtsied and departed.

Prince Gortys led us to the top of the outer walls of the palace, where we stared into the setting sun. A chill blew in on the wind. Hundreds or thousands of older women, young children, and elderly men shuffled through the gates below to take refuge within the palace.

A soldier approached Prince Gortys, said something in his native tongue, and offered the prince a sword. The blade caught the rays of the Aten along its gleaming edge, sending a flame of light across its length.

Prince Gortys took the weapon in his gaunt hand and scrutinized the jewel-encrusted hilt before looking at me. "If Father comes to fight, he may wield it. Until then …"

Princess Scylla returned, wearing a bronze breastplate and helmet. She nocked an arrow on her bowstring and squinted over the ramparts. The few armed soldiers stood either behind us or within the palace's gates.

My muscles twitched with every breath, my stomach knotting. I hadn't felt such anxiety about waiting for something since my servitude to Akhenaten. The bracelet on my arm warmed my skin, fighting off the inbound cold, and brought some comfort. Father would be watching.

The sun set and darkness fell—only the sound of faint breaths around me.

A scream pierced the still night. I jumped. The howl was so terrifying it must've been a dying man's wail, or the sound of sheer terror. Thunder clapped. Stones crashed into buildings. Lightning flashed in the distance.

The shouting of men came closer. Twenty armed soldiers raced through the streets and passed through the gate below us. They slammed the entrance shut. Wood creaked and groaned as poles were placed as braces.

Silence.

I held my breath and glanced around. The distant rumble of ocean waves escalated—seawater pounding into rock with increasing force. At our backs and well below us, waves grew to the height of a building, shimmering in the moonlight before each strike fell.

A soldier shouted and pointed out into the city.

A figure wearing a cloak appeared in the torchlight in the distance. Walking from between buildings on our left, he paused in the street, still facing sideways. He uncurled a hand, and two white birds that must've been gulls flocked to him. They landed and ate out of his palm.

The creepy scene made goose bumps rise on my arms and legs, like a defeathered duck. What was this suggesting, and why were gulls flying at night?

Wahankh swallowed so loudly it sounded as if he'd downed an entire pitcher of beer.

Screeching, the gulls fought over whatever this man held. The figure strode across the lane and disappeared into the shadows on the far side of the street.

Silence.

Water roared as it crashed into stone. The foundation of the palace shook.

Chapter 44

Journal Translation

HULKING SHAPES EMERGED in the shadows at the periphery of the torchlight lining the streets below the palace. They appeared several feet taller than a normal man, with shoulders twice as wide. This island's underworld had arrived.

Torches extinguished one by one without an apparent cause. Darkness encompassed the area, only broken by pale moonlight. Twenty Hidden Ones, monsters, shuffled for the palace as steadily as death coming for the diseased. Drawing my bowstring, I said, "I have not known better men or women than those around me right now. You will all surely claw and fight through any trials the afterlife brings against you."

"Not this night!" Princess Scylla shouted. "We will see the sun rise."

Paramessu stepped in front of me, as if I were his chariot archer, his tall shield protecting our exposed bodies.

The monsters stomped repeatedly, just out of arrow range. Vibrations and drumming echoes carried from their feet through the streets, into the palace walls, and up my legs. Men and women who'd recently entered through the gates below screamed and fled deeper into the palace. My hand shook on the grip of my bow, sweat making the wood slick. Hopefully those fleeing were not Phaistos's soldiers.

"Men of the fallen military." King Radamanthis's roar overpowered the echoes of our stomping adversaries. He stepped into the palace courtyard below, the flicker of torchlight surrounding him. "Our deaths have already been decided. Join me in the great hall for our final feast!" Thunder clapped ahead.

My hand jerked in surprise and the arrow on my string fell and clattered on the stone walkway. Retreating, Radamanthis led a large following of civilians and soldiers back into the palace. Wahankh leapt down the stairs of the outer wall and chased after them. Chisisi followed, although slower, as if still deciding.

Cowards. Did they think the king would find them a way out of this, a hope of escape or an easier death than the pain of dying in battle?

"I never liked the bully or the egocentric freeman anyway," Harkhuf grumbled, drawing his bowstring to his ear.

"We who endure will stop this madness!" Princess Scylla yelled, her volume matching the king's. "Keep those things out until I gut the traitor in our midst." She ran down to the courtyard. "I'll return to watch the last of them fall."

The monsters marched through the darkness. Bolts of lightning snapped in the sky, striking surrounding buildings and exploding blocks of stone. The rank smell of rotten eggs filled the night. Then light emerged, appearing as small sparks in the monster's midst, making their palms glow green, the remainder of their bodies still shrouded in darkness. They hurled sizzling bolts of light at the palace. Men ducked behind the ramparts, their limbs shaking. The monster's magical bolts collided with stone and wood, booming and then quaking the wall I stood upon. Smoke rose in plumes. Light collided with a man to my right. His bronze shield and helmet lit up like the sun, and he burst into flames. He toppled over the wall, screaming, and landed with a thud. His bonfire raged before the gates.

I gasped in shock, and my hand slipped on the rough sinew of my bowstring.

"Aim for their eyes!" Harkhuf yelled as he loosed an arrow. "I will blind them all!"

Seneb released his bowstring with a snap, and his arrow whistled into the darkness.

My hand quivered. Why the eyes, and what did that mean? The attacker's faces were still hidden, but I aimed for their heads and released my arrow. Projectiles rained over both sides. One beast shrieked and collapsed to the street, thrashing in pain. The others charged.

"Struck in the center of its pupil!" Harkhuf yelled, pumping his fist into the air. He loaded another arrow and let it fly.

The walls shuddered, making me stumble and sending my next arrow flying far to the left. Other arrows were incinerated by bolts of light.

Monsters smashed into the gates with a bang, beating with fists, lightning, and stone. We sent volleys of arrows, but I could not see well enough to spot their eyes. Shafts buried into their heads and shoulders. Another Hidden One shrieked and fell. The gates cracked and splintered. More soldiers were struck by bolts of light, igniting and falling like locusts.

"Time to run?" Paramessu asked, raising an eyebrow. Light snapped and collided with his rawhide shield. He sailed twenty feet behind me, screamed, landed, and lay still. His shield smoked black but didn't go up in flames. He slowly rose to his elbows and shook his head with disorientation.

"The bronze of your armor is your weakness!" I yelled. "Discard it all!"

But no one listened.

Wood groaned below. Images of monsters tearing into the feast hall and massacring men as they ate flashed through my mind. Why would the king do this? What was he hiding?

"There is something I must do!" I yelled to my comrades. "I will force the king's hand, but you must hold the wall for ten minutes!"

Fifty soldiers braced against the gates below.

Harkhuf's eyes narrowed as if he thought I was fleeing. "I guarantee you twelve minutes," Harkhuf said, releasing three whistling arrows.

I nodded. "I believe you, Master Archer."

Yanking the blood-stained garment and a rolled papyrus from my sack, I let the robe billow open in the wind. The soft fabric tugged at my fingers as it rippled. Prince Gortys stood beside me and hurled a spear. Even in his frail state, the clothing could not have been his. Lunging down the stairs, I sprinted for the great hall. A traitor with dark power still hid in the council, drawing death upon us.

Footsteps followed behind me …

Bursting into the great hall, I paused. The king was not at the table. Radamanthis lounged upon his throne, drink in hand as he muttered of days gone by. The councilmen and the fifty soldiers who'd retreated surrounded

Princess Scylla. She screamed at Prince Catreus, pinning him on his back. A sword rose in her hand.

"He is not the one you're looking for," I yelled. "And you will need every able body in this palace."

Blinking, Princess Scylla froze, her sword halting. "Leave us, Egyptian," she said. "You know nothing of the evil plaguing our city … within our city."

"I have learned some things," I said, leaping over and dropping the jeweled garment onto Catreus's squirming body. The bloody knife-strike stood out like fire in the night. If both the other princes lived—Gortys on the walls and Erythrus attacking us—then whose clothing was this?

Gasping, Princess Scylla asked, "Where did you find this?"

"At the beach where we washed up," I said. Why had Dedalos been hiking down to us just then? He'd been looking for something amongst the wreckage as well. I scrutinized Dedalos, waiting for any type of reaction. Pointing at Dedalos with one of my swords, I said, "Minutes later, Dedalos arrived with a child, looking for this very robe."

The princess wheeled around, her sword poised as she stalked the merchant.

Chapter 45

Journal Translation

"I WAS ONLY THERE BECAUSE we had just found a woman!" Dedalos said, holding his hands up in defense and stepping back to the far wall. Wavering torchlight danced across his withered features. "Radamanthis commanded me to return, and to keep the woman a secret!"

My eyes bulged. A woman? Tia? Could she really still be alive, and here?

Radamanthis stood on wobbly feet, snarling before letting loose a booming tirade of curses that echoed off of the stone walls of the audience hall.

I nocked an arrow, drew my bowstring with a steady hand, and aimed at the king's chest.

The crash of lightning and snapping of wood echoed from the gates outside, foretelling of death.

"No!" Princess Scylla screamed, placing herself between her father and me. "If Dedalos is killed, perhaps the king will be released of the curse hovering over him! Killing the king will do nothing."

"The king is already dead," I shouted, and my fingers slowly parted—as if still partially frozen—and my bow fell to the floor. I unrolled the papyrus scroll I'd tucked into my robe. Scanning the hieroglyphic message the ghoul leader had given me, I read with all of my conviction. I chanted and traced arcane symbols in the air and whispered Radamanthis's name.

"What are you doing?" the king roared, reaching out for my throat as he advanced.

I flung the bloodied robe at his feet.

Visions appeared in the nothingness overhead, below the cracking ceiling—like images in a dream. Magic! People gasped. In the vision, a less-hunched king stood upon the edge of soaring cliffs, overlooking the endless sea. Shielding his eyes, the image of the king watched the sun shine bright and sparkle over the water. His jeweled robe whipped in the wind. Waves crashed into the rocks far below, roaring like lions. A man in a brown cloak appeared, his back to us, his head hooded. This man placed the tip of a knife against the king's robe—at his ribs. Gulls circled and cried overhead.

"You will never rule my island!" Radamanthis's image yelled, the magic making his language vividly clear in my mind as his head turned to peek over his shoulder at the cloaked man. "You're a disgrace, and you were never my son!"

Prince Gortys entered the hall, inching toward us—the one whose footsteps had followed me down from the outer walls. Soldiers in the hall drew weapons and advanced on the prince. Chisisi was already inside, beside Wahankh, and pointed at Gortys. "Your traitor! I was trying to discover the same thing. That is why I retreated with the king."

"Wait!" I said, holding up a hand. Everyone stared. They would never trust my word.

The vision of the past played on.

"It had nothing to do with your appearance, Erythrus," Radamanthis's image shouted, shaking his head. "Your mother was deceived. But your vile nature and hatred are far more hideous. You cannot take a kingdom with violence and murder and expect its people's support! You have everything to learn, and no time to comprehend."

The cloaked man's blade shot forward, burying itself between ribs in the king's back. Sucking in a whistling breath, Radamanthis wobbled. The king's image spun and snatched the cloaked man's hand, holding himself at the precipice of the cliff. Waves grew larger, pounding the rock below. The king teetered …

"My son …"

The knife flashed again, cutting Radamanthis's hand. The king's eyes widened as he toppled over the bluff. His descent slowed as a violent breeze caught him. The jeweled robe blew open and flew from his body, into the air currents. Spiraling downward, the king's naked body disappeared in a splash—swallowed by the sea.

Pushing his hood back, the murderer in the vision revealed himself—a monster with one large, central, black eye. The monster peered downward and grinned as he shed his cloak. Underneath, he wore a jeweled robe identical to the king's. He reached for the sky and chanted, and storm clouds rolled in. Thunder clapped. The monster's wrinkled eyelid slid down, closing. Holding forth Radamanthis's severed finger, he chanted in a guttural tongue and shimmered as if he were made of light, changing …

The vision faded. People in the hall screamed.

I gasped in horror and shock. My knees trembled as I picked up my bow and attempted to draw the sinew string to my cheek.

"Cyclopian, or Cyclops," Prince Gortys said, cocking his spear back as if to throw at someone or something. "The Hidden One's faces are fused together on midline with a single large eye, and a wide nose and mouth."

"Their deformity gives them only one chance at vision," Princess Scylla yelled, her voice carrying out to the palace walls.

"We may be too late," Chisisi said, raising his spear as he looked back toward the gates.

"We will blind them all," I whispered, remembering what Harkhuf had said upon the walls.

Yowls erupted, ringing my ears, as the false king stumbled behind his throne. His slumping form grew and transformed as he screamed, tearing through his garments. Muscles and bone popped beneath his skin. A wide mouth snarled, and saliva dripped from jagged teeth. Shrieks of terror spewed from soldiers and councilmen. Towering over the throne, Erythrus, the Cyclops, revealed himself and his pale skin, having cast aside his disguise. He reached into the air. Light sprang forth in his hands, crackling.

I let an arrow fly for his large eye, which sucked in light like a pit. But he hurled the bolt of energy. The bronze tip of my arrow flashed, and the shaft burned to ash. Lightning streaked into a soldier beside me, sending bodies flying.

The Cyclops charged at me. I fumbled with another arrow, my throat constricting in fear. Claws like talons swung for my face. But the monster jerked, screamed, and toppled over backward.

The pale Cyclops lay on his back and his chest heaved, blowing a mist into the air that wetted my skin. Two arrow shafts protruded from his ruptured eye. Black fluid pooled around the arrows and streamed over his cheeks before splattering on the floor with a plop.

"You've had twelve minutes," Harkhuf said, leaping down the stairs after having shot the Cyclops. "I hope you have a plan, because the rest are on their way." Seneb and Paramessu followed him, as well as a horde of soldiers.

"Brother," Princess Scylla said to the dying monster. Prince Gortys stepped beside her. "I would have handed Gortys's succession over to you, if it would've prevented all this loss. Our island ..."

"I'll see you again in Hades," Erythrus said, his face contorted in pain as he covered his eye with enormous hands. Black fluid leaked in streams between his fingers.

Princess Scylla rested her palm over his heart. "You could've been Phaistos's greatest weapon against the Mycenaeans. But instead you used everything against us."

White froth spewed from Erythrus's lips as he kicked the princess's ankles out from under her. She toppled over but angled her sword and plunged it into her brother's chest as she fell. The Cyclops lurched and gasped before going limp.

The walls trembled all around us, shaking my legs and the flames of the torches. A trickle of dirt poured from the ceiling and scattered grit into my hair.

"Men and women of Phaistos!" Princess Scylla shouted, grabbing the king's sword from Prince Gortys and raising it high. "We have seen death and despair beyond ten lifetimes. We've lived through such atrocities that the monsters who'll burst through those doors should not frighten you any more than wailing children do. What each of you has already faced ... You have stared down death against all odds, and these Cyclops will hold no power over you. You will face the demons of Hades head on, and you will send them back!"

The hall erupted with a cheer so loud, the vibrations rattled my skull. Taking up arms, the people of Phaistos chanted and stomped.

Bolts of lightning splintered wood and arced into the hall. Soldiers burst into flames and flew through the air. But no one fled. Monsters with one large, central eye appeared in the entryway, towering over us. Soldiers charged, screaming and thrusting spears.

I released my bowstring with a snap, and my arrow buried into a monster's eye. Other arrows bounced off of this one's thick flesh. But the Cyclops dropped onto all fours, screaming. Another charged. Ducking and rolling away on hard stone, I unsheathed my twin swords. As I landed on my knees, a stone club swung at my face. I crossed my swords to intercept the attacker at his wrist and leaned forward. His arm's momentum slammed into my blades, jerking my weapons back and jarring my shoulders. But his club's velocity slowed, and only his fist collided with my chest. I flew into the far wall, and my spine cracked. Pain shot up my back as I slid down the wall and hit the floor. Scampering to my knees, I raised my swords in defense, but the Cyclops only gripped its hemorrhaging wrist. Tendons protruded from its skin, its club lying on the floor. I lunged and slid under its legs, swiping at the femoral arteries running along the inside of its thighs. Dark blood flowed like rivers around me. The monster collapsed, shaking the ancient palace.

Fifteen creatures poured into the room, smashing or frying soldiers. Cries of death followed, and our numbers dwindled. The princess yelled as she swung the king's sword at a massive thigh—

A large eye narrowed as it glared down at me. I held my swords up in trembling hands as lightning formed in the Cyclop's palm. Seneb howled, sinking his spear into the Achilles tendon of the monster. The beast collapsed as if made of lead. Paramessu jabbed his spear into its eye. The light within its pupil faded.

Pounding footfalls echoed down the hallway—something else was coming. Fear halted my breathing. What had these monsters brought with them?

Ragged men with long hair—the barbarians—emerged under torchlight behind the beasts. Would Sea Shepherd lead the men of Knossos against the monsters, or would he attack a weakened Phaistos? Bellowing, the barbarians charged.

The remaining Cyclops spun and charged back at the barbarians. Spear and shield collided with light and flesh, releasing crashes and screams. Many fell in a vicious, short battle, but a few monsters barreled through the men and fled out into the night.

A deafening cheer shook the hall. Men on all sides embraced.

My breathing returned and warmth rose through my chest with exhilaration. We'd defeated them! Chisisi wrapped me up in a giant hug, his limbs compressing my aching back.

"If only Radamanthis could see this," Princess Scylla said, holding her sword high.

"He can," Prince Gortys replied, wrapping his bloodied arm in a cloth bandage.

Dedalos had spoken of a woman …

I patted Chisisi's bony shoulders, broke free of his grasp, and dashed for the king's chambers. But I wasn't the first to arrive. Paramessu led the dwarves up to a cage in a dark corner. Several women were trapped within.

Tia! She was one of them.

Paramessu hacked at the sinews holding the cage shut. Tia burst out, hugged the dwarves, and jumped into Paramessu's arms. Tears flowed down her cheeks. Harkhuf collapsed to his knees, bawling like a child as his body shuddered. He held one hand over his eyes and the other out to Tia.

My eyes burned with elation.

But something was piled in the shadows beside the cage. Giant leaves of cabbage—the same herb as in the cave. My forehead pulled back in disbelief. Had we really saved Tia, or had she already consumed the herb?

Chapter 46

Journal Translation

PRINCESS SCYLLA, DEDALOS, and Prince Catreus entered the king's chambers and scrutinized the cage that'd held several women.

"I believed he was my king," Catreus said, kneeling. "I apologize for my actions. I only wanted his orders enforced, no matter how bizarre they became."

I shook my head in contempt, having little or no empathy for the rat-faced man.

"My Egyptians," Dedalos said, spreading his withered hands. "If I could've glimpsed what lay beneath your exteriors, what you were born with, I never would have doubted you. You must be of the line of pharaohs."

Born with? We were slaves … Suspicion caused my lips to purse. Was he throwing compliments so that we'd forgive him for lying to us about Tia? But we were only foreign mercenaries when he found us, not his friends. Perhaps the people on the island of Keftiu needed everyone who was still alive. They could judge Dedalos and Catreus themselves.

※ ※ ※

We spent the next several weeks in Phaistos, recovering with the locals and the barbarians visiting from Knossos. The pain in my back and twisted ankle receded as the injuries healed.

I hoped these people would find peace and prosperity, but a longing tugged at my heart and grew stronger every day.

A quiet meow called out as soft fur rubbed around my ankle. Croc!

"Where've you been hiding?" I asked and stroked along his deep orange stripes. So much for my faithful guardian and defender against monsters. But gazing upon his fur only reminded me more of Egypt, of Father, Akhenaten …

He licked at my toes and let out an irritated meow as he flicked his tail. Shaking my head, I picked him up and stroked under his chin as I followed after my companions. He purred, his gentle rumble carrying through my skin like ripples in water.

We arrived at the bluffs that the real Radamanthis had plummeted over. Princess Scylla held a bouquet of pure white flowers, which bloomed in the shape of a fan.

"Our sea daffodils," she said, holding them high so the wind that rippled our kilts also bowed their stems. "Only found on the edges of the Aegean. May they follow Father into the dark and return life to the sea. May the fish flourish again, growing to the length of a man rather than the length of his fingers."

A gust caught the petals, and white glided over the cliffs. The breeze carried the sea daffodils far out over the shimmering water.

"Like the kings of old," Seneb whispered.

"May my father be remembered for who he was, and not the traitor his son played." Princess Scylla turned to me, her brothers beside her. Tears trickled down her cheeks. "Take this, my champions." She held forth a rolled parchment. "It was Erythrus's. One of his first discoveries, before he turned away from us. May you use it for good. It is said to be an ancient summons from times long past. That is all I know."

Chisisi reached for it.

"Thank you," I said, taking the magic scroll. The others eyed me, probably with skepticism. But Chisisi and Wahankh would've seen the vision of the past that I had created in the hall.

"I know you cannot wait to see your homeland," Princess Scylla said, smiling and folding her arms. "We have our best merchant ship waiting for you at the harbor in the east. I'd offer our best warship, but we may need it soon. The merchant vessel is yours."

Prince Gortys, who'd packed on significant weight, clasped Harkhuf and Seneb in a tight embrace. "Scylla is to marry Sea Shepherd, the leader from Knossos, and I his sister. I hope she is not ugly, although I won't be as lucky as Sea Shepherd is."

Harkhuf grumbled and shoved Prince Gortys away. "No, you can't possibly be. Nor as lucky as you'd be with Tia. And not only because of her and Princess Scylla's beauty. They are as strong as any man here."

Princess Scylla and Tia glanced down and afar.

"Perhaps years from now, Greeks sailing through these isles will land and behold a Minoan society of such power, theirs will appear feeble and uneducated," Princess Scylla said.

My heart lifted with hope and awe. I smiled and nodded, wishing it for them.

"But for now," she whispered to me as the soft skin of her fingers settled onto my forearm, "I just pray they don't encounter an island overrun by Cyclops. We will terminate the pregnancies born of wickedness."

"I believe the former will be your future," I said, although my stomach knotted as I pictured the dangers still facing them. Croc meowed—my grip had tightened on his chest.

"Perhaps one day we will return and bask in the glory of your kingdom," Tia said, bowing.

"And I yours," Princess Scylla said, her eyes growing dim. "But I see much in front of you."

Emotion stirred deep within me. Princess Scylla's beauty reminded me of Nefertiti's, as well as the feelings she stirred within my soul. But Princess Scylla was so brave and intelligent, a leader of men—something Nefertiti only longed for in a partner. How could Nefertiti still hold my heart? She was everything I was not ... But could I ever feel so deeply for another? Why not for this princess, or Tia? Could anyone control what they felt, and for whom?

"There is someone back home waiting for you," Princess Scylla said, staring into my eyes, "someone you want, and who cares deeply for you. It is not right, but in this world men who hold the most power and wealth control the people. You will need all the help you can get for what you seek."

My forehead wrinkled in surprise as I stepped back. How did she know, and did Nefertiti really still love me? Did the gift of magic run through this entire royal family, deformed or not?

"Be yourself, Heb," she said, waving, "like everyone tells you. But also be better than you were yesterday."

We boarded our new ship and set sail to the south, under blue skies and the gentle rocking of waves. Salty winds blew through my stubbly hair and across my face as days and nights disappeared across the vast sea.

"How do you know where to go?" Chisisi asked one morning with a raised eyebrow. "There is nothing but water, no landmarks in sight."

"Someone taught me," I said, referring to some of the magician's books. "The Aten and the stars guide us."

Eventually, the expansive delta of the Nile opened before us, roaring as its white waters rushed into the sea. My mouth went dry, bittersweet nostalgia descending. What a wonderful yet sad world. Sometimes the greatest blessing, at other times a painful curse.

I'd return to the land of my father, but first I needed to take my companions home. They might not think the treasure of Amenhotep would be mine to claim or would want it for themselves. Wahankh and Chisisi couldn't be trusted … and Paramessu had his military vows. I'd drop them and Tia off, then take the brothers back to their family in Nubia. Throwing open the sail to catch the northerly wind, I steered us into the delta.

As we sailed south along the ribbon of the Nile, the sharp tang of the ocean was replaced by the musky scent of wet earth. The wind cleared of salt, and the moisture in the air vanished, parching my skin—the dry scorching heat of Egypt.

Tia clutched her belly and laughed at some tale of valor that Chisisi spun for her. The two had been talking nonstop since our departure, although she preferred the protection of the dwarves at night.

"Tia," I said as I pulled the rudder against the current, gliding the merchant vessel through a wide turn. "Did you consume any of that herb in the king's chamber?"

Her petite features narrowed as she brushed her hair from her eyes. "Some of the pregnant women were being forced to eat it," she said, shaking her head, "but he never touched me. Things had been tense there since we'd arrived."

Nodding, I squinted with skepticism. I wanted to believe her, but doubts flooded my mind. Did she wish to appear clean so we wouldn't worry?

"Can I take you home, Tia?" I asked.

Smiling, she shook her head. "Do you still know nothing of women?"

"What do you mean?" I asked, holding my hand over my chest.

"I was a slave woman," she said. "I …" she paused, "was forced into it from events beyond my control. My family passed away, and my uncle took care of me. I never want to see him again. My only family and friends are now on this ship." A tear glided down her demure nose as she stood, stomped away, and took a seat between the brothers, holding her face.

Harkhuf placed his arm around her shoulder. Paramessu shook his head at me.

What had I done? Had I really hurt her feelings that much? "What about you, Chisisi; you were from the delta region?"

Chisisi's sharp nose wrinkled as he scrutinized me, his hair blowing in the wind. "I've enjoyed the adventure, but perhaps I will make my way in society again … just not building Pharaoh's monuments. Tia, would you join me?"

Chapter 47

Journal Translation

MY STOMACH BURNED WITH distaste as I heard Chisisi's offer to Tia. I wanted the best for Tia, even if I didn't love her. She shouldn't fall for Chisisi—a man of exaggerated words and little action—and leave with him.

Tia's cheeks burned as she glanced down at the hull, her long hair draping over her face. "I'm flattered." She took a breath. "I'd like us all to stay together. If you must leave, Chisisi, I understand. But for me, it is too soon, with all that's happened."

I sighed in relief. Croc rubbed his bony chin against my ankle, and I petted along his deep stripes. The soft hum of his purr vibrated my skin. The only companion who'd been at my side during my previous life. And we were home.

"There will be time before we reach Memphis," Chisisi said. "If I have not won you over by then, it'll be another few weeks until the winds bring us to Thebes." He winked at Tia.

Tia played with her hair, smiling. Perhaps she liked the attention, but I hoped to the Aten that she didn't fall for him. I could tell her about Chisisi running from the Cyclops with the king, but any smart man might have done so, looking for another way out of that situation.

"Wahankh," I said. "Where will you feel free?"

Wahankh wore a smile, but it faded quickly. He'd been silent since fleeing the ramparts in Phaistos. Standing on muscular legs, he paced about, his sandaled feet slapping on the wood of the hull. "This will sound strange, and I know I haven't pulled my weight, but I've never felt so safe as I have with this group. Especially with the brothers, and with Chisisi as our leader. If you leave me in Egypt, I will worry every day that someone will recognize me and drag me back into slavery. There I will waste away, again fearing life itself. I cannot go back … I will follow the brothers to Nubia and may take up residence there, if they will have me."

Harkhuf's bearded chin jutted back and his upper lip wrinkled, but Tia reached out and tugged on his shoulder. Seneb smiled and said, "We may find a use for you."

Harkhuf glanced at Tia, his features relaxing. Some piece of him had returned after he'd helped save her. Hopefully he could do the same for his own family.

"I am ready to return home," Harkhuf muttered, his tone scratchy, as if afraid.

"Paramessu," I said, glancing at the captain. His head was leaned back, his eyes closed. "We will have to leave you a good distance from any major city, or military station, so you can't report where we are."

Paramessu nodded. "I understand."

"But tell your father everything," I said. "He cannot hold you responsible, as there was nothing you could've done."

The captain's pale eyes popped open like a surprised serpent's. "You know nothing of my father and the military," he snapped. "I am and have always been a failure. This experience will only confirm it. I knew you were the escaped slaves, and I remember whipping your flesh! And I wish I would've died fighting those creatures. I'd face them again a thousand times over rather than walk the hall to my father's quarters."

Tense silence. I swallowed.

"But," Paramessu said through gritted teeth, "you saved my life when we first met, and I told you I would not forget. I will never turn you in. I will simply"—he paused and rubbed his head and red hair as if in pain—"lie. I will say you took my ship and we sailed into the sea. The storm must have killed everyone, but a merchant found me floating amongst the wreckage. They'd never believe the actual truth anyway. Not only of the Cyclops, but that I faced off with them. I have never lied … and my father will believe me. The search for you will be over."

"You will make a great commander one day," Tia said, touching his arm.

Paramessu's eyes closed as his head slumped and his shoulders heaved. He didn't believe her.

We rode against the Nile's current, our white sail billowing like a cloud and carrying us past small towns and farmlands. The areas appeared more desolate than I remembered. We slipped through Memphis's glorious walls, which ringed the river and towered over the landscape. Egyptians at the docks carried or unloaded crates but stopped and stared as we passed.

"Most people here would still recognize a boat of the Sea People's," Paramessu said, nodding at the dock's workers, "or at least know it is not Egyptian."

"How about it?" Chisisi asked Tia. "Want to try for a family?"

Tia laughed but shook her head.

* * *

A week or more later, the bends in the river and the empty farmlands stretched for miles. Few houses dotted the desert. The Aten beat down on us like sunbathing reptiles as we approached the midway point between northern Memphis and southern Thebes. Fear tightened my throat as I thought of el-Amarna.

Spittle flew from Chisisi's mouth as he laughed at something he told Tia. Croc stretched out in the shade of the sail and mast, hiding from the midday sun. Paramessu's red hair shone brilliantly as he scouted around, likely anticipating the new capital at any moment. I wished he didn't have to go.

"Once we're a safe distance beyond el-Amarna," Chisisi shouted over the gusting wind, "you can let the soldier off."

Buildings filled the eastern bank, clustered in the center but also sprawling along the length of the river. The sparkling city of the Aten was complete. The reign of Akhenaten had ensnared all of Egypt.

Fear crept into my heart—my former master still controlling me. Ducking into the hull, I peeked over the edge in curiosity. Time slowed as I spotted unfamiliar people lying in the shade along the shore, escaping the heat. Palaces towered below the twin-peaked horizon that we'd fled over.

A bridge stretched between two tall buildings, the window where Akhenaten had appeared in my vision through the fox's eyes. Where he had showered his faithful with gifts and presented his son. How they loved him in spite of Egypt's waning prosperity. The vision must not have been false.

A great north-south road connected the palaces. Akhenaten probably still paraded himself upon it on a daily basis in his chariot of gold. My stomach burned like acid. My only consolation, and mere at that, were the two images—the Feather of Truth and an image of Bes—I'd engraved and hidden in that one mud brick I'd used to construct a small house. Wishing that one day those images would bring answers and hope to some slave, I gritted my teeth until my cheeks ached.

I needed to return my friends to their homelands and make sure they were safe. But above all, I needed to find the treasure of Amenhotep and return to face Akhenaten and Nefertiti—no matter what outcome that might bring. How long could a man live burying such rage? It had already taken its toll, probably years, on my heart and soul.

Croc was perched like a sphinx when he released a low hiss and flicked his tail. Leaping to the rail of the boat with claws extended, he glared out at the city and then down to the river. The fur on his back and tail stood on end. My fingers dug into the cracked wood of the rudder. Could the Devouring Monster still be looking for me?

The city slowly faded from view as we sailed on.

When the sun hung low in the sky and el-Amarna was miles behind us, I steered our vessel to the western shore. Sand grated against the bottom of the hull—grabbing and slowing the boat—but momentum caused me to lurch forward. Paramessu braced against the rail and stood to disembark.

"The best of luck to the greatest slaves I've ever met," the captain said, and his strong jaw clenched. He gathered his supplies and smiled at us, his gaze longing over Tia. Those pale eyes of his softened, as I had not seen before.

Tia raised a hand in goodbye.

Did Paramessu also like Tia? Sympathy rose in my chest like stomach acid. I understood what it was to love and not have the feeling recipro-cated. "We couldn't have gotten home without you," I said. "And you helped saved Tia."

Tia's nose wrinkled. She climbed over the boat onto shore and kissed Paramessu on the cheek.

My heart leapt with happiness, warmth, and hope.

"He didn't do anything more than I," Chisisi said, his tone carrying a sharpened edge. "But he should go. He's one of them."

Croc hissed. His tail puffed up to three times its normal size and his pupils dilated like orbs.

Chapter 48

Journal Translation

A LOW GROWL ESCAPED Croc's lips as he paced along the edge of our boat, staring into the river.

Water sprayed from the Nile. Jaws burst out, snapping through the erupting mist. A knife with serrated teeth and a golden hilt followed.

I gasped in horror.

The jaws protruded from beneath a draping hood of black and snatched Paramessu around the chest. With one quick twist, the Devouring Monster opened its mouth and flung the captain's limp body into Tia. They toppled over.

Hands and claws like a lion's clutched onto the edge of our boat. Reptilian eyes stared at me. I couldn't move or even breathe. Summoned from the stuff of nightmares—this monster could devour souls. There was no greater terror.

The monster sprang aboard, and our boat bucked underneath its massive weight. I fell onto my back, smacking into hard wood. The Devouring Monster stalked me and released a high-pitched hiss, its black cloak streaming water onto the hull.

The dwarf brothers leapt at the monster with jabbing spears, but the monster backhanded the striking weapons aside like reeds of papyrus, flinging Seneb and Harkhuf onto their backs.

Orange and white sailed through the air at the beast. Croc, the tiny fury, bit and clawed as he grew. The pair stumbled and fell into the river with a splash. A spray of murky water pelted my face and body with stinging droplets.

Croc!

I scrambled to my feet. As a kitten, I'd saved Croc from drowning—his greatest weakness.

The ripples smoothed out. I heaved for breath, my stomach knotting as my heart dropped. My best friend had—

"Let's get out of here!" Wahankh yelled, paddling.

"Wait!" a voice called. Paramessu's hooked nose flashed up, but his eyes were closed. Tia cradled his limp body in her arms. "We're coming aboard! I will not lose his soul!"

Harkhuf wrapped Wahankh in a bear hug so he could not continue paddling. I bounded out into the shallow water, the murk gripping to my thighs and slowing my steps. But I helped drag Paramessu back to the boat. Seneb hauled him in and laid the redheaded man in the hull. Tia climbed aboard and rowed with all her might.

I remained in the water, considering if I should dive in and try to help Croc. Could the monster swallow his—

Strong hands gripped under my shoulders, hoisted me into the boat, and shoved me to the rudder. I stumbled across the hull as a haze clouded my thoughts. Croc! But I took the oar and back paddled. Wind caught the sail and propelled us south.

Tears brimmed in my eyes with a sting as I scanned the placid water near the bank. I'd put everyone at risk by coming back here. Now I'd cost Croc his life—he must've drown by now! I punched my thigh with utter contempt, the dull thud radiating through my muscles. I was a terrible person and worse, a dangerous leader.

Tia rocked Paramessu's unconscious body in her arms and brushed dripping vegetation from his face. "It didn't devour his heart, d-did it?" Her voice cracked as her lips trembled.

Harkhuf patted Tia's head, his face almost as pale as Paramessu's skin.

Blood dripped from a row of teeth punctures running across Paramessu's chest and abdomen. Deep purple bruises formed across his body. His ribcage was misshapen, crushed from the force of the snapping jaws. But no bones or organs protruded.

I dropped the rudder and felt along the cold skin of his torso. Hard lumps ran down his side. "I think he has broken ribs," I said, recalling what I'd studied of medicine and injury. "Shards of bone can damage the lungs, but his breathing appears stable. His heart's still in place, so his soul is fine. But if that creature broke his back, he may never move again. Keep him still."

Tia trembled as she leaned back. "I beg you all, please let him stay with us, at least until he recovers. It was my fault we stopped for so long. I am the reason he was hurt."

"He needs care and love right now," I whispered, the tender words falling from my lips as if they were not my own.

"I am incapable of such emotion," Tia whispered, cradling Paramessu's head. "Like you. But I will care for him." Her eyes closed, and crystal tears cascaded down her cheeks.

"He's brought us nothing but bad luck," Chisisi said and his nostrils flared, his words probably coated in jealousy, "pursuing militia, the sea, the island. Now this. We will leave him."

"We're not dumping a man out to die," I replied.

Chisisi folded his arms and scowled. "When he gets us all killed, this will be on you." He pointed at my heart.

I returned to the rudder and steered our merchant vessel into the belly of the river. But dread filled my chest. The others glanced over their shoulders at me. What were they thinking, that I'd made a terrible decision? I already had too much death weighing on my soul.

"Harkhuf, we'll take you and Seneb home," I said through clenched teeth, "but none of you will stay with me when I return. You can choose where to go, but you *will* be getting off."

"You believe that monster wants you more than the rest of us," Chisisi said as he glanced back at me, his knuckles white on his paddle. "We all escaped el-Amarna."

"Akhenaten wants *me* to suffer and my *ba* to be consumed!" I said.

"Arrogance?" Chisisi said. "In a former—"

Chisisi's ramblings drowned out in the wind. Pain bit into my heart. Croc was gone. Emotions swirled in a jumble of love and hate, like when thinking of Nefertiti. Raising my sword to my forehead, I shaved with the sharpened edge—the blade gliding across my skin with a gental tug.

"What are you doing?" Seneb shouted, leaping and grabbing my arm, as if he were worried I was going to kill myself.

Both of my eyebrows came clean off, drifting and scattering into the wind like petals of a flower. A trickle of blood ran down the bridge of my nose, and the warm fluid sank into my eyes. "Mourning Croc's passing," I said, wiping at the blood. "It is customary for any civilized Egyptian, with the loss of their pet. And for Croc, the gesture is far too insignificant."

"Like a rabid monkey before it attacks its own tribe," Seneb said, his eyes gaping as he studied my face.

Chisisi stepped between Tia and Paramessu and covered her dripping-wet body with a robe of the Sea People's. He studied her for a moment, touched her face, and turned away to rest in the shade of the hull, alone.

Tia rinsed Paramessu's wounds as the captain drifted in and out of consciousness. When she dripped water into his mouth, his eyes fluttered and opened. He cried out in pain, then his head fell limp again.

Days crawled by. We encountered only passing vessels at a distance upon the wide river.

Paramessu eventually ate and drank without Tia supporting his head. He wiggled his toes and winced. "It hurts to breathe," he said.

But by the time we passed Thebes, he could hobble about the boat—although with his thudding limp he'd never be able to sneak up on anyone.

My heart still ached for Croc. How I wished to feel his soft fur rub against my ankle and to stroke under his chin. We used to sleep together every night when I worked as Akhenaten's servant. My happiest times ...

We sailed beyond the mysterious island of Elephantine to the farthest reaches of Egypt. The soldiers of Aswan stopped us and demanded a tariff for the use of the river. We gave them a crate of Keftian olive oil, and they happily sent us on our way.

We docked before the first cataract of rushing rapids, which roared like a pride of lions, and continued on foot with a cart of supplies. Paramessu walked and even jogged a bit before he leaned over with his hands on his knees. Tia placed his arm around her shoulders and helped him along.

An empty road led us south into Nubia. We journeyed for weeks, and I faithfully studied and trained every evening. The others joined in on the training part and sparred together and with me.

Tia grimaced as she lunged with the blunt end of her spear at Chisisi. Chisisi knocked her weapon aside, hitting her on the shoulder with the shaft of his spear. He laughed. "You can never fight a man. There's no use in you training to do so. It's like being a leader; you have to be a man to do it well."

Tia's upper lip wrinkled, and she spun away. Paramessu caught her by the wrist, stopping in the midst of sparring with me. "Let me show you." He switched her grip over on her weapon, his hand lingering on hers. "Like this," he said. He stepped away and made a slow strike with his spear, which she deflected with her shield. "You have to start slow to learn, then you grow faster. He can't teach you if his primary objective is to belittle you." Paramessu nodded at Chisisi.

"You did something well," Harkhuf said to me, chewing bread, "back on the island."

Paramessu thrust his spear at me, catching me off guard. The blunt end of his weapon jammed into my forearm with a painful crack.

Tia applauded. I groaned in frustration and rubbed at the throbbing area.

"And Heb is easily distracted," Paramessu said to Tia.

"What, and when?" I asked the dwarf, sheathing my swords.

"Someone taught you how to defang the snake," Harkhuf said.

I cocked my head.

"When you battled the Cyclops, you fought as you protected yourself, instead of using weak parries like you are rehearsing now."

"When I cut its wrist?" I asked.

"Yes," Harkhuf said. "What did that make the monster do?"

"He dropped his club," I said.

"Exactly! You defanged the snake."

"Like a black mamba with no venom," Seneb said.

Harkhuf retrieved his spear and jabbed the weapon at me. The sharpened point barreled toward my throat. I swung at the shaft to knock it down, but he was ready. Avoiding my counter, he circled around with the spear and thrust it back at my chest. My sword had already passed by, its momentum carrying my arm and defenses away. The tip of his spear stuck into my skin with a painful slice. I winced as blood trickled down my stomach.

Harkhuf lowered his spear. "Parrying can save your life, but it does nothing to defeat your opponent ... save perhaps tire him. Why not treat everything that comes at you as a target, a chance to inflict damage? I don't want any of you swiping back and forth for your attacker's face like"—he paused, his chin wrinkling in thought—"untrained people."

Seneb shook his head in disappointment at the comparison. "Thugs with knives?"

Harkhuf continued, "Your target is always out of reach that way. Now figure it out. Paramessu, jab him again."

The captain's spear shot forward at me. Ducking the strike, I swung the flat of my blade for his lead hand. Metal clanged against bone, and the vibrations carried up to my elbow.

Howling, Paramessu dropped his spear and clutched his fingers as he jumped up and down, as if the action would ease his pain.

Harkhuf roared with laughter. "Now imagine what you could do to him."

I straightened and scratched an itch from the stubbly brows regrowing above my eyes.

Chapter 49

Journal Translation

W E TRAVELED DEEP INTO NUBIA. The foliage grew thicker and more colorful, releasing exotic scents that clung to the air like perfume. The plains became more open, the jungles denser. Every so often we glimpsed what must be an endless Nile cutting through the landscape. The river was no less magnificent, but it raged with rapids, here, near its roots—even though I still could not see its beginning. Beasts with necks so long they could reach leaves in the highest trees loped off like men on stilts. Herds of antelope, in numbers greater than the men in Memphis, stampeded away. Speckled cats took down the strays. Gray-skinned beasts the size of two buildings, with huge ears, trunks, and tusks, hollered and stomped when they spotted us. We diverted our path to give them plenty of space, but their trumpeting choruses still made my ears ring.

A mud-brick fortress surrounded by deep trenches towered over the lands. A temple resided inside the walls, covered with sand and overgrown with brush.

"So this is what has befallen mighty Khaemmaat at Soleb," Paramessu said, his pale eyes passing over the southern walls. "Amenhotep the Third's governance stretched all the way to these fortifications. The last outpost against the unknown of Nubia. But not too many years ago, Egypt had to retract its borders."

I stood in awe as this forsaken land stole the moisture from my mouth. So mighty a fortress, left in ruin. Had the soldiers who'd once stood upon the ramparts fought the mysterious Dark Ones, or had they only fought other men resembling Harkhuf and Seneb?

"We have many miles to travel before we lay eyes on the kingdom of Kush," Harkhuf said, his Nubian accent having grown thicker, which made it hard to understand him. He plowed on with his head down.

Seneb nudged me, his elbow digging into my hip, and whispered, his accent also having increased a little, "His demons' voices, the ones you cannot understand, are growing louder. I must be there for him, but I fear the future." His fingers opened and closed upon the shaft of his spear.

We broke from the great road and followed a trail, hiked under trees, across grassy plains, and weeks to months later—at one time I attempted to track days on papyrus but forgot more often than I remembered—came upon a settlement.

As we ducked under the low branches of a lone tree, monkeys squawked above. The soft smell of grass surrounded us, but something else also hung in the air.

"Where is the thunder of the drums?" Seneb asked as he glanced about. "The eternal banners of foliage, calling us home?"

Huts rested on stilts, overgrown with grass. The remains of other structures—log foundations—were blackened by fire.

"No dark-skinned men or beautiful women in colorful loincloths," Seneb said, his eyes wide as he studied the village, muttering to himself. "No reed hats or beaded necklaces or hoop earrings."

Eerie quiet descended as the grasses stopped swaying.

Seneb and Harkhuf hobbled around the village for hours, as if injured, conversing in their own tongue. No people or souls remained. Seneb's wide eyes and boyish face darkened. Harkhuf cursed and smashed a fist through the straw wall of a hut. He threw his bow into the dirt and stomped around, his face contorted with emotion.

I followed behind the brothers and looked around.

Inside the dark huts, hunks of bread sat on tables, and chairs were pushed back as if the people had been forced to leave on a moment's notice. But the bread was moldy and decomposing, and everything was covered in a thick layer of dust. What could've made these people leave so suddenly, however long ago?

Surely Akhenaten's terror couldn't reach this far …

I withdrew the warm ostrich feather from my kilt and twirled it in my palms, watching the sun's rays reflect off of the deep blue. The fronds at the bottom of the feather tickled my hand. Akhenaten had given me the Feather of Truth as a reminder of how I betrayed him, but one day I'd have him remember the real truth, and I'd show all of Egypt ...

In the evening, the brothers gave up their search. We sat cross-legged on soft grass and consumed a meal of exotic roots. The pungent aroma of garlic combined with the bite of pepper and earthy starches coated my tongue and throat. A fire danced at the center of our group, its light shining on the blades of grass around us, its thick smoke mixing with the spiced food. Darkness ate away at our surroundings. What a different life I'd have lived if I hadn't grown up in a land of farmers ...

I gnawed on a white tuber as the brothers sat in silence—Harkhuf not eating and his fists still shaking.

Night's hours crawled by. "We've returned too late," Seneb said, firelight and shadows dancing across his boyish features. "Darkness spreads across the earth like a plague. Everyone is missing."

"Perhaps they just had to move," Chisisi said. "Do they follow the herds?"

"Unless they are all dead or they had to flee on a moment's notice, they would leave a trail for those left behind," Seneb said. "One you may not see, but we would."

Tia massaged Seneb's neck with her fingerstips. A tear rolled down his cheeks.

"We were gone too long, and our families needed us." Seneb cried into his hands. "I always imagined they were living in peace, ever since we were taken ..."

Why was there so much evil in this world? My eyes closed in frustration. Those who only want power and to have others suffer?

"I saw a trail," Harkhuf grumbled as he stared into the fire, his voice distant.

Silence.

"Like the footprints in the snow on the island mountain?" I asked.

Harkhuf shook his head. "Besides the remains of burnt huts, which happened years ago, there's no sign of a struggle anywhere, no overturned furniture, broken items, or blood."

"So, that's your trail?" I asked. "The lack of … but that something, or someone, who had their trust lured them away?"

"Or frightened them off," Tia said between bites of leafy greens. "They left all of their belongings, some time ago. Whatever happened, their attackers may no longer even be in the region."

Chisisi watched Tia with hungry eyes. "I say we try to find whoever or whatever is responsible and where they've gone before we leave the brothers and Wahankh in Kush. We've certainly dealt with worse."

Wahankh groaned, stood, and wandered away into the night.

"But only those responsible may know where our people are," Harkhuf said, still not blinking as orange flames reflected in his eyes. "I would like to disembowel them at first sight, or die trying, more so than anything I've ever done!"

"Therein lies our problem," Seneb said, resting a hand on Harkhuf's knee. "We must be wise in spite of overwhelming emotion. Someone with self-control must befriend whoever is responsible and gain their trust so that we may learn where our tribe has gone. The plains are too vast to find them by mere chance."

"I do not think it was a man," Harkhuf said. He held something aloft, twirling it around in the firelight. The carcass of a bug—a locust. But this one had two heads, crowded beside each other. Its glistening eyes stared back at me.

My stomach flipped with disgust. Such an abomination could not be natural, even for such a foreign land.

"I found a couple of these around the huts and along the main trail," Harkhuf said.

Seneb's mouth gaped. "Nothing's pretty at home when you haven't been there to take care of it," he whispered. "Our excuses for leaving do not matter … even if we were taken."

My heart twinged as I wondered about my home. Did I keep running on purpose, to ease the pain? But all this time Akhenaten lived the grandest life of anyone on Earth, with my Nefertiti. My fingernails dug into my palms with stabbing pain that still did not distract me from my thoughts.

I wandered off and entered an empty hut, where I lay down. Sleep eventually took me …

A lone tree appeared at the edge of a jungle in my dream. I stared into the depths of limbs and vines beyond. An antelope limped out of abyss. The tendon over its knee extruded through a gash. Absent skin revealed twitching muscles as the animal hobbled as fast as it could, its eyes wide and its breathing fierce. It glanced over its shoulder and fled.

Something stepped out of the vines—a child with black skin. Not dark brown like other Nubians, but flesh that was black and crisp, as if it had been seared by fire. The child pursued the antelope, closing the gap between them without hurrying. A Dark One? But my other visions of Dark Ones had been cloaks of black with linen-bound heads. My heart pounded in fear. I couldn't move. Sinking behind the tree trunk and down into the waving grass, I held my breath. I couldn't make myself help the animal, although I knew I should.

The hoofed feet of the antelope and the pursuing child snapped through foliage. A crinkling—from burnt skin—drew closer. The animal screamed. Then the gnashing of something chewing on flesh filled the emptiness, along with the crunch of bone. The overwhelming smell of death ... I waited in silence, stifling my breath.

A moment passed, and then another.

I peeked around the tree and over the brown grass.

The burnt child sniffed the air, as if it sensed my presence. I crouched low. I was a coward. The child turned and reentered the jungle—

Light fluttered. Warm sweat coated my brow and soaked my short hair. Wiping the perspiration away with the back of my hand, I sat up. The hut I slept in was still empty. Where was everyone?

I leapt out of the hut and down the steps.

My companions ate breakfast near the smoldering fire. The sun had risen over the eastern plains.

Tia carried a plate of colorful fruit past me and touched my cheek with a tender palm. "I thought we better let you sleep. You looked like you might be fighting an illness."

Harkhuf sat in the same spot from last night. Had he slept at all? But instead of staring blankly into the fire, he examined a cylindrical reed with a point.

"Is that a dart?" I asked.

Harkhuf grunted. "Found it buried in the straw wall of a hut. Whoever left it didn't see it and so couldn't remove the evidence."

Paramessu stepped closer and stared at the object.

"These weapons are typically coated with poison," Seneb said, standing and pacing beside his brother. "We've seen people from the jungle use it against us in the past. It can paralyze a man within seconds."

"Is there a jungle near here?" I asked, reaching for an orange root vegetable that sizzled on a pan over the fire. A vision of my dream—the burnt child emerging from dense foliage—popped into my mind.

"A few miles farther south, the road skirts the great jungle," Harkhuf said as he absently rolled the dart between thick fingers. "I will go there."

"Then we will all go," Chisisi said and bit into a yellow fruit with red-tinted skin. Juice and mush spread across his cheeks.

I inhaled the orange tuber, which left a sweet taste in my mouth, and followed the others along a dusty trail leading farther away from Egypt. Harkhuf led us with his head down, as if driven by need but not wanting to face whatever it was we searched for. Seneb marched at his heels.

Dense trees and vines emerged on our right, stretching as far as I could see.

"Be wary," Harkhuf said. "The jungle is not forgiving ... even for natives. Inside the gloom lurks creatures that can kill a man with a single bite or sting. And don't let size fool you; some of the smallest are the most dangerous."

"What is that?" Seneb asked, pointing into the midday sunlight.

A dwelling was dug into a hillside in the distance before the threshold of the jungle.

Harkhuf shook his head. "That's new. No one lives alone out here; they'd never survive."

"Only one of us will go," Chisisi said, "or whoever lives there will never believe this is a friendly visit for information. And it has to be one of you." He pointed at the two Nubian brothers.

"I don't trust myself," Harkhuf grumbled. "I will lose patience."

"I wouldn't trust you either," Seneb said, patting his brother's striated tricep.

"I will do it," Wahankh said, striding for the hill, his hands trembling on his weapon and shield. "I will earn my right to stay here."

"You won't be able to speak to them," Seneb said, grabbing Wahankh's arm and stopping him.

Seneb marched for the hillside and to a door composed of bound sticks. He lugged a sack of food—a gift—and lowered his weapons.

The entryway was shadowed by dense foliage that hung over the hill. Branches and vines reached from the jungle like fingers trying to ensnare the dwelling.

The rest of us crouched in the tall grass, watching between waving stems, as if we were lions.

Seneb knocked and shouted.

The door swung outward. A narrow face with short, black hair appeared. A lanky man stepped out and surveyed the area with a hand at his forehead. I dropped lower. He spoke with Seneb and gestured with his other hand. Seneb chatted as if he were a neighbor asking to borrow a tool.

Minutes crawled by.

The man stepped aside and allowed Seneb to enter his dwelling. The door closed. Springing up, I sprinted for the door but veered and clambered through scratching brush, ascending the hill that the house was dug into. I reached the top and beheld a scene I was not prepared for.

Chapter 50

Journal Translation

A SMALL FARM STRETCHED ACROSS the backside of the hill-dwelling at the threshold of the jungle. But there were no crops, only an array of creatures. Three goats were tied to stakes and wandered the hillside, nibbling on grass. Each had extra limbs growing from their shoulders, which hung useless at their sides. Rodents, not restrained in any way, chattered at each other while digging in the dirt … no, these creatures had no limbs at all. Hoards of two-headed locusts piled on top of each other, scuttling around a mound. The stench of rot and animal waste mixed with flowering brush. My pulse weakened, and my head spun. I wavered.

Tia stifled a scream with her hand. Paramessu heaved and vomited. The yellow froth and chunks that hit the ground began to move as finger-length worms protruded from the earth and writhed in the fluid.

My stomach flipped in disgust. Retreating, we all hid in the swaying grass around the hill and waited. Hours rolled by as terrible scenarios ran through my mind.

"I can't sit here any longer!" I said, standing. "Seneb could've been murdered and buried by now."

"It's not your family who is missing!" Harkhuf said, grabbing my bronze bracelet with a grip that felt like he might crush the metal into my bones.

I knelt back down. A breeze rolled through, making the grasses poke my skin. Itching arose across my back.

"If Seneb doesn't appear by sunset, we force our way in," Harkhuf grumbled.

We waited. The sun descended behind the trees.

Standing, Harkhuf marched for the hill, an arrow resting on his relaxed bowstring.

The door in the hillside swung open, and the lanky man stepped out into the twilight. He spotted us, his eyes showing pure white against his dark skin.

Seneb exited and waved for us to come forward with a forced smile. Harkhuf lowered his bow.

My muscles tensed in apprehension, my fingers reaching for my swords.

"This man has been cursed for eternity," Seneb said, whispering as we approached. "He has lived forty lifetimes. But they are all the same. A demon spirit has poisoned every location he's lived, and his animals. That is why he hides here, alone. And he is sorry for any trouble he has brought upon his neighbors. A child burnt in the pits of the underworld stalks the area at night but will never put this man out of his misery."

I froze, recalling my dream.

"He does not know where our people were taken and was not even aware of them," Seneb said. "But the jackals come every night he sees the demon child. Together, the beasts and this child journey into the jungle to perform evil deeds. They may've had something to do with our tribe's disappearance."

I recalled the jackal-headed Mummy Makers I'd seen in Memphis. Such dogs were always associated with the dead. An ill feeling formed in my guts.

"We could see them tonight," Seneb said, "but the size of our group will scare them away if we all try to follow them."

We waited together with the cursed man outside of his doorway.

The moon rose in the sky, growing nearly as large as the Aten. Pale light streamed around us. The wind died out, stopping the waving of the grasses. Tia hovered beside Paramessu, her shield and spear in front of them—ready to utilize all of her recent training.

"I do not trust this situation, or that man's explanation," Chisisi said, scooting over to Tia. His upper lip wrinkled as he studied Paramessu.

The cursed man rose on legs resembling the slender tree trunks around us. He pointed across the plains. Dark shapes crept through the grass and shadows, headed for the jungle.

My fingers tightened around the tense sinew of my bowstring.

One of the approaching beasts stopped, and its head perked up to scan the area. Moonlight glinted in its eyes. The jackals broke into a lope, crunching through grass like fleeing prey as they darted into the jungle.

The cursed man snuck after them and motioned for us to follow. He held up three fingers and pointed at the two dwarves.

"Only three of us can go," Seneb said.

Wahankh crept after the brothers.

The cursed man shook his narrow face and hissed something.

"You're too big," Seneb said to Wahankh. "They'll see you."

"I will face the demon," Tia said, but Paramessu quickly pulled her back to his chest.

Seneb grunted something to the cursed man, who waved his arms and replied.

"Heb is the only other who can go," Seneb said, and then grimaced. "This man is old fashioned and believes women are property and should not speak freely. He says we have given our woman too much power. She's been put on this earth to satisfy men and raise children …"

My forehead tightened with surprise and then anger. His opinions reminded me of Akhenaten and of my past. Distrust tightened my stomach like a winding cord. Tia's face wrinkled in disgust.

"He says to not let the jackals spot you," Seneb said, waving me forward. "They are the eyes of the demon child. If they see you, the demon sees you. Then we will die."

Seneb and Harkhuf crept off.

I cringed. Perhaps I should stay behind; I'd already cost too many their lives. But what if the brothers died because I didn't go? Which would be worse?

Taking a deep breath, I picked my way through dry grass and brush that wrapped around me like a cloak. The cursed man crouched next to a bush at the threshold of the jungle and pinched a tuft of fur that was stuck to a branch. Nodding in the direction the jackals had gone, the stranger led us in. Twisting shadows from a labyrinth of intertwining branches limited my visibility to a few feet.

My skin crawled, as if the deformed bugs on the hillside wiggled beneath it. Who was this man, really? I'd seen enough magic to believe his story could be true, but it seemed unlikely. But why else would he choose to live alone, way out here?

Cackles, shrieks, and whoops echoed across the canopy above—the dark shapes of animals leaping about the branches. The stubbly hair on my arms and legs stood up with fear as the bronze on my forearm turned cold. I could only imagine what creatures created such noises. The moonlight faded to a wisp. How many venomous creatures surrounded us? I shouldn't let this Nubian out of my sight.

I trailed behind the cursed man and the brothers through bushes and groves that smelled of dying blossoms. I stepped into stagnant water that rose up to my thighs—to the chests of the dwarves. The liquid rippled against my skin, its temperature warmer than the air around us. Quiet splashes sounded with every step I made. Droplets of viscous water from the swamp dripped from my arms and weapons, plopping onto the dark surface.

We exited the swamp via soggy ground that sucked at my sandals, and we clambered down a ravine. My feet and hands slipped on damp leaves and fungus until I reached the bottom.

The cursed man raised slender arms. He pointed into a clearing ahead where moonlight flooded over a rocky hill.

Chapter 51

Journal Translation

STRAINING TO SEE IN the moonlight, I squinted and studied the rocky hill within the clearing of the jungle.

A four-legged shadow of a creature ascended the peak and glanced back. Dropping to the ground as if he'd been struck, the cursed man hissed. We followed suit, and a lumpy root dug into my stomach. I peeked between low-hanging leaves the size of my chest. Reflective eyes darted over our vicinity.

A jackal.

I focused on remaining absolutely still. My lungs burned with each shallow breath.

The creature turned and slunk down the other side of the hill, its ratty tail silhouetted against the full moon, and disappeared.

Our guide crawled on all fours into the clearing and ran his hand through the short grass as if feeling for tracks. He whispered to Seneb.

"He's making sure the entire pack passed through and that one isn't luring us into a trap," Seneb said.

I swallowed. I hadn't even considered that option.

The cursed man approached the rocky hill, dropped to his stomach, and inched up the incline. When his eyes neared the ridgeline, his body jerked, and he froze. I pulled myself along, my belly dragging against sharp rock as my gaze crested the peak.

Jackals! They circled with their tails in the air, sniffing along the ground. The soft patter of their footfalls carried through the deathly still air around us. In the middle of their circle lay a pool of crystal water that reflected the sky and full moon like a mirror of the finest quality. Not a ripple disrupted its surface.

The silhouette of a child knelt at the water's edge. My hand slipped, and I wheezed as my throat constricted with terror. Pebbles tumbled from my foothold, clattering down the hill.

Ducking, the cursed man put a finger to his lips. His eyes were the size of gourds, his sweat reeking of fear.

After waiting a few minutes, we glanced back over the hill. The child was gone. So were the jackals. Ripples carried away from the center of the pool.

The cursed man said something to Seneb, and the man's tongue stuck out of his mouth as he looked to the sky.

"This is Demon's Hole," Seneb whispered.

The man kept muttering as his wild eyes darted about.

"We have to look into the face of death for answers, but he's not coming with us," Seneb said, swallowing with a gulp.

Harkhuf took a deep breath, as if these would be the last moments of his life, before he crept down to the pool. Seneb followed.

I watched for jackals, expecting them to come charging from the tree line. The sinew of my bowstring bit into my fingers as I drew it back to my right ear, and the old wood creaked with tension. Another twenty feet to the water. I inched after the brothers. Wild dogs could leap from the jungle and be upon us before we'd have time to react …

The toe of my sandal sank into cold water. "Don't everyone look down at once," I whispered, watching the tangled vines around us.

Seneb screamed. Harkhuf fell to his knees and dropped his bow.

I looked down …

The water in the pond was crystal clear, and it stretched down into earth like a tunnel. Something rested in its depths … bodies and skeletons piled together like ants on a hill.

Something whistled past my ear and stuck into my back, feeling like a poke from a thorn. An ear-piercing screech erupted from the jungle, followed by the pounding of wild footsteps. Something with skin as black as ash and white eyes leapt from the brambles onto Seneb's back. Pointed teeth sparkled in the moonlight and sank into the dwarf's neck. Seneb bellowed, his blood spurting like a geyser. My fingers tingled as if they'd fallen asleep. The arrow on my bowstring slipped and fell, and the sinew twanged in an empty shot. More whistling from flying objects carried past my head. Harkhuf ducked, raising his shield. Darts buried into rawhide. My arms and legs turned numb, my mouth opened, and my tongue slipped out. Teetering, I fell onto soft ground with a splat. My eyes were open, watching, but I could barely rotate my neck. Poison on a dart … like the one Harkhuf had found in the hut.

The demon-child raised a stone axe over Seneb's head and screamed. Harkhuf's arrow pierced the open mouth of the monster, silencing it. It fell backward. More footsteps thundered behind me. Harkhuf pivoted and released. His arrow buried into the chest of the cursed man, who swung an axe at my skull. The attacker jerked backward, the velocity of the arrow carrying his body across the grass.

My heart thundered in my chest as I fought to reach for my swords and sit up. But my arms and fingers didn't respond. Another black form burst from the bushes and lunged for Harkhuf. Seneb's spear slammed into the attacker—a woman—dropping her in death. Yipping arose from the jungle. I expected a pack of jackals to charge out.

Seneb yelled and clutched his hemorrhaging neck. Harkhuf fell to his knees as if afflicted with some terror-stricken trance. Hopefully, a dart hadn't struck him. He plunged face-first into the pool and disappeared into the ripples. I gasped as I lay there, immobile. What was he doing?

A few moments later, he resurfaced, holding the body of a dark-skinned woman close to his chest. He cradled her head and wailed, his screams echoing through the jungle. Any natural beast would be too scared to approach us now.

Seneb applied pressure to his neck as he inspected me. He didn't appear prepared for anything else that might jump from the vines around us.

"You can hear me, right?" he asked.

I tried to nod, but my body was numb, as if I were only a severed head. I blinked.

"Don't worry, the poison will wear off by morning," he said, stepped away, and leaned over the bodies of these Dark Ones. He wiped at their skin. A black substance smeared across his palm. "They covered themselves with ash, to scare their victims. There are no demons here, save those buried in the human spirit."

I turned my head as hard as I could. My face flopped over to him.

"I pretended to be a child rather than a dwarf when speaking with the cursed man," Seneb whispered, kneeling beside me and attempting not to stare at Harkhuf, whose sobs still rang out. "I believed that the cursed man was a tortured soul. But after seeing shrines to the Dark Ones inside his home, I knew he was evil. I convinced him that Harkhuf was an adolescent just learning the bow. You are much smaller than Wahankh, so he thought you would be an easy target as well. I couldn't tell you, as he said he understood Egyptian. Sorry about the dart in your back. Harkhuf knew my cues, but we couldn't risk not finding our people. It looks like the cursed man's family was taking them, one by one, to sacrifice them in the name of the Dark Ones. He told me that the Dark Ones are returning, and he wanted to be on the side of the victors."

I wanted to nod my understanding but couldn't. Hours dragged on as the brothers retrieved dead bodies from the pool.

When pink light rose in the east, I struggled but sat up and rubbed my tingling limbs. Feeling slowly returned.

Harkhuf had constructed a sled for the dead woman he'd first surfaced with—his wife? He tenderly placed her on top of a bed of leaves covering the stick frame of the sled, as if he were placing a sleeping child into a crib. Tears gushed from his eyes like waterfalls.

"Was your family not here?" I whispered to Seneb and held my breath.

Seneb shook his head. "I lost my family to the Egyptian slavers ... when they burned our village years ago. Harkhuf is the only family I have. But he will always suffer from his demons. The ones you wouldn't understand."

"I wish to know him," I said, hiking back the way we'd come through the jungle. Glancing back through twisted trunks, I watched Harkhuf as he pulled his sled away from the pond. I recalled the dwarf saying—back when we were slaves—that his tribe's death was his fault. That the slavers had burned his village and captured him. But Harkhuf had thought his wife and daughter could still be alive ...

"He is the best man I know only because of his dark past," Seneb whispered, tugging at my forearm. "I only tell *you* this, and you can never let him or anyone else know. He was a great warrior, but because of his size, he was not accepted by the others. So he practiced with the bow for hours every day, until he could outshoot anyone in our tribe under any circumstance. But still the larger men wouldn't acknowledge his abilities. Over the years bitterness grew inside of him, and because he could not be a warrior, he considered becoming a slave trader. But he'd only do so by turning in an enemy tribe—those inside this very jungle. He discovered the unsuspecting tribe's location and was thinking about selling the information to the Egyptians. I told him not to sacrifice our rivals to our greatest enemy, but he was angry at everyone, at life."

Images of Akhenaten—his shortcomings, deformities, and being treated as an outcast—popped into my mind. Such treatment led to vicious retaliation.

"I've never seen anyone love his wife or daughter more than Harkhuf," Seneb continued. "But, yes, after years of not being accepted, even though his skills with the bow were superior to any two men combined, he finally met with the Egyptian slavers. He sold out our rivals, but the Egyptians also tricked him into revealing more and tracked him home. They raided our own village. Then he experienced the nightmare he'd created for our enemies. The Egyptians bound us and dragged us away to become their dancing puppets. They burned our village while others fled."

My gut twisted in horror.

"But before you condemn my brother, remember, *that* Harkhuf has been dead for years. He now wages war with his demons every sleeping and waking minute, attempting to right some of the wrongs of his past. He has never found peace with himself, and though it seems like he may hate others, it is himself he despises the most. That is why he was so hard on you when we met. That was why he was too afraid to return. He couldn't face it. Even if his family was alive, he couldn't face his wife and daughter, not once they knew he was responsible for the Egyptians taking us and for causing as much suffering for others. He doesn't think he even deserves their forgiveness. But Harkhuf always wanted to believe his family still frolicked through the plains of Kush, laughing and missing him."

Seneb swallowed and closed his eyes.

"That woman on the sled back there"—he motioned behind us—"isn't even his wife. That was a tribe member's wife. Neither his wife nor his daughter was down there, but I think he's finally accepted their fate. He needs some type of closure and burial or neither of us can go on living." Seneb took a deep breath, his fingers quivering. "May his family frolic through the fields of the underworld or show up here one day and grant him everlasting happiness. But I don't believe he will ever forgive himself. Only death may finally grant *my* brother peace."

Yipping sounded through the trees behind us.

Chapter 52

Journal Translation

BEHIND HARKHUF AND HIS SLED, four jackals appeared at the banks of the pond.

I grabbed an arrow and nocked it. But the animals approached the dead bodies of the cursed family, sniffed, and dragged them off into the jungle.

These beasts did not wield magic; they only came to claim the dead—probably the only reason they hung around the area—simply nature at work.

I released a long breath, stashed my arrow away, and retraced our path back to our companions.

Over the next week, we retrieved and buried the victims within the pond called Demon's Hole. Harkhuf freed the goats from the hill-dwelling at the edge of the jungle and lit a torch. He touched the flame to dry brush, and the disturbing farm and house went up in a cloud of black smoke. A sickening stench similar to burning hair filled the air and scratched at my throat. I coughed and gagged. Perhaps I'd never understand this cursed man and his family. Such was the world.

But on our march back to the abandoned huts of Harkhuf and Seneb's people, my mind cleared, as if a fog were lifted by the cleansing fire.

Harkhuf remained silent, his posture broken. He hadn't eaten for days. My heart ached with sympathy for him. And if Seneb couldn't save him, then who could? Me? I attempted to imagine how he felt, his life more horrid and guilt-ridden than even mine. But how much different could his emotional turmoil be? I held plenty of guilt—betraying Akhenaten and Egypt, failing Nefertiti, Mutnedjmet, Croc, Yuf, and Father …

"I am so sorry for your loss," I said to Harkhuf early one morning while sitting around our smoldering campfire in the abandoned village. I was not sure how to bring up the subject with this gruff man.

Tia and Paramessu served starchy vegetables that wafted an aroma of fired garlic. Tia paused before me and stared.

"You can't change the past," I whispered to Harkhuf. "Believe me, I wish I could change mine. Whatever happened, the only choice you now have is to change your fate."

"Leave me alone, Egyptian," he growled. "You can't understand my suffering." He balled up a fist as if he'd strike me if I pressed him further.

Tia stepped between us. "The loss of a wife and daughter is more than I, or anyone here, could imagine," she said, her voice like a gentle breeze. "I will not downplay your suffering, and like Heb means to say, you have every right to mourn for the rest of your life. I never thought I'd love another man in this world besides my father. But I see raw emotion seeping out of the cracks of your shell, and I know you. It may not be romantic love, but I love the man you are." Harkhuf stopped breathing. "I vow to name any daughter I have after yours, the next after your wife. You will be their greatest protector."

Harkhuf stood and shuffled away, his shoulders trembling as if he might be sobbing.

Later that evening, I loosed an arrow from my bow—always pursuing my training in the downtimes. The arrow whistled and glanced off of a tree trunk in the distance, sailing into the surrounding grass.

"We fashion our bows of that wood," Harkhuf said, his face and chest appearing from the brush that he'd been silently creeping through.

I jerked in surprise.

He pointed to the dark trunk of the tree I'd been targeting. "The bow is much mightier a weapon than the spear or sword, but you should also learn to stalk your prey. And unfortunately, there's been no master archer in centuries—they say it is legend—so I'm the best teacher you'll get."

Harkhuf showed me how to assess and adjust to the wind, the weather, and elevation while sneaking along and firing. My heart soared with happiness, watching him in his element, his mind free. Although he might not ever completely overcome his past, thanks to Tia, it appeared he faced it and could go on living. My eyes closed. I didn't want to say goodbye to the brothers. I ... loved them as well ... Warmth erupted in my chest like a bonfire. My lips pulled up into a smile. I loved them?

❊ ❊ ❊

"Again," Harkhuf said a few days later, motioning for me to go out and practice, as I had been doing most waking hours. He followed me out into the waving grass of the plains, planted his hands on his hips, and watched.

I crept through the brush and released an arrow. The arrow tore through the air and buried into a tree trunk a hundred yards away, releasing a thump. The shaft vibrated back and forth.

"Thank you for helping me," Harkhuf muttered. But he'd said it so quietly, I almost hadn't heard him. This brother couldn't speak of his feelings, so I didn't respond. But the warmth and tingling I'd felt the other day carried through my entire body and soul—the feeling of helping another. I'd experienced almost nothing more moving. I'd supported this man as he looked his demons straight in the eye and walked away the victor ... Could I now face mine?

"I will miss you as much as my own family," I whispered.

Harkhuf laughed, a deep bellow. "No, you won't."

Lowering my bow, I turned and glared back at him. His dark face and beard peeked between the grasses like a hunting lion.

"We're coming with you," he said and stood straight. "I've failed my family in this life and cannot undo that. I will have to live with myself wherever I go, but the pain here in Kush is unbearable. The not-so-formidable terror of the cursed man, which thrived on trickery and fear, and plagued my people, is vanquished. I've helped them as much as I'll ever be able to, after what I did ..." He swallowed and grimaced. "But I believe some of them still roam the plains, far from here. And I've only found peace in our journeys and the hope we've been carrying."

My heart melted, and an image of Mutnedjmet immediately popped into my head. She'd once said something similar, smashed her Bes amulet in retaliation for my treatment, and attempted to help me when Akhenaten and Suty sent me into slavery. Mutnedjmet. The only true friend I'd had but was too blind to see. My heart fluttered. I'd abandoned her for far too long.

The next morning, our entire group started the trek back through Nubia, and we eventually returned to the cataracts of the Nile. Seneb's bite wound at the base his neck retracted and healed into a scar that resembled a distorted star. But the scar tissue was black.

We found our Minoan merchant vessel still hidden by brush, a hundred feet off shore. After cleaning out the boat, we sailed north with the river's current.

With all of my travels, I still had not seen the beginnings of the mightiest of rivers and probably never would. The Earth must continue even beyond Kush ...

I knew where I was headed, although I feared bringing the others. How many years had it been? I was a full-grown man now who'd experienced much. Perhaps I was even beyond my twenties. I'd never done a decent job of keeping track. The strands of time disappeared more quickly than I could've ever imagined.

At twilight, we floated past the granite mountains outside Aswan. I wished for nothing more than to see Croc alive and well, even if it meant the Devouring Monster was still out here.

※ ※ ※

Days later, the towering temples of the sandstone city of Thebes rose on the eastern banks. We'd get the supply carts and tools we'd need to unearth and empty a tomb before heading into the Valley of the Kings—although I hadn't told my companions specifically about the riches, only that we needed to find something out there that was buried.

A manmade channel stretched into the western desert, leading to the Gleaming Palace of the Aten—where I'd once asked Nefertiti to run away with me. Had that palace been left for ruin?

Taking up paddles, we steered into one of three straight canals to the east and passed only two sailing ships.

Sleeping cargo boats filled the once busiest port in the world—one of the manmade rectangular lakes before Thebes. A few scattered people sat around, watching the river or arguing amongst themselves. The workers loading and unloading crates of supplies, the whistling, and the barking of orders had vanished from this economic center.

My mind raced with memories of my encounters here: the sphinx, Akhenaten, and his Devouring Monster. I shivered.

I coasted us into the dock and slipped our boat between two empty vessels whose hulls were covered in white cloth—as if they hadn't sailed in weeks. The air was heavy and still.

Temples still towered in the distance, but the sunlight didn't shimmer off of them as I remembered. They now exuded a sense of wonder about their history rather than a present authoritative power.

"It's been a while since we've seen a boat of the Sea People's," one sun-wrinkled old man said to another, frowning and folding his arms as we stepped onto the cracking stone of the docks.

"They're not even Sea People," the other replied. "Egyptians and their dancing dwarves, although they're pretty well armed."

I led the companions away, down the sphinx-lined road. Scattered locals paced by with their heads down. The largest temple, with its towering pylon walls, lay ahead, but the entrance was barricaded with stone blocks. Was no one allowed inside to pray to false gods?

"Why's Karnak closed?" Chisisi asked an old woman as she passed by with a basket of bread.

Shooting him a scowl, the old woman hurried away, muttering, "Praise the Aten."

"We need to keep a low profile," Wahankh said, his hands shaking as he flexed and extended his fingers. "If someone recognizes me, I'll be put to death."

We searched for supplies as we wandered the streets. Wahankh hid behind us and kept his head low. The other major temple—Luxor Temple—emerged before us, its walls of stone stretching for the sky. Its entrance was also sealed by enormous blocks.

"Where can we trade for carts and tools?" Chisisi asked, grabbing a man passing the other way. The man shrugged Chisisi off and marched on in silence.

Eyes bored into us from the streets and from the entrances of houses and shops.

We approached a circle of ten men and women. They whispered to each other and dispersed as if we carried the plague, rushing into houses and shutting their doors. Two policemen glared at us from beside a building, hiding behind their spears and shields.

"We need to get out of here," Wahankh whispered from behind me, tension tightening his words. "Something is very wrong with Thebes."

We passed an alleyway. Something moved in the shadows draped across that narrow space between two houses. A blur of orange. I froze and stared. Could it possibly be Croc? We'd last seen him not too far from here, but he hadn't resurfaced from the river after attacking the Devouring Monster.

I ran into the alley, and my eyes adjusted to the dim lighting and narrow confines. Something warm lifted the hairs on the back of my neck …

Chapter 53

Journal Translation

OMETHING MOVED AT THE corner of my vision. With the patter of small feet, it darted around a corner at the opposite end of the dark alleyway.

I rushed after it. Gripping the abrasive sandstone edge of a building, I took a quick breath before peeking around to see what this thing was.

"Let's get back to the boat," Paramessu said, tugging my shoulder. "We should look for supplies elsewhere. This city gives me the creeps."

The street around the corner was dark and empty.

We hurried back to our boat as the sun set over the western desert. The others lay down in the hull, and I sat at the stern. Disappointed and unnerved, I ran my fingers along the cracks in the handle of the rudder. I could imagine everyone at Thebes was nervous because of Akhenaten, but did they know that we didn't belong here? Just because of the dwarves, or was it—

A wad of cloth was shoved into my mouth, and a sack was pulled over my head. I fought and twisted, but I couldn't scream or see. Strong hands clutched my arms, shoulders, and legs. I thrashed with all my might but couldn't free myself.

Whoever these abductors were, they bound me and me tossed aside. I landed on my back, hitting something hard with a hollow thud—like wood. A cart or crate? Other wiggling bodies were thrown in around me, probably my companions … As I breathed, the sack over my face sucked into my nostrils, delivering a whiff of dust and sweat. A stiff sheet was pulled over us, and we rolled down a bumpy street amidst the clatter of wheels spinning over dirt and stone.

After the cart stopped, the abductors yanked me out, cut the bonds around my feet, and forced me to march. Multiple doors were opened and closed before I was shoved to the ground, the dirt abrading my skin as I slid to a halt. The bag on my head was removed, although the gag remained. My companions lay beside me, but twenty armed guards surrounded us.

A man stepped before me, his face covered with the mask of a ram, curling horns protruding from its head. "What is your business in Thebes?"

Chisisi mumbled as he rose to his knees and tried to speak. The masked man yanked the gag from between Chisisi's teeth. "You don't know who you're dealing with," Chisisi said, a threatening edge in his tone. "It would be best if you let us go. We've faced more on this earth than all of you combined!"

The masked man shoved the gag back into Chisisi's mouth, and Chisisi's face turned red as his arms strained against his bonds. He released muffled shouts.

The masked man tore the gag from my mouth, stinging my lips. "I hope you are more intelligent."

Harkhuf growled.

"We are merely looking for supplies," I said, testing the rope binding my wrists behind my back—it dug into my skin and did not give, "so that we can be on our way. We're Egyptian but have been traveling for many years."

The interrogator paced, rustling his kilt. "You must've been a boy, then, when you lived here."

I nodded and jostled around, getting my knees underneath me.

He grunted. "It is unwise to go about the city questioning the old ways. There have been … many changes over the last decade, and death is the sentence for mentioning the other gods. The ears of the Hunters are everywhere. There is only the Aten and its son, Akhenaten."

"The Hunters?" I asked, leaning in an attempt to see under the man's mask.

"We could all be publicly executed by the Hunters—those who seek out and punish men who still worship the old gods," he said and paused. "If we continue, I may have to put you to death to save the other souls in this room."

I swallowed and nodded, picturing more lost souls weighing on my conscience. "I wish to know what happened to the old gods, and to Thebes."

"They are not dead," the interrogator replied, shadows stretching across the sunken eye sockets of his ram mask. "None of the other gods. Akhenaten has just forbidden them. The lands have crumbled, the people falter, and mightiest Egypt is in decline. Soon, we will fall, the last civilization of old. He says it is because we worship false gods." He spat on the floor. "Akhenaten is enforcing his one god, and only his city is thriving amongst the engulfing depression. But I am old enough to remember when Amenhotep the Third was a young Pharaoh. All of Egypt thrived in its greatest glory. The power of the Aten was rising, but we still worshipped Amun and Re ..." he paused, as if he had said too much.

"You've seen signs that Amun and Re still exist?" I asked.

"The unknown one has simply been cast aside in an attempt to erase him from history. The religions of Egypt are doomed. We've incorporated outsiders' gods into our own for eons. It has brought us peace and prosperity. These gods must all be the same, anyway ... those who created us." He took a deep breath and turned his back. "We wander on the gods themselves, they are everywhere, part of everything. Amun created the others and brought them here. The god whose is earth, Geb; the god of the sky, Nut; and Shu, who parted the eternal waters of the sky so that we may live. Re the sun god, not just a disc; Ma'at the woman, who keeps time—all the gods are subjected to her command."

My face wrinkled in utter confusion. Egypt had once been a land of pagan barbarians? It couldn't be true ... but Father had feared to speak of such things and had been murdered when he'd tried. Somehow, I was completely in the dark on this matter.

"Now Pharaoh parades himself up and down his great road, claiming the Aten and himself are one." Spittle flew from the interrogator's mask as he turned his head. "This Pharaoh once ate the heart of his own uncle, King Simut, the high priest of Amun. He did so to erase the high priest's soul, to instill fear in the people, and to create doubt in Amun!"

"I saw him do it!" I shouted, straining against my bonds and rising to my feet. "I was there many years ago. I witnessed Akhenaten devour a man's beating heart. And now I stand against him." My voice echoed throughout the chamber. A tingle of disgust filled my body as I recalled

Akhenaten biting into the heart and blood spilling down his arm. The fear in the victim's eyes. "This uncle of his saved my life. I was wounded by a hippopotamus …"

Paramessu gasped.

The interrogator didn't move. "Who are you?"

"My father was a servant of Amenhotep's. I became Akhenaten's slave."

Another man wobbled upon a cane as he stepped forward. He also wore a mask of the ram but lifted it from his face, revealing clouded eyes and thin hair as white as Keftiu snow. The time bender! A magician whom I'd encountered when I was a boy—before trying to convince Nefertiti to run away with me. He now looked as if he must've lived two centuries.

"The servant boy of Akhenaten has returned!" the time bender said, his voice hoarse. "I told you it was him." He studied me. "That is why we abducted you."

"By Amun!" the interrogator shouted, motioning for men to untie me. "You will not leave until we check with the oracle. But if you agree to help, there are many things we could use you for." His head fell back as if his muscles lost their tone. "We worked with the magicians before they were hunted and destroyed. I have waited for this moment for half of my life … as the others the magician was training have failed. If your heart is thus inclined, and the oracle confirms it, you could arise as the holy warrior of Amun." The interrogator spun about to face the people behind him. "Where has the oracle of Thebes been hiding?"

Another person in a ram's mask stepped forward but wore a dress and replied in a female's voice. "The last Theban mayor from Amenhotep's time, my husband, is the only one who knows the oracle's identity. I will bring him. But do not let any of these prisoners leave. They are an enormous liability. If they try to escape, kill them all. And do not let false hope from an old dream cloud your judgment! We've tried this many times." Whirling around, the woman strode away. The armed guards parted, giving her a wide berth.

The interrogator took off his mask, revealing a fit, middle-aged countenance. Stubbles of graying hair ran over his scalp.

"I do not even know of Amun," I said. "I cannot be his warrior."

The interrogator's chin jerked back in shock. "I would desire nothing more than to be Amun's champion. He is the ram, the unknown." He paced in a circle. "Akhenaten's motto in el-Amarna, in all of Egypt now, is 'live for the moment.' The Hunters destroy anything that names the older gods. People have been killed, their hearts eaten, and their souls lost for keeping objects in their homes, even items so simple as to use the plural 'gods.' Hordes of soldiers, including Asiatics and Nubians, roam the streets of Egypt, extinguishing the gods of old—including Amenhotep and even Akhenaten's birth name, Amenhotep the Fourth. People have reported neighbors, friends, enemies, and even family members they are upset with, whether they are guilty or not. If someone says you worship a god other than the Aten and you're lucky, the military beats you, possibly to death. If you are unlucky, the cloaked monster visits you at night and devours your heart. The unfaithful have become compliant. Pharaoh will erase all of Egypt's history."

"Perhaps Memphis and Thebes or the outside world could unite against him," I said.

"All of the taxes and tariffs are held in el-Amarna to keep the city and military strong and under his control. Thebes has entered the deepest depression we've ever known. I thought outsiders would've overthrown us by now, but Akhenaten holds many foreign kings' daughters as wives—sacrificed by their fathers in hopes of restoring relations with Egypt. And although Pharaoh disgraces our past relationships, the foreign kings do not attack because they fear Akhenaten will harm their daughters."

The Asiatic woman, Kiya, appeared in my mind—when I'd witnessed her arrival and proposal to Akhenaten inside the Gleaming Palace of the Aten.

"He has a son, a product of incest like many of his children," the interrogator said. "Pharaohs may have relations with any woman, including their sisters, and these women can bear their brothers' children, but Akhenaten is changing even the old rules. He's had relations with and is marrying his own daughters. They produce offspring who are … troubled, to say the least. Fortunately, most die in the womb, but some have survived."

Images of the demon family in Nubia and the Cyclops flashed in my mind.

"He has an infant son out of his own sister! Wretched Pharaoh will continue his lineage!" the man bellowed as he punched his open palm. "The son of Beketaten is alive and well, with only a bad leg. They are calling him Tutankhaten, Prince Tut."

My eyes bulged, and my mouth gaped—the boy I'd seen in my vision. The room tilted …

Chapter 54

Journal Translation

IMAGES OF DEFORMED CHILDREN raced through my mind. How much evil would this world see if Akhenaten's offspring were like him? Nefertiti's daughters … could they be saved? But Beketaten had his only son. Was there a chance that the child could be mine, after all these years? Probably not, unless my vision had showed the past.

My eyes fluttered. I lay sprawled out on the cool dirt floor of a small room lit by a single torch on the wall. My companions sat around me, their gags removed, but their hands were still tied behind their backs, as were mine. The interrogator and his men were gone.

"You fell," Seneb said, "like a child with seizures, but without the twitching part."

"That discussion was informative," Paramessu said. He leaned over and whispered in my ear, "But you should not believe everything they tell you. They attempt to appeal to your emotions."

I bit my lip with skepticism. A man sworn to protect Pharaoh would not be swayed by someone he didn't know. But I knew Akhenaten.

"I didn't know how messed up your kingdom was," Seneb said, rubbing his cheek on his shoulder.

Tia's face was pale. I doubted that a slave woman had much knowledge of Akhenaten's heinous acts, but her idea of an unrivaled and orderly Egypt must have crumbled.

Most of the night passed before doors banged in the distance and hushed voices carried in through the outer halls.

Armed men entered our room but grabbed only me, then shoved me out and down a long hallway into another chamber. The interrogator and the time bender stood beside a smaller figure who still hid behind a ram's mask and held a torch.

"Bring in the oracle," the interrogator said, waving a hand.

Seven shaven elderly men, whose bodies glistened with oil, stepped inside. The thick scent of olive followed them. They all wore kilts and looked identical.

The one on the far left spoke. "I am the oracle of Thebes, the original oracle of the known world. I am disguised with others, for my safety, and to preserve the future of Thebes and Amun. But only I can grant you communion and tell you what Amun allows me to see."

My forehead wrinkled in confusion, but I'd seen enough magic that I didn't entirely doubt his claim.

"Get everyone stationed outside!" the interrogator barked to the guards surrounding the doorways. "We need scouts all around. I want to know at least ten minutes before the Hunters arrive, even if it means every man here has to forfeit his soul!"

All of the guards dashed away.

The seven would-be oracles burned incense and wafted it from swinging censers. As they chanted in an ancient tongue, their voices echoed around the chamber, and they washed me with white smoke, its smell sickeningly sweet. The supposed true oracle's arms fell limp, as if he'd suddenly gone to sleep standing up. His eyes rolled back into his head, revealing only the whites. His face shook, and his wrists and elbows bent backward. Leaning over like the ghoul king, his head snapped up and his white eyes twinkled.

My skin crawled.

"I see this possibility." The voice that came from the oracle sounded as if it radiated from the bowels of the earth, shaking the walls like an earthquake.

The interrogator's eyes widened in fear. "We won't have long," he said. "To the Hunters—within the realm of magic—this will show up like a bonfire at night."

"But this one cannot achieve what it is you all hope for," the booming voice of the oracle said. "The shadows of Egypt have solidified, and you've all let them grow. This mortal will not be able to kill a god-king! He will not overthrow Pharaoh! Find another—an army!"

The interrogator and the masked woman clutched each other as the building quaked.

"Only one who has known death," the oracle yelled in my face, a warm wind blowing into my eyes and through my short hair, "the beauty of the dead, and the Book of the Dead, can defeat a god-king." He wobbled and dropped down onto all fours. "Sobek, and the extinct ones!" He lunged at my feet.

I jumped back. The air in the room turned cold, and I exhaled fog. Droplets of sweat condensed on my forehead.

"Tell me." The oracle twisted his arm around, beyond what should've been humanly possible, and thrust a gnarled finger into my thigh. "It is not I who granted you your miserable fate only to have you fail. But tell me why you fight with such hunger. What burns inside you like the pits of *Duat*? The others do not have this."

I swallowed as I remembered Father, Croc, Nefertiti, Mutnedjmet, Yuf, Akhenaten … Words burst from my mouth in a torrent of emotion, arising from some unknown region within me. "I'd rather dream with my eyes open than live in a nightmare!"

My head fell to my chest in shame. I'd always guarded my desires for fear of having my truest self known. People had thought I was a good man.

The oracle leapt straight up from all fours, and his neck cocked at an impossible angle. He laughed wickedly. "You shall see what nightmares are!" His head tilted further, as if he were listening. "They're already here!"

Screams of dying men erupted outside.

The interrogator grabbed me and drew a sword from his waist. Forcing me around, he cut the bonds around my wrists. My fingers burned as blood returned in full force.

"Get out of here!" he said. "The Hunters have arrived. Your weapons are in a chest by the back door." He pointed to an exit. "Muttuy, follow them," he said to the woman as a guard led my companions into the chamber and freed them. "Amun has little to no hope for this man, but he is the only one of the son of Hapu's trainees who has returned to Thebes. I will help him."

We raced out of the chamber, down a long, dark hallway, and found a chest before a closed doorway. The oracles, the time bender, the interrogator, and Muttuy all followed us. We snagged our gear, and I threw open a wooden door that released a long creak.

An alleyway. Darkness still hung over the city.

"No matter what happens behind you, do not stop running!" the interrogator shouted. "Head west to your boat. We will hold off these magician slayers—the Hunters."

"Run!" Wahankh yelled.

We sprinted out into the moonlit alley. Pounding footsteps and shouts echoed through the halls behind us.

An old man wailed. I glanced back.

Reptilian eyes stared from beneath the shadows of a long, dark hood. The Devouring Monster itself! It was still alive, and here to take souls ...

The monster's jaws snapped across the time bender's chest, and bones cracked before it plunged a blade of serrated teeth between the old man's ribs. A hissing sound stung my ears as the hand of a lion pointed at me. The hand was deformed, with missing fingers and claws, the wounds still red and hairless, as if ... Croc had maimed him.

"I will consume your heart," the Devouring Monster's whisper carried to me.

As I turned back to continue fleeing, a troop of Egyptian soldiers emerged from the end of the alleyway, blocking our escape with readied spears and burning torches.

The Egyptian military was also assisting Akhenaten and his monster.

Harkhuf released three arrows in rapid succession. The arrows screamed like diving eagles and buried into the chests of three soldiers, dropping them. Seneb hurled his spear into the belly of another.

A soldier jabbed wildly at my face with his spear as I drew my swords. I ducked the attack and sliced his forearms. He collapsed, screaming.

Tia deflected a strike with her shield but stumbled back. Paramessu lunged forward and skewered the soldier with a spear to the heart.

We barreled past a heap of fallen adversaries. But more soldiers poured out from the building we'd fled and pursued us as we raced down empty streets. Harkhuf and I fired volleys of arrows over our shoulders.

The clash of metal and screams from the dying oracles and guards who'd abducted us rang through the city.

My heart burned with regret. I should turn around and help these people—they wanted to resist Akhenaten as well ... But then I'd lead my companions to their deaths.

Wahankh and Chisisi heaved for breath as the rectangular lake emerged at the end of the street. The first rays of the Aten lit up the sky behind us.

We leapt aboard our boat.

Arrows buried into the hull with pounding thuds. Guards raced up the bank, closing in and slinging spears. We all dropped down onto our stomachs for cover, barely able to see over the side of our vessel. Metal clanged against wood, and a spear bounced off of the rail near my head. We'd never be able to stand up and paddle away without being struck.

The cloaked figure, the Hunter, the Devouring Monster itself, slowly approached with slapping footfalls. And Croc wasn't here—he was possibly dead. I climbed to my knees. Someone would have to stop the monster so the others could get away with their souls.

"N-no, I—I will slow him down," Wahankh said, his entire body shaking in sheer terror as he stood over me, covering himself with his shield. "I've witnessed the b-bravery you were about ..." He forced a deep breath. "The others have faced the demons dwelling in their hometowns, or plan to. I am the unluckiest, with *this* monster ... but I—I must do this." The muscular man jumped over the side of the boat onto the shore. Arrows sank into the rawhide shield protecting his frame.

The Egyptian soldiers parted for the Devouring Monster and stopped shooting arrows. My breathing stopped.

Someone kicked my shoulder.

"Get to the rudder," Chisisi said. "He's not going to last long."

Scrambling for the stern, I watched Wahankh as the others took up oars.

The mandibular bone blade flashed against the monster's black robes. Blood dripped from its serrated edge of crocodile teeth.

Wahankh stood his ground, his spear trembling as he pointed it at the attacker.

I gasped, but my hands found the wooden rudder and backpaddled.

The crocodile-blade rose slowly over the monster's head.

Wahankh shrieked, tossed his spear and shield at the monster, and sprinted back for us. We drifted farther out into the water.

The Devouring Monster chased him.

Diving into the lake, Wahankh screamed and swam faster than any man I'd ever seen.

The monster dived in and disappeared below the surface. Its ripples faded.

My throat clamped shut. Could Wahankh swim fast enough? I reached out for his stroking hands and arms. He'd be pulled under any second. Lunging, Wahankh grabbed hold of my wrist. I leaned back to help haul him in, but the water made our skin slippery. His grip slid down over my fingers. I grabbed his forearm with my other hand and heaved. He collapsed into the hull, trembling.

The pursuing soldiers boarded other docked vessels in disrepair and attempted to untie them and get them moving. I held my breath. The Devouring Monster still pursued us. We rowed like madmen, our oars tearing through the water in rhythmic splashes that soaked my face and chest.

The wake behind our boat remained undisturbed—no sign of the monster.

Finally, we careened out into the open Nile, the current grabbing our boat and propelling us north. Chisisi cheered and shook his fists. Our pursuers faded into the distance.

Stale air expelled from my lungs as I struggled with disbelief. The entire ordeal in Thebes … My heart slowed.

Paramessu collapsed, his face ghastly pale. "Discipline, society," he muttered—the same words he'd spoken when he'd whipped me. What must he be thinking now? Did a rush of images fill his mind like a nightmare transformed into reality? He'd betrayed his own military and killed a soldier for Tia. He'd be a wanted man now, wanted by his own kind. And Wahankh … he might not have fought the monster, but he'd faced it, his greatest fear—unlike me. And what had happened to the time bender? The others? Would they all lose their souls? If so, I wouldn't be far behind them. I shivered.

Shaking my head, I focused on the river. In order to overthrow Akhenaten, someone had to have known death? That was what the oracle had said through that booming voice, supposedly the words of a god. But what did that even mean, and how could I ever accomplish it—if a god said

I could not? Was it because Akhenaten couldn't be killed? My comrades would all doubt me and any attempt I made to destroy Akhenaten anyway, especially if I shared everything the oracle had said.

I glanced west, into the desert and morning light. The buried treasure out there would have to wait a bit longer—we couldn't dock at western Thebes right now, or the Devouring Monster would find us.

"Sobek, and the extinct ones?" I asked, my fingers digging into the cracks of the rudder. "Does anyone know what those are?"

Tia leaned her head onto Paramessu's back, hugging him from behind. But her dark eyes grew wide as she whispered, "Sobek is the god of my home town, Crocodilopolis."

Chapter 55

Present Day

WE UNLOADED FROM the SUV outside of Cairo. Radiating heat hit my face like I'd just opened an oven on broil. I exhaled as I studied the surrounding desert, but my breath seemed trapped inside me. We were close to where the clues of the imperfect pyramid and sunbeams from the outline of the markers at el-Amarna were hopefully leading us. Many ancient structures, even other pyramids, dotted the landscape near ancient Memphis.

Slinging my bag over my shoulder, I strode past the camels and throngs of tourists for Egypt's first pyramid—possibly mankind's first stone-cut structure—the Step Pyramid of Djoser. The odor of the camels, similar to a sheep, and the smell of hay hung about.

But Mr. Scalone already led the way.

"I'm sweatin' balls," Aiden mumbled, pointing to the camels.

"Probably easier," I said, trudging on as a camel bellowed, its voice carrying across the desert, "but not faster, after we pay and load up. We need to get to Maddie as soon as possible. Who knows what that other man will do to her if he finds out his comrade is dead. If he hasn't already."

Aiden rushed after me, carrying his tiny fox and taking a swig from his water bottle. Kaylin followed behind Mr. Scalone.

"This original pyramid was built by Imhotep, who the son of Hapu was the supposed reincarnation of," I said to Aiden. "Remember the old wise magician whose mortuary complex we visited for knowledge?"

"Yeah," Aiden said, lifting his chin. "That was my idea, and it worked."

My lips lifted into a smile despite my suffocating worry. Aiden had turned distant since Jenkins's death but was opening up again. We passed between pillars, fashioned to appear as bundled papyrus stalks, and then through the opening of the stone enclosure wall, into the tomb complex.

The pyramid loomed above us, its steps reaching for the heavens as if it were a ladder for Pharaoh to ascend into the afterlife.

"Where do we go first?" Kaylin asked, twirling her hair and waiting for Aiden and me. "There are, like, multiple buildings inside here."

"The pyramid itself," I said, pointing ahead, "or the *serdab*—Djoser's shrine. That's where they found Pharaoh's *ka* statue, a part of him that could still experience the world. The other structures you see don't have open inner chambers like regular buildings. None of this was ever meant for the living."

"No one lived inside these buildings?" Mr. Scalone asked, glancing around at all the stone monuments.

"These works of art were only meant to be used by the deceased and admired by the living," I said. "They're not for humans, who can't even enter them." I paused as a row of stone cobras stared at us. "But maybe we should split up … to be more efficient. There're about three miles of tunnels beneath the pyramid. If we don't find something obvious, or something recently destroyed, this will probably take way too long."

"I'm going inside the pyramid," Mr. Scalone said. He pulled out a medallion of an eagle with a shield, as well as a letter. Unfolding the crinkling paper, he swaggered over and handed it to a nearby guard. His letter and medallion appeared identical to the ones the Minister of Antiquities had given me.

The tall guard's eyes narrowed as he snatched the paper and studied it. Glancing up at Mr. Scalone and us, he motioned to another comrade in fatigues. A machine gun shifted in the tall guard's grip. The guards discussed something in Arabic, and the first made a call. He snapped something into the phone. But his tone changed abruptly as he responded. He nodded. After hanging up, he motioned for us to follow him around the vast walls of the step pyramid. He removed clunky keys from his belt that clinked together as he unlocked the two metal gates of the entrance.

Steel squeaked and grated as the guard swung the gates outward. No corridors or hallways led into the pyramid itself. The only way was down into the catacombs.

"What the hell?" Mr. Scalone said, turning to me with an eyebrow raised.

"Ancient tombs, up until the time this pyramid was built, were all underground," I said. "They previously used only one layer of mud brick over the dirt as a marker for the dead. This is the very first pyramid: multiple layers of stone marking the tomb below. But there are two entrances. Maybe we can use the other more public route if you don't like this one."

Mr. Scalone grunted, grabbed a flashlight, and ducked inside. "Someone has to help Maddie."

I trailed behind.

"I don't know what to look for out here," Aiden said, his eyes shining with fear as he glanced around at the clustered tourists inside the complex—as if they might shoot him. He then stared into the darkness below and pulled the fox in his arms closer to him. "I might as well come too." He stepped down into the earth, chomping his gum. Kaylin followed.

"One of you needs to watch the entrance," I said, my skin crawling with fear. "We were trapped the last time we all went underground."

"I'll stay," Kaylin said, putting her hands on her hips. "If anyone wants to shut the gate, I'll keep screaming so loudly that they'll have to kill me to shut me up."

I swallowed in apprehension as images of Kaylin also getting shot flashed in my mind. "Be careful and blend in with the tourists," I said but followed Mr. Scalone downward. My hands shook as the air grew cooler, and the feeling of something or someone watching me returned. My breathing quickened, and the hairs on the back of my neck stood up. I could see my breath in the beam of the flashlight, as if the air were freezing. It must've been dust …

As we eased through the narrow passages, I studied the walls. There wouldn't be any artifacts of importance still down here, but the limestone surroundings could hold a secret. The walls were decorated with blue faience to resemble reed matting.

Corridors of black opened at right angles. They ran into the unknown. Mr. Scalone disappeared as he strode around a bend. My throat constricted as my chest strained to breathe. Was the treasure hunter unafraid, or was he trying to leave us?

"Where do we go?" Aiden whispered from behind, his voice carrying through passageways.

"There's a burial chamber and a huge central shaft," I said. "The other chambers for Pharaoh's harem, his family, and the goods to sustain him in the afterlife would be less important for anyone leaving a trail."

"Unless a less obvious location was what they'd wanted to use," Aiden replied.

I paused, wondering. That could be true.

We wandered dark tunnels until the ground ahead suddenly disappeared into the earth. Aiden bumped into me, making me stumble closer to this shaft. The blackness reached out for me, wanting to pull me down. I yelled, leaning away and almost falling over as I shoved against Aiden.

Grabbing my shoulder, Aiden yanked me back.

His pale face leaned into my beam of light, his lips quivering as he peered downward. "A pit?"

I hugged the wall. "I'm not sure how deep it is." I shined my light downward. Only a few feet to the bottom. Exhaling in relief, I cast the light up to the ceiling. A shaft extended as far as we could see into the blackness.

"Where does that go?" Aiden asked, his voice airy with wonder.

"To the base of the pyramid," I replied. "It's a path for the deceased to travel up and out."

"But you said there's nothing inside the pyramid."

"Not that anyone has discovered," I replied. "And I don't see how we'd get up there."

"We dived into a sunken temple," Aiden said.

That was true, but having to do so was modern man's fault because of the damming of the Nile. It would be very difficult for someone in ancient times to ascend the shaft above us.

Turning away, I wandered narrow corridors, searching for any sign or clue. The burial chamber was empty save for typical images upon the walls. I strode off.

"Why do you think those hired locals killed Jenkins?" Aiden asked from the darkness behind me.

My pace slowed as I bit my lip, the pinching pressure a distraction from my guilt of letting him die. "I think that they don't want us to follow the path to the Hall," I said. "And that's why they took Maddie as a hostage."

"Why would they not want us to find this Hall of Records place?" Aiden asked. "Like, if that antiquities minister wants to stamp out crime at historical sites, what would those men have to gain by abducting Maddie and shooting Jenkins?"

I shrugged. "There aren't always answers to why people are evil."

"But even killers have their reasons." Aiden's footsteps stopped. "What would happen to us if we find it?"

"We'd reveal one of the greatest ancient discoveries in history," I said, pausing and turning. My flashlight beam reflected off of his green basketball shorts and the fox's glowing eyes. "Like the city of Atlantis."

"So we'd be rich and famous in an instant?" he asked as the sound of his fox's raspy panting filled the corridor.

I nodded. "The world's attention would be directed right here."

"So, bro, then maybe we should ask why these men wouldn't want that to happen?" He held a hand up to block my flashlight beam from his eyes.

Lowering the light, my mind raced. Was he on to something? But if someone else already knew where the Hall was, why didn't they reveal the secret and garner the glory themselves? What could they be hiding? "What do you think the Minister of Antiquities wants?"

Aiden shrugged. "I wasn't paying attention when we met with him weeks ago, and I wasn't there for your recent visit. But he seemed important. A limo, white suit, bodyguards … that's a lot for some antiquities guy."

All of a sudden Aiden seemed smarter, in spite of his appearance. And I could trust him more than the others. "Antiquities and tourism are a huge part of the Egyptian economy," I said, realizing I should be thinking more about this and not only about Maddie. I swallowed. "How well do you know Mr. Scalone?"

"About as much as you," Aiden said, scratching at the buzzed back of his head, below his dangling dreadlocks. "Dad's friend found him for Kaylin and this trip; that's all I really know."

"And Jenkins?" I asked.

"Same deal as Scalone. Why? You think they have something to do with this?" Aiden jerked and looked away, staring into the darkness, his eyes narrowing.

"Do you see something?" I asked.

He shrugged, as if he saw a lot more than the rest of us. Then he stared into my light and rubbed at his ears. Or did he hear something?

"I was just wondering about them," I said as a prickling sensation rolled along the skin of my arms. "Jenkins said something funny to me when he was dying."

"I'd say a lot of funny stuff if I was dying," Aiden said. "Mr. Scalone is a D-bag, but he couldn't have had anything to do with Maddie or Jenkins. Dad would've had his people look into Mr. Scalone better than that. He always does."

I turned and wandered down the corridor. Aiden's dad? Could that be why Maddie and not Kaylin was abducted, because her dad had arranged for an abduction for some reason? No, that was too much conspiracy theory crap. And Kaylin would be in more danger without Jenkins, her bodyguard, so it wouldn't make sense for her dad to be behind hiring these other strange men to watch us and have them kill her bodyguard.

"We'll find her," Aiden said, his crunching footsteps following me. "Maddie, I mean. And we'll be rich and famous."

My eyes closed as I exhaled, hoping for the best—at least for Maddie.

As I rounded a bend, something appeared in front of me—a face!

My stomach dropped, and I screamed. Aiden yelled.

"Calm down," Mr. Scalone said, grabbing my shoulders and shaking his head in the beam of my flashlight. "I thought you would've toughened up by now." He shoved past me and continued on into the darkness.

My cheeks burned with embarrassment. What did I think would get us down here? A mummy? As I watched the treasure hunter go, his possible intentions raced through my mind.

Aiden and I continued searching for hours before finally returning to the surface.

Kaylin sat waiting with Mr. Scalone, who was holding a brown bottle. Liquid rolled off the glass surface like rain as he pressed it to his lips and released an "ah."

My throat felt as dry as an empty creek bed that cracked under the summer sun.

"You guys were down there all day," Kaylin said, chewing on a nut-filled bar that smelled of honey. "Did you find anything?" Her voice was high-pitched with hope.

I shook my head.

"Told you," Mr. Scalone said to her. "I searched everything down there and then the entire complex outside in the time you guys looked at one thing. Reminds me of the time I was looking for gold in the Mayan Riviera with those other—"

"Did *you* find anything, bro?" Aiden asked as he exited, rubbing his head with his cap, his tone condescending. "Or was the Riviera comment referring to when you went to Cancun at forty years old and hit on college girls during their spring break?"

"Aiden!" Kaylin said, her eyes turning hard. "Stop it!"

"Don't make me club you upside the head with this bottle, junior," Mr. Scalone said, his cheek muscles bulging from his face. "Strike two against you and your nerdy friend," he said, nodding at me.

Was strike one when I'd kicked him in the face?

"So what location is your next best guess, since this isn't the correct place?" Mr. Scalone asked, tossing his black hair back and shading his eyes against the dwindling sun.

My eyes wandered as the diagram of the points of interest at el-Amarna ran through my mind—the pyramid outline, with the stepped sides, sitting within the rays of the sun. "There are about eighty or ninety pyramids in Egypt," I said. "The bent pyramid would be my next best guess of the pyramids that are still intact and resemble the clue." Did I place too much emphasis on that last clue? Or was it coincidence and the Royal Wadi actually hid the clue, one too difficult for me to discover?

Mr. Scalone didn't respond.

I wandered off and inspected a small tomb at the pyramid's base, Djoser's *serdab*—basically a sealed stone box with his *ka* statue inside. The sun set into the west and cast long shadows off all of the complex's buildings. My hand traced the granite surface, smooth except for two small holes.

"What are those holes for?" Aiden asked, making me jump. I hadn't known that he'd tagged along. But he seemed to like Mr. Scalone about as much as I did. Maybe that and Jenkins's death was bringing us closer. And I was glad he was here.

"Eye holes," I said, gazing into them. "So Pharaoh could watch the daily ceremonies, breathe in the incense, and benefit from it all in the afterlife. They are also a gateway for his soul to travel out of the box during the day."

Aiden's chin jutted back in disbelief. His fox sat at his feet, on a leash. Pointing to an image on a nearby block, one of timeworn limestone, Aiden asked, "What's the five-pointed star?"

"The North Star," I said. "These blocks were once part of the ceiling of an original burial chamber, but they crumbled and were moved. Because the North Star never moves below the horizon, the ancients thought of it as eternal, never sinking into the underworld. These early pharaohs wanted to be that star, but the next dynasty, and those after, all wanted to be the sun."

"C'mon, Gavin," Kaylin said, forcing a smile and motioning for me to come. "Let's get a room close by. We can come back tomorrow or move on to another site."

My stomach cramped, and the stress of anxiety let loose. Did Maddie have a tomorrow?

Chapter 56

Present Day

"I'M GOING TO STAY HERE, at the step pyramid," I said, waving Kaylin and Mr. Scalone away to find accommodations for the night. The stifling heat around us receded. "See you in the morning."

Kaylin stopped in her tracks. "What for?" she asked, putting a fist on her hip.

Aiden studied me as well.

"I, like, want to help Maddie as much as you do," Kaylin said, "but camping out here at night isn't going to help anything. There's a decent hotel just a short drive away. We're not in the middle of nowhere in el-Amarna anymore. You don't have to do this."

I forced a grin, the skin on my face tight and dry. My lips cracked, and a trickle of blood dripped down my chin. "I'm trying to get tougher."

Kaylin paused for moment, shrugged, and walked off. "Come get your camping supplies from the car at least," she said over her shoulder. Mr. Scalone was already gone.

"I'm pickin' up what you're laying down, Gav," Aiden said, his eyes wide beneath his flat-billed cap as he glanced around for danger. "But I don't like being out in this desert at night. I hear stuff, and those men …"

Darkness set in around us like curtains on a stage. I clicked on my flashlight, and we studied the steps of the crumbling pyramid.

Another flashlight approached. "Leave," the guard with the machine gun said, his posture rigid. His firearm reflected my light.

I pulled out my letter from the Minister of Antiquities and the cool and heavy eagle medallion. I flashed them in his beam. "We're supposed to be able to examine historical monuments at any time," I said, pointing to the letter. The red, white, and black shield of Egypt glistened upon the eagle like a diamond.

The guard's eyes grew wide, and he retreated to the exit, as if I were King Arthur holding Excalibur and he were an enemy of the Britons.

"Why is all this stuff just for dead people, and why is it so perfect?" Aiden asked, watching the guard march away. His hands trembled.

"The Egyptians fought to maintain order every day," I said, "or they'd lose themselves to the preexisting chaos … and their true belief of an ever-expanding universe all around us."

Aiden gazed up at the night sky. "I'll snag our gear," he said, picked up his fox, and rushed after the guard, "and be back before you mind hump this place and reveal its secret."

He disappeared into the night.

I shook my head. Wandering the interior of the complex, I cast my beam of light at numerous angles while scrutinizing everything. Then I glanced around, keeping an eye out for any unwanted visitors. Nothing.

Sinking down against the crumbling bricks at the base of the step pyramid, I clicked my flashlight off. Darkness, and silence. Maybe I should be at the bent pyramid instead. But I couldn't travel there and get inside tonight.

"I'm so sorry, Maddie," I whispered into the night, a feeling of hollow worthlessness overcoming me. "I'm trying the best I can. But I … we need your help."

The moon was only a sliver and veiled by a cloud. But the light grew brighter as my eyes adjusted, and stars appeared in numbers I'd never witnessed living near a city back home.

Aiden hadn't returned, and it'd been long enough. Had he left me as well? I was probably going to regret staying out here, especially with only my messenger bag and day supplies …

Shadows started to grow around the monuments, eerie shapes taking form. Goose bumps rose across my arms and legs. *Stop it. Don't be afraid. You always do this, and there's nothing out there, just like there wasn't anything in the catacombs beneath the pyramid or in Amenhotep's tomb.* But my hands still shook. *I* was actually out here, at an Egyptian tomb at night! How had my life taken this route with everything I'd avoided? None of my friends back home would ever believe this.

Taking a deep breath, I leaned back, and my mind wandered through my past. Over the years since I'd last seen Dad leave Mom's house, my parents had divorced and Dad's health had deteriorated. He'd been forced to retire and finally settle down. He'd call or visit for a few minutes every once in a while: holidays, when he really missed me, or when he was belligerently drunk. My mom was still angry with him. I'd also avoided him for far longer than I'd intended, because every time I saw him, he'd wasted further away. His intestinal disease, which I carried, had transformed him from the vibrant man I remembered and loved into a sagging skeleton, eventually too weak to even leave his house. I couldn't face staring into my own grim future.

As the years had passed, I'd sometimes answer his calls, and we'd talk for a couple awkward minutes about the weather or how I was doing. But when I was maybe fourteen, I wouldn't answer calls when I saw his name pop up on my phone. A dark, twisting feeling ignited in my heart when I ignored him—bitter revenge. I'd make him experience the same emptiness he'd made me feel as a child.

After deleting his rambling messages, I wouldn't call him back. The last time it happened, I stared at "Dad" on the screen of my phone while walking down a crowded hallway to class. Someone bumped into me as I smirked and hit the ignore button.

A few hours later, Mom called, which she never did during school.

"Hello?" I asked, my breath shallow as I waited for her to respond.

"Gavin," Mom said, sobbing. "I'm coming to get you …"

The next thing I recalled was the smell of freshly cut grass hanging thick in the chill, autumn air of the Pacific Northwest. Children screamed, playing across the street, but something had been out of place, another smell. The sun descended as Mom and I started up the long walk to the blue house with cracking paint and overgrown grass and bushes. My hands were shaking with anxiety.

"I really loved your father, Gavin," my mom had said, tears raining down her cheeks as she sobbed. "He was just always looking for an excuse to leave and travel the world, chasing God knows what—leaving us here to fend for ourselves. I just can't believe he is actually gone … for good this time." She wiped her eyes. "I hope you don't turn out like him. I just don't know what drove him to end it." She hugged me in a trembling embrace.

I swallowed and choked, holding back tears and emotion with everything I had—as young men were supposed to. We were now supposed to go through his house and things before the funeral.

"I think he was in constant pain from his disease," Mom said.

My eyes closed in regret and frustration. I'd always wanted to tell my dad about the discovery I'd finally made when I'd dug up that box from under the mistletoe—imagining how proud he'd be of me. But I never did.

I used the brass key he'd sent me nearly a year ago, in case I wanted to visit, for the first time and cracked open his front door. Dust floated into the air as the door hinges squeaked. Mom pushed past the threshold and flicked on the lights, which only showed how dreary the place was: drawn curtains, stacks of magazines, scattered beer mugs, dirty plates, and a worn leather recliner in front of the TV—his favorite spot to live for the last few years. And the sharp smell of mildew hovered in the air.

Was that what my adventurous father, who'd traveled the globe to some of the most remote regions, had become in the end? A worn-out, diseased, middle-aged man, locked inside his house? I had to escape this fate, but my disease had started even younger than his, and my symptoms were more severe.

"You'll be a doctor and help discover the cure to this dreaded illness," my mom said, squeezing around my waist as tears poured from her eyes. She too studied the recliner and his permanent imprint in the cushions—empty space like the area in my heart meant for him. "You aren't the type to chase crazy ideas and dreams of grandeur … other than realistic ones. You'll cure yourself and millions of others but also be there for the ones you love. That is something you can be proud of …"

I didn't want to disappoint her, but her words faded into silence. An image of Dad appeared, sitting in that chair, the same spot he'd relax in at Mom's house before they separated. Foam bubbled across his moustache as he lowered his beer mug with a grin. Long ago, he could talk about anything from the past and lift my spirits in wonder, no matter how depressed I'd ever been. His eyes would sparkle and vibrate, and his hands would wave as he'd spin a tale about the history of some place he'd visited and researched. He could talk about the scuffs on his shoes and curiosity would overwhelm me—not because of sheer interest, but because he was so excited about telling the story and rarely did so. But even in my imagination, his body withered before my eyes. His shoulders slouched, and the joints of his arms and his cheekbones started to protrude.

"Stop drinking so much," I'd asked him once. "Mom says you need better nutrition."

"Once you discover the cure, you can fix me." He waved me off and smiled. "But there's something I always wanted to do with you when you were old enough. Maybe after high school, if I last that long." He motioned to his emaciated frame. "You'll figure it out, though. You're a lot smarter than I am."

I'd thought he'd meant figuring out that diet probably had the biggest implication with our disease, not about visiting Egypt …

The vision of him grew more and more silent, spending more time in his chair, never traveling, tiring after only walking across the living room—a mirror of my own future. I swallowed with dread. Would this be my life? Confined against my will?

No, I'd never been adventurous to begin with. So maybe it would be easier for me to accept.

But no wonder Heb fought against his fate with all of his might, even if it meant risking everything and being forced into slavery and suffering. He'd seen his own father trapped as the servant of Pharaoh, which would become his only path in life if he continued down that road—like me becoming my dad.

Dad's image slumped down before me, his eyes closing. But not in peace—a suicide, hopefully only to ease the suffering from his illness—not because I stopped talking to him. Tense wrinkles lined his face, as if he'd left something, or everything, unfinished. He must've suffered a lot over the years, not only with sickness but with the loss of his family … My heart buckled and folded under the stamping pressure of guilt, breaking as I still fought off tears. I regretted everything I'd said and done to him in the end. It would've been easier if I'd treated him well and brought a fake plague down upon him from some greater power rather than despising him myself. Fulfilling my revenge of not spending time with him didn't make me feel any better now … He must have died thinking I really hated him like Mom did. In this regard, I suffered more than Heb.

The dark cloud in my heart only grew throughout medical school. Each day seemed harder and harder than the last. Then, in the clinical year, my lack of focus cost that poor old woman with diabetes her good foot. I still saw her face as clearly as my own dad's whenever I closed my eyes at night ...

But then I'd packed to run away from my mistake and travel to Egypt, follow Dad's letter, and find Maddie. I'd come across the black-and-white photo he'd sent to me on my seventh or eighth birthday. The kid in that picture was fearless and ready to take on the world. For the first time in years, the weight I'd been carrying lifted like a fog. I had to try to follow the clues and chase Maddie, my secret love, one last time—for my dad, for his smile in that picture, and for the tough grimace on the face of that loving kid—who I'd been so long ago when my dad was still with me. Hopefully, it wasn't too late to still have a chance with Maddie ... but in a way, I'd abandoned her. I was still becoming my dad, no matter how hard my mom and I fought against it.

I snapped back to the present, overwhelming anger making my neck and face feel as if they were in a vice, like the top of my head would have to explode. I turned and started to climb the wall of the step pyramid. Rough stone wobbled in my hands. I slipped, and gritty dirt spilled onto my chest. No, I'd better not. The walls were unstable, and the attempts to repair them lagged far behind the damage. My fists clenched as I stormed around the tomb complex.

Another half hour passed, and the pressure in my head waned. Aiden wasn't coming back.

The line of stone cobras appeared in front of me, looking like shadowed ghouls waiting to strike down anyone who disrupted Pharaoh's rest. I spun away.

The *serdab* box of granite rose before me. Its peepholes appeared to be staring, and a twinkling came from within. I peeked in. The crumbling image of the statue's face inside the box reminded me of a skeleton or mummy. I inched closer, and the inner chamber of the box went dark. My blood turned chill. I shuddered and stepped back. Wait—I could see the statue again. Was I blocking the light? Glancing down, I checked to make sure that my flashlight was still off. But some kind of light streamed through the peepholes, as if they were fashioned to receive it ...

The crumbling block with the star image that Aiden had pointed out earlier sat nearby. The North Star? Twisting around, I glanced skyward. It would be the same star that we could see back home, as Egypt was north of the equator. I followed an imaginary arrow created by the two stars at the far end of the ladle of the Big Dipper and located the fainter North Star—Polaris—as my dad had taught me. Polaris was the first star of the handle of the Little Dipper. Not terribly bright, but eternal and unmoving in relation to Earth's rotation.

Stepping aside, I searched for beams of light entering the *serdab*. I couldn't follow anything specific, but there was definitely starlight reaching the inside ... *My God*. My pulse hammered inside my ears.

Chapter 57

Present Day

GLANCING BACK INSIDE the granite box—the *serdab*—I studied the luminescence of starlight and positioned my head to the side so as not to block the light's entry.

Pale beams landed beneath the grotesque face of the *ka* statue inside. Its protruding facets left its sunken eyes and shorn nose in darkness. This wasn't a mummy, but at night it sure looked like it could be. Prickling ran across the skin of my back as if needles poked me. I shivered and shook my head.

Two streaks of light entered the inner chamber through the peepholes and converged on the statue. The false beard and the statue's upper chest received the glow, but the area had crumbled away. No wait, there was a hieroglyph. I strained to see—

Something banged beside me.

I jumped away, glancing around. My breath stuck in my chest. Only darkness surrounded me. Had Aiden returned? It sounded like stone hitting stone …

"Aiden?" I whispered. "Aiden?"

Silence. Maybe a stone had dislodged from the pyramid and toppled to its base. Or was the other abductor here?

My hand found the metal handle of the gun inside my bag, but sweat rolled across my palm, making my grip slick. I turned back to the peepholes. The faint outline of a hieroglyph lay at the edges of a crumbled region upon the statue's chest. But I couldn't make anything out. Then I dropped the gun in a shock of realization …

Starlight highlighted the damaged area of stone, which was a much lighter shade than the rest. This shade made it appear as if the area had recently been chiseled away, rather than crumbling over the millennia like the eyes and nose.

My head drooped in frustration as my stomach clenched and released a shot of pain.

This couldn't be. Not after all this! I screamed in rage into the night, my voice echoing around the complex like a stadium, my body expelling tension. *Come get me then … whoever you are.* If I couldn't save Maddie, then there was no reason to worry about myself.

No reply.

After scrutinizing the statue for at least another hour, I couldn't find any way to reconcile this clue. I'd been defeated.

Frustration and anger tore through my body, burning my heart. I leapt at the wall of the step pyramid. Coarse stone dug into my fingers and the toes of my hiking boots as I ascended, but the gaps in the crumbling wall made for easy hand- and footholds. A brick slipped loose as I pulled myself up. It tumbled downward, clattering against fallen stone at the base. But my footholds saved me from falling.

I reached the first tier, looked to the sky, and shook my fists. "Why?" I yelled.

Someone was sitting up there already. I lurched back and nearly toppled off the edge. My arms swung in circles as I tried to regain my balance.

Wait—it was Maddie whom I was seeing again, this time on the pyramid with me. Her face had burned itself into my mind, and images of her showed up when it was dark or when I couldn't think clearly. Just my imagination, beating me down for never telling her how I felt, nor acting on it, and not wanting to until I'd lost her—just like with my dad, just like Heb with Nefertiti.

I groaned. How could I ever hope to find a clue that'd been erased from the *ka* statue inside that giant box of granite? This was now impossible, like when I'd helped alter those medical records …

Could there be some sort of backup for the path to the Hall of Records, in case someone, or even time, destroyed the original? Could the ancients even comprehend three *thousand* years into the future?

Yes, they could. Ancient Egyptian society had already been around that long—according to estimates of the year that the Hall would've been sealed. They would've understood the complexity and ravaging nature of time more completely than builders from the States—with only two *hundred* and some years of existence.

I paced around the unstable edge of the step pyramid, under the starlight, and dirt spilled over into the darkness. My muscles ached and wobbled, exhaustion overcoming me. I sat down on the cool stone and reached inside my bag for the journal and a flashlight.

My hand ran over the peeling leather cover. A tingling emerged inside me.

Wait—the story inside the journal was probably from the Hall of Records, discovered and translated by Dr. Shelsher and his student. But the journal was incomplete. I couldn't just sit and read the entire thing. It ended suddenly, not too much further on, as if the student had been forced to flee the Hall and run for the tomb of Amenhotep, leaving the hieroglyphs, the translation, the story, and the life of Heb unfinished. Just like Dad's life—unfinished.

But many of the places we'd traveled to before were near the locations in the story. Not exactly the same, with places as far apart as Cairo and Memphis, and Abu Simbel and Elephantine, but they were still close. And some of them were the exact same, even if we'd skipped over other places Heb had visited. We'd just been to el-Amarna. And the companions' more recent travels around their known world would probably be too far away for a clue about a location in Egypt. Maybe the next stop was Karnak, or modern Crocodilopolis ... Wait, but Heb had not visited the step pyramid after el-Amarna and a clue had been hidden here ... But he had passed by Memphis again.

I groaned in frustration. Was I reaching now, hoping to still find the answer?

Karnak and Crocodilopolis were in different directions. If we rushed off to either, it would take days of searching. And we'd already been to Karnak and found nothing. But Crocodilopolis used to reside at the modern Faiyum region. That was far to the west of the Nile and seemed unlikely to be a primary site for the Hall of Records. I shook my head in irritation. If I chose, I'd probably pick the wrong one—just like with every checkout line and freeway lane. Then Mr. Scalone would blame it all on me, and I'd feel horrible, my choice possibly costing Maddie her life. I'd already decided incorrectly too many times. Everyone would believe it was my fault.

I pondered this before frustration overcame me again. I lunged for the next tier of the pyramid and climbed. Then I climbed another level and another, my muscles burning with lactic acid. But before I knew it, I stood atop the peak of one of the world's oldest stone monuments. A light wind caressed the cracked skin of my face and whispered in my ears. My chest heaved with exertion, and warm sweat rolled down my temples. My hands shook, my forearms swollen and pumped from the intense gripping.

There was Maddie again—in my imagination—waiting for me. She sat down and patted the ancient stone beside her before brushing aside her silky, brown hair.

Clouds sailed across the night sky like ships across the ocean. Stars and then the moon faded as clouds veiled their light. But the rest of the surrounding world was still. The wind picked up and whipped in my ears. I could imagine my comrades and all the people of Egypt stuck in time, as if frozen in blocks of ice. Only Maddie and I were alive and aware.

"Gavin," Maddie whispered, her face becoming more and more clear in the darkness. Her eyes glistened with excitement, her shimmering hair floating in the gale. She wore her sheer glasses. But those were still in my messenger bag ... My heart ached for her. "Sit down and open up," she said, motioning to the very peak of the pyramid beside her.

I slunk down at the highest point.

"Why are you out here?" she asked, gazing into my eyes.

"What do you mean?" I asked. "I'm looking for you."

"No," she said. "Here in Egypt."

"I came for you."

"And what else? How did you ever get this far?" Her perfect teeth revealed themselves inside a beaming smile. "In school, we planned to relive the past together. Then you fell off my map."

"We, I—" I paused and took a deep breath. "Some people tell you to chase crazy dreams, and others tell you to be realistic.

My dreams of reliving the past with you died, like my dad. He tried to send me out here, but I had to do the right thing, you know." I swallowed and looked away. "My mom was still alive, and Dad's life of chasing ghosts was too hard on us. His carefree and optimistic outlook, the one that drew Mom to him, eventually drove her away. And it filled them both with resentment as thick as bile. I didn't want to become him and have you eventually despise me! And it would be worth giving all of that up ... for you. Just like Heb giving up his secure life for Nefertiti." I clenched my fists in anger at my upbringing and this life in which my dad was snatched from me far too early.

"And why is Mr. Scalone out here?" she asked, placing a tender hand on my shoulder.

I scratched my cheek. "To find the Hall?" I said.

She winked. "Your decision, even if it was the opposite of what I'd wanted, would at least have been made for the right reasons."

"Wait," I said. "What do you mean?"

Smiling, she stood and opened her arms. She started whispering, then singing. That same damn gut-wrenching song she'd sung at karaoke on our college break. But her voice was so beautiful, again like velvet caressing my ears and at the same time haunting. I couldn't ignore her or tune it out. Squeezing my eyes shut and shaking my head, I hoped the dream would fade.

Lyrics rang, some over the rest as she sang in a hushed voice, this time only to me.

"There'll always be things you do not know.
When you feel is how I write.
You'll do everything so I stay alive.
Lies and truth, one's on our side.
Will you wait for me tonight?
The light is coming, look with your mind.
See the dawn of our new day's rise."

Then, suddenly, I was back in Cairo again, with the detective—as we'd been a week or so ago—to identify Maddie's supposed body.

The detective's quiet whistling carried down the dark hallway as I trailed behind him. One light flickered overhead. Double doors stood before us, opaque with Arabic letters running across the glass. The morgue. My skin prickled with an eerie sensation and a chill.

The detective flung open the double doors and strolled inside.

Bloodied surgical instruments littered a green-tiled room. The stench of formaldehyde funneled into my nose and turned my stomach. Bodies lay beneath sheets on metal tables ... The room tilted and spun, and my abdomen contracted in a dry heave. I braced myself against the wall, but the sweat caking my palms made me slip against the cold tile.

The detective stopped beside a body, pivoted around to face me, and crossed his arms. He studied me—as if he thought I might be responsible for the murder and that my reaction would decide my guilt. He reached for the autopsy sheet and flung it aside.

A woman lay beneath! Dark brown hair, petite ... Her skin was waxy under the incandescent light. My breath caught in my throat. Empty, bloodshot eyes.

This time it was Maddie! She was dead!

Green from the room spun around me and my knees wobbled. I gasped for breath. No!

The pasty skin of her neck folded, and her head flopped over, limp. But she faced me. Her eyes sprang open—vacant, lifeless. Then her lips parted as slowly as if she'd been mummified. "How could you let this happen to me, Gavin?"

Chapter 58

Present Day

RED LIGHT SHONE THROUGH my closed eyelids, awakening me. Bolting upright, I still sat atop the step pyramid. The sun just crested the eastern horizon. I'd been huddled in a ball with a thin blanket from my bag wrapped around me. Biting cold had crept into my core. My teeth chattered.

I glanced around. Off in the distance, tourists atop camels already rode this way.

Climbing down the pyramid proved harder than going up, as I couldn't see my holds as well. I finally dropped to the bottom with a thud that jarred my knees. Someone yelled.

The guard with the machine gun pointed at me, his face as red as a beet. His hands and arms waved wildly.

"*Leave!*" he shouted amongst many other Arabic words. The guard could probably put up with me looking over the monuments, but climbing the pyramid and helping it crumble might be beyond his limits.

I slung my bag over my shoulder and raced away.

I exited the tomb complex, planning on finding a cab. But a silver SUV with a boxy look swung into a spot in the lot ahead.

Aiden, Kaylin, and Mr. Scalone stepped out, hefting large packs. They talked amongst themselves.

"Morning," I said as I neared. "Hope you guys slept well."

"Gavin!" Aiden said, taking off his cap. His dreadlocks dangled around the buzzed sides of his head as he rambled. "I'm, like, asses and Kool-Aid happy you're fine. I tried to come back, but the place was sealed tighter than el Chapo's cartel. I yelled for you and waited but no one hollered back. I'd hoped you were wandering the catacombs finding the—"

Mr. Scalone smacked Aiden upside the head. The teen's thin neck bent forward. "Stop talking like a moron."

"We're leaving," I said.

Kaylin shrieked and clapped, hopping up and down. "You did it! You found the clue?"

"Not exactly, but I know where we're going," I said.

Mr. Scalone crossed his arms over his exposed upper abs, a myriad of tattoos rippling with the flexing of his forearms. He shook his head, his oily locks trailing behind. His accent was heavy. "We've stopped considering your decisions. We only use you for Egyptian trivia, remember?"

I jerked the back door of the SUV open and threw my bag inside. "Not this time."

"Oh, and why do you think that?" he asked. "Do you actually know where to go next, or where Maddie is?"

"No, not exactly," I said. "It's a hunch."

"A hunch?" Mr. Scalone shouted, throwing his arms into the air. He cursed. "Where's this hunch at?"

I was silent for a moment as I considered the options. Words rang inside my head as clear as if they were spoken to me at this moment, words virtually identical to the journal: *netjer imy.k—The god who is within you. The kingdom burning inside you should be your guide, not external forces! Don't revel and wallow in this kingdom, but use it as strength. Make your future! It's not only yours, but my last hope, to shape a dream from this nightmare. Bring your friends home. Travel Egypt, but understand the world. Journey east, north, south, and finally fade into the west. You must find the clues themselves. Then you will return. Find yourself!*

"There were two distinct possibilities," I said, "but we're going to Crocodilopolis."

"What the hell?" Mr. Scalone said. "Where is that? I've never even heard of it."

"A crocodile city?" Aiden asked, tugging his black socks up toward his green shorts.

"The current name of the city is Faiyum," I said.

"A city out in the middle of nowhere?" Mr. Scalone paced around in a circle as he scratched at his thick stubble. "We're not going there; it'll take us hours away from the important regions of Egypt. What's the other choice?"

"Karnak," I said, jumping into the soft leather seat of the SUV.

"Oh, okay," Mr. Scalone said, clapping. "Back to where we were over a week ago now. Get out of the car, I'm going to have a look at this clue."

"You can't," I said.

"Why's that?" Kaylin asked, wringing her hands as she watched us.

"Because it was recently destroyed, just as the man Jenkins shot told us in his Arabic ranting," I replied, motioning for the others to get into the SUV so we could go. "There's no marker to follow to the next location."

"We'll lose precious time driving out to a city in the desert, one whose only claim to fame is a huge oasis," Mr. Scalone said as Aiden climbed into the vehicle. "That girl you're after might suffer for it. And exactly how are we going to find a clue in an entire city?"

Heb had once said that the poison of submission that coursed through his blood might not have an antidote, but I wasn't going to keep feeding mine. I'd already waited too long. "This is taking too long," I said. "Get in the car. We have to go. Now!"

"We had an agreement," Mr. Scalone said, holding the back door of the SUV open as I grabbed the inner handle and tried to slam it shut. "You were wrong too many times. We follow the guidance of someone with more experience. This crap reminds me of the time I had to debate with a local tour guide in a Philippine jungle and we almost died of heat exhaustion. You can't go anywhere without me, so you better show me the clue here."

I shook my head and pulled on the door. "We're leaving."

"Why are you so sure of yourself now?" Mr. Scalone asked, wrinkling his upper lip.

"Because you're Kaylin's bitch," I said, my hand reaching into my bag for the gun. Would I actually need to point it at him? "She and her father own you. All I have to do is convince her that her friend is suffering and needs our help. And if that isn't enough, I'll just mention that Crocodilopolis is the last step before finding the Hall of Records. Get in and drive, or I'll jump up front and leave you here, and you can spend the night on a pyramid. Maddie needs us now!"

Mr. Scalone's head lurched back in shock. His face turned beet red, and he grunted as Kaylin climbed into the passenger seat and nodded for the treasure hunter to drive.

Chapter 59

Journal Translation

We'd sailed north for days, away from Thebes and the Devouring Monster, before docking and covering our boat with brush. My feet sank into the sopping bank as we turned to the afternoon sun and marched for the western desert. The mud sucked at my sandals and ankles with each stride.

Tia whispered something in Paramessu's ear. The former captain covered his face and shook his head. But his other hand slid into Tia's as he forced a deep breath and then stared into her eyes.

"With you, however," Tia whispered, "I cannot love, or trust." She averted her gaze. "But I sincerely thank you for saving me."

"We must move quickly," Chisisi said, bumping into Paramessu and marching away. "That Hunter thing travels swiftly and conceals itself in water. I've decided that we'll go on foot from here so that we may at least see it coming."

"I haven't seen your cat," Paramessu said to me, his cheeks as red as his hair as he released Tia. "I feel safer when he is around."

My heart ached as I glanced back to the rolling current of the river. *Croc, could you still be out there?*

"But you're not sure how to get to Crocodilopolis?" Wahankh asked, his posture more upright and proud than normal. He toted a new spear and shield atop his broad shoulders. Seneb towed a cart of supplies.

"It is to the north," Tia replied. "We must follow a branch of the river out into the desert, to its terminal lake. The city resides there. I was an adolescent when I was shipped away, but I will recognize the region when we are close."

We traversed the hot desert, the wind whistling in my ears, and followed the junction between fertile land and red sand for weeks.

The Nile forked, a branch flowing off to the northwest, away from the north-flowing river. Water spilled over the banks and flooded the surrouding farmlands. The annual inundation was underway. Babbling from the rushing water surrounded us, attempting to make me drowsy and lull me into an unwanted state of tranquility.

"This is it!" Tia said with a nervous twinge in her voice. "I remember … the water road to the Faiyum oasis—the lonely lake in the western desert."

Images of Father's *ba*, and my dream long ago in slavery, popped into my head. I'd traveled in all directions, finally now into the west.

My eyes closed. Not long, Father, and I will join you … or defeat Akhenaten.

But the oracle had confirmed I would not be able to do so. Was there another life I'd want to live? Hiding as a farmer while Pharaoh reigned with Nefertiti at his side?

My muscles twitched with anxiety. Although I needed to face Akhenaten again, thinking of the actual moment terrified me.

Tia led us along the estuary with sluggish steps. Relentless sun and arid heat encircled us like smoke, stealing the moisture from my mouth and skin. Endless desert stretched in all directions.

Tia shouted and pointed. The city of the crocodile silhouetted against a lake that shimmered like jewels. Her breathing quickened, and she held her forehead as if in pain. Paramessu placed an arm around her shoulders and whispered in her ear. Was he comforting her because soon she'd have to face the demons from her past?

Vineyards and flowers bursting with brilliant color surrounded the lake, carrying a whiff of olives, sweet figs, and dates. The blue water clashed with the expanse of red desert around it—like an island on the empty sea.

"The most fertile land in Egypt," Tia said, and the clean trail of a tear tracked down her dust-covered cheek. "Sobek, the god with the head of crocodile, protects these lands and the tombs of his people."

A shiver ran from my toes through my spine and fingers. A crocodile god?

We stood on the far side of the estuary from the city, and although the waters were not as wide as the Nile, the flooding extended well beyond the banks. It would be unwise to swim the raging current.

We wandered the area, searching for a way across. A hunchbacked old fisherman rested in the shade of a scrubby tree by the shore. His reed boat bobbed at the water's edge.

"Hello," Chisisi said with a big smile.

A sun-darkened body with white hair turned. His pupils were opaque, like blue clouds, and spider veins engulfed his face. "Who's there?" the fisherman asked. The reek of dead fish surrounded him.

"We are warriors looking for passage to the city," Chisisi said. "One of us was born here, and we wish to visit. May we borrow your boat?"

The man sat in silence. "Are you warriors threatening an old man?"

"No … not yet," Chisisi said.

I let out a breath of frustration.

"You are a decent leader, Chisisi," Seneb whispered, "but sometimes you use as much tact as a monkey flinging feces."

Chisisi cleared his throat and said, "We're looking for help in crossing so we don't have to swim."

"It is much too dangerous to touch the water," the fisherman replied. "Everyone's too afraid to sit on the shores these days. Only a starving old fool would chance it."

"Is the current that deadly?" Chisisi asked.

"Not the water itself," he replied. "But what the waters brought."

Chisisi cupped a hand over his mouth and whispered to us, "We shouldn't have to explain ourselves."

The fisherman waved a gnarled hand. "The floods always bring the horrendous gift of the children of … I am not supposed to speak his name. But I am too old to care. *Sobek.* The Aten rises and falls every day, but Sobek is always here. And this year he brought the monster itself. Sobek is angry with Pharaoh. I could be killed for speaking such, but my time is near. If you are military, you may slay me now."

"We are not," Tia said, stepping forward. A softness lifted her words. "We respect your beliefs and only wish for aid in crossing the river. But what do you mean by 'the monster itself'?"

"A woman?" The man's head perked up. "Traveling with warriors?"

"Yes," Tia said, planting her fists at her hips, "and I am the native of Crocodilopolis. I know of what dangers the floods bring, but I've never seen a monster here. Not in this paradise."

"Well, young lady," the man said, spreading his arms. "In all my years, even I have not heard of something like this. It was brought forth from the mouth of the Nile, at the gates of the underworld, cast upon us by Sobek for our weakness and treachery. People have glimpsed the beast, but no one has seen it in its entirety. Many have been taken. Everyone fears the water. It strikes when you are washing clothes, bathing, or drinking. As big as a barge. No one goes to the lake—no one but me."

Tia rolled her finger in circles beside her head to hint that the old man had gone crazy, as if nothing in this water could get that big. "Can you take us to the other side in your skiff?"

Revealing a toothless grin, the old fisherman asked, "What are you offering? There is so much an old man hasn't seen, tasted, or felt in years."

"Don't get any wild ideas," Tia replied, the softness of her words replaced with a sharpened edge. "We have plenty of food, oil, and olives from the islands."

Paramessu stepped beside her, as if for protection, but she elbowed him away.

"We have our own olives," the man said. "Food, I could use more of, but a woman ..."

"We will rid you of your monster," Paramessu blurted, probably thinking the offer would protect Tia.

Wahankh groaned. My chin fell to my chest.

Not again.

"How bad could it be?" Paramessu said, his strong jaw clenching under his hooked nose. "It's not like we haven't been doing this for years ... and I don't think Tia finds him attractive."

Folding her arms, Tia's eyes narrowed as if she didn't think the comment was humorous.

"If you throw in a month's ration of grain, we have a deal," the fisherman said. "That should last me through this life. And I'd like to see the beast gone before I go."

"Deal," Chisisi said and shook the man's hand.

We packed our supplies and half of us, including me, Harkhuf, and Tia, onto the skiff as the fisherman took up a cracked oar. He paddled into the murky waters with light splashes, angling for the northern shore. The skiff began to sink under the load, and the river rose over my dangling feet, cold and wet. I couldn't even see my toes through the silt swirling around my ankles.

"You should've seen the floods when the monster arrived," the fisherman said, his eyes wide open as he looked into the sun. "Flooding is crucial, but too much can lead to destruction. There will be a famine again this year."

The skiff held its position just above the surface as we glided through the current. Harkhuf pulled his feet up to his chest. "I hate crocodiles," he grumbled.

I pointed at the water with my index and little finger—the crocodile ward I'd once been taught.

The wind quieted and the rumble of the current subsided.

"Do not fear," the fisherman said. "If Sobek strikes, there wouldn't be anything any of us could do to stop him."

I spit out a breath in disbelief, the thought making my heart race. My mind filled with images of predators lurking in the murk below.

After what seemed like an hour, we docked. Leaping off, Harkhuf sprinted thirty feet before collapsing. My feet wobbled along the soft ground, my knees shaking. The old man returned to the far shore and brought the others.

"We need to see Petsuchos," Tia said, marching straight away.

We hiked into the city. Locals stared and muttered amongst themselves as we walked down their streets, following Tia. Dust hovered in low clouds, choking me and causing me to cough. Tia held her head high.

The walls of a mud-brick temple stretched before us, its inner chambers open to the sun. We entered and approached a pond in the center—

A crocodile sunbathed beside it!

"Holy white elephants!" Harkhuf yelled, pointing. "A crocodile's inside the temple!"

The ten-foot-long beast's eyes popped open. It raised its scaled head.

I drew my swords.

"Do not disturb him," Tia whispered, grabbing my arm.

The dark slits of the crocodile's pupils contrasted against yellow irises. White membranes flicked across its eyes as it turned. Gold and precious gems adorned its head, neck, and legs, rattling as it slunk away.

"Why's it wearing gold?" Wahankh asked, holding his shield so that he could just peek over the top. The beast sank into the pond, but its eyes remained above the sunlit surface, watching.

"That is Petsuchos," Tia said. "He is the only portal to Sobek."

"You have to be joking," Harkhuf said.

"Unfortunately, I am not," Tia replied.

"What do we do?" Paramessu asked. "Beg him to come back out and speak to us?"

"Well, I don't think he can speak," Tia said. "He's a crocodile."

The soldier's cheeks turned as red as his hair.

"We don't have to do this again," Wahankh shouted. "The old man already took us across the river; we owe him nothing. And, Tia, you are home."

"The priests of Sobek can grant you communion through Petsuchos," Tia said, glancing around, "if there are any remaining. But I doubt they'd risk their lives with blasphemies for strangers."

"So you suggest we find the monster the fisherman spoke of?" Harkhuf asked, hiding behind Seneb as he watched the unblinking eyes in the pond.

Tia shrugged. "I was hoping to get more reliable information about the locations of the attacks and the sightings first. But I must help my people."

A child appeared at the far corner of the inner temple. He was short, his head and body shaven, his kilt sparkling white. My muscles tensed. Where'd he come from? And was this child a priest?

"You are looking for it?" the child, who turned out to be a she, asked in a quiet voice.

"Yes," Chisisi replied, standing proudly. "We will rid Tia's city of—"

"Do not speak his name," the girl said, running a hand over her oiled scalp. "There are ears behind every bush and building in Egypt. Many have been killed. Souls have been lost. But if you do indeed provide the services you speak of, Petsuchos will grant your desire." She glanced at the crocodile's eyes floating within the pond. "I will tell you of the ghost in our lake."

Chapter 60

Journal Translation

"OUR MONSTER, SOME HAVE SAID," the girl, who was shaven as a priest, swallowed and whispered, "is Sobek himself. He's not been sighted by many who are still alive. They say he can swallow a grown man with a snap of his jaws. He resides in the lake, at the city's shore, but at times ventures into the river. Nowhere is safe to wash or drink."

"Can we kill this thing?" Chisisi asked.

"If it is supposedly a god," Harkhuf said and stepped forward, "and we try to kill it, what will happen to us?"

"There's no real god other than the Aten." Paramessu folded his arms.

"I do not know," the girl said, her bare scalp wrinkling. "Sobek is displeased with us, his own people. I'm unsure if a mortal can kill this beast, and I cannot foresee the consequences. It could bring further punishment to the area, but as it stands now, the people live in terror and are already being eaten. More than anything, they wish to be rid of this beast."

"Can we lure it out of the lake?" I asked. "Seneb, you're the animal expert, assuming this thing is actually an animal or part animal."

"We'd need something on shore as bait," the brother replied, pursing his lips. "And a trap."

Harkhuf tugged so hard at his beard, strands came out.

"What kind of trap can we build here?" Chisisi asked.

"We have plenty of wood," the girl replied, "because of the fertile land. But timber may never hold this monster long enough to kill it. And no one in this city will fashion mud bricks down by the shore, not while this monster is still alive."

"We will trap this Sobek," Chisisi said, grinning and puffing up his chest.

"How big of a cage do we need?" Tia asked.

The girl shrugged.

Seneb tapped his boyish chin. "People often exaggerate the size, power, and aggressiveness of wild beasts, particularly if they want others to also hate and fear the creature—like farmers with jackals."

"Then a trap large enough to fit two adult hippopotami should suffice," Chisisi replied, banging his spear on his shield.

"I will gather help," the girl said and raced off, leaving us alone in the still silence of the temple—with the holy crocodile and his watching eyes …

"I'm not waiting in here," Harkhuf said and marched out.

We followed and sat in the growing shade outside the temple walls. No one spoke. Warm sweat rolled down my forehead.

Hours later, the squeaking of wheels and rattling of wood and metal broke the silence. The girl returned with a troop of young boys and elderly people who towed carts loaded with tools and slender timber.

"Our young men have been recruited into Egypt's military and law enforcement," the girl said. "Most now live in el-Amarna, Memphis, or Thebes."

The young and aged eyes of the locals scrutinized us. A few forced painful grins and gave tentative nods of encouragement.

"Unload the timber and tools," Chisisi said as he strode to the carts and motioned for the locals to begin.

We started constructing a wooden cage.

The clatter of metal tools hacking at wood and men grunting and groaning mixed with the smells of freshly cut timber and sweat.

Reed twine rubbed between my fingers and burned my cracked palms as I tied slender trunks together in an overlapping frame of wooden bars—a gate. This gate would be held open by a rope over a pulley. Once the beast was inside the cage, we'd drop the rope and the door would slam shut, trapping it.

A week passed, every waking minute spent planning, assembling, and testing our trap. The people of the Faiyum offered us plenty of food and an empty house to sleep in but would not speak to us other than a brief hello. Did they know we'd die, their guilt already weighing heavy upon them?

"Down to the shore!" Chisisi said, pointing to the lake.

The rough bark of the timber dug into several draining blisters on my palms and fingers as I helped hoist our massive cage onto makeshift log wheels—like those we'd used in slavery to move enormous blocks of stone. We rolled our trap down to the water. The timber bars bowed and flexed as it bounded along, but the giving nature of fresh wood would make it harder to snap.

The Faiyum oasis emerged before us, its still surface sparkling in the sunlight. Waving reeds and brush ringed the shores. Slender trees stood in scattered clumps, shading small areas. The locals whispered and glanced around, their eyes showing more white than my kilt. A group of boys and elderly men turned and fled, shouting and waving their arms.

We shoved the open end of the giant trap down into the water, and I entered through a door in the back. A local man of short stature approached, leading a sheep whose wool draped from its body in dirty clumps. Our bait.

The shepherd stepped inside the trap with me, but his sheep lurched back against its lead rope and would not step through the back door. After ripping a handful of grass from between the gaps in the floor, the shepherd held it out in a shaking palm—his bait for the sheep. He clicked with his tongue. The sheep flared its nostrils as if it smelled the trap and glanced left and right. But after a minute, the animal slowly placed one foot inside, and then another and another. The shepherd patted her wool, kissed her head, and tied her to a crossbeam. With a tearful eye, he stepped out. I followed and sealed the door with reed rope.

Then we hid amongst the reeds along the sides of the trap, the rough blades poking into my legs and chest, their tips reaching over my head. The stench of stagnant water hovered around us.

A crowd gathered in the distance, beyond the waving brush. Hours passed. Locals departed one by one, like bored cats. The sheep chomped the grass at her feet in hurried bites and cried out for her flock.

My heart twisted with pity. But I couldn't fathom a better alternative. At least the sheep didn't know what terror awaited and thus didn't fear its impending death—death that would be quick.

The sun set over the endless desert as my mind and gaze wandered, my legs tight from sitting still for so long. Ancient paintings spread across a rock cliff to the north. Many animals were depicted, displaying the diversity of life at the oasis. Birds and ducks of many species, fish, deer or antelope, snakes, rodents, cows, goats, a fox, a jackal, and even hippopotami. But my eyes settled on the low-lying shape of a crocodile. The reptile hid beneath rippling waves, watching the animals above. Beside the crocodile was an image of a strange creature. A fish tail attached to the upper body of a man with his arms swimming. The image of another man, drawn upon what would be the shore, hurled spears at this creature, but not at any of the other beasts.

"Perhaps the bait at the back of this giant cage is too far from the water," Paramessu said, breaking a long silence.

"Maybe you should bring her closer to the front," Chisisi replied with a smirk.

"I don't want to be here at night," Tia said, her lips taut. "If we don't see this monster coming, it will strike and disappear before any of you can even fire an arrow. Let's get the sheep out of there and return in the morning. If this thing's as vicious as the people say, it will feed soon."

Chisisi grunted, and his stern features narrowed. He held the rope, which when released would seal the front door of the trap.

"I'll get her," Paramessu said, the burning sunset blending with his hair.

"No!" Tia said, clutching his arm.

"We don't want to lose our bait overnight," Paramessu replied. "And you do not care for me, remember?"

Shrinking away, Tia bit her trembling fingernails. Her eyes grew distant, as if she pondered something.

"I'll get her," Wahankh said, approaching the back door first.

I gasped in amazement. What had happened to this man? Perhaps I needed some of his courage.

Paramessu, Seneb, and I stepped beside Wahankh. The others kept their distance, especially Harkhuf, who was barely visible in the reeds near the rear corner of the trap. I untied the twine and cracked the back door open. Wahankh stepped inside, his knees starting to shake.

"Close the gate," I said and motioned to Chisisi while watching the water's surface.

Turning his back to the lake, Wahankh gathered the sheep's lead—

A geyser erupted, along with a wave of water. Screaming, Wahankh barreled into me. His shoulder smacked into mine, his weight flinging me into the grass. I landed on brittle brush that crunched and jabbed into my back. The front gate of the trap crashed down.

I lifted my head. The rear legs of the sheep protruded from between stained teeth. But the surrounding green jaws were more than large enough to swallow the animal whole. The sheep's legs, the beast, and the cage all started thrashing around. The entire cage jolted and creaked. And the trap hadn't fully closed—the beast was too large to fit inside. Spraying water obscured the scene. But a scaled tail, as big around as I was tall, smacked against the bars. Timbers snapped and flew in all directions. A beast as big as a barge twisted as it pulled back out of the demolished cage, into the swaying reeds, and disappeared beneath the water.

The lake rippled. Silence.

Then shouts spewed from my companions, the locals having scattered like roaches.

Gasping, Tia clung to Paramessu.

"You're still alive, hero," Harkhuf said, smacking Wahankh on the lower back. "I released a few arrows, but the giant moved faster then a cheetah. If I hit it, you'd never know. It's going to take a lot more than a cage and arrows to bring this beast down."

Wahankh fell to his knees, his body trembling so violently that it appeared he was having a seizure. "We need an army."

We shuffled back to the city, our heads hanging in defeat. Locals muttered as we passed. Tia wandered off, alone.

"We cannot sacrifice our livestock," one local woman said. "We're already starving."

Touching the bracelet on my left arm, I closed my eyes. The bronze was cold against my fingertips. We'd have to rid this city of its beast if I were to continue along the path I'd chosen.

"You're one of the stupidest people I've ever met," Wahankh said to me, his voice tense and grating.

My eyes popped open before my eyebrows narrowed, and my muscles tensed in preparation for an attack from the bully.

His arms and legs still trembled like the slender boughs in the wind around us. "Growing up in the slums, I had to fight for every meal," he said, "to gobble it down as fast as I could. I had to take from others just to survive."

"What is your point?" I asked as my hand ran across the smooth metal of my sword hilt. "I've already heard this, and I've taken as well ... from my former master."

"That is why you're stupid," he replied, his pupils dilated like pits. But he stared as if he respected or feared me. "And this crocodile the size of a house proves it. No wonder you ended up here. It's always easier to take from the weak. Like you, I've tried to take from the bigger and more powerful, when I was young and naïve. After once or twice, even against those who are smaller but willing fight, I realized it's not worth getting hurt or killed over—when there're much easier paths in life."

Chapter 61

Journal Translation

I SAT OUTSIDE OUR ACCOMMODATIONS—an empty house at the edge of the city of Crocodilopolis. Having exercised and trained, I sipped warm water from the city's rationed supply. The beast in the lake prevented people from getting water down there.

A fading twilight glow surrounded me, and the stifling heat of the desert started to wane. Aged-yellow papyrus crinkled under my fingers as I read about a soldier of ancient Egypt from millennia ago. This lowly soldier learned that his commanding officer was about to lead their platoon into a trap—one that would kill them all. He should've stayed silent, but when the orders where given to march into the Valley of the Pine Tree, he stopped and shouted a—

Sandals scuffed on dirt. I glanced up from the story as Tia tiptoed out of the doorway of the house.

"Why so quiet?" I asked.

She jumped to the side and attempted to hide her spear behind her back. "What? I need to do something. If not now, I never will. You and the others … even Wahankh … have secrets. I must do it for him." Her voice was guarded, and she didn't specify who 'him' was, but I assumed she meant Paramessu.

I shrugged. "You need help?"

"I have to do this alone," she whispered. "There's a reason why I will never have feelings for a man that I am physically attracted to." She turned away. "Tell Paramessu that I'll return before sunrise."

"You're not going after that monster alone, are you?"

She scoffed. "The demon in my past is not a beast, at least not in the sense that you are thinking." She strode off and disappeared around the corner of the building.

A grunt arose from inside our accommodations. Paramessu stumbled out. His eyelids hung as he rubbed at his face and yawned.

"Where'd she go?" he asked.

I held my hands up in feigned ignorance. "She can take care of herself."

"Perhaps, but I won't let any harm befall her." He grabbed his spear and tall shield.

"I won't be able to stop you, will I?" I asked, standing before the former captain.

"No. But if she finds out that I followed her, she'll be furious. I'll let you come with me, as long as you promise not to speak of it."

I nodded.

We trailed Tia at a safe distance. She wound between houses and buildings under moon- and lamplight, searching for something. She sat on a step with her head in her hands, crying. Paramessu gripped onto a wall, as if holding himself back so that he wouldn't run to her.

Brushing aside her tears, Tia rose and marched faster. She stopped outside the door of a meager house and banged her shield against the wood and metal entrance. The spear in her hand trembled.

"Who is it?" an angry voice barked from within. "It's late."

Tia banged harder but set her spear and shield down, leaning them against the house.

The door flew open, revealing the reddened face of a massive older man with a protruding belly and thick legs. His gaze drifted over Tia's body, his multiple chins growing. "Wh-who are you?" he asked. He grinned. "Please, come in."

The man stepped back, and Tia entered. My muscles tensed as I crept down the opposite side of the street with Paramessu to be able to see through the doorway.

Tia's back was to us, but she folded her arms across her chest. The obese man smiled, then lunged straight for her. The massive force of his heft carried through his open grip and crashed into the side of Tia's face and neck. She toppled over backward, and the large man landed on top of her, squeezing her throat.

Tia grasped at the meaty fingers around her neck, and a squeak escaped her lips.

Paramessu bolted for the door, and I followed him. But we were too far away.

Tia's other hand flashed. Bronze reflected in the torchlight. She'd pulled her knife from her dress and sank the blade into the man's offending forearm.

He shouted in pain and wavered.

Tia squirmed out from under him and kicked a heel into his large nose. Blood streamed from his nostrils before he covered his face and fell over on his side with a smack.

"I see that you haven't changed the way you treat women," she said and then finally answered his question. "I am someone you hoped to never see again. And I know that you only have one strong lunge, then you're tired and out of breath—if you haven't taken your victim by surprise."

Something flashed through my mind … the massive crocodile in the trap, its jaws crushing down …

I halted in the middle of the street, blinking in surprise. Paramessu darted to the doorway of the house. I stumbled after him as Tia sprang on top of her attacker's protruding stomach.

"What are you doing, you crazy whore?" the man bellowed.

A hefty woman the same age as Tia's attacker appeared, holding her palms out in hopes of stopping Tia. "Don't hurt him," the older woman pleaded.

"Why, has he stopped hitting you?" Tia asked and yanked her knife from the man's arm, releasing a river of blood. "Aunt."

The woman's eyes gaped. The attacker scrambled but slipped and smacked his head on the floor, issuing a hollow thud.

"T-Tia?" the man asked, his hands covering his hemorrhaging nose and forearm. "I'm so glad you've finally come home."

"You mean escaped from slavery? Which you sold me into, Uncle?"

"Well, with your behavior, I had to," the man pleaded as he held a palm out in defense and scooted away. "You were trying to spread rumors. Such accusations would have made me an outcast or put *me* into slavery.

I was doing all I could with you, but you were a spoiled, ungrateful wretch of a child!"

"Is that why you were touching me?" Tia screamed. "After Father was taken by the crocodile, you were all I had! And you took advantage of me!"

"Now, Tia," the woman said, shaking her head. "You must be remembering things differently."

Tia straightened, the muscles in her arms rippling as she approached the woman. "Rather than sympathy, you despised me, yearning for me to disappear. Because in your twisted mind, you were jealous this sick bastard was fondling me instead of you!"

"You ungrateful …" The woman stepped forward, her hand readying to slap Tia across the face.

Tia turned her knife-hand around and smashed the hilt into the woman's face, which sent her flailing onto her rear.

"I lived a life of suffering and abuse then, only to see the same as a slave woman," Tia said, pivoting and advancing slowly on the downed man. Her attacker rolled over to his back, his eyes gaping. "I have felt the hands of bad men, but none have I despised as much as yours! When Father confronts you at the entrance to the underworld, he will tell Anubis and Osiris of your misdeeds. You'll never pass the confessions. The Devouring Monster will consume your heart, and you'll be nothing."

Tia raised her knife over her head to impale the fat man.

Paramessu lunged forward, but I wrapped my arms around his toned waist, his momentum dragging my heels through the dirt. "We've all needed help," I whispered, "but we all must confront our demons on our own."

Urine trickled from under the obese man's kilt onto the floor, forming a yellow pool around his knees and reeking like a cat's sandbox. Tia kicked his groin. He groaned and flopped back. She reached up his kilt with her knife and made a quick cut. The slicing of skin sounded, and her attacker shrieked in high-pitched wails. Tia tossed two round pieces of flesh onto his chest, and blood splattered his cheeks under dancing firelight. His ghastly pale body went limp, and he sprawled out across the floor.

"I will let you live out your days with this poor woman," Tia said, a bite as cold as the snow of the island mountain embedded in her words, "a woman who knows you are the worst form of life the earth will ever know but is stuck with you. You can contemplate the days that your soul still exists." Tia spun about.

Paramessu and I dived for cover, skidding across dirt and hitting the wall of the adjoining house.

Tia erupted from the doorway and grabbed her spear and shield. Tears rained down her cheeks as she sprinted away into the night.

I lay in the warm dirt, unable to move. My companions all had demons waiting for them, haunting their pasts. And I'd brought them there … but they each faced more than I'd ever suspected, akin to my own life and the secrets I'd kept from them. Had I freed these people, tempting them to become much more than fate would've allowed? My body tingled. But the time to confront my demons would come soon … My breath gushed from my mouth as my lungs burned for air.

"You'd better treat her well," I whispered to Paramessu, patting his shoulder and standing up. "But not too much too soon … or she'll be suspicious, wondering if you know something you shouldn't."

He nodded, and we jogged back to our accommodations. We sat outside the lamplit doorway but didn't say another word—lost in thought or reliving the scene with Tia. The high-pitched chatter of the night's insects and cool air surrounded us.

Then a rustle sounded through the shadows. Footfalls grew louder, and a white dress billowed in the dry wind. My heart stilled.

Tia.

She appeared at the rim of torchlight and forced a smile. Holding her head high, she strode for our doorway. Paramessu reached out for her fingers as she passed. His touch lingered. She paused and took a slow breath. Turning, she collapsed into Paramessu's arms and sobbed uncontrollably. Paramessu held her close without saying a word.

"I love you," she whispered between cries.

Chapter 62

Journal Translation

Hearing Tia's whispered words of love to Paramessu, my heart burst with warmth. I stared at her in Paramessu's arms under the lamplight outside our accommodations. Love and hope … Nefertiti's beautiful face flashed through my mind.

Love?

The emotion prevailed, even for Tia, who'd said she could never feel its embrace again. Had I brought these two together—encouraging Tia to nurse Paramessu back to health after the Devouring Monster's attack?

I stumbled into the house, lay down, and pulled a coarse blanket up to my chest. A smile clung to my lips as I closed my eyes, my mind wandering of its own accord. Light danced across my vision before I drifted off.

A group of women stood under lamplight at the side of a road in the desert. Nefertiti's gorgeous face wrinkled as she shouted at the exotic woman, Kiya. My love's plump lips parted, revealing her teeth as she waved her arms and hands at the foreigner. Standing her ground, Kiya's hollering and movements grew just as wild. Their faces turned red and their fists clenched as firelight flickered and danced. Several girls, possibly their daughters, jumped in behind them and screamed at each other. Mutnedjmet stepped between Nefertiti and Kiya, held up her hands, and yelled, "All right!"

"Why are they fighting, Mother?" a boy asked, standing closer to me than the group of women. The boy glanced up at his horse-faced mother, his eyes unblinking in curiosity—Beketaten and

her son. He reached for her hand. The round face and features of the boy prince emerged, making me gasp.

He looked a bit like me!

Mutnedjmet stormed away from Nefertiti and Kiya, coming for me. But she paused and brushed her hand across the boy's cheek. Then, turning to face me, she knelt and reached out ... Her lips struggled to turn up into a grin, as if they hadn't done so in quite some time. A broken amulet dangled from her neck as she leaned over. Bes! The one she'd broken for me. My heart skipped and released a wave of warmth.

Love.

My eyes transferred the emotion back, staring deep into hers ...

But she patted the top of my head—which made my vision of her bob up and down—before holding my mouth shut with a strong grip. "Like a crocodile," she whispered. "You can't bite that way."

I tried to speak, to ask what in the name of the Aten she was doing, but my mouth didn't respond. Instead, after she released me and stood up, my pink tongue lolled out and licked my diminutive, furry feet—

Awakening upon the floor of our cramped room, I exhaled in relief. Had it been a dream or another vision through the fox's eyes?

My companions were still asleep. Early morning light from the Aten streamed through the windows, showering the far wall and easing the chill of the desert night. I rummaged through the sack the magician had given me back in slavery. So many books ... Rolled papyrus crinkled between my fingers—the original spell from the son of Hapu. I tucked the scroll into my kilt and strode off to visit the lake before the others woke.

❋ ❋ ❋

When I returned to our accommodations, my companions were eating breakfast. Sweet smoke hung in air.

"Where'd you go?" Seneb asked, looking up from his plate.

"I had to think," I said and tucked away the papyrus spell. I reached for a plate and spooned lumpy grains coated with honey into my mouth. The thick liquid rolled across my tongue and down my throat. Earthy but sweet. The grains crunched between my teeth.

"There's no need to put it off," Harkhuf grumbled. "What're we going to do about that thing? If it doesn't get enough food from the lake, it'll start coming closer to the city."

"Its appetite will be satiated for a few days, and it will be unlikely to strike," Seneb said. "Waiting at the water's edge for hours and days will dull our senses, like sloths who eat mushrooms. We must be ready when it's ready. This time I will see it coming."

"The most dangerous trait of the crocodile is its jaws," Tia said, her eyes growing distant. "When they snap closed, they can crush a stone block. And they target the faces of their victims."

"They strike while camouflaged and can lunge over short distances as fast as a coiled snake," Seneb said, shooting his hands out and clapping. "Dragging their prey into the water, they roll and twist their victims to snap bone. Then they dive deep until whatever is in their jaws stops moving."

"The reason we lose so many to them," Tia said, her lower lip trembling, "is that people splash in the water when bathing or washing clothes. The commotion lures them in, telling the ancient beasts that something is out of its natural environment or injured. They prefer weakened, wounded victims as much as any predator, as much as Wahankh."

I pictured a man being snatched by a perfect predator.

Chisisi said, "We need a bigger cage with—"

"Or find another weakness," I said, standing as ideas tumbled through my mind. "Its size could be its downfall." I ran out of the house, back down to the lake.

At the shoreline a few hundred feet from where the previous attack had occurred would be a good spot for my trap.

The others arrived, but they all assisted Chisisi with constructing a much larger, stronger cage. Seneb barely blinked as he and Tia scrutinized the water while we worked. Those two best understood the beast and might see signs of its approach.

I hauled twenty logs with sharpened points to the water's edge, dragging them through the tangling reeds that whipped at my face and chest. Then I dug. My hands sank into the wet ground, and the dirt coated my forearms like a cooling salve. The holes I made filled with brown water but would harbor the stakes.

"If your trap doesn't kill the beast on its initial strike," Paramessu said to me, "then we'd all be face-to-face with the monster. That doesn't sound like a situation I'd like to find myself in."

"I agree," Wahankh said. "If there's nothing between us and this beast, we'll all die."

"Again, on you," Chisisi said, pointing at my heart. "You should assist us in making this cage stronger and actually help your companions."

Bracing against the rough bark of one of my stakes, I packed dirt around its shaft and angled the tip low toward the water. "If we set stakes up now, cover them in reeds, and wait a few days, the crocodile may not notice anything out of the ordinary," I said. "We must outsmart it to gain an advantage. These could impale the beast when it strikes, using its own massive force against it."

I rolled two smooth poles of shaven timber—trunks of sharpened wood about four to five inches in diameter—from my arms into Paramessu's and said, "These are heavy and awkward but will impale the crocodile and cause more damage than our spears and arrows. Please, use these even with Chisisi's new cage."

The others also accepted two stakes each but were silent. Seneb and Tia glanced at each other as if they were skeptical ... My friends didn't even trust my judgment. I should just follow—

"They won't let us use another sheep as bait," Harkhuf grumbled, binding poles of wood together for the new trap. "Who's going to sacrifice themselves?"

No one answered.

Hours and days of work and preparation passed, me building my spear trap and my companions assembling Chisisi's massive cage.

The night before our next attempt, and a week after our initial encounter with this supposed Sobek, whoever or whatever that was supposed to be, I couldn't sleep.

Muffled voices carried through our doorway. I snuck out into the cool night, and my eyes adjusted from the dark room to streaming moonlight.

The shadowed features of a man with wavy hair covering his forehead and upper eyes emerged, speaking with another whose back was turned. I crept closer.

"Trap Sobek like a tiger," Chisisi's voice said with excitement—he was the man who faced away. "I will be the only man to have ever captured a god! When I tour the world, living like a king, people will exude respect and awe, long anticipating my arrival."

"As we've agreed, if you can trap it and survive," the other man replied, "I will have my men waiting to smuggle the monster out of the city that night."

"But I will have full command of the traveling attraction and of the men who stay to work for me," Chisisi said. The slap of skin on skin followed as Chisisi clasped the other man's arm.

The shadowed man nodded. "And I will receive fifty percent of the profits." He paused. "Is this new cage strong enough to hold the monster?"

Chisisi shrugged. "We have to test it somehow, and I'm anxious to start my new life. These people," he waved his hand behind him, "question my direction. They are too stupid to know what is best for them, too blind to see true leadership. I am done waiting for them to realize my potential and true calling in this world."

My heart raced against my constricting chest, stealing my breath. Was this the real Chisisi? Was this the hidden past he never wished to discuss, a desperation to lead? Perhaps he always longed to hold power over others, to control them by whatever means necessary—even through lies and manipulation. Perhaps he'd attempted this and failed before, then believed the easiest path to respect and leadership would be the established superiority of a freeman over slaves. He never should have left el-Amarna. Women there thought something of his tales and confidence.

"How many do you think will die," the mysterious smuggler asked, "even if your trap holds?"

"None, I hope ... but we could easily lose the bait," Chisisi replied, swallowing. "Maybe more."

I took a step back. My bad ankle—from the hippopotamus injury—popped.

Chisisi whirled around and spotted me.

Damn it.

"I will deny anything you heard," Chisisi said with a sneer. "Your leadership has only gotten others killed, and no one will believe you over me. They prefer the cage to your trap because they know you are willing to lead them all to their deaths in order to achieve your desires."

The other man slipped into the shadows and disappeared.

My muscles tensed in anger as my hands found my swords. Chisisi was a lying bastard, but was he right? I had already led too many to their deaths. Staring at him, I gritted my teeth and shook my head, but then slowly retreated to my blanket and lay down. The coarse fabric scratched at my back. What should I do? I wished Croc were here to curl up beside me and give me comfort with his soft purr. Lying awake, I listened to my heart for guidance as the magician had taught me.

A voice rang in my mind. The voice was only a whisper, but it was Father's ...

I tossed and turned for hours, sleep unable to take me.

The next morning, during a cold breakfast and on our march down to the lake, my mind raced with scenarios of how to explain Chisisi's dealings to the others and have them believe me over him. Still no clear answer ...

I crept through the prodding reeds along the side of our much larger trap. Seneb inched into the cage from the back door, holding the stakes I'd given him. "I will be the bait," he said. "I understand this beast."

"No," Chisisi said, wringing his hands. "Paramessu should ... He is tall and can cover ground more quickly."

I bit my lip. If we lost someone, Chisisi would prefer it to be Paramessu so that Chisisi would have another chance with Tia.

But Seneb stayed inside.

Chisisi's lips parted and he groaned, as if wanting to say something more.

Hopefully Seneb would be able to slip out the back in a few quick steps. Paramessu wouldn't be any faster.

I stayed beside Chisisi's trap to offer help instead of waiting at mine. The peril involved was already great, and the risk would increase if we split up. And perhaps Chisisi's idea was better. Was he the stronger leader, in spite of the way he went about it?

Murky water slipped over Seneb's ankles as he waited, his feet sinking into the muck with a slurping sound. The color drained from his face, and his legs trembled. I held my breath.

"I don't like this," Seneb whispered, looking down.

Chapter 63

Journal Translation

"SENEB, GET OUT OF THE CAGE!" I shouted, motioning through the dense reeds to indicate the back door of Chisisi's trap. "You'll never move fast enough through the mud to escape *this* beast."

Everyone stared at me as if waiting for more answers.

The wind silenced, as did the chirping birds and waving grass. The entire world around the lake was still.

I shook my head as self-doubt grew. I didn't know what to do … but Father's words from last night, and long ago, echoed inside my soul. "*Netjer imy.k*—the god who is within you. The kingdom burning inside you should be your guide, not external forces! The answers are hidden within you and everyone. You're not alone. Find yourself!"

Picturing the leaders I'd known—Akhenaten, Chisisi—I imagined what I had to become, what I had to do.

"I will not lead through fear and intimidation," I said, and energy or tension released from within me, carrying out of my body like magic, "or lies and manipulation. But as of right now, and every day forward, I am guiding myself. I will be my own bait, in front of my own trap, as that is how strongly I believe in it." Turning, I strode to my camouflaged stakes.

"Get back here," Chisisi shouted, his voice stern, as if I were a child. "We need everyone to make this work—even you."

"Only those who wish to follow me should do so," I said, making eye contact with each companion. "I've listened to those with knowledge of the crocodile, pondered it, and plan to use its weaknesses against it. But I do not know what will happen. That is the truth. Also, the truth is that Chisisi doesn't know—"

A shield smacked into the back of my head and neck and sent me reeling. But I maintained my footing and spun around.

Chisisi snarled, "This group is under my command. I'm the only freeman amongst you slaves." He spit out the last word and stepped before me.

I rubbed the back of my throbbing head as the bridge of my nose wrinkled in anger. But I forced a deep breath. "Follow your own path," I said, holding a hand out in defense.

"I will not let you scatter my followers. You've been trying since the beginning, trying to get rid of everyone by sending them home." He cocked his spear back, ready to attack.

"The others may listen to you, if they wish," I said, straightening while I looked him in the eye, "if they believe your character is one they should follow. I do not. But I will not draw swords against you unless you leave me with no other choice. Then you will regret your decision."

No one moved. My body tensed.

"What is your reasoning for this second cage, Chisisi?" Tia shouted. "Wasn't it to contain the beast so that we could kill it?"

"Yes, to trap and hold the beast," he replied, lowering his spear.

"Then what?" she asked. "What if it breaks free again?"

Chisisi stomped his foot, his face beet red. "You should not question your leader!" he yelled. "I make decisions based on what is best for the group. That is how we've made it this far. Leadership is too often in the wrong hands. It's the reason why your friend there"—he pointed at Paramessu—"lost his position as a captain in the military. It was wrongfully given to him by his father."

"A leader must answer for his actions," Tia said, stepping before Paramessu with her spear and shield raised, as if protecting the man she loved. "If he is understood, his people will trust him."

The companions focused on me, waiting. My insides tingled as my heart raced and nausea filled my stomach. What did they expect of me? I'd only let people down with my decisions and cost too many their lives. I'd never force anyone to follow me. But their eyes bored into my soul, wide and unblinking. My stomach cramped. Too much attention, like with Mutnedjmet … I saw her face and the shattered amulet she still wore in defiance. My stomach released, and my muscles relaxed. Perhaps they'd been waiting for someone to lead them for a while. Perhaps all of Egypt had. We'd been heeding Chisisi and Akhenaten ... I pictured Amenhotep, the ghoul leader, and others who had risen to the occasion, whether they liked it or not, to save their people: the valiant Princess Scylla, Muttuy—the hooded wife of the previous mayor of Thebes, who may or may not have survived the Hunter—and the girl-priest of Sobek. They all made my heart soar with pride and wonder.

"I would follow you, Heb, into the very lake if need be," Harkhuf said, pushing through the reeds to stand beside Tia. "I am sorry that I doubted your plan instead of the freeman's. But your dedication and willingness to sacrifice yourself has convinced me."

Seneb nodded in agreement and marched through the slurping muck, exiting the cage. My stomach turned, imagining his fate if he would've followed Chisisi's plan. He never would have dashed out of the cage fast enough. "I no longer fear our future, as we've faced our past," Seneb said, nodding in my direction. "I'd travel with you to the ends of the earth."

Paramessu stepped up beside Tia and folded his arms as he glared at Chisisi.

"I no longer fear the strong so much that I cannot face them," Wahankh said, joining their ranks.

A feeling of accomplishment, one I'd never experienced, invigorated my heart, making it soar. Taking my life and its decisions into my own hands ... I could sculpt my fate into whatever I could imagine. "Come with me, then," I said, motioning for them all to follow.

"I will be watching when you all die," Chisisi said, slouching and stumbling away.

He disappeared into the reeds.

Wahankh and I sat on one side of my trap and concealed ourselves in the prickly brush. Paramessu, Tia, and Harkhuf hid on the other side. Seneb stood before the hidden stakes as the bait again—his decision, as he understood the beast best. We waited. The Aten crested its zenith and sank into the west. My muscles ached from sitting still, and my thoughts drifted.

"Seneb, maybe you should splash around," Chisisi shouted as he crunched through the grass on the hill behind us. "That should get things moving."

"It is now or never," Seneb said, jamming his tree-trunk spear into the water in front of my trap. "I can't wait another entire day wondering in which second I will be devoured. And we all grow tired. Things will get sloppy." He scanned the lake, attempting to see below the surface. But the floods had brought in tons of silt, creating a vat of swirling red murk.

Seneb kicked and splashed, growing braver. Seconds dragged by like hours.

My unblinking eyes burned as I grabbed my bracelet.

> *Darkness appeared abruptly. But this wasn't from the sun setting. A vision had entered my mind. Light emerged through a swirling murk above my head. I gazed upon my companions through the eyes of another—from beneath the depths of the lake.*
>
> *Seneb stood over the water, splashing like a child in the throes of its most magnificent tantrum. The spray of water sounded muffled in my ears. Somehow, I was beneath the surface, stalking the dwarf. But I paused with suspicion, my eyes focusing instead on Paramessu, who squatted nearby. His red hair contrasted against green reeds. I moved closer ... and closer. The bank was just beyond the surface, and Paramessu was within striking distance. Energy shot through my body, and my muscles tensed as if I were getting ready to attack.*
>
> *Silence. Then a short pause—*

"No!" I screamed, the vision gone, as my real body lunged from my hiding spot in the reeds beside the trap. Pointing to the water near Paramessu, I shouted, "Get—"

Paramessu turned as he lifted his stakes—

—massive jaws erupted like a tsunami amidst the roaring spray of dark water. I sprang past Seneb.

Rows of teeth descended upon Paramessu and jaws stretched wider than Paramessu was tall. His sharpened logs lodged into the roof of the beast's crushing mouth, holding it open as it tried to chomp down. Timbers bowed and creaked.

I flew through the spraying mist and barreled into Paramessu with a crack—and a jolt of sharp pain. We collided inside the gaping tunnel of a mouth and sailed into the reeds. A drawn-out groan escaped Paramessu's lips as his stakes snapped in an explosion of splinters. I rolled over.

An eye the size of my head glared at me from between standing reeds. The slitted pupil shrank, and the jaws snapped back open, thrusting at me—

But a hiss came from the beast as it whirled away. Seneb held the shaft of a spear that was lodged into its side. The monster lunged for the dwarf.

Seneb leapt like an acrobat, his body horizontal to the ground as he spun. Sailing over the line of camouflaged stakes, he disappeared into the brush. Cracking and snapping rang in my ears. The beast's jaws slammed together, and my trap impaled its flesh.

The monster hissed and thrashed, tearing the buried stakes from the ground. Tia's spear skewered one of its eyes. Paramessu and Wahankh hurled their weapons. Grabbing a sword and rope at my waist, I leapt atop its closed snout and landed on all fours. I clung to the roughened scales, buried my blade into its thick flesh, and threw the rope ... after the big strike was a moment of weakness. The end of the rope swung around and up the other side of the beast's jaws. Cinching the rope down tight onto the hilt of my buried sword, I bound its most lethal weapon.

The monster strained. Twine stretched and frayed. Harkhuf clambered up its leg and sprinted along its writhing back like a tightrope walker. He teetered onto one leg, wobbling. But he rammed his spear down. Bone crunched as wood buried into the monster's brain. Its jaws relaxed. The crocodile slumped into the grass, and a wave of trapped air escaped from underneath its body, rolling through the reeds like a fleeing spirit.

Harkhuf roared as he attempted to pull his spear from the monster's skull. But it wouldn't budge. He pummeled the base of its neck with his fists, screaming. Chisisi bellowed and charged down the bank, driving a spear into its flank.

Blood streamed down my arms and legs—gashes from dragging against the monster's teeth when I'd sailed into and out of its mouth. But I felt no pain.

A strong hand clapped down on my shoulder and yanked me off of the monster's jaws. Paramessu embraced me, crushing my chest. "I have seen no man show more courage. You've saved my life twice. Military man or not, I am at your allegiance until the end—no matter what you are pursuing."

Warmth spread from my body through my limbs and carried out my draining blood. I smiled and squeezed around his toned chest. He fell to his knees, wincing in pain. A large purple bruise formed over his side where I'd crashed into him, which was also close to where the Devouring Monster's jaws had snapped and deformed his ribs.

Tia wiped at the bleeding cuts also running the length of Paramessu's body, then planted a soft kiss on my cheek. "Thank you! I'll take him with a couple more broken ribs. I've nursed him back from worse."

"I *hate* crocodiles," Harkhuf yelled, shuddering and sliding off of the monster's scaled head. He leaned over with his hands on his knees and forced deep breaths. "I've said that I would stay with this group, but if I *ever* have to face an animal like this again, you'll see me sprinting back to Kush." He marched for the city on shaky legs and didn't even glance back.

"Like a baby with only vegetables for dinner," Seneb said, the reeds rustling as he popped out and brushed himself off. "All the humiliation we endured for our dancing dwarf training finally paid off, for both of us." He motioned to where he'd leapt over the stakes with his acrobatic maneuver. Then he turned to me, and his chin wrinkled. "When did you decide it would be a good idea to try to bind its jaws?"

My gaze drifted to the horizon. Mutnedjmet and Tia had given me the idea—from what Mutnedjmet had said in my recent vision through the fox's eyes, unless it was a dream, and from Tia's encounter with her uncle.

A few passing locals shouted and pointed at the dead beast or rushed away to the city to spread word. Within minutes, music carried across the shore and hummed in my ears as hordes of people approached, shaking rattles and singing.

We ate and drank alongside the locals as we tended to our wounds, experiencing the euphoria of heroes.

But because of the trauma of being forced to face off with a wild beast, Harkhuf didn't speak again for three days.

Chapter 64

Journal Translation

I OPENED MY EYES, DISTURBED FROM a deep slumber. A faint flame flickered inside our accommodations—the house on the outskirts of Crocodilopolis. Someone stood before me.

Jerking, I attempted to sit up.

The girl-priest of Sobek, who disguised herself as a boy with her shaven head, was here. Putting a finger to her lips, she motioned for me to come with her. The dwarves snored. Tia and Paramessu slept in each other's arms.

The girl stepped outside, and I followed her into the dark city.

We arrived at the temple of Petsuchos. The moon cast its reflection upon the still pond. A crocodile lay at the edge of the water, the jewels around its head and its gold bracelets shimmering.

"We must do this when there are not ears around," the girl whispered. "Sobek will keep our voices confined. You need to understand the entire truth of what has befallen Egypt."

"Do you mean Pharaoh?" I asked.

"I know your story," the girl said, circling the pool. The air turned chill, causing a blanket of gooseflesh to rise on my arms and legs. "Listen to everyone, but be wary and weigh all of their words. Your master made sure you didn't understand the truth. The priests of Amun wish to make you their warrior, if the magician's other trainees all fail." She paused and stared into the pool. "And you would gladly follow them. But do not think his priests are innocent."

"The priests of Amun?" I asked, picturing the men and women in Thebes wearing ram masks, those who'd forfeited their lives in order for us to escape the Hunter.

Her eyes turned completely white. "Priests, like the others, desire control. Those who possess the ability to commune with God hold the greatest power over people. They once morphed Amun into Amun-Re, to claim the sun for themselves."

"The god, Re, is also the sun?" I asked.

She smiled. "Re rides the fiery chariot of his disc across the sky and is worshipped by the priests of Heliopolis. These priests trained Akhenaten in the ways of the gods and of the world, cultivating his mind. They paid dearly. Cursed and cast into a city in the mountains to live forever in this life … the life of the suffering. They are not the Dark Ones, but something close."

Images of the gaping jaws of the ghouls in the dead city sprang into my mind. I shuddered, repulsed. They were priests?

"You *have* seen them, haven't you?" The oil on her head sparkled with moonlight. "You've spoken with Aanen, the high priest of Heliopolis, one of Akhenaten's uncles? Aanen would not forsake Re to worship one god as a solar disc, as such a transition would grant Akhenaten unlimited power. Aanen defied Pharaoh and was punished. Like you."

"Just as Akhenaten's other uncle at Thebes was punished … devoured?" I asked.

Her eyebrow rose. "And the high priest of Ptah."

Who?

"You knew Thutmose," she said.

I gasped. Thutmose, Akhenaten's brother, the original crown prince, had been the high priest of another god?

"So Akhenaten's war with the priests and magicians is a war for supreme power," I said.

"He's revolutionized Egypt," she whispered. "Now, he decides who can worship his God and thus obtain the afterlife. He's evolved into something that no other man on this earth has ever become. The one god of the one religion."

I braced myself against the mud-brick wall, reeling. A new religion of only the living Pharaoh …

The girl looked up into the night sky and raised her hands. "You may see me as young, but I've been here before. The few remaining magicians and priests recently gathered. I spoke to the son of Hapu." Her head snapped back down, her unblinking eyes boring into the crocodile's irises. "Egypt no longer considers the dawn of time as the handing over of the throne from the god Horus to the legendary King Menes. We are forced to believe that Akhenaten is the beginning. Mark my words: A religion of one god forcing itself upon others will be the beginning of the end of mankind. And then the time of man will not last as long as the previous age of Egypt."

I stepped back, my hands shaking and my breathing quick and shallow. My desire for revenge against Akhenaten could affect the entire world ...

She swallowed. "These are not my words, but your magician's final speech. Wars will rage for centuries over nothing other than conflicting beliefs in our creator, with no proof to appease any side. There will be more violence and murder in the name of God and righteousness than from any disease upon this earth. And our greatest civilization will not be alone in its fall."

This was deeper than even I'd suspected ... And long ago, with Mahu's help, I'd saved my former master from death by pulling his drowned body from the river.

"The wisest of men has spoken but is now silenced," she whispered. "The son of Hapu passed into the underworld, taken by his own hand."

"The magician is dead?" I shouted. My insides tingled with disbelief and fear. What could I ever accomplish without his aid?

"You'd run to Nubia and had been gone for too long," the girl said. "The son of Hapu's other trainees were failing as well, and he thought you'd never return. Years of serving Akhenaten, without driving any sense into his madness, distressed the magician beyond words. He banished a group of lepers from el-Amarna, convincing Pharaoh they were unfit to live beside Egypt's faithful. It was the only thing he was able to convince Akhenaten of in all of his years."

My stomach twisted in pain. Although I didn't fully trust the son of Hapu, such hatred of other people was against his character. Perhaps he'd regretted his decision and had later taken his own life. Could I ever hope to return to el-Amarna and face Akhenaten without him?

"You can still find hope by visiting the west. He can speak to you there."

"This is as far west as I can go!" I shouted, falling to my knees.

She nodded. "Physically, but you must enter the Aten's west, descend with the sun into the underworld. You must, before facing an immortal Pharaoh. I would have you locate the Pyramid Texts, the origins of the Book of the Dead, but I fear we do not have time if we are to save Egypt."

"You want me to die?"

"I will show you the tombs of Crocodilopolis. Sobek and Petsuchos will allow it … this once. It was not Sobek's monster in the lake, but rather one created by the rising chaos." She walked up to me, her face an inch from mine. "Commit the writings to memory. Then visit the lake and call upon the extinct ones. Such creatures were drawn as cave paintings near the Faiyum over twenty-five thousand years ago. Lurking in the deepest waters of the seas, they may come if they hear the ancient summons. They wish us to believe they are gone so we will no longer hunt them. We did once, almost to the last. But in an earlier age, we worked together to gather food from the sea and lived in harmony. Then man grew greedy. He no longer wanted to share the spoils of the oceans with its inhabitants. Be wary. They despise us and will harm you, but it is the only way anyone from the council could foresee you having any chance of returning."

She took me by the arm, her oiled skin slipping against mine, and led me away in a different direction—deeper into the city. It was still and quiet, as if the locals had celebrated so hard, they'd all passed out. We walked the streets for an hour, beyond the buildings of the living, and stepped between the houses of the dead. Shadow and moonlight twisted across towering tombs of stone and mud brick.

What did this girl want from me … and why would the magician supposedly take his own life?

We approached the doorway of a tomb that was sealed by stone. Engraved crocodiles and humanoids with animal heads stood watch over the entrance. Dread rose inside of me along with the stubble on the back of my neck.

"This is the false door that the *ba* of the deceased uses to enter and exit to travel the world by day." She held a hand against the smooth stone. "A former high priest."

I swallowed.

"You will have to break in through the original door of the tomb." She poked my chest. "But don't take anything, or Sobek will return and we'll all be consumed."

She leaned over, lifted a pickax that rested beside the tomb, and pointed. "There was the opening. The mud brick is not as thick there. Read from the Book of the Dead. Learn of the Book of Gates and its spells. An early version is written inside, incomplete. But you'd have to travel far for a full retelling."

"You want me to break into a high priest's tomb and take a book?" I asked, imagining the horrors I'd face.

"You won't take anything," she said and knocked at the original opening. A dull thud sounded, as if feet of solid mud brick lay behind it. "There is no physical book. Memorize the spells."

No book? She'd just mentioned one.

"Nearly two hundred spells have been discovered by man, but they are not all in there." She shrugged and motioned with a flick of her head. "Find the ones you need. You are allowed one week."

"I'll need more time to—"

"That is all the time Sobek will allow. The damage to the entrance will be hidden, but if you're not out by then, you will be sealed in forever."

The girl lit an oil lamp that sat on the ground beside reed pens and a stack of papyrus before walking away and disappearing into the night.

I picked up the axe and chopped into the mud brick. The tip sank in with a clunk, and the shaft of wood vibrated in my hands. I worked for hours, my hands growing raw as chunks of rock-hard mud crumbled and fell inward. Air sealed up ages ago whooshed out around my head like a gusting storm. The smell of musty earth surrounded me. Time itself entered my soul, and my body tingled with fear. What guardians awaited me for disturbing their master's rest?

I squeezed into the tomb through a narrow gap I'd made and held the lamp aloft. My other hand reached for a sword. The only sound came from my breathing.

Glittering jewels, furniture, food, and figurines filled the inner room, firelight dancing across everything with flickering shadows. A mummified crocodile and linen-wrapped cats stared back at me. I shivered as I glanced around. But the walls were the most impressive. Hieroglyphics adorned every inch of every surface, an array of deep colors.

Curiosity drew me on, and I navigated between stacks of ancient goods. In the adjoining room, a sarcophagus waited. On the outer surface, scrawling writing surrounded the painted face of a man. I knew what rested inside. Turning away, I blocked out eerie thoughts and examined the walls. Spells from the ages to guide the deceased in his next journey—the Book of the Dead! And so many gods that I'd never known …

I ran a hand across the image of a man, the ancient paint as smooth as the precisely carved stone it lay upon. The sensation of someone standing in here with me pulled at my thoughts. But I read and copied the ancient secrets until the sun rose. Most of it didn't make sense, as I had a difficult time picturing things like the ferryman, portals, and mounds.

I visited the tomb every night and attempted to sleep during the day in the house we were allowed to occupy. But my stomach burned. I twisted and turned with anxiety as I tried to sleep, still unsure about what I had to do. When my time was up, would I have the important spells? Would I remember … ?

Chapter 65

Journal Translation

"WHERE'VE YOU BEEN GOING at night?" Harkhuf grumbled. My eyes opened, and I lifted my head from my blanket. He sat in the doorway of our house on the outskirts of Crocodilopolis. Sunlight streamed in over his head. Afternoon. And I still couldn't sleep.

His right eyebrow climbed up his forehead. "You've been up to something ... a woman?"

I laughed as my head fell back and bounced off of the hard floor. A dull pain followed, creeping across my skull. "I wish."

"It's time we depart," he said, glancing around. "The locals whisper and point at me like I'm a hero. It makes me nervous. And I don't deserve the title. Where do we go from here?"

My companions all entered the cramped house.

I sighed and sat up. So much for trying to sleep, although my eyes felt scratchy and dry—weariness from the long hours and nights of studying the inside of the tomb. "I wish for every one of you to come with me, until the end," I said as I stood and patted Harkhuf's muscular back.

"Let me show you the magic of the delta," Chisisi said, grinning as he planted his hands on his hips and looked at Tia. "Anyone in my company will receive a king's welcome. It is my land." His hair draped over his face as he gathered supplies.

I shook my head in disbelief that Chisisi still remained with us. He must've run out of other options, or this was typical of his behavior after his true character had been discovered. But the others didn't know of his dealings with the smuggler … I scratched my chin as he rummaged through a pack and then held it out for Tia—like Mutnedjmet had done for me when I'd been sent into slavery. My heart twinged, and my cheeks flushed with the warmth of bitter nostalgia. I should tell the others about what I'd overheard Chisisi say to the smuggler. But would Harkhuf kill the freeman or only chase him off? And would living alone out here also be a death sentence? Chisisi desired nothing more than to lead and could use power to manipulate us, but no one would heed any of his orders after the crocodile ordeal. I gritted my teeth. If I were Akhenaten, I'd have Suty kill him …

But I couldn't lead like Akhenaten. And the others had all overcome their demons. Perhaps Chisisi could as well, with more help.

"I need to visit the Faiyum again," I whispered.

Chisisi waved me off. "We've already done that. And I still helped drive one of the final killing blows into the monster."

"I have to do something at the lake before returning to el-Amarna," I replied.

"El-Amarna?" Chisisi asked, bumping into me. "Are you mad? No one in this group is ever going back there."

My hands found the cool metal of my sword hilts. Chisisi shrank away. "I don't know how to explain what I'm about to do …" I said.

"Don't tell me there's another crocodile waiting at the Faiyum," Harkhuf growled.

"No," I replied, my mind growing distant. "But you must help me perform a feat I'd be too afraid to do on my own."

Harkhuf's head jerked back. "When I'd said I'd follow you into the water if need be, I was speaking metaphorically. I won't actually go swimming in there."

"Our trials have bound us together," I said, straightening, "and each of you makes the group stronger. But I must visit the beautiful dead to determine if I can conquer my own demons—like the rest of you have. I, however, do not know if I will return."

I marched out of the house for the lonely lake.

Chisisi cursed. "I'm leaving. Go find your deaths." He stormed away in another direction.

"Finally," Harkhuf grumbled as he and the others followed me. "I thought I was going to have to beat the freeman away. He almost got my brother killed."

In the distance, water rippled and glistened under the morning sun, begging me to approach. We walked into the prickle of the stiff fronds of the reeds. A blue heron spotted us, beating impossibly large wings against the still air with a whooping sound. It lifted from the water's edge into the sky, and its feathers blotted out the rays of the sun. The Aten was only one god of *many* ...

Something splashed. I jerked, startled. Two ducks swam by. A fishing bird surfaced with shiny prey in its talons. Calling out, as if to announce its victory, it flew away with its prize.

What else lay beneath the lake? I'd read of many dangers lurking below the surface, but the creatures I imagined were not in any of my books.

I stepped into the lake, keeping one hand on my sword. Water sloshed around my feet and my body trembled. Would another crocodile erupt like a wave and engulf me?

The others stayed in the reeds. The lake water washed in cool, rising to my ankles, then to my knees. Yanking out a rolled papyrus, I took a deep breath. Could Princess Scylla have possibly known I'd need this?

"I am grateful to have shared my cursed life with each of you," I said, my back turned to them. "I'll never forget and will await you all on the other side."

Seneb gasped. "You're talking like an old man who doesn't recognize his own children."

I recited the ancient words from the papyrus and traced symbols in the air. Magic and the web of time entangled itself, summoning a sucking feeling in the pit of my stomach. Completing the spell in a crescendo of chanting and waving, I blew into the wind and then into the water.

The tiny ripples that my breath created receded. Nothing happened.

I waited another minute, then ten more.

Laughter erupted. The deep voice of Harkhuf said, "You make a better archer than a magician, and even that is nothing to brag about."

I waded back out of the lake and slumped into a patch of soft grass at the shore. My eyes blurred as I watched the wind create and carry small ripples over the water's surface, the gentle gusts whispering in my ears. Hours passed, and the evening sun set behind the trees.

Pyramid-like clouds rolled in on a high wind, dark and foreboding like thunderheads. In the midst of their abstract forms, a face appeared, twisted with pain. Father! He was watching from above … Had I failed him by not finding myself or the god within me?

Fading light crawled between a thin gap in the clouds, settling upon a lone tree on the far shore. The flowers of the tree, a tamarisk tree, blossomed—petals of sheer black …

"Now what?" Paramessu asked, patting my shoulder and disrupting my daydream or vision or whatever these images of Father were. Tia wrapped her arms around me from behind, as if to comfort me, but I was as lost as ever. At least my companions must not have seen the tree. But I had no idea where to go from here. Back to Akhenaten, to face him and die?

Light and shadow stretched across the now still surface of the lonely lake, reflecting orange and ebony.

Climbing to my feet, I groaned in frustration and let my head fall back and my eyes close. "Let's return to el—"

Muffled whispers carried to my ears. I glanced around. Circular ripples formed thirty feet from shore, rolling in the twilight. I waited for a duck to emerge. The water swirled gently at first but became a small whirlpool. My body tensed.

"You really want to go back to el-Amarna?" Tia asked.

A slender hand and arm, with skin so pale it resembled milk, stretched out from the water, reaching for the sky.

Chapter 66

Journal Translation

"BY THE ATEN!" Paramessu swore, pointing at the pale arm rising from the lonely lake. "Someone's out there!"

"Do we help her?" Harkhuf asked.

"She must be able to swim just fine," Wahankh replied.

"Like a fish with ..." Seneb said in shock.

Paramessu hefted his spear, preparing to throw. "I've seen some bizarre stuff traveling with all of you, and I don't trust this situation."

The hand retracted and disappeared below the surface without a splash. The water grew still.

"Put your spear away," I said, unsure of what to do. Or was I afraid?

The magician's old voice rang in my mind as if he suddenly stood beside me and I were his pupil once again. "Will is devotion and persistence to your wish. A wish fades with time or hardship, but will never dies."

I leapt into the Faiyum with a splash. Murky water crept up past my knees. The liquid felt heavier and more viscous than normal water, as if it would encase my legs and hold me there.

"What is he doing?" Harkhuf roared. "Heb, don't go out there!"

My feet sank six inches into loose mud as I plunged forward. Water rose to my neck. I squeezed my bracelet. "I'd rather dream with my eyes open than live in a nightmare," I whispered, encouraging myself with my own words of dedication.

"Come back to shore!" Tia shouted.

"Keep your weapons on the ground, no matter what happens," I yelled over my shoulder. "She will suspect a trap."

"Whatever is out there may not be friendly," Tia replied.

It was too late. My feet no longer touched the bottom. I tread thick water as the terror of an unknown something waiting below consumed me. My blood turned cold. Deathly silence.

Tia screamed. A great cat paced at the edge of my vision along the shore! The beast roared, and the sound carried across the lake. The orange and white figure reared up on two legs.

Something grabbed me. My head was sucked under, and cold water filled my ears with a gurgle that turned muffled.

A crushing grip encircled my bad ankle, pulling me deeper and burning like fire. Kicking to free myself did nothing. My eyes popped open in the murk as bubbles spewed from my nose and mouth. Instinctively drawing my sword, I whipped my head around, searching for my adversary. A pale woman of astonishing beauty—like Nefertiti but with skin like a summer cloud. I lurched in surprise, not expecting a woman or something with such an appearance. Her fingers held the wrist of my sword hand. I couldn't move the weapon. I shoved my knee against her bare chest. Her waxen hair drifted across her face …

Something latched on to my other arm as I reached for my other sword. Another woman, with a fishlike lower half, propelled me downward. She smiled, then winked. More hands grabbed my limbs. I released the remaining air from my lungs in a drowning shout. Struggling with all of my might, I couldn't free myself.

These creatures would enact their vengeance—upon me.

A volley of arrows streaked through the water, cascading around us. Their points sparkled, traveling along the underwater paths of the twilight sunrays.

Burning arose in my chest from the lack of air. I focused on not gasping for breath. My limbs turned numb, my head light. I sank deeper into the lonely lake.

My throat compressed as if it would collapse. My mouth popped open against my will. Cool water gushed in around my teeth and tongue, down my throat, and into my chest, bringing excruciating pain—like drinking fire. I shuddered a few times, then went still.

My eyes bulged open as I died.

Chapter 67

Present Day

OUR SUV BARRELED DOWN narrow roads out in the western desert, heading to the city of Faiyum—my best guess for following the path to the Hall of Records, and finding Maddie.

"How'd you know not to go back to Karnak, bro?" Aiden asked, staring out at the empty landscape of brown dirt and rock. His lips smacked as he chomped on a mouthful of gum.

"I don't know for sure," I said, tapping my foot and making notes with pen and paper about the desecrated clue inside the *serdab*. "But someone had to decide something. Every decision I've made, someone berates me for it. Maybe you too. That's what medical school's about. Sometimes even when you're right, those above you will tear you down, because there are still adult bullies ..."

I'd have to live with my decision either way, but I wasn't a naïve kid who didn't know anything about Egypt. I shouldn't just shut up and listen to a supposed authority—one whose opinion and knowledge I didn't trust. Mr. Scalone didn't use evidence and fact to decide anything, only gut reactions.

"Wasn't there some kind of prophecy?" Aiden asked, glancing over at me. "In ancient times, I mean?"

My dry forehead tensed with confusion. "There was an oracle at Karnak ..." Karnak. Why would he ask that?

Aiden shrugged, returning his attention to the passing desert. "Just trying to help out. I figured maybe there'd be a prophecy about the Hall, or us."

I laughed. "About us?"

I thought of Heb and his battles. Why did so many people believe someone had to be born into greatness, like royalty, to accomplish anything? My fingers found the cold bronze on my wrist.

Dad. You'd have wanted this fate yourself, but you steered me into it instead.

"I don't want to believe in fate or destiny," I said.

Mr. Scalone weaved into the congested city streets of the Faiyum, dodging people and compact cars before continuing out into the far desert. Finally, we parked near the oasis: Qarun Lake—a vast body of water in the middle of a stretch of barren land.

I jumped out, scouring the far cliffs. It was cooler here beside the water, but the wind howled, carrying dirt, grit, and the tang of the beach.

Kaylin placed her soft lips against my ear. "What are you hoping to find in the lake? And are there crocodiles in there?"

"No." I shook my head as I shouted over the gale and stepped away from her. "The crocodiles that used to reside here were killed off a long time ago. But there're strange things in this area. In a valley nearby, whale skeletons were unearthed and date back forty million years. They were carnivorous whales with five fingers on their fins, and they even had vestigial legs."

"Now you're just trying to scare me," Kaylin said, raising an eyebrow. "You said no crocodiles. I'm good with that."

Locals waded through the placid water with long fishing poles, and paddleboats dotted the surface of the lake. Tall reeds and short brush grew in clumps around the shore like school kids in cliques with their own kind. This entire desert used to be an ocean, millions of years ago. Then it slowly transformed, and oases dotted it like the lakes and ponds in Florida or western Washington. Now, this was all that was left, one of the oldest lakes in the world. Fossils of ancient sharks had been found here, as well as the world's oldest apes, and another strange mammal that had lived in the surrounding hills. It looked like nothing alive today and has never been seen anywhere else in the world. This place could mask some hidden message.

Aiden shielded his eyes as he studied my face. "A skeleton can last forty million years?" he hollered back over the wind and tucked his fox inside his T-shirt so that only her head peeked out from his collar, her eyes squinting against the wind.

"In the aridity out here," I said. In the far distance, cliffs resembling those described in the journal caught my attention. It would take us hours to hike that far. I rushed back for my bag.

Two local men in the lake started yelling, shielding their faces and bending in the increasing wind. They waved for others to follow and waded back to shore. One shouted at us and pointed at the horizon. Brown clouds swept over the far end of the lake, miles in the distance.

"That's sand," Mr. Scalone yelled as he hung up his phone and stepped out of the SUV. "The Minister of Antiquities just said they've been having more and more sandstorms in the Faiyum recently. And the people have been finding things after the ground has shifted—mostly fossils and bones. This sand better not cover up what we're looking for, but right now we need to find shelter until this passes over."

Kaylin's fingers tugged at my arm as a brown wave encompassed the horizon.

Jumping back into our vehicle, we slammed the doors shut. Mr. Scalone gunned it, and our wheels flung dirt over a group of locals trying to pack into a cart. We sped off.

The sailing grit chased us like an explosion that we were trying to outrun. Little tings and dings started as dirt pummeled the car. We were doing over eighty miles per hour by the time the brown fog reached for the back of our vehicle. My eyes bulged as I stared into its abyss.

"Stop!" Kaylin screamed, reaching for the steering wheel from the passenger seat. "You won't be able to see, and we'll hit someone or something."

Mr. Scalone's hands tightened on the wheel. He slammed on the brakes and pulled over. Darkness engulfed us before we'd even stopped. Kaylin huddled against Mr. Scalone's chest with her head down. Aiden leaned over into an airplane crash position, protecting his fox. I too covered my head with my hands and ducked below the windows in case rocks came flying through.

Squealing from dirt tearing at the metal of our SUV nearly deafened me. Loud bangs from larger debris came at random. Something smacked against the window. The vehicle wobbled side to side. I dug my fingers into the leather seat in front of me, my breathing coming in gasps. The fox yipped and whimpered, her eyes like marbles as she stared at the windows and trembled. I reached out to help comfort her and rested a hand on her wiry fur.

After what felt like half an hour, the howling receded.

Sitting up, I glanced out. The windows were covered in a thick layer of brown, as if we'd driven through a forest fire and picked up all of the ash. Mr. Scalone turned on the front and back wipers. The dirt scraped away a layer at a time with a scratching sound. He used the washer fluid, which cleared away a spot in the center of the front and rear windshields. That brown abyss behind us had faded to a hazy view of the lake far in the distance. But I couldn't see the city ahead as the dust storm raced in that direction.

"Whoa," Aiden said. "That was freaky."

I nodded. "Kaylin, Mr. Scalone?" I asked. "You both okay?"

Mr. Scalone laughed. "I've lived through a lot worse than that, like the time I had to camp on the north face of Everest."

Kaylin sat up, her face pale. But she turned and studied the lake, her blue eyes wide. "Gavin, you were headed back for your stuff like you'd seen something. We need to do this while we can, and I'm not one of those prissy girls who needs time to recover."

Floating dust tickled my throat, and I coughed. "I saw some cliffs I'd like to investigate."

Mr. Scalone wheeled the car around and drove back, our tires plowing through drifts of sand like the snow back home.

We unloaded at the lake. The local men appeared disoriented as they searched for belongings and even undressed to shake sand out of their clothing.

Grabbing my camping gear, I marched for the cliffs but kept one eye on the horizon in case of another storm.

The cliff paintings of animals that used to dot the wetlands called me onward. The same images Heb had seen, but many were faded with time, and only parts of the creatures stood out: crocodiles, fish, birds of all sorts, hippos, antelope—

Kaylin shouted, but I couldn't see her.

A sand drift towered ten feet high near the far edge of the rock cliffs—
a result of the storm. Her voice came from behind it. I ran around to the
other side.

"Oh my God, look at that thing," Kaylin said, pointing.

A mandible protruded from the earth beside the pile of sand. The
exposed teeth of the skeleton were as long as swords. Flinging piles of dirt
aside, I unearthed more teeth and a long upper jaw—a jaw almost as long
as I was tall! A crocodile that could probably have swallowed a man whole.
Aiden joined in, scraping away the dirt with a hand shovel from his gear.
Cracked and dry, the bones looked like rock. The arid desert had preserved
them like a mummy.

Something took control. I kept digging until I revealed the skull. My
hand fell into a circular hole where bone had been crushed, as if something
had been driven into its brain. I froze in awe. An image of an African dwarf
popped into my head.

Harkhuf.

The journal.

Was this *the* crocodile?

Curtains lifted in my mind like weights. Everything had been telling
me to take the story with a large grain of salt and apply modern science.
Had most of it been real? Or was it just metaphor? My skin tingled, and my
mind floated with wonder. I couldn't move, paralyzed in awe—

Mr. Scalone's phone rang.

Chapter 68

Present Day

I PAUSED FROM DIGGING hard clumps of sand away from the ribs of the monstrous skeleton of a crocodile. Shadows grew longer in the evening sun beside the lake, and the buzz of biting insects hovered around me. I took out my phone and recorded a video, taking a panorama of the entire spectacle. The skeleton lay at the base of a cliff directly below an ancient painting of a crocodile, as if on purpose. Was that a clue? One we didn't need, given the recent sandstorm?

After jotting down notes on paper, I slipped my pen into my wrinkled pants pocket and focused my camera on the chest cavity of the crocodile—still filled with sand. My gaze drifted back to the cliff paintings …

No images of humanoids living under the lake, like in the journal. I scrutinized the ancient artwork. Or was there? A cluster of paintings showed men hurling spears and shooting arrows at something beneath the surface of the water. But the thing in the water had been worn or scratched away.

Familiar images from a magazine popped into my head. There were real ancient cave paintings in Libya, not all that far from Egypt, that showed something similar to what Heb had seen painted on this cliff. The Libyan images showed people swimming. Archaeologists referred to the drawings as "cave swimmers," but some appeared to have fishlike tails. Perhaps that was what the ancient artists had believed existed when they'd seen some of the skeletons of the weird prehistoric beasts that'd once lived in this lake.

"A young woman *is* being kept near here," Mr. Scalone said, ending his call. His hair dangled around his aviator sunglasses. Shiny droplets of sweat dotted his forehead. "Someone overheard two men talking at a local shop during the dust storm. Gavin, you were right."

I nearly dropped my phone as I jerked up, my heart lifting like the rising sun. A rush of emotion followed: relief, excitement, anxiety … "Where?" I nearly screamed.

"They don't know," Mr. Scalone replied. "The Minister of Antiquities is on his way with a crew to help pin down a location. Something about a remote temple in the mountains. Just like the dying man who shot Jenkins said, a small temple. The minister's sending someone to pick us up."

I ran back for the parking lot at the far shore.

Dripping sweat, my body heaved from exertion as my feet slipped through the sand. Eventually, I approached the city side of the lake.

Aiden was only a little way back, but Mr. Scalone and Kaylin were hunched over in the dwindling sun at least fifteen minutes behind him. I downed the last of my water, and a black, boxy SUV like ours screeched into a parking spot in front of me.

The tinted passenger window slid down. A man with a huge belly spilled over the driver seat. Streaks of gray ran through his dark beard on either side of his chin, and his eyes were bloodshot.

"You Paul Scalone?" he asked in a thick accent, straightening his dark suit. The interior of the vehicle reeked of acrid whiskey. He hiccupped. Foam spilled onto his beard. "I am Kareem. The Minister of Antiquities phoned … and I owe him favor."

Was this guy drunk? I glanced back for Mr. Scalone, but my hands, tensing with impatience, squeezed onto the hot metal door of the SUV. Maddie couldn't wait for Mr. Scalone.

"Yep," I said. "And I know where we need to go."

"Jump in back," he said. "Anyone else?"

Lunging for the rear door handle, I shouted back, "No."

The plush leather and air conditioning felt like a splash of cool water as I jumped inside. I tried to pull the door closed, but a thin, pale hand reached around to the inside and held it open. Aiden peeked in. He didn't blink as he studied me, as if he could sense my agitation.

"We dashin' outta here like outlaws?" he asked.

"You aren't coming," I said, shaking my head. "The driver's intoxicated, and I don't know who's holding Maddie. Jenkins, but not you, would've been *very* helpful now." I really liked Aiden, and being hard on him—like

Mr. Scalone—made me feel bad, but he might slow me down or put himself in danger. Maddie couldn't afford that. I shouted up front, "Let's get out of here, now!"

The driver spun the tires out on the dirt, but Aiden dived in with his fox in his arms, crashing onto my lap as he slammed the door. He scooted to the other side of the back seat as we barreled away. Mr. Scalone and Kaylin's silhouettes stood straight and still beside the lakeshore in the distance before fading into the evening sun. My gaze fell as I pondered the outcome of leaving them versus delaying Maddie's rescue.

Aiden bounced along beside me, petting his tiny fox's back. Shutting her eyes, the desert fox rested her head on Aiden's lap. The driver pressed a flask to his lips as we weaved along a dirt road and crossed over unmarked desert. My grip tightened on the armrest, leaving indentations. Was this guy really still drinking? And did he think I couldn't see, or did he not care?

"Where we going?" Kareem asked.

"To the mountains," I shouted over the hum of the tires on rock and sand. "We travel to the Abu Lifa Monastery." That monastery was a small temple and dated back to the time of the pharaohs. It had to be the place that Jenkins, the abductor, and Mr. Scalone had mentioned.

Twilight lit the horizon with a red glow.

Kareem tucked the flask between his legs. "Garet Gohannam, the Mountain of Hell?"

My fingers found the gun inside my bag, squeezing its cold handle.

"A mountain from Hell?" Aiden asked.

The driver chuckled, motioning with his large hands in front of us. "Only because when sun sinks, it sets mountain ablaze in red light. No other worry about the name."

My breath slipped out from between my clenched teeth with a hiss. Would there only be the one other abductor holding Maddie? If there were more, or if they were armed, Aiden and I'd be in serious trouble. My eyes closed in regret. Maybe I should've waited for Mr. Scalone … but he could create more problems, as he had in the past. And I didn't know if I could even trust him.

"Are the police coming with the Minister of Antiquities?" I asked.

Kareem shrugged and shouted back over his shoulder. "If we confirm someone is held prisoner, then they come. But this place you send me is remote, and they don't have time for … how do you say … wild duck chases." He cupped his soft chest. "This place is in the bosom of the mountain."

Leaning forward, I examined the mirage of red flames in the distance. The mountain appeared to be on fire. My heart raced.

Desert whisked by, and darkness descended. The driver flicked a switch, and our path lit up before us as we bounded around rocks and up and down hills.

"Mr. Scalone," Kareem said.

"He didn't—" Aiden started.

"Yep?" I asked, grabbing Aiden's arm to silence him.

Kareem glanced back at me in the rearview mirror, his eyes narrowing. "We turn lights out when we get close. This could be dangerous."

"How are we supposed to find out if our friend is in there and in trouble?" I asked. "What if there're armed men inside?"

"I come with you," he replied, then burped. "Like I tell you, I owe minister huge favor. But he's far behind. They about to leave Cairo area when I left Faiyum to give you ride. He call me because I live in Faiyum." Kareem took a long swallow from his flask. "If we need them, we wait."

My stomach twisted and knotted, releasing cramping pain similar to what I'd experienced many times before having to go into the hospital for relief from my disease. I forced a few slow breaths. Was I like my dad now, on some wild adventure out in the farthest reaches of the desert? At least I wasn't stuck under Dr. Banks's thumb anymore, but could I become Mr. Scalone, arrogantly rushing in blind? No, I couldn't go that far, or I'd probably get myself and Maddie killed.

My fingers clenched, gripping the peeling leather of the journal inside my bag. The book felt warm, as did the bronze bracelet on my wrist, calling to me … The boy in the journal had escaped slavery, like me—if I wanted to dramatize my prior life. Then he'd faced monsters and beasts that would terrify me. But I never felt as if I was reading about him—more so that he still lived, and his story played out all around me. Heb was part of me, buried and linked somewhere in my soul. So which one of his monsters would await me, guarding Maddie? A ghoul, a Cyclops, a worshipper of the Dark Ones, or a crocodile? Or would I too have to die to save—

A gulley appeared in the mountain ahead. Kareem hit a switch, and everything went black. Something banged, and the vehicle bucked as if we'd hit a boulder. My head smacked into the side window, and white light flashed across my vision. Pain shot through my skull. Aiden shouted. I rubbed my temple, blinking to regain awareness.

Kareem hit the brakes and slowed to a crawl. "We go slow now. Then hike up and in. You leave dog in car. No one can hear us."

After another few minutes of rolling up a steep incline, Kareem parked the SUV and slid out. Aiden set his fox on the seat, leaving the windows cracked—although the night air had turned chill. I tucked the gun Jenkins had confiscated from Mr. Scalone into my pants and grabbed a flashlight and my messenger bag.

"If she's here and you not want to get killed," Kareem said, the sand crunching in the darkness in front of me as he approached, "then we go in the dark."

The bridge of my nose furrowed as I realized he was right. I tucked the flashlight back into my bag, and we marched up the mountain into the night. My eyes slowly adjusted to the thin moon and starlight. I could make out large rocks appearing as dark mounds, possibly with a greenish tint, like the mounds described in Egypt's underworld.

"The monks moved out here to protect themselves from Romans," Kareem whispered. "Natural protection." He pointed to the looming cliffs on either side. A faint light appeared in the distance, just over a rim of rock. "There!" He pointed and took a long drink.

I froze. Would Maddie really be in there, way out here? It was close to the Faiyum and Lake Qarun, the probable next stop on the path to the Hall of Records.

The glow ahead flickered through an open doorway. Someone was out here ...

Rose-colored stone from an ancient structure reflected the dancing flames. We crept upward over slick rocks to the gates. Aiden followed at my back. I pulled the gun from my pants. Unfortunately, I'd only been shooting with my dad a couple of times ... many years ago. Inching forward, I peeked inside the temple.

A man paced, his sandaled feet clapping on stone as firelight wavered over his body. He wore a *thawb*, and his beard was sparse and patchy—the other hired hand from the tomb of Amenhotep! My blood went cold, sending stinging ice through my limbs.

A hand grabbed my shoulder. I clenched my mouth to muffle a shout of surprise.

"How many?" Aiden asked. "And do you have another gun?"

Kareem yanked a revolver from inside his suit jacket. "I do." Firelight flickered off its silver metal. "Stay quiet. I listen."

We fell silent as the abductor carried on a long conversation, his voice agitated.

"He says he not talked to his partner in too long," Kareem said. "I not hear another voice. So, I hope he talks with someone on the phone. But he grows nervous and does not know where some American explorers are. He waits for them with the girl, so they won't proceed."

Maddie was here!

Chapter 69

Journal Translation

I DIDN'T KNOW WHAT'D happened. Something about a lake and getting pulled under, drowning …

A black expanse of nothingness surrounded me. My heart sank from loneliness and fear.

A light flickered at the end of a long, dark tunnel. I couldn't speak or think clearly, but I remembered something, something buried deep—a fleeting memory. Images, hieroglyphs appeared in my mind—the Book of the Dead, and a spell to cast …

I could speak now, and my soul took shape. "Hello?" I asked as I wandered on.

At the end of the dark passage, an old man waited, so gaunt that he looked like a skeleton. He sat, fast asleep, on a stone at the edge of a body of water. The lake behind him disappeared into the shadows beyond. Fog moved in, shrouding us. Green light drifted about the periphery.

"I wish to take the ferry," I said.

He didn't move.

I yelled.

Nothing.

I nudged him, and his frail body toppled over with a clatter, as if a pile of bones. I leapt back. But he looked up, his eyes sunken like craters.

"The ferry is not fit to make the trip," he replied in a hoarse whisper, sitting back on his rock.

A memory of another spell from the Book sparked in my mind.

"Who are you who has come?" he asked.

"I am the beloved of my father," I said, recalling the phrases and spells that hadn't made sense to me before. "I am a magician."

The ferry appeared from the darkness—a small boat of wood. It slid across the placid waters without a ripple or sound.

"Do you know of the two cities, magician?" the ferryman asked, his bones creaking as he stood.

"The underworld and the Field of Rushes," I answered, and we climbed aboard the ferry. The vessel felt light on the water as we glided through darkness and stars, crossing the Celestial River—the Milky Way.

But fog swirled around us on a ghostly wind and shrouded something—something in the lake. Black silhouettes stood in rows, up to their waists in liquid. The mist lifted, revealing faces bound in white linen.

Just like in my dream.

The figures advanced and surrounded us without making a sound. Arms concealed by black cloaks rose into the air and clawed at the sides of the ferry with scratching sounds that rattled inside my head and made the roots of my teeth tingle. I screamed and huddled against the skeleton ferryman.

"Who are they?" the ferryman asked.

"The Dark Ones!" I shouted in fear, unsure. This was not in the book.

One grabbed my wrist, around my bracelet. Biting cold seeped into skin, up my arm, and into my heart. I jerked my arm back, but the Dark One didn't let go.

"Why are they here?" the ferryman continued.

Hundreds surrounded me, and dark fingers as thin as bone latched on to my legs and arms. "I don't know!" I screamed. I'd studied all of the spells from the Book of the Dead inside the tomb and thought I had all of the answers I'd need. But *nothing* mentioned Dark Ones and their secrets. My soul was going to be dismembered ...

They began to drag me from the boat. Pain shot through my limbs and joints as they tugged at me, threatening to tear me apart.

"Because their souls have been devoured!" I yelled.

Cold hands released me and jerked away. I fell and smacked into the hull of the ferry before pushing myself up. The black figures faded back into the fog.

I exhaled in relief. Had the Dark Ones let me go just because I'd finally realized that they were the souls of the devoured? I shook my head and told the ferryman the names of the dead from the Book, and we entered Rosetjau. Towering higher than any palace, darker than any night, the great mansion emerged.

I had entered the west—the *Duat*—the underworld where the Aten spent each night. The hieroglyph for the *Duat*, the five-pointed star inside the circle, popped into my mind.

The ferry jolted, its wood groaning in protest, as we docked. I stepped out onto a bank of jagged rock and turned to bid the ferryman goodbye. But the ferry had disappeared, leaving only placid water and darkness.

I walked along a rocky path and through the open doors of the great mansion. A gate barred the way, rods of twisted metal climbing into the sky. A hunched man stood before it, speaking to whatever was on the other side. The man shook the bars and pounded his fists against them, which created a dull clanging sound. But the gates would not open. Eventually, the man wandered away. I approached, dragging my feet.

"Who approaches the gates?" a reverberating voice thundered. A face appeared, looking like the inside of a mask. Its indented face and eyes moved.

"He whose face is inverted, he who lives on snakes, hippopotamus-faced, raging of power," I said, and then named the gatekeeper, the guardian, and the herald, whose names I will not record here.

The seven gates shuddered and rose upward, releasing an ear-piercing screech of metal dragging against metal. I stepped inside, keeping my gaze fixated ahead as hordes of hideous creatures attempted to distract and terrify me—monsters whose appearance could make a man's heart stop beating from fear alone.

I believed I was inside the mansion, but now a moonlit field surrounded me—the Field of Rushes before the house of Osiris. The twenty-one portals appeared—gateways of swirling blackness that sucked in all of the faint light, as well as any warmth remaining within my fading soul.

"Terrible is the name of the door-keeper," I said and stepped into a portal.

Darkness. The swirling unknown tugged at my skin like pinching instruments, bringing tearing pain.

"Mistress of wrath who dances in blood," I shouted. "The Terrible One, Lady of Pestilence who casts away human souls, decapitates, and hacks up the dead. Who kills without warning. Who calls at the top of her voice, terrible yet majestic. Venerated Mistress of the Castle. Himself is the name of her doorkeeper."

The consuming blackness around me dissipated.

Hills and mountains of deep green or yellow erupted before me—the fourteen mounds—rumbling as the ground quaked and shook my legs. Twin peaks that resembled arrow points rose overhead, silhouetting against the pale blue moon. Hollow shrieks cried out in the distance.

Without pause, I climbed upward.

Covering my ears, I called out to the shades in the Mound of Spirits, "I know of the two trees of turquoise between where He enters and exits. Lord of Eternity, I am a Great One."

The shrieking intensified, ringing in my ears as an overwhelming taste of salt filled my mouth.

But I hailed the god of the cavern. "The Horns of Water, the River of Flaming Fire, biting with your mouth and staring with your eyes! May your bones be broken and your poison powerless, for you shall not come against me. Put yourself on your belly until I have passed. No one shall take *my* spirit. Fall!"

The voices fell silent, and the salt vanished.

I descended the Mounds of the *Duat*. A great hall of black stone arose around me. Shadowy forms appeared and hovered, grabbing me with ghostly hands that stung like the snow of the island mountain. They guided me to two opened doors of gold, then held me fast.

Sickeningly sweet incense hung thick. The great hall beyond the doorway was adorned with red and sparkling gold rugs, and a man stood before massive scales that filled a large portion of the room. He was dressed in a pristine robe and sandals, and his eyes were painted black. A contingent of humanoids with animal heads sat at the periphery, holding scepters in their closed fists. They watched.

A squawking baboon ran back and forth atop the scales, tapping the wood and plucking the twine, as if testing the apparatus. And a being with the head of a black jackal and the body of a man towered over the scene. Anubis—from the Book of the Dead!

Anubis placed something red upon one of the dangling scales, opened his jackal's mouth, and barked something I could not understand. The man being judged watched as this red thing—his heart—beat upon the scale. A single feather in the other scale stood up on the tip of its shaft. The man attempted to stand proudly, but his hands trembled.

Behind Anubis, a bird-headed humanoid with a hooked beak scribbled something upon parchment. His reed pen created a sharp scratching sound.

Thoth.

The Devouring Monster should've been sitting like a begging dog, awaiting its next morsel with its reptilian jaws spread wide. But beside Thoth was an empty green platform—the Devouring Monster had been summoned to do Akhenaten's bidding in the world of the living …

The scales sat even for a moment, and the man on trial smiled. A *ba* with the body of a falcon and the head of the man on trial flew about but landed on the man's shoulder and flapped its wings, the whooshing of its feathers the only sound within the still chamber. Another massive form, shrouded in shadow, sat in silence at the far end of the room. The face of a man rested atop this giant being, his skin deep green. He sat atop an enormous gold throne and glanced down at a woman standing beside him.

Osiris himself!

My heart raced with fear. Four small creatures with gangly limbs scuttled around Osiris's throne, squeaking and pointing at the scales.

The scales creaked and tipped, and the heart descended. Every humanoid in the room shouted at the judged man as he screamed and waved his arms wildly. His *ba* shrieked and flew over my head, soaring out of the hall.

Anubis howled, the shrill sound making goose bumps rise across my arms and legs. The hall turned silent. Striding over to the scales, the jackal-headed god scooped up the still beating heart and tossed it over his shoulder.

The organ landed with a splat in a pile of other hearts beside the Devouring Monster's empty platform. It beat one more time, and then the heart stopped. The dead man screamed and fled with his *ba*, sprinting past me with a rush of cold wind and pounding footfalls.

"Run away before the Devourer returns for your vile soul," the booming voice of Anubis rang out. "But soon you will be lost to the fabric of time."

Wailing echoed throughout the mansion as the dead man fled.

My heart pounded louder, but it was not within my chest. The organ sat in my open palms! Its contractions shook my arms.

I was dressed in a fine white robe unlike anything I'd ever worn. And before I could think, the ghostly hands ushered me forward into the hall. The golden eyes of the jackal fell upon me. Snarling, he reached for the beating heart in my hands …

Chapter 70

Present Day

KAREEM MOTIONED ALONG THE walls of the small temple surrounded by rock cliffs. The abductor still paced around inside, under firelight, ranting on his phone. His footsteps echoed.

"We need know how many men are here, and where girl is," Kareem said. "You two look. I stay here and watch. When he sleeps, we go in."

Aiden pulled a small shovel from his pack, as if it were a weapon. Sneaking off and following the outer wall by the pale moon- and starlight, we glanced through entryways and windows. No other men.

I turned a corner around the back, grabbed the smooth stone of a windowsill, and peeked inside. Light flickered through the doorway of a room, landing upon a chair. Someone was tied to it. Long, dark hair dangled over her face as her head rested on her chest, her body slumped forward in sleep—or death. My stomach sank and cramped, feeling as if it would pull me down with it.

Maddie!

Dirt covered her exposed skin. Her chest moved with respirations.

She was alive! But her posture and appearance made me grimace. Sympathy tugged at my core. I needed to get her out of there.

Pointing inside, I whispered to Aiden, "She's in there."

Aiden's eyes bugged out as he gripped his shovel tighter. Rising on his tiptoes, he glanced in. His face dropped in shock.

"Is she here?" someone asked from the darkness.

I jumped back as Kareem crept up to us, his bulk wobbling side to side—he had circled around the other side of the temple.

"Yes," I whispered. "We need to get her out—now!"

Kareem's face stiffened, the night's shadows growing long across his cheeks. "No other men stay here. But chances are best for no one to get hurt if we wait for him to sleep. It's far past midnight. He should go to bed soon."

"Maybe the minister and his police will show up by then," Aiden said, glancing down at the shovel in his hands. His teeth chattered.

I sighed through a constricted throat that made the air rushing out feel gravelly. But going in would not only be dangerous for us, it could get Maddie killed.

We waited a couple of hours, anxiety gnawing at my gut every second. Was she okay? What had she been through already?

The man inside yelled and shouted, stomping around.

My stomach spasmed, sending a wave of cramping pain through my belly. Nausea followed. I gagged, leaned over, and my stomach heaved several times before I vomited into the dirt. A splatter sounded at the base of the temple, the vomit hidden by darkness.

"You all right?" Aiden asked, resting a shaky hand on my shoulder.

I nodded as acid burned my throat. "That's not too weird for me, especially in a stressful situation like this." I wiped my mouth with the back of my hand. "We need to go in."

Something shattered against a wall.

Kareem shook his head. Beads of sweat glistened in the moonlight as they rolled down his brow. "He still talks on phone. The person he talks to knows something happened to his partner a while ago but just told this man the news. Now the person on the other line is trying to calm him, but this man grows angry."

"Really?" I said sarcastically, standing and taking a deep breath. Was he going to hurt Maddie?

"You stay," Kareem said, slapping my back as he motioned with the barrel of his gun. "I go around front and take him out. Give me five minutes. When you hear shouting or shooting, come in and grab girl."

Nodding, I stiffened my resolve. I pulled a knife from my bag to cut Maddie's ropes. Whatever was going to happen, this was it. We couldn't wait for the Minister of Antiquities or for the man inside to do something.

Kareem slunk off and disappeared. Waiting made my mind race with scenarios of bad things: all of us getting shot, dying out here in the empty desert, and leaving Maddie to this abductor.

Aiden grabbed my hand. "How can *we* do this? Fight a terrorist who's armed and has Maddie?"

I swallowed, thinking. "His wish is to stop us," I said, squeezing the gun and picturing Heb from the journal. "Wishes fade. Our will to save her will not die."

Aiden stared at me, unblinking.

Someone shouted in Arabic.

I tensed but stepped inside the back door. Sneaking along a short corridor, I followed the voices and firelight. Running footsteps. Wood grated on stone, as if the the abductor dragged a chair behind him. Maddie screamed.

My pulse hammered in my ears as thick sweat coated my palms. The metal gun in my hand slipped around. Aiden hovered at my back.

Men shouted just ahead. Approaching the lighted room, I peeked around the corner.

Firelight danced at the far side of the room. The abductor stood behind Maddie, who was still tied to a chair. Kareem stood on the other side of them, his gun pointed at the abductor's face.

Maddie's head flicked back and forth. Her feet stomped the ground in fear.

Kareem spoke in Arabic to our previous hired hand, then released the hammer of his gun and lowered the firearm. The abductor shouted back, waving a large knife wildly about. He positioned the blade against Maddie's back and pointed at Kareem.

I froze in horror, my breathing halting. What could I do? Would Kareem be able to talk down this crazy man who'd been holding Maddie for a couple of weeks already?

Probably not.

I blinked to get control of myself.

Kareem spoke again. "You speak English? It is easier for me, as I am not native-born Egyptian." His gaze drifted over the abductor's shoulder to me as he held his hands open and set his gun on the floor.

His lie must have been for my benefit.

The abductor shouted back in Arabic, but then, in a thick accent, said, "You leave or I kill. The matter of woman is far greater than any of this world. I care not if I die. She still live only to stop others like her."

My gun hand shook with apprehension, the handle becoming slicker. I inched closer for an easier shot.

"I cannot leave her with you," Kareem said, backing away from his gun. "There will be many police, and they take her from you."

The abductor jammed his knife against Maddie's back but didn't impale her yet. His entire arm shook and veins popped out from his skin.

Chapter 71

Present Day

M Y GUN HAND JERKED. I needed to do something—right now, or the abductor would impale Maddie with his knife!

Aiming, I squeezed the trigger of my gun. My eyes closed at the last instant.

A bang resounded throughout the room, ringing my ears—then a shriek and tearing of cloth. Maddie screamed in agony. The abductor fell to the floor, clutching his chest. His knife was buried into Maddie's back.

He'd still stabbed her!

A pool of darkness spread across Maddie's shirt like a wave. In the dim lighting, I couldn't see color, but it had to be red …

I lunged for her. Kareem picked up his gun and jumped on the attacker. Aiden hit the assailant over the head with his shovel—

Dropping my gun, I used my knife to cut into the thick cords holding Maddie to the chair. Her face was ghastly pale. Her breathing came in forced gasps. She couldn't catch her breath. And her eyes didn't focus on me. My hands and arms trembled.

Laying her on her side, I applied pressure around the knife to stem the loss of blood. I lifted her shirt. Blood poured around the weapon lodged between two ribs in her back.

Maddie gasped slower and slower. She was going to die …

My breathing stopped. Removing a lodged object outside of the hospital was a huge risk. If the weapon had pierced a major vessel, the blade itself could be blocking further internal hemorrhage. Pulling it out might release that hold and lead to a massive bleed—without a surgeon on hand to ligate the damaged—

Maddie gasped again, her entire chest leaving the ground as she fought for oxygen. She wouldn't last long enough to get her anywhere, just like Jenkins and the other abductor …

Grabbing the handle of the knife, I yanked. The blade withdrew, grating and vibrating against bone and leaving a trail of blood.

Maddie attempted to scream in pain, but it came out as barely a whisper.

Her chest and now even her stomach heaved. Her tongue turned dark, hanging out of her mouth. The gaping hole in her upper back or her punctured lung must be acting as a one-way valve. It would trap pressured air inside her chest, further collapsing all of her lung tissue. The light in her eyes faded …

"Help," she whispered as she stared blankly out into the night.

My hands shook. Rifling through my pockets, I located a pen and bit out the ink tip and rear cap. I jammed the hollow casing in through the hole in her back.

She gasped.

Air spewed out through the tiny tube with a high-pitched hiss. After a few seconds, it stopped.

Placing my lips around the pen casing, I repositioned its inner aspect and sucked, expelling air out through my nose.

Maddie groaned, long and loud. The color returned to her tongue, but she still heaved for breath. I continued removing air for a couple of minutes. But the inner valve-effect could still be trapping air outside her lung with every breath.

"Aiden!" I shouted, holding my thumb over the tube so that air wouldn't be drawn back into her chest. "Give me your gum."

Aiden spat a wad of green gum into my palm. I jammed it into the pen's opening—sealing the tube—and used the blanket in my bag to apply pressure around the rest of Maddie's wound.

"Press it tight," I said to Aiden, motioning for him to take over.

His shaking hands held the makeshift bandage in place.

Lifting Maddie, I sat her up and elevated her arms over her head to help expand her chest cavity.

A sparkle returned to her eyes, reflecting the firelight. She blinked.

"Gavin?" she asked, her face dirty but streaked with clean tear tracks.

I threw my arms around her and hugged her, trying to avoid her wound. All of my emotion released, making my body limp as tears trickled down my cheeks. "I thought you were dead," I said.

She groaned and reached around to the wound on her back.

Grabbing her hands, I said, "Leave it alone. I may need to use the makeshift chest tube again before we get you to a hospital."

"Save me," the man I'd shot said between shallow breaths, the light in his eyes already gone.

"I'm sorry, I'm not a doctor yet," I replied.

"For sake of mankind, not open Hall of Records," he whispered. "Future of world depend on it."

He fell flat against the floor with a thud.

Maddie's face went white. "Wh-what happened?"

Staring into her eyes, I grasped her head behind both ears. "You're going to be fine."

She stared back. The first rays of dawn's light streaked through the doors and windows, illuminating the room.

I reached into my pocket, pulled out the sheer glasses she'd dropped when she was abducted, and slid them over her nose and ears. Finally, back in the right place.

She smiled, squinting against the sun as she tucked her hair back behind her small ears. Yellow and pink light showered my face, and hope lifted my heart. I didn't know what'd just happened, but warmth radiated through my body. The image of the world below this mountain, the ancient seabed—the one we'd left behind—was painted with the flawless magic of morning sunlight. It stole my words.

I studied Maddie as she gazed upon the wonder and pointed. She was beautiful ... alive. How lucky I was to have traveled the curvy road of indecision, just like Heb. I'd learned so much about ancient Egypt, my dream, *and* how to save lives. My eyes closed, picturing my gallivanting dad. All along, I knew he'd helped the less fortunate throughout the world, living a life of purpose. I should've been proud of him, not angry ... I imagined my realist mom and the doctor's path she'd steered me down. I was thankful for both of them and their differences—together a balance of extremes.

Fear of my future receded like a vanishing tide. Whatever lay ahead, it was not predetermined by either my mom or my dad.

As I recalled the magician taunting Heb about not following a straight path, I saw Heb as clearly as if he stood before me … the years of journeying and heartache he endured before returning to chase his own love and dreams …

My heart melted with love and relief. But my hands still trembled. I stared at Maddie, a smile creeping across my lips. The sun rose, its orange disc fully visible through the doorway as it climbed over the horizon and left the underworld behind.

"Like an eaglet opening its eyes and witnessing the majesty of the world beneath its soaring wings," Maddie whispered as if she'd been reading the journal with me the entire time—a tear in her eye. "Sit down and open up, Gavin," she said, patting the floor beside her.

I knelt. "Maddie, I love—"

She pressed her soft lips against mine and held me tight.

About the Author

R.M. Schultz has been enthralled with ancient Egypt and its lost secrets for decades. He lives with his wife, daughter, and many pets in the Pacific Northwest.

Note from the Author:

First off, thank you for choosing to spend your time reading this book. There are so many stories to choose from, and I am thankful that you decided on this one.

To express my gratitude, I will forward you a draft chapter from the third and final book of the Era of Shadows series. If interested, please visit my website at: http://www.rmschultzauthor.com/ and send me a message under the "contact" page.

Also, if you enjoyed the story, please consider rating and reviewing it on Amazon.